Moon Spinners

Moon Spinners

A SEASIDE KNITTERS MYSTERY

Sally Goldenbaum

AN OBSIDIAN MYSTERY

OBSIDIAN
Published by New American Library,
a division of Penguin Group (USA) Inc.,
375 Hudson Street, New York, New York 10014, USA
Penguin Group (Canada), 90 Eglinton Avenue East, Suite 700, Toronto,
Ontario M4P 2Y3, Canada (a division of Pearson Penguin Canada Inc.)
Penguin Books Ltd., 80 Strand, London WC2R 0RL, England
Penguin Ireland, 25 St. Stephen's Green, Dublin 2,
Ireland (a division of Penguin Books Ltd.)
Penguin Group (Australia), 250 Camberwell Road, Camberwell,
Victoria 3124, Australia (a division of Pearson Australia Group Pty. Ltd.)
Penguin Books India Pvt. Ltd., 11 Community Centre,
Panchsheel Park, New Delhi - 110 017, India
Penguin Group (NZ), 67 Apollo Drive, Rosedale, North Shore 0632,
New Zealand (a division of Pearson New Zealand Ltd.)
Penguin Books (South Africa) (Pty.) Ltd., 24 Sturdee Avenue,
Rosebank, Johannesburg 2196, South Africa

Penguin Books Ltd., Registered Offices:
80 Strand, London WC2R 0RL, England

First published by Obsidian, an imprint of New American Library,
a division of Penguin Group (USA) Inc.

First Printing, May 2010
1   3   5   7   9   10   8   6   4   2

OBSIDIAN and logo are trademarks of Penguin Group (USA) Inc.

LIBRARY OF CONGRESS CATALOGING-IN-PUBLICATION DATA:

Goldenbaum, Sally.
Moon spinners: a seaside knitters mystery/Sally Goldenbaum.
p. cm.
"An Obsidian mystery."
ISBN 978-0-451-22988-5
1. Knitters (Persons)—Fiction. 2. Murder—Investigation—Fiction. 3. Massachusetts—
Fiction. 4. Mystery fiction. I. Title.
PS3557.O35937MJ66   2010
813'.54—dc22   2009049584

Set in Palatino • Designed by Elke Sigal

Printed in the United States of America

This book is dedicated to my sisters and brother—
Jane Pitz, Bob Pitz, and Mary Sue Sheridan.

And to Sister Rosemary Flanigan,
for years and years of friendship and support.

Acknowledgments

It takes a knitting village to write a knitting mystery, and I'd like to acknowledge and thank my village:

• The people who maintain the many Web sites and blogs that provide ready resources for knitting, yarn, facts about fiber, and knitting tips. To mention one is to miss hundreds, but a special thanks to knitty.com, Knitting Daily, and the energetic Ravelry community.

• Joey Ciaramitaro and his Good Morning Gloucester blog (http://goodmorninggloucester.wordpress.com/), a daily feed that provides grist for my writing mill and keeps me in touch with life on Cape Ann, with the world of fishing and living by the sea, and with the fascinating people who live next door to the Seaside Knitters.

• John McElhenny for his gentle editing tips on what works and doesn't work for Cape Ann life and lingo, and the Cape Ann Historical Association, Rocky Neck Art Colony, Rockport's Bearskin Neck businesses and many other *real* places on Cape Ann that have provided a model and inspiration for the fictitious town of Sea Harbor.

• The many readers whose supportive notes and comments keep me honest—and writing.

And a special acknowledgment to Sandy Harding, who has enriched the Seaside Knitters (and their author) with her wisdom, skill, and attention.

Moon Spinners

Chapter 1

*I*t was worse than canceling Christmas.

At least that was Izzy Chambers' first thought when she got Nell Endicott's phone call. Friday night on the Endicott deck with her uncle Ben's martinis, grilled halibut, and dear friends was sacred. What was her aunt thinking?

"Now, Izzy, that's not you talking," Mae Anderson said. The yarn shop manager had listened to her young boss grumble her way through sorting an entire shipment of bamboo yarn. "It's that awful diet soda you drink, missy."

But it wasn't the diet soda that bothered Izzy. It was the lost shipment of walnut knitting needles that the carrier couldn't trace. It was the leak in the shop's roof, and the injured bird that had flown into the display window, cracking both the glass and its poor wing. It was the influx of summer people before she was quite ready for them.

And suddenly it all crashed down on her, and Izzy felt a need as intense as needing water in a desert to spend Friday evening with friends and family on the Endicott deck. It was tradition, after all.

But this Friday night it was not to be. This week, Nell said, they'd all be at the Sea Harbor Yacht Club, enjoying Laura Danvers' wonderfully planned charity event.

Cass Halloran took the news even harder. After putting in ten-hour days checking and baiting traps, banding lobsters, throwing back those that were too big or too small or pregnant, and repairing a nasty gash on the *Lady Lobster*'s helm, Cass needed the Endicott deck in a most serious way. She was ornery and she was tired the night she got Nell's message, a volatile combination.

But, as Nell knew would happen, Izzy would come. And so would Cass.

"Bring Gracie Santos along, too," Nell had added. "She could use a break from working on her new café, and I need one more person to fill the table."

Birdie Favazza hadn't offered an opinion, something that caused Nell far more concern than the others' dramatic complaints. Birdie always had an opinion, but in recent days she had been unusually preoccupied. Even Izzy had noticed, and wondered aloud if there was a counterpart to PMS that afflicted eighty-year-olds. Birdie was rarely cranky and always dependable, but for the first time since Nell could remember, she had missed their Thursday-night knitting session the night before.

"Laura Danvers is adamant that all the tables be filled for this event," Nell told each of them. "I think there will be some press attention, and she wants it to look good."

And then she had added the clincher: "But the real reason you should come is because it's for a wonderful cause—the community center at Anja Angelina Park. Part of it will be used as an activity center for kids—a place for them to go after school if there isn't a parent at home."

"Only my mother can use guilt more skillfully than you," Izzy said before hanging up.

Nell smiled without comment. Her sister, Caroline Chambers, was a hundred times more accomplished in that arena. Nell didn't like to play the guilt game. Unless, like tonight, it was for a good cause.

Nell slipped into a sea-green summery dress. It felt good against her bare legs. Storing away woolen sweaters and slacks in the cedar closet was a pleasurable task, and she welcomed the lightness of summer clothes. She slipped a filmy lace shawl over her shoulders and walked across the carpet to the bedroom windows. A breeze came in off the sea, soft and caressing, like a lover's touch.

The Endicotts' master bedroom was in the back of the spacious, airy house, and from the window Nell could see the moon reflected in the blackness of the night sea. It was an extraordinary view, day or night, and tonight, for reasons unclear, it seemed especially vivid. The enormous full moon hung just above the treetops, nearly brushing the branches. It was a mysterious moon—a white, shimmering globe, its light blinding against the blackness of night.

It was a night for the Moon Spinners to begin their task. Nell stood in silence, imagining the women of the ancient Celtic myth pulling the silvery strands of light from the sky and winding it on distaffs, until weeks later the waning moon would disappear completely, leaving the world wrapped in a blanket of darkness, the tides quieter, creatures safe from the hunter.

She wondered who else was standing at a window at this exact moment, or walking through the darkening shadows of the beach, or relaxing on a deck, transfixed by the sight above them.

"Hmmm," Ben said, coming up behind her and wrapping his arms around her waist. He looked out the window, following her gaze. "It's extraordinary," he whispered into the curve of her neck.

Nell nodded against his chest, her body welcoming the support.

"Some think a full moon has magical powers." Ben spoke against her hair, his eyes on the moon. He stood there for a minute longer, then stepped away and walked over to the mirror to knot his tie.

Nell wouldn't know later what it was—the strain of staring at the bright light or the anticipation of the party? But the moon seemed to grow larger beneath her stare, a moon lacking the comforting, gentle smile of her childhood when she'd lie flat in a Kansas field and look up at it, making wishes, telling secrets.

Tonight it wasn't a smile that passed down over those thousands and thousands of miles. The moon's light and shadow had mixed in an ominous way. Nell felt a foreboding—like the green sky before a tornado rolled across the Kansas plains or the unsettling quiet before a nor'easter surged down on Sea Harbor.

Instinctively, she took a step back and looked away, wrapping her arms around herself and shivering slightly.

Ben caught her reflection in the mirror. "Nell?"

Nell diminished the slice of fear with a slow smile directed at her husband. She walked over and touched his cheek.

"You're looking quite handsome tonight," she said with a catch in her voice. "Come—we've a party to attend."

Chapter 2

*T*he Sea Harbor Yacht Club was casual as yacht clubs go, but tonight it was elegant, bathed in rich golden hues. Flickering candlelight, small pots of tiny yellow roses, and delicate amber bowls filled with chunks of lobster swimming in a saffron wine broth had transformed the casual club into an elegant summer party.

"The dinner was amazing," Izzy conceded. She dropped her napkin beside her plate and sat back in her chair. "Sorry I was such a pill about coming, Aunt Nell."

"No apologies necessary. I know the yarn shop was hectic this week."

"I shouldn't be complaining, should I? Business is great. Knitting is fantastic therapy for people. I think that's why we're so busy. Tommy Porter came in yesterday, proudly decked out in his policeman's uniform, and asked me if I'd start a class for men only—he thinks it would help the police force in times of stress. And yesterday I had twenty-five customers knitting lace without a single moan or thrown needle." Izzy lifted a corner of the filmy shawl that covered her bare shoulders. "Like it?"

The shawl was as light as a feather. It draped over Izzy's shoulders and arms like an intricate spider's web, the ends collecting on her lap in a silky puddle the color of the sea. Nell had seen Izzy pull out the silk-and-merino yarn two weeks ago at their Thursday-night knitting group. She needed to make a sample for her lace class, she'd said.

She must have elves that finish things while she sleeps. A mere mortal could not whip together such a lovely piece so quickly. Izzy wore it with a simple dress with spaghetti straps. Her niece looked beautiful and elegant—and she didn't have a clue that heads had turned when she'd walked around the room looking for the Endicott table. But Nell knew that now that people had seen Izzy in the spidery shawl, she'd have a waiting list for the next lace class. And they would all want to look exactly like Izzy. Unassuming. And beautiful.

"Izzy's right," Cass said. "If we had to be anywhere other than your deck tonight, this will pass. Sorry I grumped. Handling two hundred and fifty lobster traps is getting to be a burden. And now Pete wants to add fifty more." Cass sat back in her chair and picked up her slender martini glass. A lone olive sat on the bottom. She rolled the stem between the pads of her fingers and looked at it accusingly. "But I did tell the bartender that he needs martini lessons from Ben. This is most definitely not an Endicott martini. No thin icy layer on top. Too much vermouth. No anchovy in the olive."

"I'm sure you endeared yourself to him." Birdie Favazza patted Cass' hand.

"I agree with Cass on the martini front," Ham Brewster said. "But I suppose one Friday won't kill us." Ham didn't forgo his Friday martinis lightly. He and his wife, Jane, worked hard all week, not just creating their own art, but making sure Sea Harbor's Canary Cove art colony was running smoothly. And they depended on their longtime friends' deck to keep them sane and happy.

"Kill who, Mr. Brewster?" Stella Palazola appeared at the artist's elbow. She was balancing several plates of strawberry meringue pie drizzled with dark chocolate fudge sauce. She grinned familiarly at the group and set one plate down in front of Ham's wife, Jane, then another in front of Gracie Santos, Cass' childhood friend.

"Figure of speech, beautiful," Ham said. He smiled up at the young waitress. "Tell me, Stella, how did they manage to get the finest waitress in Sea Harbor to work this party? Rumor has it you were giving up waitressing for the summer?" He eyed the tray of pies.

Stella grinned at Ham and then across the table at Birdie Favazza. "Miz Birdie sprung me for the night. You know my sister, Liz? Of course you do. Well, she, like, manages these fancy affairs, and they needed an extra waitress." Stella nodded toward the woman standing over near the main doors of the dining room. Liz Palazola looked like the loveliest guest at the party—her short dress showing off an enviable figure. But her watchful gaze and alert demeanor hinted at the management skills that earned her rave reviews from yacht club members. "She'll run the whole damn town someday," was Ben's assessment after a recent board meeting.

"It's a well-deserved break, dear," Birdie said to Stella. "Liz was very smart to ask you."

"Not that I need a break, Miz Birdie. You pay me way too much for hanging out with your housekeeper and that husband of hers. Ella and Harold don't even need me half the time. It takes more than a broken ankle to keep Harold down, that's for sure. He hobbled down those carriage house steps today and I swear he'd've taken off in your Lincoln if I hadn't been out there. He looked like there was a fire and he had the only hose in town. Turns out he woke up from a nap and he was missing Ella, as if his wife can't go off on her own." Stella dropped the tray to her side and put one fist on her hip. She looked sternly at the older woman. "You need to talk to him about women's rights, Miz Birdie. He's, like, a little behind the times."

Birdie held back an answer, and Nell tried to read her thoughts. She and Birdie had been friends for years, and despite the nearly twenty-year difference in their ages, they often stepped into each other's thoughts. But tonight Birdie's expression was puzzling, her thoughts about her caretaker and housekeeper hidden in the lines of her face. But she was worried about something, that much Nell could tell.

"Well, Stella," Birdie said, "I hope that proves that I need you. Harold Sampson can be stubborn as an ox, and we need that broken ankle healed—he isn't a spring chicken, you know. It was a complicated break, the doctor said, and it's been only a couple months. He won't be pulling any more mud and pine needles out of my eaves, that much is for sure. I know your mother misses you at her restaurant, but I selfishly think I need you more."

Ben and Nell both suspected that Birdie hired Stella as a way of padding the young woman's freshman-year college fund. Stella was taking all the jobs she could get to make sure she could afford Salem State in the fall. And her mother would be grateful for Birdie's help.

After Stella's father died, Annabelle Palazola demonstrated the grit fishermen's wives were made of and opened a restaurant to give Joe Palazola's children the college dreams their father had spun for them. The Sweet Petunia was a hometown success, but Annabelle had four children whose dreams demanded attention.

And Birdie Favazza was known for helping make dreams come true.

Stella brought two more desserts to the table, placed one in front of Nell and then leaned near to Birdie's ear, talking in a stage whisper as she set the other plate down. "I'm not joking about the Lincoln, Miz Birdie. The extra keys you gave me, like, disappeared from the kitchen hook today. You need to talk to Harold."

Birdie nodded, a frown pulling her thin eyebrows together. "Don't worry about them, dear," she said. "I'm sure they're around someplace."

When she looked at the others, Birdie had erased the frown with a smile. "Stella keeps track of us all quite nicely. I don't know what I'd do without her."

Birdie seemed to welcome the shadow that fell across the table just then, diverting attention.

An elegant woman appeared between Cass Halloran and Gracie.

"Good evening," Sophia Santos said in a distinctive voice.

At the sound of her aunt's voice, Gracie immediately pushed back her chair and started to stand up.

"Sit, please, *cariña mía*," Sophia said, kissing Gracie lightly on each cheek. Although Sophia's greeting to everyone was gracious, her accented words held a note of urgency. "Please," she said, "continue talking. I need one moment with Gracie." But without waiting for the chatter to pick up and cover her words, she leaned over and set one hand firmly on Gracie's shoulder, as if Gracie might somehow flee if she let go. She spoke quietly, but in a voice that contrasted with the festivity around them.

"I have been trying to reach you, Grace," she said. "I must speak with you. Please come to the house tomorrow morning." Sophia spoke with the same kind of authority her husband did. Requests did not require answers. Gracie would stop by.

"*Es urgente*," Sophia added.

She straightened up, pushed an imaginary stray hair into place, and apologized again for interrupting.

"Nonsense," Birdie said. "It's always nice to see you, Sophia."

"The Santos and Delaney construction companies are doing a wonderful thing, helping with the community center," Nell said.

"It is, how you say it, a 'unique' partnership," Sophia Santos said, but the words lacked amusement, and her striking face remained expressionless.

"Unique is probably an understatement, Sophia," Ben said. "Who could have imagined those two men agreeing on anything?"

"It's all show," Birdie said. "They're both teddy bears beneath those tough exteriors."

"Teddy bears . . ." Sophia repeated, trying unsuccessfully to put the image into a context that made sense in her own language.

While Birdie tried to explain, Nell looked over at the bar just as Alphonso Santos walked in from the bar's terrace. He wiped his hands on a white handkerchief, then joined the mayor and the Sea Harbor police chief. The three men sat at a table, their faces serious, and fell into a discussion that Nell suspected revolved around the community center tonight's party would benefit. Work had already begun, but the complications of multiple companies working on a civic project were always evident.

Nell had rarely observed Alphonso from afar this way. She felt slightly guilty, rude, perhaps. *Never stare*, her mother had always taught her and her sister, Caroline. But then, looking at someone across a crowded room wasn't exactly staring.

Alphonso lifted his head and Nell was taken aback by what an utterly handsome man he was. Thick, graying hair and an imposing stature enhanced his look and emphasized the strong bones of his face, the piercing eyes. With family homes in Boston and Sea Harbor and several Massachusetts businesses contributing to his wealth, he was a powerful force on Cape Ann.

Alphonso looked up, his eyes meeting Nell's. He acknowledged her with a nod of his head and a slight lift to the corner of his lips.

Amused? Nell wondered. Then his gaze moved beyond her, across the table to where his wife stood tall and regal next to his niece.

The trace of a smile dropped from Alphonso's face, but Nell couldn't quite read the look that replaced it. Perhaps it was simply the look of a man watching his wife from afar, viewing her the way strangers did, admiring the elegant beauty that turned heads.

The screech of a microphone hushed the crowd and drew attention to a small stage set up at one end of the room.

Laura Danvers, party hostess and planner, stood behind the microphone and blanketed the crowd with a smile.

"A lovely welcome to all of you," she said, her carefully modulated voice not at all the one the knitters were used to hearing when Laura found her toddler rearranging Izzy's cubicles of yarn in the shop.

"As you know, the money raised tonight will go to the children's portion of the community center in our own Anja Angelina Park. It will support staff, playground equipment, computers, and video equipment, and even a nurse's room for administering vaccinations."

There was polite applause.

"And none of this would be possible," she went on, "without the generosity of two Sea Harbor companies. Without their gracious donation of reduced labor and supply costs, the community center with its children's wing would be nothing more than architectural lines on a piece of blue paper."

Nell glanced over at Gracie. Her aunt had disappeared when the announcements began, probably to avoid the limelight. Sophia Santos was a private person, polite, gracious, but removed from the fray, as Birdie sometimes put it. Nell had known Sophia since she and Ben moved from Boston to make Sea Harbor their home. But in all that time, they had never gone beyond casual conversation. Sophia could be difficult, people said—there weren't many shades of gray in her worldview. She had a compulsion to speak up if she thought something was unjust, unfair, or just plain wrong. But that side of her rarely came out at cocktail parties, and Nell knew her only to be pleasant, slightly mysterious, and a bit remote.

Birdie had mentioned recently that Sophia didn't seem to have many friends—but she was showing surprising kindness to her housekeeper, Ella Sampson, driving her to Mass each day since Harold broke his ankle and was unable to do the task.

At the microphone, Laura Danvers continued in her carefully modulated voice. "Will David Joseph Delaney and Alphonso Nicholas Santos please join me for a moment to be properly thanked?"

Ben leaned toward Nell. "I hope Laura stays between the two of them or we may have July fireworks a month early."

Nell held back her smile. Though not exactly a Hatfield and McCoy–type family feud, the relationship between the Delaneys and Santoses was far from amicable. And not one that pulled them together easily on a stage.

Across the room, she watched D. J. Delaney push back his chair. His diminutive wife, Maeve, looked at him with pride. D.J.'s eldest son, Davey, sat next to his mother. Named after his father, Davey was the spitting image of him—square face and body, built like a bull. It was Davey, Ben had told her, who was angling to take over the family business. Though he was a hothead, Ben suspected he'd be good at managing the projects.

On the other side of Maeve sat "young Joey"—as the thirty-six-year-old had been called from the day of his birth. He had his mother's mellow brown eyes, smooth skin, and light hair.

Nell looked from Joey over to Gracie, her platinum hair brushed to a sheen and hanging softly around her shoulders. Her narrow face was calm, a pleasing smile in place, not disturbed by the Delaney and Santos' fanfare. Gracie Santos could speak to the volatility of these families better than any of us, Nell thought. She'd been intimately involved with both, the Santoses by blood, the Delaneys by marriage.

D. J. Delaney reached the riser first. His seersucker suit was stretched tightly across his broad shoulders and his bright flowered tie was a perfect match for his ruddy complexion. If Nell hadn't known better, she would have thought he had just run the Sea Harbor marathon.

Laura shook D.J.'s hand and stepped back to accommodate the imposing figure of Alphonso Santos. The two men nodded to each other, and Laura stepped again to the microphone, praising the company owners effusively for their support of the center. Alphonso appeared as he always did—in control, the powerful businessman in a fine Italian suit. D.J. shifted from one foot to the other, eyeing a squat glass of Irish whiskey that he had handed off to a waitress before standing up beside Laura.

Although the Santoses and Delaneys had competed on every major development project on the North Shore, a little pressure from the mayor had brought the two together to provide crews and supplies at cost to make the children's project truly a community effort.

The unlikely alliance didn't fool anyone.

"It can't hurt either company to please the city council and mayor," Birdie declared when the brief thank-yous were finished and the applause died down.

Gracie put down her dessert fork and brushed her hair back over one shoulder. "Not to disparage my uncle, but I'm not sure either of those men ever did anything that didn't hold personal gain. Some people are just like that."

"Like what?" Joey Delaney came up beside Gracie's chair, leaned over, and kissed her on the cheek.

Gracie smiled and offered him a chair.

"Nope. Thanks. Just came to say hello. You look great, Gracie." A wave of dark brown hair fell across Joey's forehead.

"So what's up with you, Joey?" Cass asked. "Will you be working on the community center or are you still hiding behind numbers and books?"

Joey laughed. "I'll be working my fingers to the bone, Cass; you know me." He held up two hands, then looked embarrassed at the dark sauce smudging his fingers.

Gracie pulled her brows together, feigning disapproval.

Joey picked up her napkin and wiped off his fingers. "Sorry, ladies. See what happens without you, Gracie? I can't get through a meal without making a mess."

Gracie allowed a small smile. "You can take care of yourself just fine, Delaney."

Nell watched the exchange. If divorce had to happen, Joey and Gracie were certainly a model for how to go about it. Although Gracie had filed divorce papers months before, it didn't seem a pressing issue. And in recent weeks, Nell had seen them around town together, laughing, sharing a beer. The bitterness sometimes connected to divorce was nicely absent. She wasn't sure of Gracie's feelings, but Joey Delaney still seemed totally in love with Gracie.

"So how's the fish shack coming?"

"It's not a shack, Joey."

Nell watched the interplay. They were certainly an attractive pair. Gracie's delicate cheekbones, straight blond hair, and enormous blue eyes complemented Joey's square chin and Irish smile. He was the most handsome of the Delaney boys, a tall, well-muscled man.

Joey Delaney had loved Gracie Santos, the story was told, since the day she pushed him off his Big Wheel in third grade and broke his wrist. She decorated his cast with a red heart and signed it, "Sory Joey. Luv, Gracie." The die was cast at that moment, Joey would say with a laugh as he told the story. And he still had the cast, shellacked and stored away, just in case anyone wanted to see it.

His wedding to Gracie had been a photographer's bonanza, from the enormous baskets of yellow roses filling Our Lady of the Seas church to the reception in the Santoses' lavish gardens. And the fact that the families stayed rigidly on either side of the church during the ceremony and spoke little at the festive affair that followed was covered up by the joy of the young couple and of their friends and neighbors.

They'd moved to Gloucester, away from the families, for a chance to start out on their own. But now, four years later, they were both back in Sea Harbor, each one pursuing a separate life.

"Well, whatever," Joey said. "Let me know if you need help. I'm pretty handy with a hammer or paintbrush." Joey touched Gracie's shoulder, waved at the others, and wandered off toward the adjacent bar area, where a group was staring up at a flat-screen television tuned to the Sox game.

"Nice offer," Cass said, her dark brows lifting the sentence into a question.

Gracie laughed. "He's actually been a big help lately. He must be on some kind of medication. When we were together, I never saw him. Now he anticipates when I need him before I do. But that being said, he's not so hot with a paintbrush. Our bedroom ended up with a wavy orange ceiling. Besides, he says his father is putting pressure on him to step up to the plate at the company. Sometimes I think Joey is the only smart Delaney brother. They need him more than ever now that—" She paused.

"Now that what?"

"Oh, you know, just the usual, I guess. Joey hasn't said much, but the construction business is always open to criticism. You don't use the right kind of nails or stones or insulation or whatever. Some of the mud is probably slung at the Delaneys by my own family— Alphonso and Sophia."

"Well, I can help paint, Gracie. And I *am* hot with a paintbrush," Izzy said. "I'll drag Sam Perry along. He's not as good as I am, but that long, lean body of his is useful for getting high spots."

"I'll bring the beer," Cass offered.

"You're great, every single one of you," Gracie said. "And I never turn down free help."

"The place is looking good," Ham Brewster said. "Ben and I scoped it out the other day when we went fishing. It's just what we need down on the pier. When do you open your doors?"

"Hopefully by Summerfest. The summer solstice." She tipped her chin up and grinned. "It's my thirty-sixth birthday, too—being born on the solstice is supposed to bring good fortune. The café is my birthday present from me to me."

"The Lazy Lobster and Soup Café." Jane Brewster laughed. "I love it. It sounds down-home, a place that should be featured in a movie, like *Fried Green Tomatoes*." She leaned over and tugged playfully on her husband's graying beard. "And speaking of down-home, I think it's time to dance with the one who brung me—hopefully before he falls asleep."

Ham groaned and gripped the sides of his chair, pushing himself up, feigning difficulty. In the distance the band struck up an easy swing melody and people moved toward the small dance floor.

Jane's shoulders began to sway to the rising beat. Her loose salt-and-pepper hair moved to the rhythm and a long purple skirt swished about her legs.

Ham looped one arm around her. "Who can resist the likes of my Janie? She's a dancin' fool."

Nell watched her friends walk off. Founders of the Canary Cove art colony, Jane and Ham had lived in Sea Harbor since the late sixties. Their pottery and paintings had a large following. But what Nell and Ben valued the Brewsters for even more than their artistry was their unwavering, devoted friendship. "I swear Jane gets more beautiful with every gray hair," Nell mused.

"She's not the only one." Ben slipped his arm around the back of her chair and massaged her neck with his fingers.

"Hey, you two, none of that monkey business in here," Cass said.

Gracie shushed Cass and turned to Ben and Nell. "I love that you do that," she said. "Don't ever stop."

A flurry of movement and loud voices nearby interrupted Nell's response. She turned toward the sounds.

Alphonso Santos stood near the entrance to the dining room. Although he faced the club lobby, with his back to the room, Nell could see a drink glass clenched in his hand. He seemed to be look-ing at an attractive middle-aged woman dressed in jeans and a white silk blouse, coming in the front door.

The woman's face was lit with anger and her coal-black hair was a wild flurry about her face, but beneath the chaos was a face as beautiful as a Madonna's—a long nose, firm cheekbones, and well-shaped lips. A face with perfect parts. But it was the pitch to her voice, not her beauty, that attracted the attention of those close enough to hear.

"I hate her, Alphonso," the woman hissed. "She's stealing from you. I wish she'd disappear from our lives forever."

Nell looked around at the others sitting at her table. They were trying to continue conversations, trying not to listen.

Alphonso's answer was inaudible to the diners. He reached out to touch the woman's shoulder.

She jerked away, taking a quick step backward and nearly tripping on the edge of an Oriental rug. Steadying herself, she looked at Alphonso again. Her voice lifted above the din of plates being cleared and cheers from the bar for a Sox home run. "She's the one you should cut out of your life, not me." The words were hurled across the marble lobby and traveled to the tables closest to the dining room entrance.

As if powered by her own words, the woman lifted one hand into the air. Her fingers were coiled around the neck of a beer bottle.

Ben pushed out his chair and headed for the entryway.

It was Joey Delaney and Liz Palazola, with Ben just one step behind them, who stopped the bottle from being hurled in Alphonso Santos' face.

Joey grabbed the woman's wrist, and Liz and Ben stepped into the fray, distracting her.

Cass bit down on her bottom lip and looked over at Gracie.

She was clenching her napkin with one hand. The other lay stiff on the white tablecloth.

Birdie reached over and covered Gracie Santos' rigid fingers with her blue-veined hand.

Gracie's narrow shoulders lifted in a slight shrug. "You know Mom—she never misses a party."

Chapter 3

*G*racie quickly turned her back to the lobby. She wanted to disappear—to suddenly become Lewis Carroll's Alice and slide down the rabbit hole. The others at the Endicott table ached with empathy.

When Julianne Santos' voice and hand dropped, Alphonso indicated to Ben, Liz, and Joey that things were under control. He cupped his sister's elbow in the palm of his hand and walked her out of the yacht club and down the wide fan of front steps.

Liz motioned for the men to follow her to the bar area, where she ordered them drinks—compliments of the house—and thanked them profusely.

The club manager's smile slipped back into place, her savvy control over the awkward situation evident. It came as no surprise to Nell when Annabelle Palazola's eldest child became manager of the yacht club. She had brains and common sense as well as beauty.

When Alphonso walked back into the dining room a short while later, he didn't glance at his niece. Instead, he scanned the room, looking over groups of diners, people moving about the festive room greeting friends and neighbors.

The band in the corner began to play another set.

Finally his gaze settled on a quiet seating area in the corner. Sophia sat on the couch with Mayor Stan Hanson, Beatrice Scaglia—

a longtime council member—and several other civic leaders. The mayor's body was hunched forward, his face serious. Across from him, Sophia's hands moved with her words—definite, decisive movements, pausing occasionally as if to pull out the proper English word to match her Spanish expression. From where Nell sat, Sophia was winning the argument, whatever it might be about.

Alphonso stood still for a moment, watching the exchange. Then he nodded to a waiter to bring him a drink refill and disappeared through the French doors.

Nell turned back to the table as Cass asked Gracie if she had known her mother, Julianne Santos, was back in town.

Gracie shook her head. "I never do. You know that better than anyone, Cass."

Birdie ran her fingers through her short silver bob. "I've known your mother for a long time. I watched her grow up. She's not a bad person."

"Good or bad, Julianne Santos will never win the mother of the year award," Cass said.

Nell couldn't blame Cass for her sharp words. She'd grown up with Gracie and had seen too much to empathize with Julianne. Since she was a teenager, Julianne Santos had lived on the edge, disappearing on a moment's notice for parts unknown, returning weeks or months later when she ran out of money. On one of the returns, she brought Gracie with her—but soon left again, leaving Gracie behind. Nell had always hoped those stories were exaggerated, but no one had ever refuted them. Gracie's childhood hadn't been an easy one.

Her uncle married late by Sea Harbor standards, and when Alphonso finally brought Sophia home to the big house on Ravenswood Road, Julianne's visits became even less frequent. She and Sophia were like fire and ice. And that was putting it nicely, Cass had said.

It was unspoken, but understood, that with Julianne gone, her brother, Alphonso, would raise her daughter.

And he did.

"I'm fine," Gracie said to everyone. "This isn't new. Just Julianne's way of saying hi."

Ben appeared then, as if on cue, carrying a tray of tall narrow glasses with sprigs of fresh mint sticking out the top.

"Uncle Ben to the rescue." Izzy took two of the glasses from the tray and handed Gracie a fresh drink. "The bartender may have failed martini school, but he makes a mean mojito."

"The best," Ben said. "And when we're finished, I am going to challenge the lot of you to outdo me on the dance floor."

Nell laughed and pushed back her chair, planting a quick kiss on Ben's cheek. "I can't compete with Ben on the dance floor," she said. "What I need is some ocean air."

"I'm right behind you, Nell. If I had even one of those Cuban drinks you'd be scooping me off the floor." Birdie pushed herself up from the table.

"Birdie." Ben looked up. "Didn't you tell me Izzy was driving you over tonight?"

Birdie turned and glared at her friend, her white brows nearly touching each other. "Are you checking up on me, Ben Endicott? Shame on you! I told you I'd drive at night only when necessary."

Ben laughed. "Of course not. But I saw your big Lincoln drive into the parking lot a while ago. I was curious."

"I'd never attempt that windy road in the Lincoln—not if I thought you'd find out about it anyway. Izzy and I had a pleasant drive over together in her car, thank you very much."

"Hmm," Ben said. "Could Harold have come by?"

"No. He's home with a broken ankle and not driving these days. You must have seen someone else. Possibly you should be wearing your glasses more often, my dear Ben." She smiled at him sweetly and planted a kiss on his forehead.

Ben looked properly chastised. "Sorry, Birdie. I should know better than to doubt you."

"Yes, you should," Birdie said, and turned to follow Nell to the terrace doors, her silky kimono wrap billowing about her.

Nell knew Ben wasn't convinced, and as soon as she and Birdie were out of view, he'd walk outside and check again. Birdie's Lincoln Town Car was hard to miss.

"It was getting a tad warm in there," Birdie said as they stepped out onto the cool terrace. She took a deep breath and tipped her chin up to catch a breeze.

"Julianne Santos' arrival didn't help cool it off." Nell sat down on a stone bench near the railing of the softly lit terrace. In the distance, the sound of waves lapping against the shore mixed with the dance music coming from inside. Above, the enormous moon bathed the stone terrace in a soft glow.

"I almost didn't recognize Julianne. I haven't seen her for a while."

"And she often changes her look. Sometimes red hair, sometimes platinum. I haven't seen her next door for a while, though the Santos house is so hidden from view I can't really see much."

"She's a beautiful woman."

"I remember Julianne when she was a teenager. She was always in one kind of trouble or another. Running off with men she barely knew. I used to think it was because her parents were gone so much. She had to work extra hard to get any attention. These days I rarely see her."

"Sophia would be a formidable sister-in-law."

"But a decent aunt to Gracie."

"And driving Ella Sampson to church every day while Harold's laid up is a sweet thing do."

Birdie agreed. "Ella enjoys it. I think it's good for her and Harold to have their moments apart, though Harold is not happy that Ella has someone other than himself to talk to."

Birdie sighed, then went on.

"They've been arguing day and night. Two of the gentlest,

most wonderful people on earth, and suddenly they are at each other at every turn. If Harold says something is black, Ella says it's white. They're a mess."

"Maybe Harold is just frustrated that he can't be off fishing or fixing lawn mowers or pruning trees. That bum ankle probably gets him down."

Birdie nodded, but Nell could tell she wasn't convinced. "Well, this too will pass." She patted Birdie's hand.

"Yes it will." They both fell silent then, the way old friends do, a comfortable respite from talk, each alone in thought.

The sounds of laughter and light chatter floated over the terrace as small groups drifted out for fresh air and after-dinner drinks. Nell spotted Alphonso standing alone a short distance away, his palms flat on the stone railing. Collecting himself, Nell supposed. He looked slightly disheveled, his tie askew from the altercation with his sister. It was an unnatural look for him.

A group of guests moved across the terrace, headed for the steps leading down to the beach, and Alphonso disappeared from Nell's view. When the space cleared, a waitress was walking his way with a tray in her hands.

"Mr. Santos?" Nell heard her say. "The manager sent this out, compliments of the house." She handed Alphonso a crystal glass.

Nell watched Alphonso's face soften, appraising the beautiful young woman, his eyes roaming over her full figure. She responded with a slow, flirtatious smile, then turned and walked back into the club, her tray empty and her practiced walk attracting attention.

Alphonso took a slow drink, watching her walk away. Once she disappeared inside the club, his pensive look returned.

"Alphonso has had better nights," Birdie said, looking in that direction.

"Gracie, too."

A shadow fell between the two women and Alphonso. It was Sophia, car keys dangling from her long fingers. She stood straight and regal, her elegant form a shapely silhouette against the low terrace lights. Her voice carried over to Nell and Birdie on the breeze.

"Your *hermana* . . . she is gone?"

"Yes. My sister won't be back. Not tonight, at least."

Sophia stood close to Alphonso for a moment longer, looking at her husband but not speaking.

"I saw you talking to the mayor. The beach access?" he asked.

"Yes. The mayor is a stubborn man. But the land is mine, Alphonso. The access will remain closed. The neighbors will have to find another road. Another beach." She lifted her hand again, the keys catching the light of the moon. "I am leaving you now. I have an important day ahead. Save time for me, my husband. We will have things we need to discuss. Good night, *mi amor*."

Sophia touched his cheek lightly with two fingers, her eyes locking onto his. Then she turned and walked back into the yacht club, her lacy wrap draped over her arm, her head held high, and a weary smile easing the lines of her face.

Alphonso stared after her, his look so electric that Nell and Birdie looked away. They felt like intruders, eavesdroppers, witnessing an intensely private moment, one they were not meant to see.

It was the sound of a Scotch glass, flung against the stone floor, that caused Nell and Birdie to look back. He stood alone, surrounded by crystal splinters. As he turned back to the sea, their eyes met, and it was only then that Birdie and Nell saw the look of total anguish in Alphonso Santos' eyes.

Chapter 4

The white moon hung so low above Devil's Cove that Sam Perry was sure if he reached up, he could touch it. His first night dive, and as the dive guide had promised, it was a perfect one.

He pulled himself from the black water and waded over to the rickety dock on which the divers had stashed their gear bags. He slipped his diving mask to the top of his head, hoisted his tank onto the dock surface, and braced his elbows against the edge. The moon was eerie in its brightness. It had an iridescent glow, not the usual milky haze of lazy summer nights. Sam played with the ring of his underwater camera—recently focused on moon snails and lumpfish and lobsters disappearing into nests of wavy seaweed. He tilted the lens upward, focusing on the sky.

The wet suit was a slippery second skin, and the photographer's elbow slid along the plank. He steadied it, then looked up again into the night sky, his eyes shifting from the pinpoint light of stars to the mysterious moon.

A movement on the rocky cliff above the diving beach distracted Sam for a second. At first he thought it was a falling star. But the lights moving erratically along the upper terrain, bouncing in the darkness, told him differently.

Sam frowned, instinctively moving the lens of his camera from the sky to the cliff, following the lights.

It was a car, and it was going too fast for the curvy road that outlined the high ledge. Devil's Cove had hosted its share of accidents, teenagers out for joyrides and grazing the granite boulders that bordered the lookout area, or a driver with a few drinks in him, screeching to a stop just before the land took a downward turn. But mostly people were careful along Devil's Cove Road, warned by the slow-down signs that lit up when car lights hit the neon paint.

Sam called to the other divers who were surfacing in the water behind him. Wordlessly, they focused on the dancing headlights. Sam lifted his camera again and adjusted the telephoto lens to pull the image closer.

"Slow down, you crazy fool," someone murmured behind him.

Then, as if sensing an audience, the two beams of light turned abruptly toward the ocean. Sam squinted, blinded momentarily as he stared into the looming headlights.

In the next instant, the car was airborne, sailing in front of the moon like a toy, its small shape a stark silhouette against the glow.

As if at a tennis match, the divers' heads moved as one, following the trajectory of the car. Helpless, they stared in awful amazement at a bright red car flying through the sky like a comet, then hurtling to the rocky shore below.

Chapter 5

*N*ell had fallen asleep that night as soon as her head hit the pillow, unaware that five miles away, a group of divers would get little sleep at all.

The next morning Ben teased her that she was half-asleep on their way home from the party. "Even those police sirens didn't get a rise out of you. Why didn't you sleep in today? It's Saturday—no board meetings, no grant writing classes to give."

Ben's words of advice were hollow ones. He knew Nell hadn't slept past seven since she was a college student pulling all-night cramming sessions. And that matched his own habits just fine. He liked being the first one up, around five or so, as was his habit. And then he liked watching Nell walk down the back stairs and into the kitchen, her hair still tousled or sometimes damp and wavy from a shower, her lazy gaze moving over him like sunlight.

He fell in love all over again, every time he saw her come down those steps, he had told her once.

"Was sleeping in what you had in mind when you woke me a while ago?" she asked with a playful lift to her brows.

"You got me there." Ben coughed in mock embarrassment and opened the refrigerator. He took out the half-and-half and Nell's scone mix, ready to be dropped on pans and placed in the oven.

"I wonder what those sirens were about last night," she said, picking up a spoon and stirring the mix. She dropped spoonfuls of batter onto the cookie sheet and wiped a dollop of batter from her finger. "I dreamed about them, I think." Nell forced her mind back to her sleeping hours. "Sirens frighten me. They can signal lives changing in an instant."

She slid the pans into the oven.

"It was probably just some kids joyriding around Devil's Cove. The police chief told me his men are clamping down on teenage shenanigans before summer gets into full swing and someone gets hurt." Ben unrolled the *Sea Harbor Gazette* and spread it out on the kitchen island. "Whatever the ruckus was, it was too late, probably, to make the paper."

But Ben was wrong. It hadn't been too late to make the paper. And—as Nell had predicted—it meant lives would be changed in an instant.

Nearly filling the top half of the newspaper was a photo of Alphonso Santos' red Ferrari, smashed like a used soup can against the rocks of Devil's Cove. It didn't need identification; even wrecked and lying on the shore, it was a car that everyone in Sea Harbor knew.

Before Nell could react, the sound of tires and slamming car doors announced that they had company. As she stared at the photo, Nell suspected whoever was coming wasn't coming for blueberry scones.

Sam and Izzy came through the front door and across the family room to the kitchen island. Both wore running shorts and damp T-shirts. Izzy's hair was a multicolored tangle of waves, held together haphazardly by a bright blue scrunchie. The scent of sea air followed them across the room.

Izzy held a copy of the morning paper in her hand.

"Can you believe this? Sam was right there. He saw this happen." Her enormous brown eyes filled her face as she looked from Nell and Ben to Sam, and then back again.

Nell pushed her reading glasses to the top of her head. "This is awful. We saw Alphonso shortly before we left—out on the patio. He was upset about something, maybe that scene with his sister."

Sam spoke up. "It wasn't Alphonso who was driving, Nell."

Nell looked at him, not understanding, and then she and Ben stared again at the newspaper, reading for the first time the two-inch headline that stretched across the page.

MRS. ALPHONSO SANTOS
DIES IN CRASH ON DEVIL'S COVE

"Sophia?" Nell's eyes widened in surprise.

"We were coming up from a dive. The car crashed to the shore, right at the edge of the water on that jagged pile of boulders the kids like to climb on. We thought it was Alphonso, too, and ran over to see if by any miracle we could pull him out of the tangled metal. Right away we saw it was a woman, but we didn't know it was his wife—it was hard to tell." His voice dropped.

"Did Alphonso survive?" Ben didn't want to hear the answer. No one could have survived that crash.

"There wasn't anyone else in the car. She was alone."

Of course. The scene on the patio came back to Nell—Sophia holding up the keys and her cryptic message: *I'm leaving you, Alphonso.*

When she had repeated it to Ben on the ride home, he said it could have meant anything. Leaving him alone on the terrace. Leaving him to get a drink. Leaving him to go home.

It was the logical explanation, Nell admitted, in spite of Alphonso's odd reaction. Ben was right. She was leaving to go home. Alone.

"She was weaving all across the road," Sam went on. "And then the car spun off the road and over the edge. One of the guys thought the driver had to be drunk, it was that kind of driving."

But Sophia rarely drank. And she had been as steady as a trapeze artist when she walked out onto the terrace the night before.

Last night. It was only hours ago that Sophia had stopped by their table to say hello, elegant as always. She'd given Gracie a hug—brief, in an urgent manner, Nell remembered. "Does Gracie know?"

Izzy nodded. "Cass and Pete are going with her to Alphonso's," Izzy said.

"Alphonso must be devastated. And Gracie's mother?"

"No one seems to know where she is. But—"

Izzy's words dropped off, interrupted by the front screen door opening and closing. Birdie walked across the room, her sneakers silent on the floor and her face flushed from the bike ride across town. She pressed one hand to her chest to catch her breath, then walked over to the island. "Clearly this wasn't a day to stop at Coffee's, my original destination."

"I suppose the news is all over town?" Nell said.

Ben looked up at the kitchen clock. Nine o'clock. "I suspect that's so." He handed Birdie a glass of water.

"It's an awful thing. Such a shame for poor Alphonso."

Birdie pulled her small frame onto a stool and pushed her sunglasses to the top of her head. "The Santos house was lit up like the Fourth of July, but never did I imagine anything like this. I thought Alphonso had invited some people over after the party for brandy and talk. They did that sometimes. Sophia wasn't much into late nights, but Alphonso was another story. His energy well never went dry."

"What was the scene at Coffee's?" Izzy asked. The coffee shop patio was a popular spot all mornings, but Saturdays especially.

"It was packed. I could sense the talk more than hear it—you know how it is. There's something in the air when the unexpected happens. First people are shocked, then sad, and then the inevitable speculation and gossip start. Was she drinking? Was she on drugs? Suicide? It's a shame, but I think people feel a need to come up with logical explanations for tragedies. It makes them feel more in control, a kind of insurance that this couldn't happen to them because they would never do whatever Sophia did to have her life end so tragically."

It was human nature's way of handling tragedy. Nell glanced at the newspaper photo again and then looked up at Sam. "What an awful thing to have witnessed, Sam—to see someone die in such a violent way."

Izzy pressed into Sam's side as if her presence would make the images go away.

Sam wrapped one arm around her shoulders. "What was awful was to know what was about to happen and not be able to do a damn thing to stop it. As a photojournalist I've seen my share of bad things. But this was . . . personal, I guess."

Nell walked over to the stove and slid the warm scones onto a platter. "I don't imagine sleep came easily." She carried the platter to the island.

"I can't quite get my arms around the erratic driving description," Ben said. "Sophia was almost too cautious with that car. I don't think she liked driving it. And the car itself hugged the road and took curves better than any car around here—it's hard to imagine that a careful driver would run off the road."

"Why do you suppose she was alone?" Izzy wondered. She picked up a scone and slathered it with the sweet butter Ben had set out.

Birdie took a sip of coffee, then slipped a scone onto her plate. "Sophia and Alphonso often drove to parties separately. Sophia didn't like to stay as late as Alphonso. But even if they went together, Alphonso was quite resourceful, and I don't suppose he'd have trouble finding a way home after she left."

Birdie's words hung in the silent air for a few seconds. She hadn't intended them to carry innuendo, but Alphonso Santos was rich, powerful, and good-looking—and most certainly resourceful. And the combination elicited persistent rumors of extracurricular activities that none of the friends gathered in the Endicott kitchen had any intention of addressing—at least not this morning.

"It makes one wonder . . ." Birdie said.

"About?" Ben refilled the coffee mugs.

"The vagaries of life. Here we have one person dead. But maybe if Alphonso and Sophia had left together, we'd be mourning two people today. Or maybe, with a different person behind the wheel of that powerful car, no one would be dead. Or maybe, if Sophia hadn't driven on that road . . ." Her voice trailed off.

"Lots of what-ifs," Nell agreed. "That's always the way."

Ben and Sam leaned over the newspaper photo again, examining the wreckage.

"It was his dream car," Ben murmured. "Alphonso didn't talk much about possessions—but when he got this car a few months ago, he made us all leave a community center board meeting to go out and look at it. It was last March—a beautiful spring day, I remember. He was like a kid on Christmas morning—or as much as Alphonso could seem like a kid." Ben took a drink of his coffee. "He loved that car something fierce."

Sam agreed. "I took some photos of it for his office. Joey showed up that day—he's a car nut, too—and Alphonso let us inspect it inside and out. I even have pictures of the engine. Then Alphonso topped it off by letting us take it out for a spin. We ripped up a couple back roads. It was amazing."

Birdie frowned as she pulled their thoughts together about Alphonso Santos' dream car. "That's right. He loved that car. And then suddenly, a week later, it was Sophia's car."

"And he never drove it again, it seems," Nell added softly.

The room grew silent. Sophia had been the only one driving the car since that first week. And she drove it like an old lady, some said. To meetings, to church, to the supermarket. Carefully. Cautiously. Joylessly.

"Sophia Santos didn't even like cars," Birdie finished. "Especially the one that she died in."

"The gift from hell," Izzy finished.

Chapter 6

"Two houses so close together and so vastly different," Nell mused, looking out at the carefully tended lawn of the Santos estate.

"They fit the personalities of the people who live in them." Ben drove slowly up the long driveway. "Can you imagine Birdie living behind locked gates and pruned bushes shaped like birds?"

Nell laughed. Birdie's three-story captain's house next door commanded the same view and equal acreage as the Santos home, but it was casual and comfortable. Nell never hesitated to drop her shoes at the door and curl up in one of Sonny Favazza's deep leather den chairs that still, all these years later, smelled of Birdie's first husband's cherrywood pipe. The Favazza home welcomed sandals or bare feet, jeans, cutoffs, or designer slacks. It never mattered.

In the Santos home, Nell was always a guest, something she'd never in a million years be considered at Birdie's.

The brick drive was smooth and shiny from a recent hosing, and tiny gaslights cast slender shadows into the carefully maintained flower beds. Nell looked around at the wide, illuminated grounds, the curved granite benches, and lights shining up into the trees. Statuary—cherubs, decorative urns, and Greek gods in awkward poses—were placed around the main house, gazebo, and flower beds. Nell remembered Cass' stories of playing with Gracie on the expensive statues and breaking an ear off a unicorn poised for flight. It was a misdeed that Nell suspected was never confessed to Alphonso.

The steps in front of the brick and stone house were lit, too—each one holding a pot of tulips. For a moment Nell regretted the container of lobster stew that was cushioned tightly in the car trunk. It was habit, she supposed—one took food when paying condolences. But suddenly it seemed an awkward gesture.

"Out, my love," Ben whispered in her ear and only then did Nell realize that he had parked the car and was holding open the passenger door. In his other arm he carefully balanced the box containing the soup.

Nell slipped out of the CRV, glad to have Ben at her side. Ben was comfortable in situations like this, a product of his many years in a boardroom. An experienced semiretired business owner with business and law degrees, Ben Endicott rarely encountered a situation that either his sense of humor or his intelligence couldn't carry him through. Even the lobster stew, Nell thought with a smile, would seem the correct thing with him carrying it up the steps.

Nell fell in step beside Ben, her dark summer dress moving against her legs. A breeze lifted her hair, and she pressed it back into place with the palm of her hand and looked up at Ben's profile. "Birdie will meet us—she's walking over."

"Over the river and through the woods . . ."

"No river, though." Nell looked back into the thick stand of trees that separated the two properties. It did, indeed, look like a woods.

"I suppose that access road that Sophia had gated off might be considered the river," Ben said, following her look.

The narrow stretch of land that led from the road to the ocean lay hidden in the middle of the thick stand of trees—but everyone knew of the pathway. For decades, families on the south end of Sea Harbor had loaded up their beach blankets and toys and headed down to the cove below. A curving arm of land kept waves at a minimum and protected the sandy beach. The Children's Beach, it had been dubbed by the locals.

"I don't understand Sophia's blocking it off," Ben said. "It's not a good way to win friends."

"I'm not sure Sophia was about winning friends. I think she simply liked her privacy. For whatever reason, Birdie said she was passionate about this issue."

Ben nodded. But when push came to shove, they both knew that the residents inconvenienced by her bold action wouldn't easily accept the need for privacy as a viable reason. The woods prevented anyone walking down to the beach from being seen from the big house. "Unreasonable" and "irrational" were words hurled Sophia's way when the topic was discussed.

"Sam, Izzy, and Willow are probably here. I think Gracie was soliciting friends tonight."

Gracie had told them that her uncle would be receiving people for a short time on Sunday night. "Receiving" was the word he had used, one Gracie felt awkward repeating. "It somehow seems so . . . so obligatory," she'd said. And then she'd managed a laugh and added, "But if you bring food, Nell, well, that's worth receiving."

The heavy walnut doors were opened by a butler. Nell and Ben stepped into a foyer filled with crystal vases of flowers—lilies and white roses in such abundance their fragrance was nearly overwhelming. A maid appeared instantly and took the soup tureen from Ben, acknowledged it with a slight bow of her head, then disappeared without making a sound on the marble floor.

Ahead of them, Alphonso stood tall and sedate in a black suit, a polite smile on his darkly handsome face, greeting each guest in turn.

Nell waited in line, listening to the murmur of condolences. She watched the guests move forward, as if mysteriously choreographed, shaking Alphonso's hand, nodding to friends, then making their way to one of the bars set up in the dining room and out on the terrace.

The mayor was there, along with many Harbor Road shop owners, neighbors, and people with whom the Santos Company did business. Nell spotted Joey Delaney over near the terrace doors. Joey had probably come for Gracie. To be a support. He was alone, out of the way, but there if Gracie needed him. A guardian angel, Nell thought.

Behind her, a steady stream of people filed through the door. Nell looked around and noticed Birdie's housekeeper, Ella Sampson. She was standing alone, her slender frame slightly stooped, as if the weight of the occasion were too much for her. She started to get in line, then noticed where it was leading—to Alphonso Santos—and quickly stepped aside and disappeared into the dining room.

All around her, Nell heard muted conversations about the accident. The speed of the car. Sophia being alone. The erratic driving. All disparate pieces of conversation that subtly asked for answers that no one could offer.

Alphonso's deep voice drew Nell's attention back to the man now in front of her. He spoke to Ben, then shook Nell's hand, his controlled smile in place. But when Nell looked up into his eyes, she saw sadness and felt a sudden press of Alphonso's hand, more firmly, as if convincing her of something.

"Sophia was a good woman, a good wife," he said in a low voice. "I loved her, no matter what."

His steel gray eyes locked onto Nell's. He clasped her hand firmly.

"Yes," she said. "I know you did, Alphonso."

But she didn't know that, not really. And it wasn't her business to know it. She smiled again and slid her hand from his grasp, allowing Harry Garozzo to take her place, his beefy baker's hand now clasping Alphonso's.

A maid directed them into the expansive dining room, where a series of leaded French doors opened onto the terrace. The polished mahogany table held mounds of shrimp and crab legs in silver bowls, elegant configurations of fresh fruit, and an assortment of crackers and imported cheeses, light salads, toast points, and caviar. Another table was laden with desserts.

At the end of the room, Liz Palazola stood quietly, motioning to waiters and waitresses, checking trays and bowls, smiling at guests.

She looked lovely, striking, even with a line of worry marring her forehead. Nell wondered if Liz had ever looked ordinary. Beauty was effortless to Annabelle's eldest child. And with each passing year she grew more striking. A simple black dress slid over her full breasts and was transformed into a lovely garment. Liz was totally unaware of the effect, Nell imagined.

Ben began filling a plate with shrimp and crab, reminding Nell that the last meal they had had was a cheese and spinach omelet that morning at the Sweet Petunia.

"It beats our leftovers," she said with a smile. She picked up a glass of wine from a passing waiter and walked over to Liz.

"I wondered who could possibly have pulled something like this together on such short notice. It's lovely, Liz."

"Thank you. Alphonso said if people took the time to come, they should at least have something to make up for the dinner they may have missed. Sophia would have wanted it to be perfect. To be elegant, just like she was, he said. It was the least I could do. This is such a horrible time for everyone."

"It looks very much like Sophia, not at all the mushroom soup and bean casserole we're used to at Father Larry's church receptions."

Liz smiled and nodded toward a gray-haired man standing at the French doors, engaging Ben in conversation. A heaping plate of food was held in one hand, and with the other, Father Northcutt punctuated his words with a wineglass.

"I don't think the good padre minds the variety."

Nell laughed. "No. I don't suppose he does. Father Northcutt loves good food. I'm glad he's here to support Alphonso—especially since I understand the funeral won't be in his church."

Liz motioned to a waiter to refill a water pitcher on the table. "Her family is there," she said. "In Argentina, I mean."

"But Alphonso didn't have to do that. The husband has rights, and if he wanted to bury her here, to keep her close in that way, he could have insisted."

"Here?" Liz seemed surprised at the suggestion, but before she could pursue it, a loud crashing noise came through the kitchen's swinging door. "I'm sorry, Nell, I need to take care of this."

As Liz hurried through the door, Nell spotted a heap of shattered glass and mess of caviar on the floor. Liz Palazola would have that under control in a matter of seconds, she suspected.

The room was buzzing now, the wine loosening tongues. Waiters wove their way through the groups of people, pouring, picking up empty glasses, offering appetizers. From where she stood, Nell could see the front door and the wide staircase that curved to the floors above, a massive crystal chandelier in the center. She spotted Ella Sampson again, walking down the stairs, one hand gripping the banister. Ella glanced uneasily around her, and Nell suspected the majesty of the house and the formal attire of the guests was overwhelming to the gentle and simple housekeeper. She wore a plain collared dress with a narrow belt, and a cardigan sweater over it. A cloth purse hung heavily from her arm.

Nell noticed a book sticking out the top of the bag. The chandelier's light bounced off the gilded pages. It was too big for Ella's bag, a teal leather volume that stretched the opening of the narrow purse.

As if she felt Nell's look, Ella reached over with her other hand and tried to shove the book farther into her purse. Then she looked around once more and hurried out the front door.

Curious, Nell mused, but before she had time to process her thought, Izzy appeared at her side.

"Come," she said, and looped her arm through Nell's, leading her toward the doors. "We're on the terrace."

Gracie, Willow Adams, and Cass sat at a patio table with Birdie. Cass' brother, Pete Halloran, Sam, and Ben stood nearby discussing the Sox's wicked rousting of the Yankees earlier in the day. Father Northcutt had moved on to greet a group of parishioners on the other side of the terrace.

A lively Baroque concerto filtered out through hidden speakers. The ambience bespoke an elegant cocktail party.

"No offense, Gracie," Cass said, "but as lovely as all this is, I want you guys to say good-bye to me down on the beach near Perry's place with endless pitchers of Ben's martinis and a clambake. Throw in Pete's band and I'll be a happy camper."

Gracie's smile was halfhearted. "This was Alphonso's idea of what Sophia would have wanted. It really didn't matter what anyone else thought."

"It feels elegant, just like she was, dear." Birdie reached over and patted Gracie's slender arm. "I think he did the right thing."

"I suppose. But I bet half the people here never even met Sophia. And at least some of the rest didn't like her much."

"I'm not sure about that," Nell said tactfully. "I think most people simply didn't know her very well, myself included. Sophia was always lovely, but she didn't talk much about herself."

"You're right, sure. I didn't know her very well myself, even though she tried to be an aunt to me. Sophia never shirked her responsibility, which is what she considered me, I think. Sophia and Alphonso always seemed okay with my being here when Mom took off. They weren't exactly warm and fuzzy, definitely not the Cleavers, but they took me in, and that was good. They didn't have to, I suppose."

"They were your family," Cass said. "Of course they had to."

"I suppose. And I guess the bulk of it was on Sophia because Alphonso wasn't around much. Someone had to make sure Cass and I didn't tear the house down or smoke in the bathrooms." Gracie took a drink of wine. "Weird as it may be, I think she cared about me, even though it wasn't her choice to marry a man who would end up with a preteen under his watch."

"You were lucky," Willow Adams said softly. The youngest in the group, Willow's eyes reflected the experiences that made her seem older than her twenty-three years. "It's hard when your mom isn't there. Before she died, my mom was kinda like yours, I think. Sometimes she wasn't there, even when she was. You know?"

Nell watched the young fiber artist, knowing the words were spoken with difficulty. Willow had come to Sea Harbor a year before, searching for a father she had never known. And by summer's end she had worked her way into their hearts. When she decided to stay and make the Canary Cove art colony her home, just as her father before her had done, no one was happier than the Seaside Knitters.

"Speaking of mothers," Cass said, "what happened to Julianne? Does she know about Sophia?"

Gracie shrugged. "I left a message on her cell phone. At least I think it's her cell phone. Who knows if she has it with her or if it works or if she checks it."

"She'll come. I know she'd want to be here for you and for her brother," Birdie said.

Nell noticed the lack of conviction in Birdie's voice. Julianne was hard to predict. She'd clearly wanted something from her brother last Friday. Probably money, Birdie had said. The elder Santoses' will left everything to their son, Alphonso, with the directive that he provide for his younger sister from a designated fund, keeping her safe. It was a demeaning but necessary situation for the willful Julianne, but it didn't stop her from asking for money, usually to spend on some low-life man who would inevitably take advantage of her. It was hard for Alphonso to say no because he felt guilty—or at least that was Birdie's view of the situation. But when he married Sophia, she encouraged a firmer stand.

"It might be better if Julianne doesn't come," Gracie said. "It will be one more thing for Alphonso to deal with. She's probably worlds away after their argument Friday night."

Nell looked into the dining room and saw Alphonso at the bar, alone for that brief moment. He stood still, his blunt fingers wrapped around a drink glass, his brow creased, and the weight of the world showing on his face. Liz came up and offered him a plate of food, but he shook his head, and she soon walked away with the plate still in her hand.

Instead, Alphonso gestured to the bartender to refill his glass, then turned and wandered onto the terrace, his face composed again and his hand held forward to a business associate who moved to shake it.

"Did you see Joey?" Nell asked, looking over toward the young man still standing at the terrace doorway.

Gracie followed the nod of Nell's head. "That's nice of him. Especially since Sophia . . ." A movement beyond the railing distracted her and her sentence fell away.

"Oh, Lordy," Cass moaned. They all followed her look to the edge of the terrace.

A slender figure wearing a bright red tank top and a silky skirt that looked more like a slip moved along the flagstone pathway on the back side of the house. She held one hand aloft for balance, as if walking a tightrope.

"Alphonso?" she called out, looking up to the terrace. "Are you there?"

Nell had a sudden image of Zelda, moving dramatically toward her husband, F. Scott Fitzgerald, her slender body waving in the breeze, a martini glass held aloft in her hand. A strong breeze would have toppled either of them.

Gracie started to call to her mother, then stopped abruptly, suddenly aware that people were standing on the terrace, watching. She took a deep breath and stood still as her mother came closer to the terrace steps.

In three long strides Alphonso was at the top of the steps. Without looking at Gracie, he motioned with his hand for her to stay away.

"Julianne," he said calmly.

Julianne stopped at the sound of her brother's voice. She looked up. "I heard about Sophia, Alphonso. You're sad, I know. She's dead." Her muffled words traveled up on the breeze, accompanied by the faint smell of whiskey. She stopped on the bottom step, gripping the handrail.

"Let's go into the house, Julianne. I'll get you something to eat." He took one step toward her.

Nell looked at Gracie, wishing she could sweep her up and protect her from the scene her mother was about to make. Out of the corner of her eye, she saw Joey moving across the terrace to Gracie's side. He placed one hand on the small of her back, but Gracie stepped away from the support, standing alone, resilient from years of practice.

Other guests had stopped talking and an eerie silence fell upon the terrace. Even the music seemed to have stopped for Julianne's entrance.

Alphonso held out his hand to his sister as one would to a child. "It's okay, Julianne. Come up."

Nell watched the play of emotions on Julianne's face, an awful mix of sadness and anger. She looked like a tragic heroine, beautiful and bereft, confused. Her beauty was a *worn* kind of beauty, Nell thought. Like a beautiful doll that has been played with too much or too roughly.

Julianne held one hand up in front of her as if to stop her brother from moving toward her. Her head moved slowly from side to side.

"Don't be sad, my Alphonso," she said. She spoke with effort, her voice louder than necessary and her eyebrows lifting crookedly into a sweep of scattered bangs. "That woman didn't belong here in our parents' house. Not ever. She was bad for you. For me. It's better that she is dead, Alphonso."

Before her words could completely settle on the shocked gathering standing in stony silence above her, Julianne Santos released her grip on the railing. With the grace of a ballet dancer, her body folded over on the wide granite steps.

Chapter 7

$\mathcal{N}$ell walked into the Seaside Knitting Studio, weaving her way around customers leafing through patterns on a rack near the front door. She waved to Mae, Izzy's store manager, and headed toward the back of the shop.

It was the color that caught her eye and caused the detour—but not a color, really. The yarn was brilliant and white as snow. As if pulled by a magnet, Nell wandered into the small room defined by floor-to-ceiling cubicles of yarn. On the one wall with open space, Izzy had hung framed photographs of sheep—the Bluefaced Leicester, a California Red, even a Navajo-Churro—all reminders, she told her customers, of the amazing animals from which the raw fiber came. In the center of the room on a small round table was a giant wicker basket. And overflowing its edge was Izzy's new shipment of handspun wool. Nell picked up a soft, luxurious skein of Cormo wool and held it up to the light, resisting the urge to press it against her cheeks. "Amazing," she murmured. She fingered the spun fibers and wondered about the hands that created it. A true art.

"Hello, dearie," a voice behind her chirped. Nell turned and only then noticed Esther Gibson sitting in the room's one rocking chair, her gnarled hands working a large multicolored glove. She looked at Nell over the top of rimless glasses and smiled, her fingers continuing to loop yarn over needle.

Nell smiled, an effect the police dispatcher always had on her. "I didn't see you there, Esther. You're as quiet as a church mouse."

"Quiet can be good," Esther said brightly. "That young crew at the station house thinks quiet breeds ill. If they aren't chattering and telling their silly jokes, they're playing pounding music on those tiny boxes."

Nell laughed. "Tommy Porter tells me you keep all the young police officers in line. They need you, Esther."

"Well, yes, they do. Not that sweet Tommy, though. He'll be chief one day, if he sticks around long enough." A short cane was hooked over the arm of the rocker, a concession to a bad back suffered from nearly thirty years of sitting in an unforgiving wooden chair as Sea Harbor's police dispatcher. She lifted it now and leaned forward on the worn handle, her voice dropping to a hushed level. "Nellie, tell me dear, what is all this gossip about Sophia Santos? We're getting calls, people going on and on as if they had good sense. Let the dead lie in peace, is what I say—God rest her soul."

"What kind of calls?"

"Silly calls, the kind a dispatcher doesn't have time to dally with. Everyone has a theory. Everyone wants a say. You'd think there was a reward out there, the way people are acting. But for what, I ask? My goodness. A lady called today to tell me that Sophia was drunk, and she could have killed someone. She said she was calling to report it. Why? I'm wondering to myself. So she'll get a ticket, for heaven's sake? So I said to the caller—nicely, of course, but quite firmly—I said, 'She did kill someone, dearie. She killed herself, and that's a very sad thing, and it doesn't need your gossip to paint it another color, now, does it?'"

Nell thought about the unsuspecting caller, sweetly put in her place. "Rumors can be nasty. But people don't mean harm, I don't think."

"Sometimes they do, dear." Esther settled back into her chair and picked up her knitting. Her glasses slipped down her nose as she looked down and counted the stitches with the bent tip of her index finger. Then she looked up again. "But sometimes people just don't think before they open their mouths, and they say or do things that add fuel to rumors, maybe not meaning to. They jump-start those rumors, you might say." She paused for a moment, her thin brows pinching together across her nose, gathering her thoughts. "And sometimes others are hurt by those thought-less rants."

Esther was trying to be delicate, Nell thought, not mentioning names. But it was clear that the news of Julianne's outburst had already hit the airwaves—or at least the police station. And Esther wanted Gracie protected from her mother's words.

The police dispatcher had watched the youngsters of Sea Harbor grow up for more years than anyone could count, and she considered it her personal responsibility to protect them and warn them of supposed or actual danger. Nell remembered how Esther had taken a teenage Izzy under her ample wing, even though Nell's niece wasn't a native and only spent summers in Sea Harbor during those years. Esther adopted them all. Loved them all. And they remained under her watchful eye, even when adulthood found them running businesses, with spouses and babies, and having houses of their own.

"Gracie will be fine, Esther," she reassured the older woman. "She's strong beneath that Alice in Wonderland look." And Nell believed her words to be true. Although Gracie's willowy frame looked like a strong gust of wind would topple her, her life had prepared her well for storms.

Though she was being discreet, Esther probably knew all the details of what had happened the night before, how Ben and Alphonso had lifted the inebriated Julianne from the steps and helped her into the house. Gracie had trailed behind, but returned shortly after. "It will embarrass her to see me," she had said. But Nell suspected it was more than that. The ties between Gracie and her mother were so tenuous they couldn't carry the stress of the day. And speaking ill of Sophia—the one woman who had tried to help Gracie through her teens—would not have settled comfortably in Gracie's mind.

Esther nodded without looking up, a smile lifting her lips. "And now I need to finish this glove, Nelly. I have the five-o'clock shift at the station, you know."

Nell's return smile went unnoticed, and she placed the skein of Cormo wool back in the basket, leaving Esther to finish the ribbing on her bright plaid glove. A gift, no doubt, for one of Sea Harbor's men in blue. Esther had lobbied for years for a more colorful uniform.

Izzy and Birdie were busy piling skeins of a new wool blend on the wooden table when Nell walked down the three steps into the back room. "It looks like I am almost in time to not be useful," she said apologetically, eyeing the rainbow of greens, yellows, blues, and gold of the sock yarns.

"You don't know how to be *un*useful," Birdie said, piling the skeins into baskets. Purl, the Seaside Knitting Studio's resident feline, was curled up in the middle of one of the empty baskets, her green eyes following the movement of Birdie's hands.

"There wasn't as much to do as I thought," Izzy said. "And Birdie is a taskmaster—one quick lady."

Although Mae would close the knitting store soon, Izzy's Sassy Sox class would keep the shop lively. The class was full to capacity, Izzy had said, and she had begged the Thursday-night knitters to help her with beginners. "Socks scare people," she said. "Silly, but true."

Nell needed little encouragement. She loved knitting socks, and the methodical rhythm of knitting and purling was exactly what they all needed to replace the troubling thoughts of Sophia's death and Gracie's mother's outburst. Ben was meeting Sam for a drink at the Gull and they'd all meet up later for dinner. Maybe drive over to the Franklin in Gloucester. The chef's garlic grilled calamari and a spinach salad would top the evening off perfectly.

Laura Danvers and two of her friends arrived for the class

about the same time Cass and Willow snuck in the back door off the alley. Beatrice Scaglia and several women from Beatrice's council committees were next.

Nell spotted Mary Pisano taking a break from her chatty newspaper column to knit socks, although Nell suspected her motivation centered more on picking up news tips. Mary attacked her column for the family-owned newspaper with the zeal of a Pulitzer prize–winning journalist, and a chatty group of women in a merry mood and safe environment could unearth enough grist for Mary's mill for a summer's worth of columns.

"This is what we need to take our minds off the awful ending to our party Friday night," Laura announced to those within earshot.

Beatrice Scaglia sidled up close to Laura, her narrow heels clicking on the hardwood floor. As always, Beatrice was dressed for a New York board meeting, though she'd come from the Sea Harbor city hall three blocks away—a business environment where khaki pants or a cotton dress were considered dressy. "You were a very gallant hostess, Laura," Beatrice said. "We were all proud of you."

Nell watched the exchange, amused. Laura, married to a young bank president, was becoming a viable community leader, just like her mother before her. And Beatrice, with her eye still on the crown, as her husband, Sal, called the mayor's job, would do anything to pave the way for next year's mayoral election. Bucking a minor scandal the summer before, Beatrice had poured herself into so many generous causes that most people had forgotten it—or at least forgiven her. Her attempt to protect her good name by getting rid of evidence in a police investigation hadn't hurt anyone, which made forgiveness easier. And somehow, in the mysterious way marriages work, the couple's unlikely marriage had remained intact.

"I did nothing, Beatrice," Laura said, "but thank you. It was unfortunate, though, that the evening had to end in tragedy."

"Of course," Beatrice said, slightly chagrined that she hadn't been the one to address the tragedy first. She pulled out a chair at the table and sat down, tugging a skein of bright pink yarn from her bag. "I *knew* Sophia, you know," she murmured with a certain pride.

Nell noticed that Beatrice didn't add what everyone around her knew to be true—that while she may have known Sophia Santos, Beatrice didn't like her very much. Sophia was causing headaches for the City Council by locking up the beach access road that many Sea Harbor residents considered their own property. Beatrice Scaglia cared about keeping her constituency happy. Happy voters portended good election outcomes. And they expected her to get that access road reopened before the ocean warmed enough for the children to swim.

Several people came in from the front of the store, carrying knitting bags and new packages of bamboo needles. There was an influx of vacation people, both men and women, young and old, with sunburned noses and eager faces. In minutes the room was humming with activity as people helped themselves to the bottles of soft drinks and the cookies Izzy had rushed down and gotten from Harry Garozzo at the last minute. Having a bakery and a deli so close had saved the day more often than the Seaside Knitters could count. And Harry was always generous, throwing in a few extra. Knitting kept his wife, Margaret, happy, and that was worth its weight in cookies.

The room quieted when Izzy stood up on a small platform near the windows. As the voices faded away, she welcomed the crowd with the same magnetic smile that had captivated jurors in Izzy's past life as a defense attorney.

"The very best rule about knitting," Izzy began, "is that there are no real rules. And when working up socks, we can apply that with a vengeance. Socks can be sweet or sexy—high fashion or cuddly feet warmers." She pointed over to the window seat where Birdie and Purl were comfortably settled. "We'll start with sassy—

maybe even a tad sexy. Birdie Favazza will demonstrate what I mean."

Soft titters passed through the group as their oldest member stood up to her full five feet to demonstrate a sexy sock. Birdie waved to everyone and pulled a long stocking from her bag. "Why give flowers when you could be giving socks?" she asked, lifting her white brows and eyeing a very handsome young man sitting on the steps.

Birdie had used a four-ply soft merino wool to knit up the Rowan pattern. The panels of lace stitches ran the full length of the knee-high sock and added a distinctive and lovely look. A silky black bow at the top screamed "sassy," Birdie told them.

"I love it," Laura said. "Birdie, you're a sassy socks genius."

"And an expert knitter," Izzy added when the laughter died down. "So we won't be trying anything quite that complicated to start with, though who knows what you'll be knitting up in a month or so?"

Izzy went on to explain the model sock they would knit for starters—three inches or so when finished. "But it will teach you everything you need to know, and next we'll move on to the real thing."

In minutes the entire group was working on a tiny pair of socks, knitting and purling the ribbed edge, working down the very short leg of the sock.

"Turning the heel," Mary Pisano sang out. She stuck her pencil behind her ear and picked up her needles. "Do you have any idea how much I've yearned to turn a heel?"

The group laughed and Izzy, Cass, Birdie, and Nell moved through the groups of people to help when a stitch was dropped, to admire balls of soft blended yarn, to encourage the reluctant few who were still slightly fearful of knitting anything that had a shape.

It was after seven when dozens of tiny socks were folded into knitting baskets and their proud creators thanked Izzy profusely for beginning them on a new knitting journey.

In record time, the last drink bottles were in the recycle bin, the bits of yarn swept up, and the baskets of needles and markers put away. Birdie poured them each a glass of wine and held her own up in the air. "To Izzy's successful Sassy Sox class."

"Here, here." Their voices joined in the now-quiet air.

"It was a good group, though I can only imagine what Mary Pisano's heel looks like—she scribbled on her pad of paper between every row."

"If she wrote down everything people said about poor Sophia Santos, she'd have enough for a hefty book," Nell said.

A movement outside the window caught her eye, and she walked over to the side window, peering out into the alley. Ben and Sam stood beneath the alley light, their hands in their pockets, their heads bent in conversation. Ben turned slightly, and it was then that Nell noticed concern on his face.

As if feeling her look, Ben stopped talking and looked up at the window. He waved halfheartedly, as if caught doing something he shouldn't have been doing.

Nell frowned and opened the alley door. "What's up?" she asked.

Izzy was right behind her. "You two look like you were caught sneaking a smoke or something."

The two men walked across the gravel alley and up the three steps, pushing smiles across their faces.

"Is everyone gone?" Ben asked. His voice was low, as if to hide his presence from any knitting students still in the shop.

Izzy nodded. "Everyone's gone."

"So, like what?" Cass asked. "You're acting weird."

Birdie walked over and sat back down beside Purl on the window seat. She picked up her lacy sock and concentrated on starting a new row. Purl pressed against her leg.

Nell watched Birdie out of the corner of her eye. Knitting supported Birdie through so many of life's events—happy, sad, distasteful, difficult, joyful. She wondered what vibe Birdie had caught that had sent her looking for her needles. She hoped it wasn't the same one she was feeling herself.

"Were things lively at the Gull?" Nell asked, hoping her brightness alone could change the mood.

"Jake had a crowd," Sam said. "Pete's band was playing. It looked like a good time."

"But not for you?" Izzy said.

"Not so much. Chief Thompson walked by. He spotted us coming out."

"You were carded?"

Cass' joke fell flat.

"Jerry was talking on his cell. He asked us to wait and then hung up a couple minutes later. It was a reporter, he said. The news was already out. Maybe we could help keep the talk sane and honest. And Sam, after all, had been there, seen it all, he said. People might listen to us when they digested the news tomorrow morning."

"What are you talking about?" Nell asked. "What news?"

"It's about Sophia's . . . well, her accident. They finished the preliminary autopsy. They did two autopsies, I guess you'd say. And the results of one of them weren't good."

Ben paused, cleared his throat, and then continued.

"It seems it wasn't really an accident. It looks more like Sophia Santos was murdered."

Chapter 8

*M*urdered.

The word hung like a heavy cloud over the room. It didn't fit into the beautiful summer evening. Nor the sun-drenched town. Nor the room that a short while before had held laughter and needles clicking together and piles of soft yarn being knit up into miniature socks.

"Food always helps." Ben took out his phone and put an order in at Harry Garozzo's deli down the street. Fried calamari, chicken cacciatore, and a Caesar salad. They would eat together, right there in the Seaside Knitting Studio. No one was up to a noisy, happy restaurant meal, but all the knitters needed more time together—and more answers than Ben and Sam had offered.

Nell walked over to the cupboard as the knitters busied themselves with ordinary things, things they understood and could control—pulling out place mats and flatware, putting yarn away to protect it from Harry's tangy red sauce, getting out glasses and pouring water.

Sam had walked down the block to pick up their order, and when he returned carrying Harry's thick white bags, he had added a couple bottles of wine to the stash.

Between bites of the crispy squid, the group dissected the bits and pieces of Chief Thompson's conversation and worked their way through the heavy sadness they felt for themselves, for the town, for Gracie, and most especially for Alphonso Santos. No matter how they pulled apart the police chief's words, the message always came out the same:

It hadn't been alcohol that caused Sophia Santos to drive like a demon, just as those who knew her had insisted all along. Sophia could nurse a single glass of white wine through an entire cocktail party—and there would still be some left.

Nor was it drugs—which was a crazy idea from the beginning, Gracie had told them. The idea of Sophia doing drugs was about as believable as Sophia mud wrestling. Having ruled out the list of things that didn't cause Sophia's death, the rest of the coroner's initial report on Sophia Santos was plain and simple:

Alphonso Santos' beautiful Argentinean wife was as clean and pure as holy water. Clean of drugs, of alcohol, of poison. She was clean of any unusual substance other than the Sea Harbor Yacht Club's fine lobster stew—which, the club chef admitted, had a sprinkling of fine sauvignon blanc in it.

But the second autopsy—the one on the Santoses' brilliant red Ferrari—the love of Alphonso's life, or so some people would say—did not bode so well.

Tampered Brakes, read the official report—and a fine job of it, one that left the Ferrari's prized Brembo brakes useless.

As police chief Jerry Thompson predicted, the newspaper and radio were filled with the news, and by the next morning, the talk along Harbor Road had abruptly switched from Sophia driving while drunk to a rumored plot to ruin the Santos Company, to reports that a fired worker thought it was Alphonso driving and had tried to off his boss, to a radio talk show caller declaring that the Boston mafia had intended to kill Alphonso for taking away union construction jobs. "It was their modus operandi," the young man declared.

"That was Gus Egan. I recognized his voice," Cass said. "He went to Latin school for a year and has probably been waiting his whole radio life to use those words."

. . .

They sat on the pier in the late-afternoon sunshine—Cass, Izzy, and Gracie. They were lined up like fishermen, their bare feet hanging over the edge. Painting was the excuse, but holding off the rest of the world, the gossip and sadness, was the intent. Cass and Gracie had spent the afternoon working on Gracie's lobster café, cleaning up debris, sanding, and planning table placement. Gracie said working held her together and might keep her sanity intact.

Izzy had walked over as soon as she could get away from her yarn studio. She sat next to three open pints of paint, color samples Gracie had brought out for her to look at. She swirled a paint stick absently in one.

Birdie and Nell had come by, too. They'd come to help, they said, but more than that, they had come to assure themselves that Gracie was okay. They sat next to each other on a weathered bench near the three younger women. Behind them was the rough shadow of Gracie's lobster café, its walls uneven and gray, the glass in the windows bearing the manufacturer's stamp, and a pile of lumber leaning up against the front of the restaurant. Paint cans stood on the front steps.

Gracie's eyes were swollen and red, her hair pulled back in a ponytail that settled between her shoulder blades like a long question mark. "It isn't like I've lost a mother—Sophia never tried to be that. Or even a friend. We didn't have that kind of relationship. But she was a decent lady, and my uncle—for all his faults—is having a hard time with this. I can't imagine anyone wanting Sophia dead. Wouldn't you think you'd have to really hate someone to want that person dead? People didn't know Sophia well enough to hate her."

"Does Julianne know this latest news?" Cass asked.

Nell was wondering the same thing. She supposed Birdie and Izzy were, too. Whether or not Julianne knew Sophia well enough to hate her, she had let an entire gathering of the Santoses' friends and neighbors know exactly what she thought of Sophia Santos.

Did Gracie's mother know that someone had murdered the woman she'd proclaimed to want dead?

"Joey said she knows. The police are telling anyone connected to the family to stick around the area until they get the information they need. Can you imagine containing my mother anywhere longer than a day or two? That'll be harder on her than a prison sentence would be. Joey found her. She's been in Gloucester, staying with our friend Mandy White—not Alphonso, which is a wise move. A little distance between the two of them will be good."

"Ben saw Jerry Thompson at a meeting this morning. The whole thing baffles the police. Some think the target must have been Alphonso, not Sophia. They connect a Ferrari with a man, I guess. And Alphonso had probably made his share of enemies as he grew his business. Power does that."

"But everyone knows that Alphonso didn't drive that car," Izzy said. "Customers sometimes joked about it. It was Alphonso's dream car, but it was Sophia who drove it to garden club meetings and church."

"And yacht club parties. You're right, Izzy. It was strange," Birdie said. "I would see him out there in his driveway, alone or with one or two of his groundsmen, polishing that car like it was going to be in a parade.

"Alphonso practically slept in that car the first week he had it—and he drove it everywhere," Birdie continued. "And then suddenly—nothing. The polishing continued, but as far as I know he never drove it again. It was always Sophia. Ella, my font of all knowledge, told me Alphonso *gave* it to Sophia—and that she surely deserved it."

"Yes, he gave it to her," Gracie said.

"So?" Cass asked. "What's the story about that?" She pulled the bill of the Sox cap forward to shield her face from the sun. Her bare arms were tan and firm from the heavy lobster traps that she and her brother, Pete, maintained. "That's weird, isn't it? Why would he give the car he dreamed of to someone who didn't want it?"

Gracie was quiet for a few minutes, as if wondering whether she was revealing family secrets. "I'm not sure why. It happened shortly after Alphonso bought the car last spring. He didn't buy it for Sophia. It was his baby. He loved that car. And then one night there was some kind of an argument between Sophia and him. I was staying in the carriage house while my new condo was being painted." She wrinkled her forehead and thought back over the months.

"I heard Alphonso drive in that night. It was late. I remember it because Sophia had been in Argentina visiting family and had been back only a couple days. And in my judgmental way, I was wondering why he wasn't spending those nights with his wife instead of driving around in a Ferrari. But anyway, later Sophia came out on the terrace and Alphonso followed her. My windows were open and sound travels because it's so quiet up there. Birdie, I'm surprised you didn't hear it, too."

Gracie pulled her feet up and wrapped her arms around her knees. "They were arguing, Sophia in Spanish—so I didn't really know what the fight was about. It was unusual, though. Sophia rarely argued. It was almost, like, well, like, beneath her.

"The next morning I went over to the big house for coffee, and I saw a fancy key case on the kitchen counter—leather and elegant—with a diamond 'S' in a beautiful silver rectangle on it. And next to it was a cream-colored card."

Gracie paused and her cheeks colored slightly. "Okay, I didn't mean to read it. I don't usually do things like that—honest. But it was sitting open, right next to the coffeepot. Being a klutz, I accidentally splashed coffee on it, and when I tried to blot it up, I recognized Alphonso's fancy scroll. He wrote that the new car was the one material thing he loved more than anything in the world. And as proof of his respect for her and as testimony that he would always be there for her, he wanted Sophia to have it."

"Geesh," Izzy said. "Some makeup gift."

"Proof of his respect for her? That's an odd way to put it," Nell said.

"Was Sophia happy with the gift?" Izzy asked.

"I don't think so. She didn't seem to like Alphonso as much after that either, although they were both so proper it was hard to tell. But as for the car, it frightened her a little. And she didn't like the attention driving a fancy red sports car brought. But for some crazy reason, she kept it and drove the darn thing everywhere. In his take-charge way, Alphonso had donated her other car to some charity, so maybe she didn't have a choice. I think it used to drive my uncle crazy, though, because people teased him that a Ferrari should always be driven at an absolute minimum of eighty miles an hour. But not Sophia. She never went over fifty on the highway. In town it was more like fifteen."

Nell noticed that Birdie had grown quiet, listening to the talk around her but bringing her own unspoken thoughts to it.

"Birdie?" Nell said.

Birdie shook her head as if to shake away the thoughts. "Nothing. It's an interesting story, is all. I know Alphonso loved the car. And why he'd give it to Sophia is a mystery. I do know that Harold would watch with pure unadulterated envy, though, when Sophia would pick Ella up for Mass each day. Imagine, riding to Mass in a Ferrari."

The group chuckled at the thought of plain Ella Sampson riding up to Our Lady of the Seas in a red Ferrari.

"And going fifteen miles an hour," Cass added.

"Speaking of Ella, how is she doing with Stella helping out, Birdie? She's so quiet and efficient and in charge that it could be difficult for her to give things up."

"Yes, she's very proprietary. But she has her hands full with Harold. And both Ella and Harold needed more help. We're trying to keep Harold from moving around too much until his broken bone heels. Crazy man should never have been cleaning out gutters on that rickety ladder. Now he's spent nearly two months not doing much of anything. So I need Stella. But Ella doesn't make it easy on her. For one thing, she speaks to her in Spanish, which Stella doesn't understand."

"Ella speaks Spanish?" Cass asked. "I thought she was from Boston."

"Yes. But her parents were from Mexico and spoke Spanish at home. Harold doesn't know a word of it so Ella rarely uses it. Just with Stella. It's Ella's nice way of telling Stella she doesn't really need her. And the more time she was spending with Sophia Santos, the more she turned on the Spanish, because she and Sophia spoke it all the time when they were together."

"I bet Stella handles it just fine. I can't imagine her letting it get to her," said Nell.

Birdie nodded, her face lacking its usual emotion. "Maybe," she said. "But with Ella becoming the dominant one and Harold not wanting her to stray far from him, it's a household to handle, believe me."

"I think reinforcements are here," Nell said, turning toward the loud footsteps walking down the pier.

"Ladies, let's get this show on the road. I thought this was the work crew." Sam shifted a camera hanging around his neck.

The three women on the edge of the dock twisted around. "About time," Izzy said.

"We thought you'd be done by now," Ben said. "Up and at 'em."

"Aye, aye, sir," Cass mocked and scrambled to her feet.

"Just planning our approach," Gracie said, lifting herself effortlessly from the floor. "Planning is all-important." Her cheeks were flushed from the remaining rays of sunshine, and she started across the wide concrete pier to the future home of the Lazy Lobster and Soup Café. It was to be a lobster *café*, she'd told her uncle when discussing the investment with him. Unique. Delightful. Family dining at its finest.

"I hope you've brought beer," Cass said.

"Pete was in charge of that. He'll be here soon." Sam wrapped an arm around Izzy's shoulders. "So, beautiful, into tattoos now?" He touched her cheek, then tilted his sunglasses so Izzy could look into them.

She squinted, then wrinkled her nose and touched the streak across her cheek. "We're testing colors. Like it?"

"Hmmm," he said. "Terrific. My very own painted lady." ·

"You say that to all the girls, Perry," Izzy said. Then she leaned down and dipped her finger into a can of periwinkle blue paint. She straightened up and spread it delicately across Sam's cheek. "Periwinkle Perry," she said in a husky voice. "Who can resist him?"

Sam took her hand and held it behind her back, then gave her a quick kiss on the cheek. "Careful, Iz. A paint war would be a bad thing."

"Yikes," Gracie yelped. "Behave, you guys. Can you imagine my permit people wondering how the famous Sea Harbor Pelican Pier turned red?"

"Why the camera, Sam?" Nell asked.

"Have you ever seen him without it?" Cass said.

"Well, not when I have potential award-winning subjects all around me. Beautiful women. Blue water." He slipped a camera from his bag and snapped a close-up of Izzy. "'Girl with Yellow Cheek,' I'll call this one."

Izzy tossed her head and laughed. "It's *wheat*, Perry, not yellow. Some artist you are."

Once inside, the group worked like a well-rehearsed dance team, grabbing old shirts from hooks along the wall, pulling on a collection of baseball caps Gracie had thoughtfully provided, and checking out the colorful swooshes they had applied to one wall last Saturday. Since then, the place had been deserted, but Nell suspected getting back to the task at hand was exactly what Gracie needed. Distractions were vital at times like these. Wringing hands rarely brought resolution.

"It's shaping up, Gracie," Ben said, grabbing a hammer and chisel from the wooden tool chest on the floor. "You're doing a great job."

Gracie smiled and pushed a strand of hair away from her cheek. "I hope so, Ben. I really want this to work. For me. And for Alphonso, too—I want to prove to him that I'm not like my mom when it comes to managing money. And I want the whole bunch of you who have pitched in to help to be proud of it." She looked over at Cass, who was smoothing out nail holes with a sandpaper block. "Cass kinda had to—she's known me too long to say no. But the rest of you didn't."

"Sure we did," Izzy said, leaning into the conversation. "Birdie said we had to."

Gracie laughed. "Good for Birdie." She looked over at the small figure squatting on a wooden stool, carefully sandpapering a strip of new woodwork.

"You'll have lines weaving all the way to the parking lot," Nell said. She sat back on her knees and looked around at the space that had once housed a bait and tackle shop. She could hardly remember how it appeared the first time they had seen the inside. The dust and dirt had been so thick they'd covered their mouths with tissue, and beams of light from the holes in the roof fell down on piles of discarded debris—old fishing lines and hooks, unpainted buoys and weights. The windows were broken and dirty glass littered the floor. It had taken a leap of faith to see beyond the mess to Gracie's dream.

Back then, she couldn't imagine people laughing and chatting and walking through the restaurant door. She couldn't imagine tables or chairs or lobsters served on bright white platters—or chunky bowls of thick chowder to offset winter's chill.

But today, it already looked like a welcoming place—and big enough to house the twenty or so tables that the permit allowed. The main room was anchored on either side by a small kitchen, storeroom, and one bathroom with a new sink and stool. Gracie's biggest splurge was a fireplace—necessary if she was going to serve chowder in the winter, she'd rationalized. Joey Delaney had stepped up and offered to build it—his contribution to her project, as he called it. It was fronted with Cape Ann granite, sturdy and thick, and soon they'd add a mantel carved by a Canary Cove artist. The back wall would be all windows and doors. Beyond them, hanging out over the harbor water like an airplane's wing, was a wide rustic deck. For family dinners in the summer, Gracie had said. And there'd be big heaters for spring and fall. Wouldn't the kids love it, sitting at picnic tables, waving at the gulls, and watching the harbor seals play off the far shore?

Pete appeared soon with pizzas and a cooler of beer. He set it down near the kitchen door. "Sorry I'm late, folks."

"And where were you, dear bro?" Cass asked, her brows lifting suggestively.

Pete made a face at his sister and pushed a lock of sandy-colored hair from his eyes.

"It's nice of you to give Willow a hand," Birdie said from her perch on the floor. "And you leave him alone, Catherine."

Cass laughed. "I think it's nice, too."

"She's fixing up her dad's studio," Nell said. "I'm glad she's making it her own."

"Yeah. It's looking great. She's moving things around, adding some display stands for her fiber art. But she's keeping Aidan's spirit there, too. His wooden sculptures are everywhere—but none of them for sale."

Nell smiled at the memory of their friend who had been dead a year now. His daughter was working hard to make sure people wouldn't forget him.

Pete began snapping the tops off cold bottles of Sam Adams. "It'll always be Aidan's place. But there's lots of Willow appearing in bits and pieces."

"Willow is creating a hanging for the restaurant—I saw the sketch and it'll be perfect for above the fireplace," Gracie said. "It's her first commissioned piece, she said."

The ringing of a cell phone cut through the conversation and several hands slapped jeans pockets to identify the source.

"It's me," Gracie announced, lifting her phone into the air. She stepped outside to take the call.

"The beer was a good idea, Pete. Thanks," Ben said.

"Maybe we need to take a break before we begin? Prime the pump?" Cass offered, eyeing the pizza.

The others laughed, and Birdie pulled some paper plates and napkins out of a bag next to her. "That's one of the many reasons we love our Catherine," she said. "She always has her priorities in line."

Cass' husky laugh traveled across the room and she blew Birdie a kiss.

The door opened and Gracie walked back into the room, her face serious. "That was Julianne," she said. She tried to keep her words light, but they fell as heavily as an anchor onto the dusty hardwood floor. "The police have questioned her. They called her a 'person of interest.'" Gracie looked around, her eyes as big as saucers in her narrow face. "That's not good, is it?"

Chapter 9

$\mathcal{T}$he only sound in the hollow room was the shuffling of a pizza carton as Pete made a space next to him for Gracie to sit. She folded her legs and collapsed on the floor, accepting the bottle of beer that Pete handed her. She took a deep breath and looked around. "So, what do we think?"

"Do you want me to go down to the station?" Ben asked. He had pulled over a bench and sat next to Nell, a plate of pizza balanced on his lap.

Gracie shook her head. "She called from the Gull, not the police station. Fortifying herself, I guess."

"So they didn't keep her?"

"Nope. Just asked her a lot of questions. Like why she was at the yacht club that night. And where she disappeared to after she talked to Alphonso. And was she hanging around the parking lot. And how much did she know about car brakes."

"Did she have answers?" Ben asked.

"I don't think she remembers that night very clearly. She'd had way too many beers. She thinks she just wandered down to the beach after confronting Alphonso. She sat there for a while, so that's what she told them. Then, when her head cleared, she got back in her car and drove over to Gloucester to spend the night with Mandy. Things had gotten too tense between her and Sophia this past year for her to stay at Alphonso's."

"It's not a surprise the police wanted to talk to her," Nell said. "They'll be talking to everyone. You, me."

"And unfortunately, Julianne's scene at the club and the house were well reported," Birdie added.

"I remember Julianne saying things like that ever since Alphonso married Sophia," Cass said. "She would have hated anyone he married, don't you think, Gracie?"

"Maybe. But maybe not as much as Sophia. Sophia was so black and white—the opposite of Julianne. And she judged Julianne harshly, not that she didn't deserve it."

"Alphonso doesn't listen to many people, but he seemed to have valued Sophia's opinion," Birdie said. She was sitting on the floor leaning against one wall, her short legs sticking straight out in front of her. Her gray eyes were thoughtful as she followed the conversation from person to person. "That couldn't have sat well with your mother."

Gracie agreed. "My grandparents didn't leave Julianne her own trust, not outright anyway. It was for her own good, Alphonso said. That was probably true. She had to ask him for money if she ran out. Which she did often because she couldn't hold a job."

"Not to mention the men that took advantage of her," Cass added.

"That, too. Sophia thought that you rewarded the good, punished the bad, and Julianne, in her mind, didn't often fall into the 'good' category. She encouraged Alphonso not to be an enabler. I think that was the word she used."

"It's the tough love approach," Birdie said.

"Exactly. But Julianne knew that when Alphonso turned her down, it was probably because of Sophia. And she hated her for it. That caused problems."

"Your grandparents meant well," Birdie said. "They were good neighbors and very kind to me when Sonny brought me to his family home next door. I think they tried hard to do the right thing for their daughter."

"Who's your mother with now?" Ben asked. "Alphonso?"

"I don't know, but she'll be okay. She's a survivor." Gracie's voice fell off and Pete filled in the silence by finding some work music, as he called it, on his iPod.

A fresh pizza box was passed around as James Taylor, crooning about fire and rain and finding a friend, filled in the background.

Nell looked at Gracie sitting on the floor. She wanted to say something to ease her worry. But what? She reached down and squeezed her shoulder gently, reading the emotions that played across her narrow face.

Gracie was looking around the circle—the unlikely group of friends who'd stay all night if she wanted them to. They'd stay and spackle or sandpaper, sweep the dust and wipe up the floor. They'd stay as long as she needed them, and then they'd stay a little longer, to be sure she was okay.

"You guys are the best," Gracie said. She caught her bottom lip between her teeth, as if thinking through what she should say next.

"Julianne isn't a bad person," she went on. "She just can't hold things together very well, that's all." Her eyes grew moist.

"She may have her faults, but she's not a murderer." Gracie was shaking her head now, as if she were talking to herself, convincing herself. "She could no more kill Sophia Santos than she could be mother of the year. She just couldn't, that's all."

The knock on the door was soft, but in the stillness of the room, it echoed harshly. Joey Delaney opened it slowly, then stepped inside, and looked around. "Hey, everyone. Am I interrupting?"

He filled the doorframe, the tall shadow of his body falling across the group. He looked around until he spotted Gracie on the floor, an untouched plate of pizza in front of her.

"Gracie," he said. His voice was hesitant. "I just left your mom at the Gull . . ."

It wasn't until Joey walked around the circle, his eyes never leaving his almost ex-wife, and crouched down beside her, that Gracie's tears flowed freely.

Chapter 10

They stayed later than they'd planned, leaving only when darkness and limited electricity forced them from the building.

It was therapy of a sort, Nell supposed. At the least, the night of work, pizza, and friends seemed to lift Gracie's spirits.

"How was Julianne?" Nell asked Joey as she helped him finish spackling the fireplace.

Joey sat back on his heels and shrugged. "She seemed okay. She's the kind of person who can weather just about anything. She says she didn't do it—though the evidence is stacking up against her fast. But it's Gracie I'm concerned about. Her mom is good at shaking things off. Gracie, not so much."

"I can see that. I think it helped that you came by."

"I wanted to be sure she was okay," he mumbled, then pulled himself up from the floor and reached out a hand to help Nell up.

Nell brushed the dust and sand off her jeans and straightened her spine, pressing her hands into her lower back. "Well, Gracie needs friends. All of us."

"Her mom can be a handful—I saw a little of that firsthand when Gracie and I lived in Gloucester. But Julianne and I, I don't know, we've connected lately. Maybe it's because we both can mess up good things and know what it's like to lose something . . . someone . . . important." He pulled his keys out of his pocket.

"She wasn't fond of her sister-in-law, that seems clear."

Joey was silent for a minute, and it seemed to Nell he was weighing his words. But when he spoke again, his tone was non-committal, neutral. "I don't know much about that," he said. "Everyone has their side to things, I guess." He looked over Nell's shoulder and waved at Gracie. "Hey, gorgeous Grace, I'm out of here. Call if you need anything."

He gave his fireplace one more approving look, waved his key chain in the air, and disappeared out the door.

Gracie walked over to Nell and wiped her hands off on her worn jeans. She watched Joey through the window. "Julianne talks to him sometimes. He'll help her through this if she needs it. Better him, maybe, than me."

"He seems to like your mother."

"Especially these last few months, whenever she's shown up in Gloucester or here. He's seen her more than I have," Gracie said.

"He cares about you, too."

Gracie shrugged her narrow shoulders. "It seems we should be married, have kids, live in a little cottage by the sea, doesn't it? But it was complicated."

"Matters of the heart can often be."

"We were married almost four years." Gracie glanced over at Ben, then back at Nell. "I guess that doesn't seem long to you. But at times it seemed like a lifetime to me."

"Maybe some people are meant to be loved and not married."

"Maybe so."

"You and Joey have made this divorce process seem, well, *comfortable.*"

Gracie looked out the window again. Joey was fastening his helmet and revving the engine of his coveted Agusta bike. "It's been an emotional roller coaster. We moved to Gloucester just to put a little distance between family and us, though Joey came over to work every day. I don't know, maybe I had too many expectations for marriage. Maybe you should just let it unfold. But I wanted a husband who was a partner, available. Joey was gone a lot. I wanted kids. He didn't—not for a while, he said—but that 'while' kept stretching out and I finally realized he didn't really want kids at all. We never seemed to have enough money. Things were a mess. It was just a bad scene, and finally we both agreed the divorce was the best solution. He moved out, back to Sea Harbor, and I stayed until the lease was up a few months later. I didn't see him at all during that time. Then when I moved back, I don't know, it's been different. Recently, he's been a real friend, so attentive. He seems to understand me better. I swear I've seen him more in the last three months than the whole time we were married."

Izzy walked over and handed Nell and Gracie chocolate chip cookies.

"When will the divorce be final?" Nell asked.

"Soon. Sophia and Alphonso finally stepped in and insisted I talk to the family lawyer."

"Sophia was okay with the divorce?"

Gracie nodded. "She never wanted the marriage. He was a Delaney, after all. She used to say the only thing I could have done worse would have been to marry Davey Delaney. These past few weeks she was at me all the time to finalize it and get on with my life."

"I suppose with the restaurant and all, you needed to get things in order," Izzy said.

"Alphonso was helping with the loan until I had my own money. I thought Joey and I lived pretty simply, but you know how that is. Money doesn't last long. Even the wedding money our families gave us dried up. So Alphonso agreed to cover the restaurant investments until I could take over."

Nell watched Gracie's face while she tried to explain her marriage to Izzy. It held a wistfulness, and Nell couldn't tell if it was for Joey, for the kids and the cottage by the sea, or for something she was missing entirely. But she wasn't at all convinced that Gracie wanted this divorce.

Nell wondered about her own words to Gracie—*Loved but not*

married. She had said it sincerely, but did she believe it? Nell looked at Ben. He was sitting on the wooden bench with Sam Perry, his elbows resting on his knees as he listened intently to Sam, who was probably explaining some new photographic technique, or a new sailboat he'd seen—a passion the two men shared. Ben's head was slightly turned, his strong nose and chin prominent in profile. *He needs a haircut*, Nell thought, but the slightly shaggy look, his full silver-touched hair just hitting the collar of his knit shirt, brought back memories of walking around Harvard Square together, her long peasant skirt swooshing around her knees and a headband anchoring her long brown hair. Ben would have been wearing a T-shirt stretched across his chest, something from a Simon and Garfunkel concert or a peace rally. They'd both be gesturing as they walked, their shoulders bumping, their voices lifting now and then in laughter. And underneath their conversation on war and peace and zero population growth, there'd be a warm, rushing current of happiness and desire.

Some people, well, some people were meant to be married. That part of the equation she knew firsthand to be true.

"We're closing up shop for the night," Gracie announced, calling Pete in from the kitchen. "Everybody, out. Get yourselves a life." She looked over at Ben, Pete, and Sam. "I owe you guys big. All of you."

"Oh, pshaw," Pete said, and reached for a green garbage bag. "We'll pull in the favors. Don't worry. I'll know where to camp out when Nell's kitchen is closed."

They picked up pizza cartons and bottles, then emptied them all into the recycle bin. Purses and backpacks were gathered and Gracie found her noisy ring of keys and ushered them out the door.

"Nell, dear, you are my wheels tonight," Birdie said, reminding Nell that they'd come together. They had been there so long that they'd nearly forgotten how they got there.

The group wandered off, dispersing in different directions,

heading home or for a nightcap at the Gull, where a new band that Pete wanted to check out was playing. Nell and Birdie walked up the pier to the harbor parking lot, their sneakers silent on the wooden walkway.

Nell shivered in the evening breeze and slipped her arms into the blue denim sweater that Birdie had knit for her last year. She had watched her knitting it, carefully working in the gentle cables, for two long months. And all that time, she never knew that the gorgeous cotton and linen sweater was to be hers. Not until she found it beneath the tree on Christmas morning, wrapped in tissue and tied with a bright red ribbon. It was a perfect sweater for this time of year, a touch of warmth before the hot days heated the nights, soft and comforting against her skin.

The moon and gas lamps lining the pier guided them to Nell's car. She could feel night settling down over the town, the light of the moon growing brighter as it pushed away the last shadows of daylight. Was it just five short days ago that they'd looked up at that same moon on the yacht club terrace? Five short days since a wayward car had sailed toward the moon, then spun to earth, crashing against a pile of granite rocks?

They pulled out of the parking lot, heading south into the hilly neighborhood known for its large homes and well-kept yards. The houses along Ravenswood Road had been built in the days when Cape Ann provided a hefty proportion of the entire country's fish supply. Some of the dwellings, like Birdie's, were captains' homes that had been updated into lovely rambling estates; others were built by Boston barons who used them as vacation homes and entertained lavishly, then built them even bigger into permanent residences. The heavily forested land hid one house from another, a fact many owners considered a good thing.

Nell glanced over at Birdie as they pulled into her long drive off Ravenswood Road. She was sitting quietly, gazing out the window with a pensive look on her face.

"A penny for your thoughts, Birdie."

Birdie's laugh was halfhearted. "They're not worth that." She snapped free of her seat belt and opened the car door. "Would you like a nightcap? I could use the company."

Nell paused. She'd told Ben she'd be home in twenty minutes, but then, Ben knew that she and Birdie often forgot about time when they were busy solving the world's problems. He had nodded wisely and told her he'd be there when she got there— whenever that might be.

"Let's do that," Nell said and turned off the ignition.

Birdie stood beside the car and looked over toward the carriage house. It sat above one of her two garages. Sonny used to fix his car parts in it, and Birdie kept it sparkling clean. The lights were on in the apartment, and through the glare, Birdie and Nell saw Harold hobbling slowly across the room like an injured ghost. He walked toward the window, spotted them in the drive, and pushed the casement windows open. Birdie thought she heard music. Rock music—not a usual choice for Harold.

"She's gone," Harold shouted down to the drive.

"Who's gone?" Nell turned to Birdie.

"Ella," Birdie said quietly. She walked closer to the carriage house. "Did you let Stella know?"

"Stella is an abrupt young lady, Miss Birdie. And she's making so much racket. I won't be able to sleep."

He cast his eyes downward to the garage below his home.

Although the large garage doors were shut, yellow beams of light poured through the small windows. And with attention turned in that direction, Birdie realized that the garage was the source of the screeching electric guitars and banging drums, not Harold's apartment.

"You sit back down, Harold," Birdie called. "Put your foot up on that stool I brought you. I'll take care of it."

Birdie hurried toward the garage and grabbed the handle of one of the doors. The door was three times taller than she was, but she tugged until it swung wide open. Instantly the recorded sounds of the electric guitar filled the night air. Inside, sitting cross-legged on the cement floor, her face smudged with dirt and her head moving from side to side to the music, was Stella Palazola.

At first Stella was so absorbed in the music and twisting a stuck cap on the riding lawn mower that she didn't realize she wasn't alone.

"Stella?" Birdie said.

Stella jumped. Her glasses slid down her nose. "Miz Birdie! Where the he—heck did you come from?" She smiled at Nell and pushed her glasses back in place. "Hi, Miz Endicott. Were you guys standing there long?"

"No, dear, we just got home. What are you doing?" Birdie eyed the nuts and bolts scattered across the floor.

"Fixing this machine. Harold can't mow and I might as well do it, but the mower is broken."

Birdie shook her head. "You don't need to do that, Stella."

"I want to. There's not enough to do around here. Ella chases me out of the kitchen every chance she gets and revacuums any room I touch. I might as well do this. Harold can't get down the stairs fast enough to stop me, and I like fixing things. Our dad taught Liz everything you'd ever want to know about keeping things working. She's an expert—way better than our brothers at car repairs. Liz can fix anything. She's taught me a little here and there."

Nell watched Birdie's small body sigh. Her normally smooth and peaceful household was losing its calm. She hoped for Birdie's sake that Harold was up and around soon.

"Stella, Harold says Ella is gone," Birdie said.

"She just went for a walk, is all. I saw her leave, carrying that big leather book with her like it was a Bible. Maybe she'll meditate or something and come back nice."

"Stella and Ella don't like each other much," Birdie explained to Nell. "I think it's because their names sound too much alike."

Stella frowned at Birdie, ignoring her attempt at humor. "She's just nasty. And she's especially mean now that Mrs. Santos is dead. It's making Harold as cranky as a trapped lobster."

"Why would it affect Harold?" Nell asked.

Birdie answered. "That once-sweet man is jealous. He's always depended so on Ella—and she on him—and he didn't like God or Sophia or anyone else taking his place. It was an odd friendship, but a real one."

"Harold hated it," Stella blurted out. "He didn't like Ella spending all that time away from him. In fact, he didn't much like Mrs. Santos."

"Well, I suppose that's true," Birdie conceded.

Stella wiped her hands on a rag and stood up. She looked at the lawn mower proudly. "I think I got this baby working again."

Birdie managed a smile. "Stella, dear, why don't you go on home now? Or go out and meet your friends. Have some fun. You work too hard sometimes." Birdie pressed some extra bills into Stella's hand.

Stella looked down, then frowned at her employer. She shoved the money into the pockets of her jeans and then impulsively collected Birdie's small frame in her arms and gave her a tight squeeze.

"I want to be just like you when I'm old, Miz Birdie," she said.

"Thank you, dear. Now would you please tell Harold that Ella just went out for a walk, and Nell and I will make sure everything is fine?"

When Stella had collected her things, yelled up at Harold, and driven off in the small Volkswagen her sister had given her for her high school graduation, Birdie took Nell's arm and walked her over to the main house.

They settled into overstuffed wicker furniture in the back sunroom—a charming addition that allowed access to the outdoors on three sides, even when the weather turned chilly. In winter Birdie filled it with golden grasses and mums and tropical plants, but in summer the pots were filled with wildflowers, tall lilies, and roses.

Nell buttoned her sweater against the early-June breeze coming through the open windows. Soon sounds of Segovia's guitar filled the small room.

"There. Time to relax." Birdie lit the hurricane lamps, then poured two glasses of wine and held one up. "To my crazy household," she said, lifting her glass.

Nell laughed and clinked her glass against Birdie's. "It's a little energetic, true. But if you didn't seem worried about it, I'd find the whole thing entertaining."

Birdie leaned to the side and pulled a ball of yarn from the knitting basket beside the couch. She fingered the soft wool absently and settled back into the chair. "Some days it seems humorous. Some not so. Ella has been acting peculiar. Sophia's death has not only saddened her, but depressed her, too. I'm wondering if I should take her to a doctor."

"Not that she would let you. Those two are stubborn."

"Stubborn isn't the word for it. I love them dearly, but sometimes they are challenging. I know for a fact Harold will hobble down those steps tomorrow and redo every bit of work Stella did on that lawn mower. He won't let anyone challenge his mechanical skills."

"Harold has always seemed so dear. The thought of him being jealous of Ella's time surprises me."

"They're both dear—but they have their idiosyncrasies. When Harold came to work for us after he married Ella, they pretty much kept to themselves. Sonny and I became their family, I guess you'd say, and they seemed perfectly content with that. Stella was right about Harold wanting Ella all to himself. And for all those years she didn't seem to mind a bit."

Outside the wind picked up and tossed pine needles against

the window. The warm rush of the wine and cleansing breeze felt good against the emotional heat of the past week. Nell sat back in the chair and sipped her wine, her thoughts on the sweet couple that had been part of Birdie's life longer than Nell had been.

"So her friendship with Sophia must have been quite a change in their lives, especially for Harold," Nell said.

"It wasn't that Sophia and Ella played bridge every day or were on the phone constantly." Birdie picked up a pair of bamboo needles and began casting on the first row of a sweater Izzy had talked her into trying. It was a swingy cardigan the color of the sky on a clear day. She was eager to get some inches on it so she could imagine the finished project.

"But they went to daily Mass together."

"That's true—and occasionally they'd walk in the woods when Harold was napping. Ella would sneak out, I guess you'd say. Stella teased her about it last week, which didn't settle nicely."

The thought of the elegant Sophia and the quiet Ella acting like teenagers made both women laugh. Birdie poured them each another inch of wine and leaned her head back against the chair. "I suppose everyone needs a friend. What would the four of us do without our Thursday nights? And we certainly are a good match for Ella and Sophia in blending differences. We're the most unlikely quartet in town."

Nell laughed. They certainly were that. *Dear friends . . . and as different as the colors of the sea.* Nell had brought Izzy dinner at the Seaside Knitting Studio that memorable Thursday night a few years ago, knowing her niece would be working late. Birdie had come by for several hanks of Peruvian mohair that Izzy had ordered for her. Cass was lured in by the enticing aroma of garlic, herbs, and butter in Nell's clam pasta.

And so the four women had settled into an unlikely friendship, one nurtured by Nell's soups and pastas and grilled vegetables, by Birdie's fine pinots, and by Thursday evenings spent knitting, talking, laughing, and shedding an occasional tear in Izzy's cozy back room. It was a friendship that had become as sacred to them as Sophia and Ella's visits to Our Lady of the Seas church.

Nell paused, her wineglass raised midair. She frowned, then turned and looked out the window. "Birdie, do you hear that?"

"The wind?"

"No. Voices."

Birdie pushed the button on the remote and silenced the simmering sounds of Segovia's guitar. She frowned and turned to look outside.

The sky was dark now, but gaslights lit the drive and surrounding grounds. "I don't see anyone out here."

"There, I hear it again. It sounds like someone's in trouble."

Wordlessly, the two women moved as one out the back door and across the drive.

"I wonder if Ella is back," Nell said out loud. Harold's lights were still on, but he wasn't at the window.

The sound of voices was louder now, but still muffled and indecipherable.

"It's over there," Birdie said, pointing toward the woods. "There's a path next to the carriage house that leads to the Santoses' property."

"It sounds like a woman. Ella must be out there, but who would she be talking to?"

"*¡Que la mató!*"

The voice was louder now, and clearly Ella's.

With the moon lighting their steps, they hurried toward the voice, avoiding tree roots and fallen branches that straddled the pine-strewn path.

Just before they reached a curve that marked the end of Birdie's land and the beginning of the Santos property, they were stopped by a man's voice.

"Go home, Ella. I'll walk with you so you are safe. It's dark."

It was Alphonso Santos, his voice low and controlled. Birdie and Nell stepped into the darkness of an apple tree grove and peered out into the small clearing.

"Don't touch me." Ella's back was to Nell and Birdie, but they could see the shadow of her hands, out in front of her, as if warding off evil.

"I won't hurt you, Ella. But you can't keep coming here like this, to my home."

"Sophia's home," Ella said, her voice muffled.

"Of course. Sophia's home. But she's gone, Ella. She's not here. Sophia died."

He spoke as if it were a child standing in front of him, his voice calm and measured.

Birdie and Nell looked at each other, puzzled by the scene unfolding in front of them. They held their silence. Waited.

Finally Ella spoke again, her voice a hiss in the night. She flung her words toward Alphonso with a vengeance.

"You killed her," Ella said. "*Que la mató.*"

Before Alphonso could speak or Birdie or Nell could react, Ella spun and ran back through the woods, never seeing the two figures standing beneath the trees.

Chapter 11

"An evening away. Dinner and drinks. It can be beer and burgers, hot dogs. But we're going."

Ben was adamant, and Nell agreed. The week was taking a toll, and a Wednesday night away from Sea Harbor might be just what the doctor ordered. Putting a bridge and a strip of highway between them and the rapidly accumulating pile of rumors about Sophia Santos would be a good thing.

"If any of our friends want to run away with us," Ben told Nell, "they're welcome. But I, for one, am going—and I prefer it not be alone."

In the end it was Izzy and Sam who showed up at 22 Sandswept Lane and joined Ben and Nell for the ride into the city.

Izzy shared Ben's need to escape. "The rumors in the yarn shop were so loud I nearly wore earplugs. All I heard all day were motivations for killing Sophia Santos, a woman I can't imagine anyone wanting dead." Izzy climbed into the backseat of the CRV. "One thing everyone seemed to agree on is that the murderer had something against the Santos family. I think the fact that no one thinks it's a crazed murderer wandering the streets is making people less afraid than they'd otherwise be."

Nell had noticed the same thing earlier that day when she'd had her hair trimmed at M.J.'s Salon. There was talk of Sophia's crash and the expected expressions of sadness. But the heart of the discussion was a curiosity about who could possibly have disliked Sophia enough to do such a terrible thing. Surely no one they knew. The police would figure out who did it. Surely.

"One person who hated another," Harriet Brandley had announced with some authority as a dark brown dye was brushed onto her graying head. Harriet and Archie had plenty of books in their Sea Harbor bookshop that detailed similar stories, she had explained to those around her. Two people. One crime. And that left everyone else in the town safe and sound. And in that manner, a safety net was carefully built around the residents of Sea Harbor.

Nell wondered at the well-intended logic of the conversations. The fact that a murderer could still be walking the streets of Sea Harbor—perhaps sitting right there in the salon, listening to all the chatter while waiting for a color treatment or a cut—somehow didn't play into the conversations—or was intentionally left out. A shield, was how Ben explained it. People play mind games to protect themselves.

Ben pulled the CRV onto 128 and headed west. "The police are encouraging that kind of thinking to keep the level of worry down. Maybe they've bought into it a little themselves, although they are checking all leads."

"What could Sophia have done that would make someone kill her?" Nell asked, a question someone seemed to ask hourly.

What, indeed? The answer wouldn't be simple. She suspected they were only just beginning to know who Sophia really was. But the fact that people closely connected to Nell's life were already affected by this tragedy—Ella and Gracie, especially—made Nell hope it was resolved soon.

"Birdie and I overheard an interesting conversation last night," Nell said aloud. She detailed the encounter between Alphonso and Ella in the clearing.

"Ella accused Alphonso of murdering Sophia?"

"That part isn't so unusual, Iz." Ben pulled onto the highway.

"They usually look at family members first in murder cases. Ella probably watches a lot of television—she knows that, too."

"I think it's strange that Ella would attack him that way. What does she know? Gracie was a better witness to that relationship, I think, and she hasn't painted it as dysfunctional—though she did say that it seemed to her Sophia visited their Beacon Hill place more often since they had that bad argument in the spring."

"Sometimes people kill out of—or for—love," Nell observed. She looked out the window as the trees gave way to shopping malls and highway intersections. Ben merged onto 93 and headed south.

"But how does Birdie's housekeeper fit into all this?" Sam asked.

Nell repeated the story of their friendship, and Ella's grief over Sophia's death.

"I've seen them together a couple of times, walking down Harbor Road in the morning as I'd open the shop," Izzy said. "They were always talking, gesturing, happy to be together."

"Speaking rapid Spanish. I'm sure it was nice for Sophia to have someone to talk with in her native language."

"Losing her friend must have been difficult. But I don't understand why Ella would lash out at Alphonso." Izzy leaned forward again, her face intent. "Do you think she knows something, Aunt Nell?"

Nell had wondered the same thing. Ella didn't seem the type to throw blame around haphazardly. Nell suspected there was more to it than a grief-stricken friend seeking to place blame on someone.

"Okay, folks," Ben interrupted. "I'm taking this next exit and heading toward Somerville. Or Cambridge? You have exactly eight minutes to let me know where we're going."

"A place that's not fancy or noisy," Nell suggested, "but has tasty food."

"And out of the way, so we won't see anyone we know," Izzy added.

"Give me a pint of Guinness and some curry fries and I'll be a happy man," Sam said, his words measured and suggestive. He lifted a brow.

The others laughed at Sam's subtle suggestion.

"The Thirsty Scholar Pub it is, then." Ben headed toward Beacon Street and the pub that had become Sam's second home when he lived in Somerville—one of the best-kept secrets in Boston, a reviewer had said—which was one of the things Sam liked about it. Ben maneuvered the car through the narrow streets, past the student apartment buildings and small homes, and pulled into a space between two Jeeps.

The foursome walked along the sidewalk in the June night, the smell of charcoal grills filling the air and loud music pouring from open windows.

"Good choice," Nell said to Sam as he held open the door and ushered them into the brick-walled pub.

They found a table near the wall and, as if by magic, a tray of Guinness appeared on the table. The creamy heads were lined up like pristine chefs' hats, each one a mirror of the other. "Mussels and curry fries to follow soon," the waitress said, giving Sam a thumbs-up.

"They haven't forgotten you here," Izzy said, watching the young waitress wiggle around the tables on her way to the bar. She lifted one brow.

"I think I paid for her first year of college," Sam said, ignoring Izzy's look. He stretched his long legs beneath the table. "Big tips equate to Guinness at the ready."

Ben picked up the tulip-shaped glass. "Perfect."

"It feels like we're on another planet. As dearly as I love Sea Harbor, a getaway is good. Not to mention the comfort food they serve up here. Running away is good." Izzy took a long drink of the dark beer and moved her arm as the waitress slid a platter of fries with a pot of curry sauce to the center of the table.

Nell nodded. She slipped her black cashmere sweater to the

back of the chair and brushed a wave of salt-and-pepper hair behind one ear. She wasn't sure if it was the dark bitter beer with the sweet aftertaste or the lovely company—or watching Sam's large, competent photographer's hand absently touching Izzy's fingers, then her wrist, then tugging on a strand of her uncontrollable waves. But whatever the reason, the heaviness she'd felt that day in the salon gave way to the sweetness of a cool summer evening. And she was happy.

First came the mussels—juicy and plump in a smoky chili broth. The group fell silent as they eagerly speared the mussels on forks and sopped up the sauce with bread like starving sailors. Their orders came shortly—shepherd's pie, Irish bangers and mash, meat loaf and gravy.

"Comfort food at its best," Sam said. "It kept me hale and hearty while I was working for the *Globe*."

Izzy nibbled on a piece of soggy bread. "I'm surprised they didn't have to roll you from one photo shoot to another."

"So you think you're keeping me lean, Izzy girl?" he asked. He looped an arm over the back of the chair and rubbed the soft yarn of Izzy's sweater between his fingers.

Nell enjoyed the interplay, but wisely asked few questions regarding their relationship. Her sister, Caroline, had pleaded with her to get the scoop. Izzy provided her mother with few details.

But Nell knew Izzy like her own soul, and stepping into the privacy of her niece's heart would not be wise. Since Sam appeared in Sea Harbor to teach a photography class two years ago, his relationship with Izzy had visibly changed from the surprise of running into an old family friend to a far more intimate one. They were *good* friends and depended on each other, that was unquestionably clear to all those around them. But by the end of Sam's first summer in Sea Harbor, the friendly teasing had deepened into conversations, looks, and touches that made everyone who knew them happy. And although she wouldn't pretend to predict the future, Nell was quietly hopeful she'd be there to see it unfold.

Ben remained true to his goal in getting away from the week's traumatic events, and talk focused on Sam's photography exhibit at the ICA in Boston and the work being done on the community center in Sea Harbor.

"They have a great group agreeing to help out once the building is finished," Nell said. "Annabelle Palazola wants to have cooking sessions with the kids, Joey Delaney is going to do some wood-working with the boys, and even quiet Sal Scaglia volunteered to teach about quarry history."

They laughed at the thought of the reticent director of deeds taking an unruly group of teens on field trips.

"Jane said there's a slew of Canary Cove artists donating time," Sam said. "Willow is at the top of the list."

"She'll be a good teacher. The kids will love her."

"And fall in love with her on the side. Willow is magical. And a gifted artist, too," Sam said. "Sometimes it's hard to believe she's only twenty-three. I see Pete around her Fishtail Gallery a bit. What's that about?"

Izzy laughed. "Cass is keeping an eye on it, too. For now, they're being helpful friends to each other. That's a good thing."

"Friends. Hmmm. That's how it starts. I need to have a talk with Pete," Sam said. He picked Izzy's hand off the table and kissed it lightly.

"You're scaring me, Perry," Izzy said, frowning.

"What, I'm nice and thoughtful and romantic and take you to my favorite restaurant—and you're scared?"

Izzy looked at Ben and Nell. Her face was flushed, and for once in her life, Izzy Chambers had no retort.

By the time the cheery waitress returned to talk Sam into the evening's dessert special, plates were clean and stomachs were full. It was unanimous that they call it a night.

Nell looked at Ben. "This was a good idea, Ben. Getting away was great therapy. I'm ready to go back."

Nell and Izzy made a quick trip to the ladies' room while Sam and Ben split the tab and collected their credit cards. The foursome met at the front door.

"And we didn't see a single soul we knew," Nell said, tucking her arm in Ben's as they started down the street.

"Well, except for one," Sam said.

"Who?"

"Liz Palazola. I noticed her when I went over to the bar."

Izzy and Nell stopped walking. "Why didn't you tell us?"

Sam shrugged. "She was with a guy. A date, maybe, from the way she was looking at him."

"Who?"

"I don't know. His back was to me, but they were leaning close to each other, and Liz seemed far more intent on him than seeing someone from Sea Harbor. So I didn't bother her. Maybe she had the same goal we did—to get away, be anonymous."

"You're probably right," Nell said.

"So let's go," Ben said, noticing the women had stopped moving.

Nell and Izzy took a few hesitant steps, then stopped again while Sam and Ben went on.

In retrospect, Nell didn't know why they turned back, or why she looked through the tall narrow window of the Thirsty Scholar Pub. It wasn't planned, nor was it like her to invade another's privacy. But she did exactly that—turned and stepped close to the window. Then peered through.

At that precise moment, Liz rose from her chair, her smooth blond hair falling across her shoulders. She half-turned from the window, a lovely smile lifting her lips as her light wrap appeared on the arm of her companion.

As he held open the sweater for Liz's waiting arms, the man lifted his eyes and looked toward the window. And in that briefest of seconds, Alphonso Santos looked directly into Nell Endicott's surprised blue eyes.

Chapter 12

$\mathcal{B}$irdie began pouring the wine as soon as Nell had finished her story about their dinner at the Thirsty Scholar Pub.

"Liz . . . and Alphonso Santos?"

"Are you sure?"

"Did they see you?"

The questions cascaded out of Birdie and Cass without time for answers.

Not that there were any answers, Nell thought. Yes, Alphonso had seen her. Or had she imagined it? It was so quick, a lift of a head, a shifting of a glance, and then he'd turned away. Or had she turned away first? The surprise of seeing Birdie's widowed neighbor with Liz Palazola had unnerved her in a way that made recollecting it accurately nearly impossible.

Sam had said Nell was probably thinking about everything going on back in Sea Harbor. Maybe Alphonso was on her mind and that's why she thought she'd seen him with Liz. Sam had seen the man, too, and he hadn't immediately thought it was Alphonso Santos. But when pushed, Sam admitted that he hadn't really looked, hadn't really wondered *who* it was, and that he'd only seen the back of his head.

"Did his head look . . . well, older?" Izzy had pushed. "Were there gray hairs?"

But Sam said that the couple was sitting in shadows, and he

couldn't really say what color the guy's hair was. He probably didn't even look at his hair. The two people were leaning toward each other, their heads nearly touching, so it was hard to see much of anything. Besides, he said, Liz was the one who usually attracted the attention, not the person she was with. And then he had added, tipping Izzy's chin up with his finger and trying to make her smile, "Unless, of course, it was you, charming Izzy. Then I'd know every detail of every color of every hair on your head. And there are many."

"Men!" Izzy had grumped, pushing away his hand but allowing a trace of a smile to return. And then she softened her complaint by suggesting to Sam that if he wanted to grow up to be a famous photographer, he'd better start noticing details.

Nell walked over to the bookcase and plugged in the Crock-Pot.

"Let me help." Cass appeared at her elbow and lifted the large Tupperware container out of Nell's cloth bag. She pried off the top and leaned over it, breathing in the smell. "I knew it!" she said, pouring the thick, chunky soup into the pot.

"It's one of Nell's summer secrets. I can smell the curry from here," Birdie said from her chair near the fireplace.

"It was a little chilly tonight. The kind of night that isn't sure if it's April or June. Soup sounded like a good choice."

"Perfect," Birdie said from her favorite spot near the fireplace. Purl sat on her lap, purring happily.

Izzy walked over to the coffee table and picked up a glass of wine. "I agree. It's perfect. It will help us think."

"About?" Birdie said, slipping her glasses onto the top of her head.

"Who killed Sophia," Cass shot from across the room. "I'm concerned about Gracie. Her mom is worrying her. Julianne is wandering around like a beautiful lost soul. Gracie thinks she might just up and leave if something doesn't come to a head soon."

"What are the police saying?"

"Nothing. Maybe that's part of the problem. There're only telling Julianne that she can't leave the area."

"It's only been a week. They're making some headway," Nell said. "Ben told me the car was badly smashed, but they were able to retrieve the brake line to determine the cause of the failure. And they're talking to the yacht club's security, waitstaff, anyone who might have seen anything that night."

"The person would have had to get under the hood, right?" Birdie said, playing out the scenario in her head. "Sophia was so afraid someone would ding that car that she always parked in the most remote space. I spotted her car when Izzy and I arrived that night. It was as far from the clubhouse as possible, hidden by those pretty islands with greenery all around. It would be difficult to see someone out there."

"It had to be someone who knew what he was doing," Cass added. "I've worked on cars, and you need to know what you're messing with, especially on a Ferrari."

"What's that awesome smell?" Jillian Anderson, one of Mae's teenaged nieces, flew down the steps, taking all three in one graceful leap. Jillian and her sister, Rose, were Izzy's regular weekend help, but once school was out for the summer, they were willing to come nearly anytime she asked them. Birdie said they did this because they were sweet and generous, but Cass and Izzy suspected it was to keep their cell phones in texting mode.

"It's roasted vegetables in a sweet potato soup. A splash of wine, some grilled chicken and—voilà—a chilly night surprise," Nell said.

Jillian glided to Nell's side, looking down into the chestnut-colored soup. Flakes of parsley and slivers of roasted yellow pepper floated to the top as Nell stirred.

"Looks yummy." Jillian pressed a hand against her flat tummy. "You're an amazing cook. Aunt Mae says she sometimes hangs around here longer than she has to on Thursday nights so she'll get a taste."

Nell laughed. Mae would love her secret ploys being revealed by her teenaged niece.

Jillian reluctantly turned away from the food and looked at Izzy. "I'm the last one here, boss. Aunt Mae had to go to a meeting and asked me to lock up. So I'm, like, out of here. You guys need anything?"

"We're fine, Jillian. Thanks."

"*De nada.*"

Izzy's brows lifted. "You're taking Spanish, Jill?"

Jillian's smile fell away. "Well, I was. I mean I suppose I still am, but I'll probably flunk out next year."

"Flunk? That's silly. Why do you say that?" Cass asked.

"You have me mixed up with my twin, Cass. She's the smart one." Jillian offered a lopsided smile. "It's because of Mrs. Santos. She was helping some of us. She was so great. And now she's . . ." Jillian looked back up the steps as if there might be someone there, ready to grab her words and run away with them. She looked back at the knitters. "She's, like, dead."

Birdie looked at Jillian. "Yes, dear," she said. "It's a terrible thing."

"Did you say she was tutoring you?" Nell asked.

"Yep. Mr. Rodriguez—you know him, Miss Birdie. He's that cool dude who used to wait tables at the Edge on Sundays. I know he used to wait on those little old ladies you'd take in there for wine."

Nell held back a smile. Those little old ladies were all Birdie's age, though Jillian clearly set Birdie apart as the young chaperone. The group had gathered at the Edge each week for over forty years, though their meetings of late were less frequent and smaller. "For tea," they would say, though no one had ever seen a teacup grace their table.

"Jimmy Rodriguez comes in here a lot," Izzy said. "He's a good knitter."

"And an awesome Spanish teacher. He said some people

needed extra help, so the principal got him, like, an assistant. Mrs. Santos helped those of us who were having a hard time. Flunking, I guess is what you'd say was happening. She was, like, so smart. And wow gorgeous. Most of the guys in the class had a thing for her. Dweebs. As if she'd look at them."

Nell looked over at Birdie. She hadn't known that Sophia was tutoring at the high school either. Sophia Santos was proving to be a bundle of surprises.

"We—we think maybe she, like, had a lover." Jillian looked over at Birdie, her cheeks pink. "You know, like a boyfriend, but more? And he killed her because she wouldn't leave Alphonso Santos. I mean who would leave Alphonso Santos? He's, like, richer than God."

And then, before she divulged more of the Sea Harbor teenage dissection of the Sophia Santos murder, Jillian was gone, calling out over her shoulder that she was off to decorate for Sunday's regatta and she'd be locking the front door behind her.

"Good grief," Birdie said when the front door slammed shut. She put her needles and yarn down on the table, got up, and walked over to the long center table that now held the soup, a set of hand-made soup bowls, and crusty hunks of French bread wrapped in a linen cloth. "We have more to digest tonight than Nell's soup, so we better get started. Now we have teenagers accusing Sophia of having an affair. What's next?" Birdie shook her head.

Cass' laugh mixed with the aromas of garlic and ginger as she followed Birdie to the table. "Well, it's not with Jimmy Rodriguez, that's for sure. I used to babysit him. He's not much older than Willow. But if Sophia was having an affair, Jimmy might know something. Maybe we should ask him. Maybe it's important."

"And maybe it's teenage gossip," Nell said.

It took some minutes to fill the bowls with the chunky soup. The contents of Nell's Summer Surprise depended on her refrigerator, and tonight's held bits of grilled asparagus, sautéed squares of Vidalia onions, wild mushrooms, and red and yellow peppers, all swimming in a bath of sweet potato broth and wine. Juicy strips of grilled chicken bobbed on the surface like Cass' lobster buoys.

Izzy programmed her iPod, refilled wineglasses with Birdie's sauvignon blanc, and brought the basket of warm bread over to the coffee table. In minutes they were all settled on the Endicotts' old den furniture, enjoying the comfort of one another, the soft worn leather, and Nell's soup.

"I think Sophia's like these Vidalia onions," Izzy said, capturing one with her spoon. "We'll be pulling off layers for a long time."

"It's interesting to think that the people who may have known her best were high school kids and Birdie's housekeeper," Nell said. "I wonder what that tells us."

"That there could be lots of motives for killing her that we can't begin to imagine," Birdie said softly.

For a few minutes they savored the soup in silence, listening to the soft strains of Dar Williams singing about family.

You are my family.

The words settled inside the knitters as warmly as the soup. They *were* family. A friendship wrapped around a love of soft yarns and bamboo needles. Random lives woven together just like their sweaters and hats and shawls. Izzy often said she couldn't quite remember what it was like *before* Thursday nights at the Seaside Studio. And Birdie would wisely say, "And thankfully we don't have to, Izzy dear. *Today* is what we have to think about. Today is what we have."

Cass finished her soup and then began soaking up the remains with a piece of bread.

"There's more, Cass," Nell said.

It was a meaningless comment. Of course there was more. Nell didn't know how to cook for four or five. There was always enough for drop-ins or to stash in empty refrigerators. One of the things Cass counted on every Thursday night was returning home with enough of the meal to avoid canned beans for another few days.

Cass refilled her bowl and sat back down. "I didn't think I

was anything like my mother, but I'm beginning to think I got her worry gene."

"Gracie?"

Cass nodded. "She told me last night she was going to figure this out herself if the police didn't let her mother off the hook soon. I think she's worried about what would happen if Julianne disappeared."

"They haven't completely ruled out that Alphonso might have been the intended victim," Nell said.

"Because of contract disputes?"

"That's one thing. And competitors dislike Alphonso. D.J. and Alphonso had a showdown at a recent council hearing. D.J. suggested Alphonso was using his wife to smear Delaney's reputation."

"What does that mean?" Izzy took a sip of her wine. She pulled out a skein of lavender baby alpaca. "Is Alphonso in danger?"

Nell glanced over at the pattern lying open on the table in front of Izzy. The belted sweater was beautiful, perfect for someone long and lean like her niece. She would attract attention in a potato sack, but this sweater would cause people to stop her on the street.

"No. There's too much scrutiny to do anything to Alphonso," Nell said, still looking at the pattern.

"Well, I think it's all hogwash." Birdie leaned forward and set down her soup bowl. "Everyone around here knew Sophia was the only one who drove that car. And we know for a fact that Alphonso had his truck at the club that night. THE SANTOS COMPANY is painted across the side of it as big as a moose's head. It was even in some of the photos on the society page that had been taken that night. After he gave up the Ferrari, Alphonso always drove that behemoth of a truck. Free advertising, I guess."

"It might have been someone we know, someone sitting at a table in the same dining room, eating the same food." Izzy shivered and the group grew silent, pondering the disturbing thought.

Strangers were one thing; friends and neighbors were another. But someone had killed Sophia. Someone had become angry enough with her or disliked her enough to end her life. And that was fact.

"I wonder if Alphonso and Sophia were having problems. One never knows what goes on behind closed doors." Nell pulled her knitting from a large bag at her side. "That story Gracie told us about Alphonso giving Sophia the car indicates something happened between them."

"She said they argued. And it must have been a doozy to merit a Ferrari as a peace offering. Which I think is downright weird," Izzy said. "And now . . . seeing him with Liz Palazola. So *intimate* like." She looked up at Nell. "That's how you described it, Aunt Nell, even though I know you don't want to think that."

Cass picked up Izzy's thought. "Why would Liz be with Alphonso? And in an out–of–the–way place, not even a week after his wife was murdered? They didn't just bump into each other there." Cass wagged a knitting needle in the air. "Okay, let's just get it out there—were they having an affair? She's about as gorgeous a woman as he'd find anywhere, besides his own wife."

"Younger, but that shouldn't matter. There are plenty of women Liz's age who would give their heart to Alphonso if he'd ask."

Nell collected the empty soup bowls and set them on a side table. "I don't know what to think about it. But seeing them together reminded me of how solicitous Liz was at the wake. Almost as if she could anticipate what Alphonso would want of her, would like—the way people do who know each other very well."

Nell mentioned the conversation she and Birdie had overheard at the club when Sophia was leaving. It occurred to her suddenly that they might have been the last people to have seen Sophia—along with Alphonso. "She could have just meant she was leaving him to go home. But what if she knew there was someone else?"

"So if we're talking suspects, Liz and Alphonso belong on the list," Birdie said with some force. "Having Sophia out of the way would definitely benefit them. Sophia was so religious—I'm not sure divorce would be acceptable to her."

"Liz is a really fine woman," Nell began.

"Of course she is, Nell dear. And so is Julianne. Liz is also a woman with fine mechanical skills." Birdie repeated the scene with Stella fixing the lawn mower. "Liz could fix anything, Stella said. Including cars."

"So we're officially trying to find the killer?" Izzy said, her voice lifting. Her brows shot up.

"Someone has to," Cass said, "And before Gracie goes and gets herself killed. No matter what her relationship is with Julianne, Gracie can't abandon her—and a lot of people are pointing their fingers directly at her. Gracie went down to the police station today and she nearly made Tommy Porter cry, bombarding him with questions, telling him that her mother needed to move on with her life."

"Poor Tommy," Izzy said, feeling instant empathy for the young policeman. "He doesn't do well under stress."

"Gracie felt sorry for him, too, so she backed off. And once she was being nice again, his lips loosened and he told her that they had to question her mom because everyone knew she hated Sophia Santos. It would be irresponsible not to, he said a little solicitously, Gracie thought. But then he added that he personally thought they needed to look more closely at the owner of the Gull Tavern, Jake Risso."

"Jake?" Nell said. "Jake is a curmudgeon, not a killer. Tommy is probably upset because Jake always cards him when he goes to the Gull. He won't let Tommy grow up."

"No, it could be more than that," Birdie said. "Jake's been on a toot lately. He rented the Pisano house after old Enzo died last year. Mary Pisano inherited the house from her grandfather and she couldn't do much with it until Enzo's estate was all settled. Jake said it was his dream house—so Mary rented it to him for the year while the family decided what to do. Why a widower needs an eight-bedroom house is beyond me, but it's none of my business, now, is it?"

Nell smiled at the irony in Birdie's statement. Her own home—the one Sonny Favazza carried her into on their wedding night—had at least eight bedrooms, and more living spaces than any of the knitters had ever attempted to count. Had she been questioned about living alone in a big house, Birdie would have said she didn't consider it a "house" in that sense—a building with bedrooms. The Favazza home and land was a part of Sonny. A part of her. *It would be like selling my soul*, she would have said if anyone had questioned her.

"I always thought that the beach access land belonged to the Pisano house," Cass said.

"It did. But when Sophia offered Enzo an enormous amount of money for the access land not too long before he died, he sold it to her. He thought it would be less trouble for Mary when he was gone. He never thought Sophia would close it off the way she did, though, or he wouldn't have done it. Enzo loved having the whole neighborhood traipse down to the cove on his little trail. Once he even made a wooden sign and posted it right at the road. It said, 'Enzo's Access. Welcome one and all.' And he stuck a hook on it with plastic doggy bags attached for anyone who needed one."

"I remember that," Cass said. "Mary wrote a nice story about it in her column."

"But how does Jake Risso figure in this?" Nell coaxed. Birdie told wonderful, colorful stories and knew more about Sea Harbor than the town historian, but sometimes it slowed down the issue at hand.

"Jake didn't know Enzo had sold off that land. Jake thought it went with the house and he signed a year's lease with Mary. Poor fool didn't read the contract carefully, I guess, because he was in such a hurry to live on Ravenswood Road.

"When he found out, he went a little crazy. He had counted on that land as a way to get his boat into the water. Jake is passionate about his fishing—ever since his wife died, he pursues it with a frenzy. And now that he's finally allowing his son more time to run the tavern, it's truly his first love."

"So he can't get his boat into the water there now?" Cass asked. "That's a bummer."

"Well, he can, but he shouldn't. Jake is nothing if not resourceful. He's found ways, mostly breaking Sophia's locks and going down the pathway just like everyone always did before Sophia closed it off.

"Then she bought new locks. And Jake broke those, too. Finally Sophia called the police—that's probably why Tommy thought of Jake as a suspect. They gave Jake a ticket for damaging property. He paid it happily. Then the next day, he did the same thing."

Cass laughed. "I didn't know Jake had it in him."

"Apparently he does. But in the end, Sophia won. That week before she died, she had four concrete posts anchored into the ground. No boat is going to go down that road again."

The sky above the knitting studio darkened while they talked, casting long shadows across the hardwood floor. The wind picked up, whistling through the two pine trees that marked the corner of the knitting shop. Izzy got up and pulled closed the windows facing the ocean. "It's so beautiful out there," she murmured, half to herself.

"Too beautiful to be tarnished by murder, that's what you're thinking," Nell said, putting her knitting aside and walking over to Izzy. They stood silently for a few minutes, looking out at the same scene that had convinced them a few years ago that the abandoned store with the big back windows was the perfect place for Izzy's yarn shop. In the distance was the breakwater, and on the farthest tip of visible land, one could glimpse Anja Angelina Park.

Ben had built the seat beneath the two long windows before they'd even begun to clean up the dingy building, and Nell had fashioned the soft cushions that Purl now considered hers. But the view was the same, the colors changing with the season, the life of the sea changing daily.

"It's not just Gracie's mother I worry about," Izzy said to Nell. "It's Liz. And Annabelle. Think what it will do to her if Liz is implicated in this mess. The Delaneys will surely be questioned, even Joey. Those boys are all so loyal to their father. And Gracie won't be able to move on with her life and her business and her peace of mind until all this is behind her."

Nell nodded, her thoughts paralleling Izzy's exactly, as often happened. Their friends, too many of them, would have their lives thrown into chaos if this weren't settled quickly. But it was even more than their friends. It was the whole town. The aftermath of murder didn't just fade away. It would be there every day, staring them in the face, causing an anxious current along the narrow roads of Sea Harbor until the murderer was caught.

A ringing cell phone broke into her thoughts and Nell automatically felt her pocket.

But Izzy had claimed the call as coming from her phone and she stepped into the galley kitchen to answer.

"Birdie," she called a minute later. "It's Esther from the police station. She wants to talk to you." Izzy's expression was a question mark.

As Sea Harbor's longest-running dispatcher, Esther Gibson was in the know before almost anyone. Sometimes, Ben would tease her, before things even happened. "Our prescient Esther," he'd call her.

Izzy handed Birdie her phone. "She said she didn't have your number handy and she knew you were here because it was Thursday. God help us if we ever change the day or place."

Nell saw a flicker of worry pass across Birdie's face. She'd be wondering if Ella and Harold were all right. But Stella was at the house, doing some painting for Birdie. She would have called if anything was wrong. Surely.

"Yes, Esther, dear," Birdie was saying. "No, it's not mine. It belongs to the Santoses. . . . Well, of course I will tell them . . . Yes . . . Right now . . . That's fine, Esther. Go back to work now, dear, and don't worry your head about my daffodils or those new bushes that Harold planted this spring."

Birdie set Izzy's phone down on the coffee table and began folding her knitting into her backpack.

She looked up at the three faces staring at her.

Birdie sighed. "It seems we underestimated the power of one Jake Risso. Esther says Sophia didn't win the battle of the road after all. And the police are on their way."

Chapter 13

"Esther was concerned that the police would trample my new bushes," Birdie explained as Nell drove quickly down Harbor Road.

Izzy and Cass had piled into the backseat and leaned forward to listen. "Bushes, yarn, flowers. Esther's worries know no bounds," Izzy said.

"She's sweet to think about the plants, I suppose." Birdie nodded. "But I'm more concerned about Harold and Ella. Apparently Ella called the police and was single-handedly taking on Jake Risso."

The police were a short distance ahead of Nell, the light spinning around, and she pulled over on the easement, right behind Tommy Porter's black-and-white Chevy. Birdie was out of the car before Nell's engine died, running across the road as quickly as her short legs could take her.

Jake Risso sat atop a small tractor aimed at one of the round cement posts that Sophia Santos had strategically planted at the end of the pathway to the beach. Three posts had already been pummeled, broken off at the base by the force of Jake's self-designed battering ram. He had one more to go, and it was looking wobbly as Nell, Cass, and Izzy rushed up behind Birdie.

"Jake, what the hell are you doing? Get off that thing."

It was Tommy Porter, his stuttering gone in the heat of the moment, his voice strong. Several police spotlights added definition to Jake's machinations and emphasis to Tommy's words.

Birdie's attention shifted from Jake to her housekeeper, whose narrow body was planted in front of the one remaining post. "Ella, dear, I don't think that's a good place to be. Come over here now."

Birdie's words were gentle, but her voice was stern.

Ella shifted her glare from Jake to Birdie, then back to the source of her anger. "I'm protecting Sophia's property."

"I tried to stop her." Stella stood nearby, her purple hoodie wrapped tightly around her. "She's crazy. I told her it wasn't her business."

"It's police business now, right, Tommy?" A tall figure, standing directly behind Tommy, stepped up next to him.

"Danny Brandley, that you?" Jake said.

"Hey, Jake," Danny said.

"He's with me," Tommy mustered. "He's riding with me tonight."

Jake turned off the tractor's engine and silence fell around them. He looked over at Tommy and Dan, the bookstore owner's son. "Here's the deal," he said. "The lady's dead now. Finally. Game's over. We need to get things back to the way they used to be."

Nell looked over at Ella. If looks alone could kill, Jake would be lying on the ground at that moment.

The group moved closer to the police car, all of them, and Stella whispered to Cass, "That guy's hot."

Nell glanced at Danny Brandley, who either hadn't heard, or had graciously ignored Stella's comment. Danny must be in town visiting his parents, she thought. She made a note to drop by the bookstore and say hello.

"The way I hear it, Jake," Tommy said, "is councilwoman Beatrice Scaglia is fighting your battle nicely—and legally—with the council and Mr. Santos."

"That takes too long," Jake pushed. "Even Beatrice is at her wit's end. Couldn't get Sophia Santos to listen to common sense."

Dan Brandley spoke up. "Tommy here knows what he's talking about."

"Aw, come on, Danny. I've known you since you were a snot-nosed kid. No harm done here. I'll clean up the mess. I know you're a big-shot reporter now, but this is small-town stuff."

"He has no right to do this," Ella blurted out, her shaking finger pointed at Jake Risso.

Birdie walked over to Ella. "The police will take it from here, Ella. It was brave of you to come out in the dark, but why don't you go back to the carriage house and check on Harold? He must wonder what all the ruckus is about."

"That Jake's a crazy man. Not right in the head," Ella said to Birdie. "This was so important to Sophia. So very important. He made it so hard for her." Ella looked over at the crushed cement. "Sophia wasn't selfish, no matter what they say. It was for her sister, it was all for her sister. Jake Risso has no right—"

Nell, standing on Ella's other side, nodded, although she wasn't sure what Ella was saying nor why Sophia had blocked the path for her sister. In fact, she didn't know Sophia had a sister. But she was fairly sure about Jake Risso. He clearly had no right.

Ella looked once more at the chunks of concrete littering the ground. Then she sighed loudly and walked back up Birdie's long driveway to check on her husband. Nell had no doubt that Harold would be waiting on the small deck, peering into the darkness and worrying about his wife, who had suddenly turned into a social activist.

As Ella disappeared from sight, another vehicle came up the hill, sending Tommy into action. "It's . . . d-dangerous for all of you to be hanging out here near the road like this," Tommy said. "It's dark. Cars might not see you."

The car drew closer, slowed, then came to a sudden stop. Behind the wheel of a canary-yellow BMW convertible, his jaw set, sat Alphonso Santos.

"What the hell . . ." Alphonso's voice flew up over the car door and through the dark night. He turned off the engine and got out of the car. His body towered over Jake Risso. "What's going on here, Jake?"

"H'lo, Alphonso. Just burning the midnight oil. Opening up this walkway so the ocean isn't just for a privileged few. No need to bother you about it."

They all turned toward Alphonso. Although Nell had never witnessed his temper, Ben had seen it at yacht club board meetings. Nell's good friend Rachel Wooten had been the object of Alphonso's ire a few weeks before, and it had shaken the always-composed attorney considerably. It was over the beach access, Rachel had told her. As a city attorney she'd hoped to convince him the city would keep the walkway maintained if he would consent to open it again for the convenience of the neighborhood.

But he'd turned red, Rachel had said, and in angry tones that called the entire office to attention, he bellowed out that it was his wife's wish, her land, and if they tried in any way to dishonor it, there'd be hell to pay.

Now, in the bright light of Tommy's spotlight, Alphonso pulled his brows together, but his face was expressionless. Nell watched, wondering if the famous Santos ire was making its way to the surface.

Alphonso looked around at the gathering for the first time and nodded a hello. Nell thought his look lingered on her a second longer than the others, but there was no change of expression, no indication that he had seen her the evening before—in an out-of-the-way restaurant . . . with another woman . . . less than a week after his wife's death.

Alphonso turned to Tommy. "Who called you?"

"Mrs. Sampson, sir," Tommy said.

Alphonso frowned. He shoved his hands into the pockets of his slacks and stared at the mess of busted concrete. "Ella Sampson," he said quietly, "of course."

Nell watched his face and tried to detect an emotion. A thought that might accidentally slip out and play itself out on his face. But all she saw was a man deep in his hidden self, in thoughts that he had no intention of sharing. He looked like he was standing alone, without anyone else in sight.

Finally, he looked over at Tommy. "Good job, Tom, but I think it's under control now. I'm sure there are other needs in our fair city greater than this misunderstanding."

Misunderstanding? Nell looked at Birdie, whose puzzled expression matched her own. Jake Risso had destroyed Sophia's clear attempt to keep her land private.

Alphonso continued talking in his distinct, authoritative way. He started back toward the shiny new car, but turned his head so his words were clear. "Jake here will somehow get the other post out. Right, Jake?" Without waiting for an answer, he continued. "Then he'll clean up the damn mess he made, and then, folks, drama is over. Curtain down."

He opened the car door and slid onto the leather seats. "The path is now open, folks," he called out as he turned the key in the ignition. "Use it in good health."

Before anyone could respond, Alphonso revved up the powerful engine and stepped on the gas. He pulled the car back onto the road and, with the wheels spitting gravel in all directions, headed up the road to the Santos estate.

Chapter 14

*B*en was already at the kitchen table, the Friday paper spread out in front of him, when Nell came down for coffee.

"Restless?" Ben said. "You tossed and turned last night."

"I dreamed I was going to be bulldozed from here to Boston." She had told Ben the saga of the cement posts when she finally arrived home the night before.

Ben was as mystified as she was.

"I'd much rather have you dreaming about me than Jake Risso and his foolishness." Ben handed her a mug of coffee.

Nell smiled. It didn't deserve a response. She didn't need to dream of Ben; she had him close by, a warm person to reach out and touch. "I'm still puzzled by Alphonso's quick turnaround."

"One thing is clear—the closed access was Sophia's pursuit, not Alphonso's. But I agree that it's strange for him to give in so quickly after her death, especially after that fuss he made with Rachel Wooten. There's a civic planning meeting at the club today. Maybe Alphonso will be there and I can get his take on things." Ben got up and rinsed his cup out. He walked over and kissed the top of Nell's head. "I've got an early meeting with Sam about the regatta. But we're still on for tonight, right?"

"I think if we were to cancel two Friday deck suppers in the space of a month, worse things than being bulldozed by Jake Risso would happen to us."

Nell could see that she wasn't going to have much time for herself today. What she'd like to do was go to the yacht club for lunch with Izzy or Birdie and accidentally run into Liz Palazola. She instinctively wanted to protect Liz—but from what, she wasn't sure. Maybe she was wanting Liz to tell her that there wasn't any way it could have been her in the Thirsty Scholar with Alphonso Santos. She had been working all that evening, right there at the club. Nell would breathe a great sigh of relief.

That scenario, however, seemed unlikely, unless Nell's latest vision check was completely wrong.

But no matter, it wouldn't happen today, not with grocery shopping, a meeting at SeARTS in Gloucester, a short talk to the library guild on the future of nonprofit organizations. No time, even, for a short hike or stopping by Birdie's to figure out what in heaven's name had happened last night. Additional information would have to wait until tonight.

It was late when Alphonso had driven off, and they had all left promptly—Stella and Birdie going back to the house to figure out how to tell Ella what Alphonso had said, and Izzy and Cass catching a ride home with Nell.

They left Jake sitting on his tractor, stunned at his unexpected good fortune.

"Good things come to him who waits," he said to the knitters as they walked away.

"I didn't see you doing much waiting, Jake," Cass shot back.

"But it's finally settled," Nell offered. "That will be good for everyone."

"Not quite everyone," Izzy murmured.

"Not so good for Ella," Jake said, answering Izzy's unheard words. "That lady'd like to see me disappear right off the face of the earth. Send me to the moon. Now she can spit out her murderous venom on Santos."

Which is exactly what the knitters figured Ella would do.

"Ella's very upset," Birdie confirmed that night when she arrived for dinner on the Endicotts' deck. She handed Nell a bag of sourdough rolls that Ella had baked that day. Baking and cooking proved to be an anger-management tool for Ella, and Birdie heartily supported it.

"I never thought of Ella as a crusader. She's always seemed so quiet." Izzy pulled herself up onto a kitchen stool, her long tan legs straddling it.

"She has spunk," Sam said. "That's not all bad."

"No, but this new zeal seems a bit over the edge. I was almost afraid to leave her alone tonight. If Alphonso ends up dead, there will be absolutely no question in my mind who did it."

"Her feelings are understandable, though," Izzy said. She picked an olive out of a bowl and popped it into her mouth, her face thoughtful. "Sophia was her friend, and it was her wish the road be blocked off. Now that she's dead, Ella is carrying her torch. And then Sophia's husband turns around and goes against his wife's wishes and there's nothing Ella can do about it." She looked up at Sam. "Don't ever think of crossing me when I'm dead, Perry. I will come back and haunt you something fierce."

"I'm afraid to cross you in life, Iz. No way I'd do it in death."

Izzy smiled, satisfied, and Sam dropped a kiss on the top of her head.

"Hello, ladies—you, too, Sam." Ben walked in from the deck with Cass trailing right behind him. They each held a martini glass. "We didn't know you had come in. Cass was just filling me in on Tommy's traveling companion last night."

"Geesh, there're no secrets around here," Cass said to Ben's back.

"What secrets?" Ham and Jane Brewster walked across the family room, carrying a basket of peaches they'd picked the day before.

Cass added an extra olive to her martini. She had pulled her dark hair back tonight and it hung in a single fat braid down her back. A fitted blouse and jeans showed off a figure firm and tan from dragging traps and hauling lobsters.

"Ben may make the best martinis in the universe," she said, "but the man does not have bartender potential. He can't keep a secret. But here's what I told him, lest your imaginations do harm to my fine reputation. I asked Ben if he knew that Dan Brandley was back in town. You know—Archie and Harriet's son. He lifeguarded at the club when we were wild teens, Iz. And, as Stella Palazola so delicately put it last night when he showed up on Ravenswood Road in a police car, 'He's hot.'"

"Hot?" Ham speared a tiny onion out of his martini.

"Archie and Harriet's son?" Jane said. "He was working on his computer on the Palate deck the other day. A nice guy. I haven't seen him since he was a teenager."

"He was at the yacht club party, too, with his parents," Nell added.

"Now, how did I miss that?" Cass spied a platter of rosemary crackers on the island and took one.

"He works for the *Globe*," Nell said. "Archie is very proud of him. I think he's doing some writing while he's here."

"So he's not a real policeman?" Izzy set out a bamboo tray with a round of Camembert and the basket of rosemary flatbread.

"No," Ben said. "He's a special-assignment reporter. He probably wanted to see how things worked on a patrol just in case he ever had to do a story about it. A Boston cop might not be as amenable to it as Tommy Porter."

"He handled things nicely last night without showing up Tommy Porter," Birdie said.

"I thought so, too," Cass said. "That's what I was telling bartender Ben."

"You've lost me. What brought the police to Ravenswood Road last night?" Jane asked. "Is there news on Sophia's murder?"

"Nell, it's your story," Ben said. "We guys are off to poke some coals to life."

"And make another pitcher of martinis," Sam added, following Ben and Ham onto the deck.

Nell pulled a pan of pork tenderloins from the refrigerator. The fragrance of fresh garlic, ginger, and soy sauce filled the room.

Cass sighed. "Have I told you lately that I love you?" She wrapped her arms around Nell dramatically.

"And I love you, too, Nell," Jane said patiently. "But I'd like to hear what happened last night."

A light knock on the front door, then footsteps signaled another guest. "I told Gracie to come by," Cass said. "She needed friends. And she's too skinny to run a restaurant—people will think the food isn't good if we don't fatten her up."

"Zip it, Cass," Gracie said, picking up the end of the conversation. "Cooking expertise does not depend on body fat." She handed Nell an arrangement of daffodils mixed with bright green fronds. They were cut low and nestled in a thick glass bowl with colored pebbles at the bottom.

"How beautiful!" Nell took the flowers and placed them in the center of the butcher-block island.

"I thought my café needed window boxes, so Joey built me some. These are my first plants." She touched the tip of a bloom. "So now I have window boxes—but no place to put them."

"But you will soon, sweetie," Birdie said.

Gracie's smile was halfhearted. The week had taken a toll on her. Cass was right—she looked thinner—like a reed blowing in the wind, and a strong one just might topple her.

"I need to figure out some financial things with Alphonso before I can have the equipment delivered, but he has enough on his mind right now. I'm giving it a rest for a few days."

"You have paint. We can at least finish that up," Cass said.

"Come, Gracie, you need a touch of deck magic." Nell picked

up the bouquet and motioned toward the deck doors. "It heals all ills."

Gracie brightened. "I love your deck. I have memories of being out on here with Cass and Izzy one summer. Izzy was having kids spend the night after a swim meet—I think you had put up a tent in the yard. And, Birdie, you suggested that since I was six months older than Cass, I would be a great chaperone."

"Hah!" Cass said, holding open the door.

"'Hah' is right," Gracie said, laughing. "I was one of those kids who started the trouble but looked innocent, so I never got blamed for anything."

"I got blamed," Cass said, passing around a platter of bruschetta dripping with chopped tomatoes, olives, and olive oil. "Even the nuns thought Gracie could do no wrong. I think it was because she had those silky golden waves when she was little, like there was a halo around her head. She got picked to be an angel for the Christmas play. Not me."

They all laughed and settled in deck chairs. Ben refreshed drinks and Izzy put out the platter of Camembert and crackers on a low glass-topped table.

"So now," Jane said, smearing cheese onto a cracker, "I want to know more about Cass' hot Brandley guy and what he was doing on Ravenswood Road with the police."

Gracie leaned forward in her chair. "Police on Ravenswood Road?" she said.

"See?" Jane said. "It's not just me. Birdie, tell all."

Birdie explained the late-night event once more. "It was Ella and Jake causing the ruckus," she added.

"But the biggest surprise of the evening was when Alphonso showed up in a snazzy new car," Izzy said.

"A new car? You're kidding," Gracie said.

"It's gorgeous—a canary-yellow BMW."

Gracie choked on her martini, coughed, and set it down on a table. "Are you sure? Canary yellow? Alphonso is pretty much a red and black kind of guy when it comes to cars. I suppose he's replacing the Ferrari."

The group nodded.

Replacing Sophia's car.

The thought hung in the air, unspoken.

"Seems kind of soon," Gracie said finally, her voice soft. "He's got other cars—"

Nell knew they were all thinking the same thing. But Gracie was the only one who would be free to voice it.

Nell went back in the house and returned with the platter of tenderloins, handing it off to Ben. Izzy followed carrying a large grill basket filled with fresh vegetables and a sprinkling of basil leaves. The meat sizzled as Ben dropped it onto the hot grate.

"I don't get it," Gracie went on. "What's Alphonso thinking?"

Nell and Izzy had shared that same thought earlier in the day when they'd talked on their cell phones, Nell parked in her car outside Shaw's Market, and Izzy on her knees in the yarn shop, filling the pattern rack with new magazines. They were both trying to make some sense out of the evening before. Going against a dead wife's wishes and buying a flashy new car somehow didn't easily fit the mold of a grieving husband.

But then, Nell reminded Izzy, there were no rules for grieving.

Izzy wasn't deterred. "It sounds more to me like a man who is feeling suddenly free. A man who is having an affair," she had said bluntly. "It puts Alphonso right smack in the firing line of suspects, don't you think?"

Nell had agreed with Izzy, but they certainly had no proof of anything. Having dinner with a woman or buying a new car wasn't proof of an affair. And even if it were true, an affair didn't signify murder. At least not always . . . but it raised antennae.

"Alphonso is difficult to understand," Gracie said.

Ben got up and tested a piece of meat with a fork. "I think your uncle likes people to think that. It gives him an edge in business. But some parts of Alphonso are right out there for everyone to see—he's a brilliant businessman, articulate, interested in the community. Think about it—you're all talking about the car, but no one's talking about the fact that he quelled a minor riot among city council members and the neighbors up in his and Birdie's neck of the woods—all who could buy and sell this town if they wanted to. He didn't have to open that path back up and he gains nothing from it—except maybe a line about being a generous neighbor in Mary Pisano's column."

"Line? Hell, he'll get a paragraph for that," Ham said.

"That's true," Nell said, "but Alphonso is also going against his recently deceased wife's wishes by opening it up. That's the part that's hard to understand. None of us knew why she felt so strongly about blocking it off, but it's almost harder to understand Alphonso backing her while she was alive, and then so quickly disregarding her wishes after she's gone."

"It all depends on how you look at it," Sam said. "It's difficult for those who believe that Sophia is still with us in some spiritual way. But for those who think that everything ends with death, it may not seem so awful."

"I don't care what Alphonso believes or doesn't believe," Gracie said. Her eyes flashed with anger. "At least he could have waited until the dust settled on her grave." She stopped and took a breath of air, then went on. "Or, while we're on my uncle's questionable actions, for going out and buying a fancy new car."

"And that brings us to something far more easily digested. Dinner, anyone?" Ben's thick brows lifted humorously, and soon the mood of the evening changed to one of pleasure and happier thoughts of Nell's grilled vegetables with a tangy cucumber yogurt sauce, fluffy, fragrant basmati rice, and slices of pork so tender no knife was needed.

While Izzy lit the hurricane lamp on the long teak table, a recent addition to the deck, Cass put in a new CD of an old Stephane Grappelli jazz album, and soon Grappelli's fingers on the violin filled the night air with a lively version of "Blue Moon." Sweaters were buttoned against the night air, chairs pulled out, and platters placed between the candlelight. Nell was the last to sit.

Ben raised his glass and looked down the table. He smiled into Nell's eyes first, just as he did before every toast. And then he looked around and brought in the rest of the group. "To dear friends, to family," he said. "Shalom."

The group raised their glasses and echoed Ben's words, just as they always did. Glasses clinked, smiles grew, and soon platters competed with one another as they were passed around the table to laughter and talk and the sounds of friendship.

It was a while later—just as Nell was scooping up ample servings of cherry crisp with the buttery topping dripping down the sides— that the sound of a doorbell filtered out to the back of the house.

Ben stopped in the middle of a story about a family vacation fiasco in Colorado. "The doorbell?"

"Willow said she might come by . . ."

"But she'd never ring the doorbell," Izzy said.

"Nor Pete," Cass added. "And he has a gig over in Rockport." She licked the buttery sauce from the tip of her finger.

"There's an easy solution. I'll answer it." Nell pushed her chair back and went inside, leaving the French doors open behind her.

They'd all been wrong. Joey Delaney stood beneath the porch light, looking embarrassed.

"Joey, come in," Nell said, opening the door wider. "You're just in time for dessert."

"Sorry for bothering you, Nell. I know this isn't a good time to barge in, but I'm looking for Gracie. I got Pete on his cell, and he said chances were good she was over here." He paused, then tried to lighten his tone. "Pete said next to a paying gig this was the only place to be on a Friday night."

"Well, Pete's right. And you are welcome anytime. Gracie's inside. Come in."

At the sound of her name, Gracie appeared in the hallway. "Is everything okay?"

Nell could see as soon as Gracie posed the question that she didn't think everything was okay. And the look on Joey's face told them both that she was right.

Joey looked down at the sisal rug beneath his boots. He shoved his hands in his pockets. He was nearly a foot taller than Gracie, a well-built man, but when he looked down at her, it was with a tenderness that belied the strong muscles visible beneath his knit shirt.

"Hey, Grace, sure—everything's fine. Alphonso is seeing what can be done. He called and asked me to look for you."

"What can be done? What do you mean?"

Ben walked in from the deck. He stood in the hallway, just behind Gracie. "Hey, Joey. Can I help?"

"Hi, Ben. It's Gracie's mom—Julianne," Joey said. "They've arrested her for manslaughter. They think . . . Well, they say she killed Sophia."

Chapter 15

$\mathcal{G}$racie accepted Ben's offer to go with her to the police station. Joey seemed relieved—he'd come over to the Endicotts' on his motorcycle—not a great way to get Gracie to the jail. But Gracie asked Joey to ride along with her and Ben, and he readily agreed, apologizing for leaving his bike in the drive. The police had arrested Julianne a couple hours before, Joey explained, and she'd used her one call on Alphonso. Probably a good move, considering his influence.

Alphonso thought it wouldn't be difficult to set bail. But he'd been wrong, an unusual happening for Alphonso Santos.

When Ben returned from the police station later that night, he slid into bed next to Nell and leaned back against the downy pillows, tired to the bone. Nell slipped off her glasses and put down her book. She rubbed his arm.

"Judge Wooten was called in," Ben said. "Rachel's father. He's an honorable man. But a smart one, too. And as he so wisely put it, Julianne Santos was a bigger flight risk than a seagull."

And the crime, the judge reminded everyone, was a serious one.

So there would be no bail, even with the murdered woman's husband offering to provide both the money and the oversight.

"Have the police found something? Is there a reason Julianne was arrested today?" Nell asked.

Ben wrapped an arm around her, gathering her close to his body. "The police received an anonymous tip. The caller suggested they take a look at Julianne's car, that they might be surprised at what they found. She'd been seen opening the trunk of her car at the club that night, though the caller never said who saw her.

"So they went over to Gloucester where Julianne was staying— it's the same apartment house Joey and Gracie lived in while they were married. Her car had broken down in front of the house and hadn't moved, the landlord said, since Julianne arrived the night of the murder.

"Julianne was coming back from a walk when the police drove up. She readily gave them the keys. She had nothing to hide, and they could have the car if they wanted it, she said. It didn't work."

They checked the trunk as the caller had suggested, and that's where they found the books, stuffed inside a cardboard box. Self-help manuals on everything you'd ever want to know about your car, from A to Z—and computer printouts of the most current information. Step-by-step solutions to every automotive problem, from fluid leaks to stalled engines to noisy mufflers.

And highlighted with a yellow marker were sections on brakes. Domestic-made brakes. Foreign brakes. Even Brembo brakes. Dual cylinders in Ferraris. How to repair them. But of more interest to the police were the trouble-shooting sections outlining what can go wrong with brakes—and what the consequences are. There was even a subtitle in one, meant as a touch of humor, called "How to cut a brake line without breaking your fingernails." Stuck in a paper bag behind it were a mess of things—a box of throw-away surgical gloves, a suction device, wires, a pointed metal probe.

"Gracie is stunned," Cass said the next day.

She and Nell walked along the waterfront on Harbor Road, their heads held back to catch the morning breeze. The wind was gusty, lifting Nell's hair from her neck and tossing it against her cheek. An invigorating June day.

Cass wore a floppy gray cotton hat that Izzy had knit for her, and she pulled it down tight on her head, holding her mass of dark hair in place. "She doesn't know what to think."

"Ben said it doesn't look good."

Cass nodded. "A pile of books on how to screw up brakes. Plus a bunch of printouts from Internet sites that explain exactly how to do it. And top that off with her outburst at the club and again at the wake. No, I guess it doesn't."

"But even with the books and tools and comments we all heard Julianne make, something is missing. Julianne was so wobbly that night that I don't think she could have hit the side of a barn with a beach ball, much less dismantle the brakes on a sports car."

"Gracie said the same thing. Her mother didn't learn how to drive until she was in her twenties. She hates cars, as is evidenced from that jalopy she drives. Maybe because her brother loved them so much. And she absolutely denied that the books and bag of tools were hers. Someone planted them there, she said."

Nell looked out over the ocean as if there might be answers floating along the incoming tide. The harbor was dotted with dozens of sailboats, their billowing white sails brilliant against the blue sky. "Everyone is taking advantage of this perfect day," she said. "Even Ben and Sam, using Willow as an excuse. She's determined to learn to sail the fancy Hinckley sailboat she inherited from her dad, and Sam and Ben immediately signed on as her instructors."

"It's great to be out on the water on days like this," Cass said. "But all this awful stuff in the air is enough to take the wind out of anyone's sails."

Nell smiled, but Cass' pun carried the sad truth. The vibrancy that she loved about early-summer days was dulled by Sophia's death. The smells of summer—salt air laced with coconut oil, the perfume of wild roses spilling along the roadside, the sweetness of Scoopers' cotton candy and rich ice cream. She'd hardly noticed them.

It was too close to them—and not just Sophia's dying, not just Julianne's arrest—but all those tangled up in the web of her death.

They walked past the Ocean's Edge restaurant and along narrow, windy Harbor Road, past Jake Risso's Gull Tavern and M.J.'s Hair Salon. Past all the small weathered shops with blue and green and yellow shutters framing the windows and colorful hand-painted signs above doors. All the mix of things that defined the town they loved fiercely.

They reached Harry's Deli, his windows decorated today with wrapped cheeses, bottles of olives, capers, and wine, all piled high in enormous wicker baskets. Scattered about the cheeses and baskets were arrangements of forsythia, purple cape daisies, and blue and yellow violas, freshly cut from Margaret Garozzo's lovely garden.

Nell looked in the window and saw her own reflection, wind-blown salt-and-pepper hair full and billowy around her fine-boned face. Her prominent cheekbones were pink from the salty gusts. She smiled into Harry's bountiful display, masking her troubled thoughts, and pushed her hair back into place as best she could.

"Your hair looks great," Cass said, holding open the door. "I like the messy look. Sexy." She followed Nell into the blended aroma of simmering broth with a trace of nutmeg and the smell of homemade bread baking in Harry and Margaret's stone oven. Nell looked over the counter to a pot of steaming soup. "Smells amazing, Harry."

The deli owner wiped his wide hands on a once-white apron. "Stracciatella, my dear ladies. Delicious. My mother's own secret recipe—nutmeg, but also with a hint of cinnamon." Harry pressed his finger and thumb together, kissed them loudly and flung his hand out into the steamy air. "The cold soups will come soon, but one finale of the season for my stracciatella. A table for two, ladies?"

"For four, Harry."

"Izzy, Bernadette, and you two beauties, if I may be so bold as to guess. Right this way."

"Bernadette?" Cass spoke to Harry's back.

Nell laughed. "I don't think there are too many people around here who know Birdie's real name, Harry."

"Of course I know her real name. I knew Sonny Favazza, too, and her other three husbands." He chuckled as they walked across the room. "Four husbands, imagine that." His hand flew out in the air as he talked. "And all fine fellows, but none held a candle to Sonny Favazza, people say. I was just knee-high to a grasshopper when he died like that, so sudden. Who woulda thought? A heart attack for such a young man? But my parents talked about it, and the beautiful Bernadette, a new bride, like a ghost in that big house on the cliff. It was like one of them novels."

Nell imagined the spirited Birdie back then. Alone, devastated, building a life for herself without the love of her life. Of course she hadn't known Birdie then, but she knew the woman she'd become. And she'd sat in the warmth of Sonny Favazza's den and listened to Birdie's stories, wandered through his ancestral home, and knew of the things Birdie's husband had built for Sea Harbor—Pelican Pier, a library, a clinic. Through his home and his legacy, Nell suspected she knew Sonny Favazza nearly as well as anyone—except for his beloved bride. His Birdie, as he'd affectionately nicknamed her.

Harry led them to their favorite table, right next to the back window where the gulls sat on the windowsill and the diners could nearly touch the top of sailboats pulling up to the moorings along the concrete wall.

He pulled out their chairs, first Nell's, then Cass', then took a deep breath and leaned over the table, a serious expression pushing away his broad smile.

"Julianne Santos is in jail," he said in a low voice.

Nell nodded, picking up a menu. "Yes, Harry," she said.

Everyone knew about the arrest; there was no reason for Harry's whisper. It had been on the news and in the morning paper. Even Mary had written about it in her column, beseeching the "powers that be" to wrap it all up quickly and bring the summery days of wine and roses, as she'd colorfully put it, back to Sea Harbor.

And then Mary had launched into a thank-you to Alphonso Santos for his generous, kind gesture, reopening the Ravenswood Road beach access just in time for tiny feet to find their way to the sandy cove. A gift for the whole town. Alphonso Santos was "a good neighbor," Mary had written. "A generous man," indicating clearly that others were not so kind.

Mary hadn't mentioned Sophia Santos at all.

"People are relieved," Harry said, taking Nell's silence as encouragement for him to continue. "People are happy."

"Happy, Harry?" Cass asked, her eyes peering across the top of the menu. "Someone has died."

Harry nodded his nearly bald head solemnly. "Certainly Sophia Santos was a decent lady and she will be missed and mourned. She came in here often. She loved my gnocchi especially. *Magnifica!* she used to say to me. It is sad for Alphonso, sad for us to have lost this lady. But it's a good thing to be rid of the worry and to stop wondering if there is a murderer walking our streets. Someone who could harm our children. Who knows why Alphonso's sister did this awful thing? Maybe she had a good reason—jealousy or some personal thing, But whatever, it's over now."

Izzy came up behind him and caught the end of his monologue. "It's not over, Harry," Izzy said. She pulled her brows together in a look that Nell suspected had driven opposing attorneys crazy when Izzy was in the courtroom.

Squeezing her body around Harry's ample girth, Izzy sat down in the window seat across from Nell and Cass and looked at Harry. "They didn't say Julianne did it, now, did they? They said they *think* she *might* have done it. She's innocent right now." Izzy smiled, then, the generous wide smile that made people feel warm and wanted, even if her words were strong or contrary. She gathered her tangle of waves back from her face and slid a scrunchie around the fistful of hair.

"It's been a crazy morning," she said to Nell and Cass. Then she took a long drink of water and pulled a half-finished sock from her bag. She lined up several balls of a soft wool-cotton blend on the table in front of her. "This will calm me down. I need calming down." She picked up her needles, balanced them on her hands, and moved from one double-pointed needle to the next, the needles clicking like chopsticks.

"Harry, dear. Please move so I can sit down," Birdie said, coming up beside the baker and tapping him gently on the back.

Harry looked down and greeted Birdie with a broad smile. He took a step back and Birdie settled next to Izzy, hooking her backpack over the chair.

"Now," Birdie said, looking up into Harry's round face. She slipped her arms out of her light sweater. "I think we could use a glass of your fine mango tea and those delicious bread sticks to nibble on, don't you?"

Harry's jowls swung slightly with the nod of his head and his smile grew as it always did in Birdie's company. It was only his stance that showed his reluctance to leave an unfinished conversation. "Coming up," he said finally, and moved his large frame slowly through the maze of tables, back toward the counter.

"Sweet Harry," Birdie said. "He means well, but he's like a bee spreading pollen, taking bits of conversation from table to table."

"But what he says is usually the consensus of what he's heard. Which means this morning's crowd thinks Julianne is guilty and the case is closed," Izzy said. She held up the sock cuff. "These socks are for you, Nell. They're knee-high hiking socks. Perfect for the fall when we hit the Ravenswood Park trails. Or maybe if you take up biking with Birdie?" She pointed to the secondary yarns she would use on the narrow stripes around the calf. "Mellow yellow, ship-shape blue, and rich red. Perfect Nell colors."

"I'll love them, Izzy," Nell said. She reached over and fingered the soft yarn, then touched Izzy lightly on the cheek. "And biking isn't out of the question."

"This is what's keeping me sane," Izzy went on. "I want to curl up in a corner and knit. The shop was nuts this morning. Mae and I spent half our time fielding rumors. I don't know why people think we'd know anything—maybe it's just that knitting can lend itself to lots of conversation, but it was wild."

"What are people saying?" Cass said.

Before Izzy could answer, Harry's wife, Margaret, came over to the table to take their order, a smile filling her small lined face. "Try the stracciatella," she urged, already scribbling it on her clean pad.

They all agreed, declaring her Italian soup the best in town and the flowers in the window gorgeous. Margaret left the table happy and discreetly, as was her way.

"Both Rose and Jillian were working today, and they repeated the teenage scuttlebutt."

"That Sophia was having an affair and her lover killed her when she wanted to break it off?"

"That's the one," Izzy said, pulling a bread stick from the basket. "I think it's from some soap opera they watch. And Jillian says she saw this man, the *lover*, with her own eyes. And her best friend saw him, too. He picked Sophia up at the high school one day. He was 'way cool,' Jillian said. Younger than Sophia by a century, or maybe a decade, was her friend's take."

"And the 'he' is?" Cass rummaged around in her backpack for the beginnings of her mysterious fish hat.

"A mystery man. They didn't have a clue who he was."

"I don't think the police are looking into mystery men," Nell said. "Ben thinks they'll concentrate on building up their case against Julianne, and they have a pretty good start. It's their job, of course."

"Even though she says she is innocent?" Birdie shook some sugar into her tea and stirred it with her spoon.

"So many people heard her wish Sophia dead," Izzy said. "And she had plenty of motive. With Sophia out of the picture, Alphonso would be much more generous in giving her money."

"We know she was at the club that night. And then there's the box of books telling her how to do it, and tools to help her," Birdie said.

"But Gracie said her mother's mechanical ability would fit in a thimble. If she wanted to kill Sophia, she'd have been far more likely to put some poison in her tea. She'd never fool with the inside of a car." Cass ran a hand through her hair. "I think Julianne has been an awful mom to Gracie. I've always resented her for that. Living with that probably brings its own kind of life sentence. But I don't think Julianne Santos could possibly kill anyone."

"You sound convinced, Cass," Izzy said. She moved her yarn to the side as Margaret placed a big bowl of soup in front of each of them, then disappeared, as quiet as a kitten.

Cass was silent for a moment, thinking about the lineup of things against Julianne Santos and trying to give them a fair shake. She picked up her spoon and played with the tiny threads of egg swimming on top of the soup.

"Yes," she said finally, "I am."

Birdie sat up straight in her chair, her spine not touching its back. "That's good enough for me. I am with Catherine," she said. "I watched Julianne Santos grow up. She had plenty of problems, that's for certain. She was a beautiful little wild child—and her parents traveled so much there wasn't anyone to nurture that spirit and make sure it developed in the right directions. She's done crazy things and she's been a terrible mother. But I would bet on my sweet Sonny's urn that she could no sooner kill anyone than fly."

Nell played with her fork, lightly tracing a pattern in the table-cloth and listening.

"We've tossed out ideas willy–nilly. Without clear design. We'd never knit a cable sweater that way. Or a pair of hiking socks. Not even a hat."

"So . . . ?" Cass said. They waited for Nell to continue.

"So if we want to put an end to all this and get our summer back, we need to figure out what really happened that night. And I'd say we had better begin now."

"Today," said Birdie.

"Or sooner," Izzy added.

A shadow fell across the table and stilled their voices. They looked up into the perspiring face of Harry Garozzo. He'd come from the warm kitchen and smelled like garlic and onions.

"All right, ladies. I admit you're right—this is a sad time, not a happy time," Harry said without preamble, as if he were simply continuing a conversation they'd all been a part of. "I just don't like the fear and the uncertainty. It affects business, our life here. All the goings-on up and down Harbor Road. So when they say they have the person who did this awful thing, that's good."

"If it's the right person," Izzy said.

Harry went on as if she hadn't spoken. "But I am always honest with my friends—" His large arms spread out as if to embrace them. "So I will tell you that I have my doubts, too. My Margaret—she's as quiet as a church mouse and she minds her own business. But she hears things sometimes because people don't even know she's there, like a ghost. Sophia came in here after Mass sometimes with Ella Sampson. They were an odd couple," Harry said, his eyes twinkling. "That beautiful Sophia and straight, simple Ella. But both nice ladies, sure. They stopped in after Mass on the Tuesday before Sophia died. Margaret remembered it because it was her week to arrange the altar flowers and Sophia and Ella told her how pretty her flowers were. Margaret uses the flowers from her own garden. She has a green thumb."

Harry looked over his shoulder to see if he was needed behind the counter, then turned back.

"Sophia looked worried that morning, but she was always so beautiful that worry was hard to see on that face. Margaret put plates of mushroom brioche in front of them and poured their coffee without them even knowing she was there. They were quiet that Tuesday, not chattering in Spanish like they usually did. Just looking out the window and drinking their coffee.

"When Margaret came back to the table to refill their coffee cups, Ella was gone to the ladies' room and Sophia was turned away, still looking out at the ocean, concentrating something fierce. She was mumbling quietly, in Spanish at first. Margaret heard the word 'marriage.' *Matrimonio*. It's like the Italian. *No marriage*, Sophia said. And then, just as Ella walked back from the ladies' room, she said something in English, as if she'd just learned a new phrase or a saying and was trying it out. It sounded awkward, coming from her, Margaret said. 'Over my dead body.' That's what Margaret thought she heard. 'Over my dead body.'"

Chapter 16

*N*ell didn't know if it was Margaret's overheard conversation or simply the week's events that were tiring her, but she might have canceled their plans for later that day if Ben and Sam hadn't been sitting in the family room when she got home, drinking beer and listening to Pete tune his guitar.

"You're coming, right?" Pete looked up. His mouth curved in the grin that his mother said got him through Our Lady of the Seas grade school. "The good nuns couldn't resist it," Mary Halloran said. "They turned a blind eye to Peter's mischief far more times than they should have."

Nell decided Pete's grin had aged well, maintaining its effectiveness, even though the grin was going on thirty. "Of course," she said. "I wouldn't miss it."

The farmer's market stayed open until eight on summer Saturdays to showcase the town's musical talent as well as vegetables, fruit, and flowers. Tonight was Pete's band's moment in the spotlight. And of course Nell wouldn't miss it.

Ben and Nell picked up Izzy and Sam at Izzy's, a small white framed house just a few blocks from the Endicotts', and drove the short distance to the pier. The market booths spilled out into the green area that sloped down to the water. A small platform stage was set up near a curved row of benches, where they could see the top of Pete's head in the distance.

Rain had threatened off and on in the late afternoon, but by seven o'clock the sky had turned to a dusty purple and everyone breathed a sigh of relief. "My guitar doesn't do well in the rain," Pete said, as they walked up. Willow and Cass held plugs and a maze of cables.

"Sometimes your guitar doesn't do well in sunshine," Cass retorted, trying not to trip over a tangle of extension cords.

"Peace, you two," Willow scolded, waving to Merry Jackson as she carried her old Casio keyboard to the stage.

"I'm hot tonight, Pete," Merry called out. "We're going to wow 'em."

Ben and Sam brought a cooler of water bottles from the car and set it down next to the speaker. They watched Merry flounce onto the platform, her bright blond ponytail flying over a bare shoulder.

The co-owner of the Artist's Palate Bar & Grill had more energy in her little finger than Nell had in her whole body. Tonight she'd be using it singing backup and playing the keys.

Merry plugged in her keyboard and dragged one finger along it, causing the microphone to screech. "Oops," she said and waved happily to the group.

"How does Hank keep up with her?" Sam wondered aloud. Merry's husband was nearly twenty years older than his irrepressible wife.

"I don't think he even tries," Ben said.

Andy Risso walked up next, dragging his drums on a dolly behind him. Andy's scruffy beard and long brown hair were a bone of contention between him and his dad, Jake, and Nell wondered if that was the reason Jake hadn't turned over the keys to the Gull to his son so he could spend his days fishing. But no matter how he looked, Andy was a gentle, nice person and, frankly, Nell thought he added a bit of civility to the Gull Tavern. His degree in English lit made him one of her favorite conversationalists.

Andy doffed his floppy hat to the group and began setting up his equipment.

"Isn't it time you named this motley group?" Cass asked.

"We have a name," Pete said, feigning offense.

"What is it?"

"Merry, tell Cass our name," Pete said. He strummed his guitar, then tightened a string.

"Sure, we have a name, Cass. All bands have names," Merry said.

"So what is it?"

"Andy, tell the fine folks our name."

Andy pulled his brows together and looked down at his drums in fierce concentration. Hair fell across his face, all the way down to his chin. Finally he lifted his head in an explosion of brown locks and shouted, "And henceforth thou shalt be called the Fractured Fish!"

"Fractured Fish," Pete and Merry echoed to a chorus of laughter.

"We'll be back, Fractured Fish," Ben said. "If Nell doesn't get her zucchini and corn before they run out, it won't be a pretty sight."

Sam stayed behind to help the band set up, but Izzy followed Ben and Nell across the lawn to the crowds of people squeezing melons and smelling small pots of herbs. The line of booths stretched across the green area opposite the pier, almost all the way to the water.

"I saw Chief Thompson for a while this afternoon," Ben said in a low voice. "We talked about Alphonso—and I mentioned Liz. It seemed it was going to come up, so I might as well mention it—for whatever it's worth."

Nell shivered. She wasn't sure if it was from the wind that had picked up or the thought of Alphonso and Liz being implicated in a murder, but she slipped her arms through the sleeves of her sweater and pulled it close.

"And?" Izzy prompted.

"He had already talked to Alphonso, even before they'd arrested Julianne. An anonymous caller had had suggested they check into an affair."

"An anonymous caller?"

"Esther took the call. She was pretty sure it was Ella Sampson."

Ella. That might explain her intense anger toward Alphonso a few nights ago. She suspected an affair. She'd have to remember to ask Birdie if she knew any more.

"What did Alphonso say?" Nell stopped at a counter and began checking the silky ends of a cob of corn.

"He became very angry and said that it was none of their business, that his personal life had nothing to do with his wife's murder, and they should stop grasping at straws and find out who did it."

"That's a little shortsighted. Of course his personal life is important to the case."

Ben agreed. "It was the first time Jerry had seen Alphonso uncomfortable. But he covered it up quickly with anger."

"I suppose the police talked to people at the club, waitstaff, security guards, bartenders?" Izzy asked.

Ben nodded. "A lot of people wandered in and out during the dinner and dancing, but no one was seen in that dark corner of the lot where the car was parked. But Jerry says that tells them nothing—that corner was pretty well hidden. Alphonso went out for a cigar once or twice—but the security guard seemed to think he stuck close to the bar. Again, it's hard to say."

"I suppose they talked to Liz, though I can't see her puncturing brake lines in that elegant dress she had on," Izzy said.

"Liz attracts attention, whether she wants to or not. I don't think a security guard would have missed seeing her walk all the way across the parking lot," Ben said. "She had her finger on everything happening that night, according to her staff. It was her responsibility. They claimed they couldn't sneak a smoke without

Liz knowing they were gone. Apparently even Sophia went out a couple of times—for some fresh air, the bartender thought, though she ran into Davey Delaney outside the bar patio and it turned into a shouting match."

"Sophia was shouting?" Nell said.

"Davey was shouting. Sophia was composed, as always. A security guy had to calm him down."

"Did they say what it was about?" Nell dropped the corn and zucchini into the bag and paid the merchant.

"They said it was just Davey, the way he is. He can get in a snit at the drop of a hat, especially if anyone disparages the company—and apparently Sophia had done or said something he didn't like."

Ben took Nell's bag and he and Izzy started back toward the stage where Pete was standing front and center, strumming his guitar and singing about "times they are a-changing."

Nell felt a quick intake of breath next to her. She turned and found herself face-to-face with Maeve Delaney. The diminutive Delaney matriarch was looking up at Nell, her small frame seeking height.

"Maeve, I'm so sorry," Nell said. "I didn't see you standing there."

Maeve's small round face was clouded with concern. "They've arrested Julianne Santos." Her tone was definitive. "It's done."

Maeve pulled several bills from her wallet and handed them to the merchant. "I think the police know more than I do and more than you do. I trust they are doing their job, and I suggest that you do the same."

She started walking away from the market area, headed toward the parking lot. In the distance, standing in front of a large truck, Nell saw D.J. Delaney watching the two of them.

Maeve saw him, too, and waved, then turned her back to him and spoke quietly to Nell. A cloud of worry fell over her face. "My son Davey sometimes speaks out of turn. He needs to rein in that temper. Sure, and he doesn't like anyone coming up with a bad word about his father's company. Act like a gentleman, I tell him. Be more like Joey, I say. But he's a good man underneath it all." She sighed. "You don't ever stop worrying about them, though, no matter how big they get." The last words were so soft, Nell could barely hear them.

"Did Davey and Sophia dislike each other?" she asked gently.

"Sophia upset all of us, but we don't speak ill of the dead, God rest her soul." She swatted the air as if dismissing a fly. When she looked at Nell again, the worry seemed to have been pushed back to some hidden place. In its place was a serious and stern expression, one she might have used to speak to a recalcitrant child.

"It's all over now, Nell. All of it. Let it go. We must bury the dead and get on with living."

She touched Nell's arm then, a firm, pressured touch. Then dropped her hand. But the pressured feeling remained the whole while Nell watched the small Irish mother, her back as straight as an iron rod, walk up the hill to her waiting husband.

Chapter 17

Overnight the winds changed, coming in from the south and driving out the chill that had brought out sweaters the night before.

On Sunday morning Nell walked over to her dressing table and picked up a brush. "I'm counting on a lazy, quiet hour, a creamy omelet, some knitting, and the *Times*. We both could use it." She slipped on a light blue blouse. Black slacks, a wide leather belt, sandals, and Nell was ready.

"Sounds fine to me. But it'll never happen." Ben followed her down the back stairs and into the kitchen. He took the car keys off a hook beside the phone and headed out to the garage.

Nell followed close behind, pulling the door shut behind her. "What do you mean, it'll never work?" She climbed into the CRV.

"We've been having Sunday brunch at Annabelle's Sweet Petunia for . . . how long? More years than I can count. And you've never made it through a breakfast without talking to at least a dozen people."

Nell ignored Ben's teasing and looked out the window as they drove down Sandswept Road, down to the beginning of the Harbor Road shops, then turned and drove over the bridge to Canary Cove. The short strip of land, just before the galleries and boutiques began to crowd the windy road, was green and lush, a welcome emptiness in the middle of Sea Harbor. On either side of the road, the sea lapped gently against the scrubby terrain, and off in the distance, large whale-watching boats moved slowly out to sea, their passengers leaning on the railing and waving at anyone who would wave back. Sailboats puffed their sails and some die-hard fishing boats that didn't know to take a day of rest headed out beyond the breakwater to find some giant cod before the waters got too warm.

The galleries didn't open until noon on Sunday, and the road was quiet as they passed the arts foundation building. Nell strained to see the new display of glass beads in Rebecca Marks' blown-glass lamp gallery as they passed it and vowed to get back soon—without Ben. Better to browse. Across the road, Willow's Fishtail Gallery was taking on a new, more feminine look and becoming her own. Several pieces of her fiber art added vibrant color to the window display. But outside the door, guarding the studio, was one of her father's life-sized wooden mermaids. Nell imagined the spirit of Aidan Peabody somehow embodied inside the carved figure, protecting his daughter from harm.

Ben turned left onto the narrow gravel road that took them up the wooded rise of land to Annabelle's Sweet Petunia restaurant.

"The lot is nearly full," Ben said. He circled once, then found an open slot near the walled-in garbage area where most diners chose not to park. He pulled the car into the space and they headed toward the restaurant.

"I think I spotted Birdie's bike. This is quite a hike for her," Nell said as they walked up the steps and into the shadowy interior of the homespun restaurant.

Stella Palazola stood behind the podium, grinning at them and holding a stack of menus in her hand. "I'm just seeing you guys everywhere this week," she said. "That's cool."

"Stella, I swear, there's not a person on this earth who works as hard as you do," Nell said.

"You tell that to my mom. My sister, Liz, is the one who usually wins that award, but I'll catch up. Just watch me." Her glasses slipped down her nose. She pushed them up with her index finger, then laughed and pulled them off entirely. She waved them in the air. "Guess what? These are soon to be a part of my past. Forever."

Ben narrowed his eyes and framed her face with his fingers, seeming to survey the new look of Stella Palazola. "I have to say, you are gorgeous with or without glasses, Stella, my girl. But those brown eyes are amazing. You'll knock 'em dead at Salem State."

Stella blushed.

"You're getting contacts? That's wonderful."

"They're all ordered and paid for, thanks to my guardian angel, Miz Birdie. My graduation present," she said proudly. "And speaking of the queen, she's waiting for you. We snagged a table big enough for whoever. You guys seem to collect people like flies."

Ben tossed Nell a knowing look that she easily ignored and followed Stella out to the deck.

It was true that they never knew whom they'd find on the Sweet Petunia deck or who would stop by their table and stay awhile. But there had definitely been times when she and Ben had had a table alone, just the two of them, times when Ben got to read the whole Week in Review section of the paper without a single interruption. Not too many, maybe. But there had been times. Surely.

Nell spotted Father Northcutt on the deck, sitting with Pete and Cass' mother, Mary Halloran. Nell felt sure that Our Lady of the Seas would fall directly into the sea itself if it weren't for Mary. She did everything from arranging altar committees to keeping Father Larry's books. And at Ben's suggestion, the good padre had actually made it a paying position recently. Mary was probably filling him in on everything he needed to do for the next week, chastising him for the things he neglected the week before, and, Nell noticed, she was forcing him to eat fruit and granola, something Father Larry would never, ever have chosen on his own.

Alphonso Santos was there, too. He was sitting alone at the small corner table, more private than the others, reading the paper. He looked more relaxed than Nell had seen him for a while. His silk shirt was open at the collar, his slacks casual. Odd, she thought. His sister was in jail. His wife was dead. Was it a time to relax? And then she quickly brushed the thought away. Who was she to dictate how he handled the loss of his wife?

Birdie sat a few tables down on the wraparound deck. Her yarn and nearly finished socks were on the table and a cup of Annabelle's strong coffee sat in front of her. She was knitting without looking at her stitches, her short needles moving beneath her fingers like magic wands, knitting and purling. In front of her on a ring were index cards, helping her know where she was in the lacy knitting. But her attention was clearly focused elsewhere, though Nell couldn't be sure on what. She was looking out over the treetops to the Canary Cove art colony below, or maybe to the blue waters beyond and the parade of boats making their way out to deep water. But what was going on in her head was hidden. Nell thought about Harold and the Lincoln. In his talk with the chief the day before, Ben had learned that he wasn't the only one who thought he saw Harold Sampson at the club that night. The bartender swore he saw him sitting in the dark car, parked beneath a tree. Perhaps that was it.

Dan Brandley sat alone at the next table and Nell stopped and asked if he'd like to join them, rather than eating alone.

"Thanks, but I'm waiting for my folks," Danny said.

"I know they're enjoying having you back," Nell said. "And how are you enjoying being thrown into the thick of Sea Harbor happenings, like neighborhood squabbles?"

Danny laughed. "At the great bulldozing of the concrete posts, I guess you mean."

"Just another summer night in Sea Harbor." Ben laughed.

"When Tommy offered to take me along, I jumped at the chance. You never know what's going to be grist for the writing mill. But who knew I'd end up in the middle of a neighborhood feud? At best, I thought we'd catch some teenagers smuggling beer under the pier."

"People didn't like that pathway being blocked, as Jake clearly demonstrated."

"I'm glad it was settled before the National Guard had to be brought in. Alphonso Santos does things like that, I hear."

"His wife was the one who closed it off."

"So Tommy explained."

"Did you know Sophia Santos? I'm sure you've heard about her murder."

For a minute Danny was quiet. Then he shook his head.

"I think Alphonso did the right thing," Ben said. "It can't worry Sophia now, and it's a good thing for the neighborhood. People used the path for years."

"I suppose that's true," Nell conceded, still bothered by Alphonso's disregard of Sophia's wishes.

At that moment Harriet and Archie walked up to the table, and before his mother could reach out, her thirty-nine-year-old son quickly brushed a wayward strand of hair off his forehead.

The Brandleys greeted Nell and Ben. "Isn't it wonderful to have him back, Nell?" Harriet gushed with great enthusiasm.

Nell smiled. Harriet looked years younger. What amazing effects children can have on their parents. "How long will you be here, Danny?"

"We'll hang on to him as long as we can," Archie answered.

The whole town knew that Archie and Harriet's secret wish was that Dan would someday take over Sea Harbor Bookstore, the store that meant everything in the world to them—second only to their son. Sometimes Nell thought Archie made changes in the store, not just for all the people who loved Sea Harbor Bookstore, but for Danny—so he might come back and fall in love with it the way Archie and Harriet had. In recent years they'd created cozy getaway places in the bookstore, places to curl up and read—or snooze, as some regulars often did. They added outlets for computers and sturdy tables to hold cups and laptops, had the building wired for Wi-Fi. Rather than compete with a friend, Archie bypassed putting in a coffee bar and instead encouraged customers to "get coffee from Coffee's—but drink it here."

"You're here on assignment?" Ben asked.

"One of those drawn-out, investigative series. We have a team working on it, but since Mom and Dad live here—and some of the work involved talking to people up here—they asked me to do it. Saves on per diem expenses."

"How is it coming? Interesting subject?" Ben asked.

Dan shrugged, noncommittal. "I'm actually inching my way out of it to have time for some other writing I want to do—and to spend some time with Mom and Pop. I'd forgotten what a special place this is."

A waitress appeared, carrying a tray filled with platters of eggs and muffins, and began moving things aside to fit them on the table.

With a wave Nell and Ben left the Brandleys and headed to the table where Stella had already poured them mugs of steaming coffee.

Birdie put down her knitting and looked at the enormous watch on her wrist. "I've timed you two. It takes you fifteen full minutes to walk from the restaurant door to the table."

Ben looked at Nell and lifted one brow. *I told you so*, his eyes said.

"Ben Endicott, you talk as much as I do."

Ben held out her chair. "My bride has a hard time admitting when I'm right, Birdie. What do I do about that?"

"You keep it to yourself," Birdie said. She took a drink of her coffee and fingered the silky yarn in her sock absently. "Stella has already decided we're getting the special. It's a lovely chard and wild mushroom something."

Nell handed her menu to Ben and he stacked them, closed, at the end of the table. She slipped on her glasses to look again at Birdie's sock.

"It's a shouting match of fun, that's how I see it," Birdie said of the curving lines and lacy texture. "I've decided to give the finished pair to Ella. She needs someone to pull her out of this terrible state she's in."

Nell laughed. Somehow the lacy socks looked more like Izzy or Liz Palazola or Willow, someone who could carry off a slight edge to their attire. But who knew, maybe sassy socks were just what Ella needed right now.

"She's grieving her friend, I suppose," Ben said, pulling the sections of the *Times* apart. He put the stack on the empty chair and folded the Week in Review in front of him.

"Yes," Birdie said. "And that's certainly understandable. But it's so hard on Harold. He can't imagine her missing anyone when she has him. Especially someone like Sophia Santos, whom he didn't like much. It's very sad."

Ben started to say something about Harold, but stopped when Stella appeared with a basket of warm corn bread, crusty and sweet on top and buttery moist, with a touch of hot pepper inside. She lifted three plates of cheesy chard omelets from her tray and put one down in front of each of them. Annabelle had drizzled a design over the top of each omelet with a mild hot sauce. It curved around the plate like a lazy river. Fresh sprigs of parsley and mint finished off the plate with a brilliant spot of green.

"Beautiful. Your mother is an artist, Stella."

Stella looked at the platters and bit down on her lip as if to hold back a retort but failed in the effort. "Liz did that. She thinks Ma is too plain. I don't think she's plain at all."

"Liz is helping out today?"

"Not helping. No, not much. She just comes in the kitchen and tries to take over sometimes. It's the way she is."

"She handles things at the club fine," Ben said. "But no one can beat Stella when it comes to running Sweet Petunia's."

Stella's smile didn't quite make it to her eyes. Her sister's artistry seemed to have blocked out Ben's nice words.

"Whatever," she murmured and set a small pot of sour cream on the table, then walked off to the kitchen.

"She was happier when we walked in," Nell noted. She took a forkful of omelet and savored the taste of fresh tarragon mixed with chard and eggs.

"Sisterly rivalry, I suppose," Birdie said. "Stella is an absolute dear and can do just about anything she sets her mind to. She's smart as a whip. But following in Liz Palazola's footsteps would be a formidable task for anyone, especially someone as conscious about how she looks as Stella is."

"I think Stella's proud of Liz deep down, but the more she comes into her own, the more she wants that shadow to go away so she can just be herself and not beautiful Liz's little sister."

Birdie agreed, then nodded toward the doorway that led into the restaurant from the deck.

Nell twisted slightly in her chair, turning her head to follow Birdie's look.

Liz Palazola stood just outside the door, talking to Dan Brandley.

She and Dan were probably in school together, Nell guessed, calculating their ages.

Liz was smiling her gracious smile, but she looked pale, Nell thought. She seemed to be trying hard to focus on what Dan was saying.

But the most striking thing about Liz, as was usually the case, was her appearance. Today she wore a canary yellow sundress with a low neckline and an Empire waste. The dress moved softly over full breasts. The color matched her cascade of hair, smooth and shiny and falling over her shoulders like sunshine. The look was that of an impressionist painting—all golden with soft and lovely curves.

"It's canary yellow."

Nell looked up. Stella stood next to the table, clearing their empty plates.

"The dress, you were looking at her dress, right? It's Liz's favorite color. Her couch is that color, too, can you believe that? And she painted her kitchen yellow. Sometimes Liz can be obsessive."

"It's a pretty dress," Nell said, moving beyond the awkward moment.

"I guess," Stella answered, then brushed off the crumbs on the table with a towel. She glanced back at her sister, then refilled their coffee cups and disappeared down the deck.

Nell looked again at Liz, leaning against the door in her bright canary-yellow dress.

"Yes," Birdie said aloud, reading into Nell's thoughts. "The color of Alphonso Santos' brand-new BMW convertible. Liz's favorite color."

It was over an hour later when they finally packed away knitting and newspapers. The deck was nearly empty, although Alphonso Santos still sat quietly at the back table, his head down, his long legs stretched out beneath the table. He held an iPhone in one hand and tapped into it with the other. His food was gone, the table cleared. He looked like he was settled in for the day.

Nell had tried not to be nosy earlier when Liz appeared on the deck—it was certainly none of her business, after all. But when Liz opened the door to go back inside, Nell looked up to see Liz pause for a moment, one hand on the door, looking back to the corner table. Alphonso's answering look was intense. Nell wondered if the diners sitting between Alphonso and Liz had felt anything pass by their way. Sizzling electricity. Electric shock, perhaps.

"How about if we give you and your bike a lift home, Birdie?" Ben asked when they had made their way out to the parking lot. "I haven't had my fill of your company." Before Birdie could answer, he walked off to the metal rack to collect her bike.

"He's a bossy one," Birdie said, looking after Ben. "But don't trade him in."

Nell followed her husband with her eyes, took in his purposeful stride across the gravel lot. His attention to Birdie was unobtrusive—and always caring. The sun had warmed the air considerably while they'd sat on the deck, and the bike ride back to Birdie's home involved several hills. Ben had decided four wheels back was better than two. "Trade him in?" she said to Birdie. "Not likely."

The lot had cleared out considerably, and Alphonso's convertible stood out even more than it had on the darkened road a few nights before. It was parked in the shade of a maple tree on the other side of the lot, its polished surface catching the filtered rays of sunlight.

"Our car is the other way," Nell said. "Near the back door." She pointed to the CRV nearly hidden in the shadows of the shed that held Annabelle's Dumpster and garden supplies.

As they walked toward the car, Nell spotted Liz Palazola standing on the back steps of the restaurant, just beyond the shed. She was nearly hidden by overgrown bushes that shielded Annabelle's back garden from general view. As Nell approached the car, she could see her more clearly. Her head was hung low, and she was gripping the side railing tightly, as if for support.

At first, Nell thought of walking out of the shadows and asking if she needed help, but before she could move, the screen door opened and Stella walked out.

Nell and Birdie turned away, toward the car, where Ben was fastening the bike to the rack.

Stella's voice followed them.

"What are you doing out here?" she asked her sister. Her tone was harsh and unforgiving—a voice neither Nell nor Birdie had heard before.

"Stella, leave me alone," Liz said. "Just go away."

"How can you do this to Ma? What were you thinking? You're supposed to be the perfect one."

"I'm not perfect. I never pretended to be perfect." Liz's voice was soft.

"But this . . . this isn't the way our pa would have wanted it. Not like this."

Birdie slipped into the backseat of the car and Nell circled to the front, anxious to get out of earshot of the private conversation.

But just an instant before Nell pulled the door closed, Stella spoke again. This time the harshness in her voice had all but disappeared, and her words came out in plaintive regret.

"How could you do it? Not this way. A baby, Liz? A baby?"

Chapter 18

Ben sat with his hands on the steering wheel. He looked over at Nell, then turned to Birdie.

"A baby," Birdie murmured as her eyes met Ben's. "This complicates things."

The voices in the distance grew softer, the words muffled. The opening and shutting of a screen door. Then silence.

Ben turned the key in the ignition and brought the engine to life. They drove away in the silence of their thoughts, past the galleries now alive with visitors and along the narrow strip of land near the bridge. The only sound in the car was that of the soft breeze blowing in over the granite outcroppings along the shore.

Liz Palazola was pregnant.

Ben was already slightly late for the regatta by the time they dropped Birdie and headed back to 22 Sandswept Lane. Sam was waiting at the house, and the two left together for the teenage sailing competition at the club.

After two hours of errands, cleaning, and other distracting tasks, Nell retreated to the deck. She poured herself a glass of iced tea and settled her laptop on her knees. It wasn't just the cleaning and laundry that had taken a backseat this week. She'd barely begun to gather her notes for a talk she'd promised the Beverly Women's Group. She could talk about nonprofit organizations effortlessly after years of directing a large Boston foundation. But she liked to customize her talks to the group's interests. Add a touch of new life. The woman who called had asked her to talk about the basics, and Nell would give them exactly that. How to write a grant proposal. Where to find grant money. Who's who in the foundation world.

Very basic indeed. Life should be so basic and simple. But the hows and whys and wheres that were tugging at her thoughts, distracting her from gathering her notes, were not simple at all.

The notes for the talk refused to come together. Each time she looked away from the computer screen, she saw Julianne Santos . . . in jail. Or Liz Palazola . . . her face pale and her fingers white as she gripped the rail to fight off morning sickness. Or a relaxed Alphonso . . . driving a canary-yellow convertible, while the tangled metal remains of a red Ferrari in a warehouse somewhere bore testimony to the tragic loss of his wife.

Nell looked over the tops of the trees that marked the back edges of the Endicott property. Beyond it, as the tree branches waved and bent in the late-afternoon breeze, she glimpsed the sea. Gulls swooped and dove in aerobatic perfection. Nell breathed in the tangy air and closed her eyes for a minute, soaking it in.

Comforting. Familiar.

She loved it all dearly. The changing colors of the sky, the sound of the sea, the smell of the salt, and the feel of the sand—the immense beauty that enhanced and informed the life they lived in this small seaside village.

Maybe it was that startling contrast that made murder in this town so difficult to grasp—so wretchedly awful.

Or maybe murder was simply innately awful, all by itself.

Nell slipped a sweater over her shoulders. Whether from the disturbing thoughts or the chilly air, she couldn't be sure, but the sweater was oddly comforting.

"Nell, where are you?" Flip-flops slapped across the family room floor. Izzy and Cass appeared at the doorway to the deck.

"The front door was open," Cass said, then popped the last bit of an ice-cream cone into her mouth.

"And a closed door would have stopped you, Cass?" Nell lifted her eyebrows in a tease and pushed her glasses up into her hair.

"You're happy to see me. You know it. We brought you a cup of double-chocolate fudge. It's in your freezer."

"Did you know it takes exactly one triple-scoop ice cream cone to walk from Scoopers to your front door?" Izzy sat down opposite Nell and curled her bare legs up beneath her. Her white shirt was decorated with a dribble of strawberry ice cream and Izzy dabbed at it, frowning.

"All right, you two. What's on your minds? You didn't walk up here to decide how big your ice cream cones had to be."

"We came for several reasons. One is that we just left Gracie and she's a mess."

"Left her where?"

"At the Artist's Palate," Cass said. "Joey was meeting her there. But here's what happened—the three of us were going to meet for a drink—"

"Because someone told Cass that Danny Brandley loved the Palate's deck and often went there to write," Izzy interrupted.

"Oh?" Nell said.

Cass threw Izzy a look. "No 'ohs' necessary. Danny was there. He bought us a beer. And then I lost out to a shiny aluminum Mac-Book Pro."

Nell laughed.

Cass continued, hiding the faint blush behind a voice that was slightly too loud. "Gracie was late and she'd been crying, I think, something Gracie doesn't do lightly. Her mom had asked her to visit."

"Julianne was acting strange," Izzy said.

"Strange, how? It would certainly be understandable if she was depressed."

"No, that's the strange part. It's just the opposite, Gracie said. She was calm, coherent, and a totally different person than most of us know. She seemed resigned to the fact that people in the town are happy to have her be the murderer."

"But that's not true," Nell began.

"In a way, it is," Izzy said. "She's been around Sea Harbor so infrequently that I think people view her as an outsider. They don't know her. And it's much easier to think of an outsider murdering Sophia."

Nell closed her computer and set it aside. "You may be right." Harry Garozzo had voiced the same opinion. "Did Gracie say if Alphonso's been to visit her?"

"He's been too busy," Cass said. "Or so he told Gracie."

"I see," Nell said. Too busy, though he'd just spent a morning relaxing on the deck of the Sweet Petunia restaurant. Again, Nell held herself in check. Who knows what he was doing with his phone? Texting Julianne's lawyer, maybe. Building a team to protect his baby sister. Preparing for a future without his wife.

"Why did she want to see Gracie?"

"That's what bothered Gracie the most, I think. Julianne told her that she was at peace and that Gracie should be, too. Although she didn't kill Sophia, she deserved to be punished. That's what she wanted Gracie to know."

"That doesn't make sense. You don't take a murderer's punishment because you've made bad decisions in your life."

Cass nodded. "Exactly. Gracie argued with her, told her that was ridiculous, but Julianne told her—very calmly, Gracie said—that this was as it should be. She'd done many terrible things in her life, and the worst of them all—worse than murder, she said—was that she'd never been a mother to her only child. And there was no punishment great enough for that crime."

Nell looked away for a moment, swept away by the emotion that must have filled Gracie to the brim. "How terribly sad," she murmured.

"Gracie thinks Julianne might even confess to the crime to speed things up."

"And the worst part is, no one seems too interested in who else might have done it," Izzy said. "It's awful that the real killer could be walking the streets. And awful that an innocent person might be punished for it."

"It ups the ante," Cass said. "If Julianne didn't do it, who did? That's the only thing that will resolve this."

Nell was silent for a long moment. Her thoughts went back to Liz Palazola. The overheard conversation had been a quiet one, but maybe important, in the light of things.

"Aunt Nell," Izzy said, leaning forward and touching Nell's arm. "You have something on your mind, and I think I know what it is. Did you talk to any of the Palazolas today when you and Ben went for breakfast?"

Her eyes met Nell's.

"Yes, you did." Izzy answered her own question. "You're wonderful at keeping confidences, even when you're not asked to, but it's not a secret about Liz. Laura Danvers came in the shop today. She's pregnant again—number three. Can you believe it? She saw Liz in the doctor's office."

"That doesn't mean . . ." Nell began.

Izzy shook her head and a tangle of waves fell across her cheek. She forked her fingers through her hair, pushing it back. "No, normally it wouldn't. Except Liz got sick in the waiting room, and Laura took her to the restroom. She told Laura that she was almost three months pregnant."

Nell settled back in the chair. She repeated the conversation they'd heard at Annabelle's. "It was disturbing," she said. "An affair is one thing, but a baby takes it to a new level. They'd have known about the baby for a while."

"Long enough to ask Sophia for a divorce."

"Which she might not consent to."

No marriage, Sophia had whispered in Harry's deli. *No marriage . . . for Alphonso and Liz?*

"Having a baby should be such a happy time for her," Nell said out loud.

They fell silent then, the thought of an innocent baby somehow caught up in the tragic drama unfolding around them.

"My tap dancing class went well." The non sequitur was from Birdie, standing in the open doorway. "I'm knitting each of the ten ladies in my class a pair of fake fishnet stockings. And then we will have a performance, and you will all be invited."

Birdie walked over to an empty chair and sat down. "In the meantime, fill me in." She looked at Nell. "I heard from one of the ladies at the retirement home that it's almost a closed case. Julianne has all but confessed. And I don't believe one single word of that."

Nell got Birdie a glass of iced tea while Izzy and Cass filled her in on Gracie's visit to her mom and confirmation of Liz's pregnancy.

Birdie looked over at Nell. "Stella ran some errands for me today, and she needed little encouragement to talk about it. It seems that she and Liz saw us and suspected we overheard their conversation."

"Did Stella confirm the father?"

"No. Liz refused to talk to her about it."

"I suppose she told Annabelle about the baby," Nell said.

"Yes, who was loving and understanding—but angry, too, according to Stella. For her most responsible daughter to get herself in such a fix was hard for her to stomach. At least that was Stella's take on it."

Birdie paused, then pulled another sock out of her backpack and checked it against a copy of the pattern. She looked up as if to speak, then thought better of it and concentrated again on the sock pattern.

Nell saw worry play across her friend's face and recognized

the attempt to brush it away with knitting. A ploy that nearly always worked. But today the worry stayed. "Birdie, what are you not saying?" Nell handed Birdie the glass of iced tea.

"Nothing, probably. But this murder has touched everyone. And until there's real resolution, people are going to be angry and afraid and accusing each other of things—"

"Are you talking about Harold and Ella?" Nell asked.

"In part. Ella is almost like a crusader these days. I see her walking along that path between our house and the Santoses', coming and going. I don't know what she does when she gets over there. She probably just sits and hopes that it's all a grievous mistake and Sophia will walk out of the house and ask her to go for a walk. My sweet, lovely Ella has become militant. This has all taken such a toll on her. She's determined that Sophia's murderer be brought to justice."

"She doesn't think it's Julianne?"

"No. She's sure it's not."

"Why?"

"Because she has it in her head that Alphonso wanted to end his marriage and finally figured out a way to do it. And she thinks he's getting away with murder."

$\mathcal{B}$irdie quickly went on and explained that even though Ella believed it on one level, she had no proof. It was pure emotion on her housekeeper's part. And frankly, Birdie was upset about the whole thing. Ella was coming close to harassing Alphonso on his own property and she wouldn't blame him for having her arrested for trespassing.

But on another level, Birdie said, she thought accusing Alphonso came from Ella's intuition, knowing that he hurt her friend.

Either way, it was unnerving.

Cass and Izzy left shortly after, and Nell suggested she and Birdie grab a bite to eat at the Ocean's Edge.

The regatta coaches and team would be eating at the club, Ben said when he called. Their team had been victorious, and that called for a celebration. Nell could hear the pleasure and pride in his voice. The rough-edged gangly boys that he and Sam had rounded up from the Boys' Club last summer didn't know a jib from a daggerboard back then. And here they were, winning their first race of the summer.

"You'd have thought they'd just won the America's Cup," Ben had said like a proud father.

Nell climbed into the passenger side of Birdie's Town Car thinking, as she sometimes did, of what a great father Ben would have made. But when that didn't work for them, life moved in and filled that space in mysterious and sometimes surprising ways. Izzy, for starters, as close to them as any daughter could be. And his work with the Boys' Club program, filled with kids without dads. Even Sam—who'd never known his own father—had formed a close bond with Ben that satisfied something important in him. And Ben's sailing team could now be added to that list.

"I wouldn't ever admit this to Ben," Birdie said, "but I miss having Harold drive me around. I don't enjoy driving this car anymore."

"I imagine Harold misses driving it, too."

"In the worst way. And he'd probably be fine driving, but it seems safer to wait until the brace is off. And by the way—he didn't drive to the club that Friday night."

Nell looked at Birdie in surprise. "Oh."

"I asked him. He said if he was going to sneak the car out, he sure wouldn't go to the yacht club."

Nell wondered whether to say anything more, to mention that others had seen Birdie's Lincoln there, too. Not just Ben. She finally decided it could wait. "Well, no matter who's driving this car, Sonny would be pleased at the way you care for it."

"Some traditions are hard to let go of, even if they are silly in this day and age. Sonny had his car polished, detailed, and the carpets shampooed the first Friday of every month, whether it needed it or not. Have you ever heard of such a thing?"

"And you do the same," Nell said, knowing that even though Birdie had outlived three husbands after Sonny—and loved each of them sincerely—Sonny Favazza lived on in her life in a very special way. And so, it seemed, did his car.

They drove north on Harbor Road, passing by the shops and restaurants and Pelican Pier. Birdie had had a new brass sign posted in the green area near the pier that boasted the name in tall golden letters.

Sonny Favazza had named the pier himself after he'd spotted a lone brown pelican in the cove behind his house. Brilliant, he had said to Birdie, his eyes twinkling. For decades people will wonder why a pier in Massachusetts bears the name of a southern bird. *His* bird. And he'd gathered Birdie in his arms and sang to her of a pelican in Massachusetts, as they danced around the widow's walk.

Birdie passed the Ocean's Edge, a large clapboard restaurant with a wraparound deck, and saw at a glance it was packed. Sounds of laughing and conversation poured from the porch and open-air bar in the back.

"I have a better idea. Ella has been taking some of her anger and sadness out by cooking," she said, passing the restaurant by and heading straight on Harbor Road toward the Ravenswood neighborhood. "We can make some chicken sandwiches. I swear she roasted ten chickens this week."

"Better chickens than Harold."

Birdie laughed. "Those two are like wet hens these days. Some days I think I should put them in time-out."

Birdie pulled into her driveway and drove the car into the garage. When she pulled the keys out of the ignition, they slipped from her fingers and fell to the floor.

"Butterfingers," she muttered to herself, running her fingers around the dark floor beneath the driver's seat.

Nell pulled out her cell phone and made a quick call to Ben to pick her up at Birdie's on his way home from the club. She walked around the car. "Find them?"

"Yes, and also this." She pulled a rugged twill cap from beneath the seat. "It's Harold's."

Nell recognized the cap. Ella had given the chauffeur's cap to Harold as a joke when he started driving Birdie's Town Car around town—and Harold had loved it, insisting that he wear it whenever driving the car. He'd had it for years, and treated it with great care.

"I wonder why it's here," Birdie said.

"He probably dropped it after driving somewhere."

"No. Not unless he's been driving in the past week. The car

was detailed the day of the yacht club party. The first Friday in June."

Birdie stood still, fingering the visor on the cap, thinking.

Nell looked up toward the house. She saw a light go on in the kitchen. Ella, expecting Birdie back, probably, and fixing dinner.

Birdie started walking toward the house and Nell followed. She could read her friend's thoughts as clearly as if she'd spoken them aloud. Ben swore he had seen Harold driving the Lincoln the night of the party, but Birdie had been resolute that he was at home. Especially after Harold said he hadn't been driving the Lincoln.

The cap suggested a different story.

Harold had been driving that day.

"It had to be that day," Birdie said aloud. "Stella mentioned the keys being gone, so I looked for them the next day. I found them on the hook beside the door in the kitchen, right where they always were. I assumed Stella had overlooked them."

They walked through the back door to the kitchen.

"I'm home," Birdie called out to Ella as they walked through the back hall and into the kitchen.

Birdie's kitchen was large and airy, a renovated space that held a commercial-sized gas stove and plenty of windows that looked out onto gardens and the ocean. A round table sat in front of the windows. Sitting at it, his long fingers wrapped around a glass of water, was Harold Sampson. Ella was nowhere in sight.

"Harold! You surprised me," Birdie said. "I thought Ella was in here."

Everything about Harold was long—his face, his chin, his arms and legs. When he lifted his head, looking at Birdie, even his attempt at a smile looked long. "Ella's gone again. I thought it would stop. But she's out, walking somewhere."

When he saw the cap in Birdie's hands, he frowned. "That's my cap. Thanks, Miss Birdie. Where was it?"

Birdie set it on the table in front of him and opened the refrigerator door, moving around an assortment of plastic-wrapped bowls. "It was in the car," she said, taking out a platter of sliced chicken and setting it on the long island. "You must have dropped it there last Friday."

Nell stood near the counter, almost feeling sorry for Harold. He was clearly distressed.

"Were you driving on Friday, Harold?"

Harold focused on the hat, his brows pulled together in deep concentration, as if sorting through possible answers and wondering which ones would get by Birdie.

"It's all right, Harold," Birdie said. Her voice was firm but kind. "I just want to be sure your ankle heals. Where did you go?"

Harold looked at Birdie and took a deep breath. His chest rose and fell. "It was Ella," he said. "She's my life, you know. But she was moving away from me so quickly. Not around when I needed her. It had always been Ella and me. And then Sophia came and took her away from me. I had to do something."

"They were friends, Harold," Nell said gently. "That's all."

Harold shook his head in disagreement. "Ella changed when that woman came into her life. That Friday night I couldn't find Ella anywhere. You were gone, Miss Birdie, and Stella was gone, too. I thought maybe Ella had gone to the yacht club with Sophia Santos. And I couldn't take it anymore. I snapped. I wanted my Ella back."

Birdie and Nell looked at each other, not wanting Harold to go on. Not wanting to hear what he was about to say to them.

But Harold went on.

"So I drove over there to bring her home. That's where I went and that's why. But she wasn't there. I parked there for a while, not sure what to do, just watching people come in and out. Mr. Santos came out once—for a cigar I think. He saw me sitting in the car, so I asked him to go get my Ella for me, that she was with his wife. He told me she wasn't there, that his wife had driven over alone. So I turned around and I came back home."

"When was that?"

"Early. It was still light. Maybe eight o'clock or so?"

"And Ella?" Birdie asked.

"She was home, mad as a hatter that I'd gone out in the car when you told me not to. I made her promise not to tell you."

His eyes settled on a point beyond Nell and Birdie, near the kitchen door.

Nell and Birdie turned.

Ella stood in the doorway. "Are you all right, Harold?" Her eyes took in the platter of chicken on the island, then traveled back to her husband. She looked back at Birdie. "What's going on?"

"We wondered where you were, Ella," Harold said. "I never know these days. You're here and then you're gone."

"I was walking in the woods, Harold. I came back, just as I said I would."

Harold set his jaw. He looked frustrated and sad, Nell thought, unusual emotions for the even-keeled man.

"You won't find her in the woods, Ella," he said. "She isn't anywhere. She's gone, and she's not coming back."

For a moment, Nell wasn't sure what Harold was talking about. But when she looked into his eyes, they were clear and focused, and she realized who "she" was. And that she was, indeed, not coming back.

Ella's head jerked around and she glared at Harold as if he had let loose with a string of profanity. When she looked back at Birdie, an enormous sadness seemed to be pressing down on her narrow shoulders. "I will fix you some sandwiches," she said.

"No, Ella. It's fine. Nell and I will take care of ourselves. You and Harold can go back to the carriage house and relax."

Harold stood up and walked across the kitchen, limping. His eyes were steady and focused on his wife, and he spoke softly, as if they were the only two in the room.

"She's not coming back, Ella. Not ever. This was supposed to end it all, to give us our life back. We are finally rid of her." He touched Ella on her arm as he walked past her, an oddly loving touch.

Ella stepped away.

Then Harold walked through the door and out into the night alone, his shoulders weighted with loneliness.

Chapter 20

*W*hen Ben picked Nell up a short time later, he was sunburned, tired, and not readily given to conversation. "I'm spent," he said, leaning over and opening the passenger door. He kissed her on the lips.

"Teenage boys will do that to you," she said. "And you loved every minute of it. And I, too, am spent, though from boys a whole lot older than the regatta team."

Ben didn't press for details, and they said little on the trip home, each sinking into the privacy of their own thoughts. Decompression time, Ben called it. But whatever it was, it was one of those silent understandings between soul mates that never failed to fill Nell with gratitude.

The exchange with Harold stayed there, playing at the edges of her thoughts. Troubling.

He was tired, Birdie had said, and not talking sensibly.

Or maybe they—Birdie and Nell—were tired, reading unintended things into the words of a man who clearly loved his wife—and thought he was losing her.

Or maybe he meant exactly what he said.

And maybe Harold Sampson was lying.

An hour later, showered and comfortable in soft sweats, Nell and Ben lit some candles, slipped a Dave Matthews CD into the player, and wandered out to the deck. It was a ritual they held sacred when schedules and weather allowed, and on this cool Sunday evening, Nell knew the night would be kinder to her and sleep would come more readily, if deck time with Ben came first.

She handed Ben a glass of Scotch, then sat down on the padded chaise next to him. They stretched out, side by side, looking up at the wide sweep of stars overhead. Some nights they sat in silence, content with the closeness of each other's body and the constellations in the sky. Other times they rehashed the day and put worry or concerns to rest before they went inside to watch the news or head upstairs to bed. Tonight was for collecting thoughts. Putting things in order.

The air was still, a change from the pleasant gusts that had propelled Ben and Sam's team to victory. But chilly, the way June nights in Sea Harbor often were.

"Was Liz at the club tonight?" Nell asked. Her mind had wandered over a long string of happenings and people vying for attention. The most disturbing, Harold's outburst just hours earlier, was still so foggy in Nell's mind that she decided to tuck it away. Maybe, as she and Birdie had both halfheartedly agreed, it would make more sense in the morning.

"No. Liz wasn't feeling terrific, the bartender said."

"Her pregnancy isn't a secret anymore. It was mentioned at Izzy's shop today, though she thinks people don't know who the father is."

"No, probably not. I would certainly never have paired Alphonso and Liz up together. I imagine that will be a surprise."

"I was thinking about Alphonso giving Sophia the Ferrari. A gift of something he truly loved. I wonder what happened that night that made him do it. I wonder if Sophia had found out about their affair."

"Or the baby."

"It would have been a terrible shock to her."

"That's what we would think, isn't it? But the Sophia Santos I know from cocktail parties might not be who Sophia is—or was—

at all. Maybe it wasn't a terrible shock. We didn't really know her, did we?"

"What do you mean?"

Ben thought for a moment before answering. "Didn't you tell me Izzy said we'd be peeling off layers of Sophia, like an onion? I think maybe that's right. The woman I knew was beautiful, gracious, and polite. The perfect hostess and a perfect mate for one of the most successful businessmen in town. But in just these few days, there's another picture emerging, one of a woman who may have been all of those great things, but who was also strong-willed, rigid, forceful. And maybe things we are yet to know. Beatrice Scaglia was at the club today and had some strong words to say about Sophia. The mayor agreed that she was unbending. Always gracious, he said, but tough as nails. It was difficult for her to listen to others' opinions. He considered Alphonso much easier to work with than Sophia."

"It's uncomfortable to speak this way of someone who just died," Nell said.

"It is. But when someone's been murdered, it's probably not helpful to elevate him or her too quickly to sainthood. It can get in the way of the truth."

"Not that anyone is actually trying to find the truth." Nell told Ben about Gracie's visit to the jail. "Even Julianne is willing to go along with the police's story of how this all played out. Why would anyone look further?"

"There's truth to that. You're right. But Julianne may be telling her daughter she is innocent as one last attempt to look good in her eyes. How do we know for sure she didn't kill Sophia? She'd been drinking that night. She hated her brother's wife. I think we need more than instinct and Julianne's word to write her off completely."

"Maybe," Nell said, her voice lacking conviction. "But we also need to look into all the others who could have done it. I think if we look into everyone who was at the club that night, who would have had a chance to tinker with Sophia's car, who had a motive for killing her, we might be able to shed some light on it."

"You don't think that's someone else's job?"

"Whose, Ben?" Nell rolled her head on the chaise pillow and looked at her husband's profile. "Who would do it? Not the police. Not now that Julianne is practically confessing."

Ben was silent. He drank his Scotch slowly, ice cubes clinking against the side of the glass. He pulled his brows together in thought.

"I know what you're thinking, Ben. It could be dangerous to nose about in this messy business. It was a murder, after all, not a traffic violation."

"That's my worry, Nelly. Absolutely. Jerry Thompson helped us today with the regatta. He said the evidence right now is circumstantial, but there's probably enough of it to convince a jury— witnesses who saw Julianne head off to where the car was parked, her tirade at the funeral. The things they found in her trunk. And simply the facts—that Sophia stopped the ready flow of Santos money into Julianne's pocket, and she hated her for it."

"Gracie says she is all but accepting the guilt as if it's her due, as if it's God's way of punishing her for being a bad mother. That's wrong, Ben."

Ben agreed. "The chief says Julianne is not the beautiful, erratic, slightly crazy damsel we've seen the past days. Years, for that matter. She's being pleasant, cooperative. Even sweet, Jerry said, which isn't a word people have used much to describe Julianne Santos. She blames no one for anything, except herself. It's making the force nervous. They don't know how to treat her. They have to remind themselves that she's an accused murderer, not a beautiful woman they're bringing dinner to and being courteously thanked for doing so."

"Has Alphonso been very visible in all this?"

"He's paying for her attorney. It's probably complicated."

Nell supposed it was. The family relationships involved were fodder for a Shakespearean play. "Margaret Garozzo heard Sophia say that only over her dead body would there be a marriage. Or something like that. Sometimes her words are a little difficult to understand. A divorce would have been hard for her."

"How do you know that?" Ben's smile was one of bemusement.

Nell felt the smile in the darkness. "Women just know these things, Ben Endicott. Just like I know you are about to fall asleep on me if we don't move that big lug of a beautiful body upstairs." Nell slipped off the chaise and picked up their glasses.

"Hmm. Beautiful body?" Ben swung his legs to the side and looked up at Nell. "You like this body?"

Nell glanced at him briefly in the light of the waning moon, a suggestive look lifting the corners of her mouth. Then she blew out the candle and walked slowly into the house.

It was a while later that Nell finally slipped into a lovely sleep, wrapped with Ben in a tangle of sheets. And when sirens punctuated her dreams hours later, Nell pushed them into the deep recesses of her subconscious.

These couldn't be the sirens that spoke of danger. Not the sirens that changed lives.

Nell slept.

Chapter 21

"Aunt Nell, it's Izzy."

Nell carried her coffee over to the kitchen table, the phone cupped between her shoulder and ear. "Yes, sweetie?"

"It's about the restaurant," Izzy began.

Nell glanced at the clock. Eight a.m. What restaurant was Izzy talking about at this hour? She was usually in the shop by eight on Mondays. "Izzy, were we supposed to meet somewhere? I must have forgotten."

"No, it's the Lazy Lobster. There was a fire last night . . ."

There was a crowd hovering around the restaurant when Nell arrived at the pier. A policeman stood on one side of Gracie. Joey Delaney was on the other. Gracie wore a pair of old jeans and a sweatshirt. Her blond hair waved carelessly around her flushed cheeks, and from all appearances, it had been a while since she'd slept.

Nell spotted Pete, Willow, and Cass a short distance away talking to a fireman. She hurried over.

"What happened? Is everyone all right?"

"Everyone's fine," Alex Arcado, a tall ruddy-faced fireman, answered. "Seems someone saw a good place to sleep last night. Only problem was, he tried to build a fire."

"It must have been someone sleeping along the beach. They

walked out here and saw an easy way to enter." Pete pointed to a window hoisted up and then left open.

"Built a fire?" Nell looked skeptical.

"It got a little chilly in the middle of the night," Alex said. "Especially when the wind picked up again. I suppose he saw the fireplace. Might as well light one. We found traces of a pizza box and some old newspapers."

"He?"

"It's usually guys who bum around the beach in the summer. Safe as Sea Harbor is, I wouldn't want my daughter out there," Alex said. "But I don't think the police know who did it. It's probably not a high priority. Not too much damage done, and the fire was most likely an accident."

"It was primarily smoke damage," Pete said. "The fireplace is a mess. The guy wasn't too bright. He didn't know enough to open the flue."

"Someone spotted the smoke and called us quick," Alex said. "That's what saved the place."

"That would be me," Birdie said, walking up beside Nell. "I couldn't sleep last night—I had too many things on my mind—so I went into Sonny's den to relax and look out over the water."

Nell imagined the scenario. What relaxed Birdie more than anything was gazing through Sonny's telescope—sometimes at the sky or out to sea, but most often swiveling the brass neck over toward Canary Cove, and without much effort, Birdie could check on teenage parties at Anja Angelina Park, not to mention interesting late-night activity around the harbor.

"I'm sorry for your loss of sleep, Miss Favazza," Alex said, "but it was a mighty good thing for all of us that you were awake. Not too many people are up at three a.m."

"You're a fine bunch of men. You do a good job, and we're exceedingly proud of you." Birdie patted the sleeve of his yellow jacket. "Now you're the one who needs some sleep."

Alex tipped his helmet toward Birdie, a slight blush adding to his perspiring forehead and cheeks. "I expect I will do just that. The place is safe now. Just needs a little cleaning up and that fireplace'll need some work. This is the second small fire this June."

"Another restaurant fire?" Nell asked.

"Yeah. A stove over at Jake Risso's Gull. Poor Jake burned some of his hair trying to put it out. Not that he has any to spare." The fireman touched his helmet again and was off down the pier, dragging an ax and a fire extinguisher with him.

Nell followed the others into the restaurant to assess the damage. The firemen had opened all the windows and the wide doors at the back to help release the fumes. "The smoke smell is still strong," Willow said. "But we can get a professional fire-cleaning service in here to take care of that. Maybe some fans would help. I have some in my studio I'll bring over. Come on, Pete, let's check the deck." She walked away, small as an elf, her short self-cut mass of thick dark waves bouncing about her head. Next to her, Pete Halloran looked oversized, a tall, gangly man. But watching them standing out on the deck, Nell suspected that the difference in their height was the furthest thing from their minds.

Nell walked over to the fireplace for a closer look. The fireman was right—it had seen better days but could be repaired. The smoke and flames had curled over and up the granite wall, scorching it. In places, the grouting was loose and chunks fell out onto the hardwood floor. Gracie had been so proud of it. She looked at the debris still in the fireplace and could see the edge of the pizza carton sticking out. The trespasser must have eaten, drunk a few beers, then settled down in front of the fireplace to sleep. When the night grew cold, it just made sense to light a fire and warm himself up, she supposed.

Cass walked over and picked up a broom. "Izzy had to go back to open the yarn studio but said you should check in with her later—and not to forget about the socks class today."

Nell nodded and rubbed her finger across a thick swatch of soot coating the granite fireplace.

"Imagine the guy's surprise when the room filled with smoke. It must have scared him half to death." Cass began to sweep the fireplace debris into a pile.

Nell nodded. "He probably got out in a hurry. It's too bad Birdie didn't catch his escape." She found a trash bag and dustpan nearby and crouched down beside Cass. "Has Joey seen the damage?"

"Gracie called him as soon as she got the call from Esther Gibson."

"He's been a good person to lean on."

Cass shrugged. "Gracie doesn't talk about it much, but he's certainly been around when she's needed him."

"Do you know why they separated?"

Cass stopped sweeping for a minute and leaned on the broom, thinking about Nell's question. "I wasn't in touch with Gracie much when they lived in Gloucester. I'd see her once in a while, but she was always alone. Joey was doing sales for Delaney & Sons then and was gone all the time. Gracie wanted babies, and Joey wasn't interested. I think they argued a lot. But some of their problems had to be family-related. She didn't just marry Joey. She married the whole clan."

"That included Davey, I suppose," Nell said.

Cass nodded. "Hotheaded Davey. He's overprotective of his dad, as if D.J. needs protection—the man can be a bulldog if it means getting what he wants. Davey's also a little bit paranoid. He's always on the watch for someone trying to harm the company."

Nell remembered Ben's comment about Davey taking over someday. It made sense that he cared about the company he hoped to run.

Cass went on. "Davey acted weird when Joey and Gracie got married. He tried to blame it on the Delaney–Santos competition, that it couldn't be good for the family. What if Gracie were a spy?"

The thought of Gracie as a spy made Nell laugh. "Where was all that coming from?"

"I think it was all cover-up. I think Davey wished Gracie had married him. In fact, I think he still feels that way."

"I wondered about that myself."

"Joey is the smart one in the family and that probably bothers Davey, too. I think he works extra hard so his dad will notice him. That's probably why he comes out fighting when the company's reputation is at stake. Pete said he was in the Gull a couple weeks ago ranting and raving and knocking over beer bottles. Jake finally made him leave."

"What was the problem?"

"I only know bits and pieces, but there was a rumor that Delaney & Sons might be violating codes or something. Or maybe it was manipulating numbers, I don't know. A reporter followed up on it and actually went to the plant, asking questions. Davey Delaney was furious about it. Uncontrollable, Pete said."

"Who would have made such a claim?"

Cass began sweeping again, pulling ashes out from the corners of the fireplace. "I'm not sure. But he was throwing Sophia Santos' name around, right along with the beer bottles."

Nell took a deep breath. So many rumors. She looked through the window at the two figures standing just outside. The policeman was still talking to Gracie, and Joey was standing a few steps behind her. He looked angry, too, but not the kind that she imagined caused thrown beer bottles. He looked angry and protective at once.

On the floor, Cass had gone back to her sweeping. She reached one hand up to Nell. "Would you hang on to these? Might be something Gracie needs." She dropped a key ring into Nell's hand and sat back on her legs. "It looks like whoever did this ate all the pizza. Only charred remains."

Nell took the items and shoved them into her pants pocket, then leaned over to hold the dustpan for Cass.

Cass swept up the last of the ashes. "There, finished."

"We're just in time, then," said Gracie, walking through the door. She and Joey looked at the fireplace. "Thanks. The police and firemen say we're lucky. The damage is light, thanks to Birdie. I hope she starts sleeping during the day and continues to watch over us at night."

Birdie came in from the deck and caught the end of Gracie's sentence. "Do they know who started the fire?"

"They think it's a guy who comes through here every summer, poor fellow. No money, sleeps on the beach. He's harmless."

"Well, this wasn't harmless," Joey said. He crouched down and peered into the fireplace pit. "Was there anything left in here?"

"Part of a pizza box. We swept it all out," Cass said.

"This could have been bad, Gracie." His brows pulled together, and when he straightened up, Nell saw the worry in his eyes.

"Joey, do you think something else happened here?" she asked.

Joey waited a few seconds before he spoke, but his answer was even and thoughtful. "No, I guess not, Nell. It's probably what the police say it was. And the fireplace isn't a problem. I can fix it. It's just that this could have been a lot worse." He looked over at Gracie. "It could have been more than a building that was damaged, Gracie. It could have been you. And I don't know what I can do about it."

The end of his sentence was barely audible and Gracie looked away, out the window, then back to Joey.

"Well, maybe you can stick around a little bit more. Fix the fireplace." She lifted both shoulders, then lifted her hands in the air. "I give up, Joey. Maybe I'll even let you paint a wall or two."

Chapter 22

"Jillian and Rose have been amazing this summer," Izzy told Nell. "They are wanting as many hours as I can give them. It makes my life so nice. Sam and I actually had a long lunch date today."

"Where did you go?" Nell began stapling the pattern copies together for Izzy's sock class.

"His place. We went for a walk along the beach, took some pictures of dogs chasing Frisbees, and then sat on his deck and ate Sam's gourmet sandwiches. That means he piled everything in his refrigerator on some of Harry's great nutty bread and slathered it with a spicy cucumber-yogurt sauce you gave him. Then he put it on a plate with a fancy toothpick holding it together. It was delicious, and probably half of it started life in your kitchen."

"A good break in your day."

"Sam is a good break almost anytime. He's a very special guy—I think I'm beginning to like him."

Nell was noncommittal, calm, knowing that Izzy was cautious when talking about her feelings. She reached for Izzy's box of supplies and began filling small baskets with scissors, needle gauges, measuring tape. Low-key or not, she almost felt guilty for the pleasure that washed through her in nice gentle waves when Izzy talked this way about Sam. It wasn't her business, she told herself often. But she thought the world of Sam Perry. And Izzy was the daughter she never had. She and Ben had seen Izzy through low points of her thirty-three years. Witnessing the high points was pure pleasure.

"Izzy, you've liked Sam for some time."

"Of course. Even when I didn't like him, I suppose I liked him. At least a little. But when you're thirteen, you don't like your brother's geeky friends. It's not cool."

"I can't imagine Sam geeky."

"Geeky in a good way." Izzy got up, found her iPod on the shelf, and plugged it into the dock. Strains of the "Four Seasons" filled the yarn shop's back room.

Nell lifted her head. "Vivaldi?"

"One of the men who's coming today plays violin over in Rockport—Sam and I met him one night at a concert. He wants to learn how to knit."

"So you think the music will impress him?"

"No, but if he's comfortable, he may catch on to purling a little faster." Izzy grinned. "It's all about comfort, I say. You do what it takes." She sat down at the table and touched a ball of pale green fingering yarn in the basket.

Nell could almost see the image of a tiny green sweater, made up in organic cotton with a sweet floppy hat to match, pass in front of Izzy's eyes. There was a shift occurring inside her niece, and it would be nice to see where it led.

"As often as I see Sam, I want to see him more," Izzy said. "I like that we can sit in the same room reading and not talk for an hour, but it's a million times better than sitting in that same room alone—the air feels different and the funny sound he makes when he clears his throat is comforting. And then when we do talk, sometimes we say the same thing. I like it that some nights we can sit out on his deck and talk until the sun rises right up out of the ocean. I like it that he teaches those goofy kids how to sail and you'd think when he comes home that they were the ones teaching him."

"I like Sam, too."

Izzy laughed, a full deep laugh that often caused her customers to smile for no reason. "You're so coy, Aunt Nell."

Mae stuck her head in the door. "I'm leaving, Izzy. Jillian and Rose will handle everything—don't worry for a minute. We've had a couple more sign-ups for the class, so turn a fan on. Some of these youngsters could use a little lesson in body hygiene. Sweaty, if you know what I mean."

"Thanks, Mae. We'll be fine."

Cass and Birdie hurried in a few minutes later. "What can we do?"

"Lemonade. Ice. And a fan, I guess." Izzy pulled open a drawer beneath the wall of bookcases and took out a collection of sock samples that she lined up on the table. They ranged from baby socks to anklets to heavy wool hiking socks.

"Izzy!" Jillian Anderson stood triumphantly in the doorway. "Guess who's here?" Jillian's long hair flew in all directions as she tossed her head, and she pushed it back happily with her hand. "Ta-da," she said, stepping aside and holding out her arms as if announcing a star onstage.

A tall, very handsome man appeared in the doorframe, frowning at Jillian. "Cool it, Miss Anderson," he said. Then softened it with a grin that showed a perfect set of white teeth.

"Jimmy Rodriguez," Cass said, dropping her bag on the table and walking toward him.

The young man reached out his arms and gave Cass a hug, then released her. "This can't be that old cranky babysitter who made me eat canned beans."

"I didn't know how to make anything else, Jimmy."

He leaned down and whispered loudly in her ear, "Just between you and me, Cass, no one has called me Jimmy since seventh grade."

"Whatever," Cass said, brushing off his words. "Izzy says you're spending your whole salary on yarn."

"Seems like it sometimes. I'm ready for winter—two cable

sweaters already finished. But damn if these socks don't scare me. Izzy claims I can master it. We'll see."

"You will, you will," Izzy called across the table. "What you already do is much harder than socks."

"I hear you're teaching Spanish, Jimmy—Jim," Birdie said. "That's just wonderful—though we miss our favorite Sunday waiter at the Ocean's Edge. I would guess you are a wonderful teacher."

"He's the best," Jillian said, still standing in the archway.

"She's trying to get points." Jim inclined his head toward Jillian.

"I need them now that Mrs. Santos won't be there to help." A jingling of the bell and her sister shouting, "Jillian, where are you?" sent her scurrying off to the front of the store.

The Spanish teacher's smile faded. "That's a big loss, Jillian's right. Mrs. Santos was good with kids like Jillian. She'll be missed for sure."

"That's what Jillian tells us," Nell said.

Jim walked over and picked up one of the socks from the table, fingering the stitches. Several women walked in behind him, and Izzy began handing out patterns and pointed out the iced tea and platter of cookies.

"How did Sophia become involved in tutoring kids?" Cass asked, staying close behind Jim.

"It was Father Northcutt's idea. Mrs. Santos and he were buddies, and he knows I worry a lot about the kids who have a hard time catching on. The language classes are too big—I couldn't get to all the kids who needed help. So somehow Father talked Mrs. Santos into helping. She was great with the kids. Stern. Matter-of-fact. Didn't put up with any crap. But they responded—and they learned."

Jim stepped away from the table so others could admire the collection of socks. He moved closer to Birdie and Cass and lowered his voice.

"It's an awful thing. Really awful."

"How was she, at the school I mean? Friendly?" Cass asked.

"Polite, not especially friendly. The guys were all half in love with her, but they were certainly not friends with her. No way. She wouldn't even see kids individually. There were always at least two of them. I thought it was a little overkill, but she set her own rules."

"What about teachers, administration?"

Jim shook his head. "Everyone knew she was there a few days a week because you couldn't miss her. She was drop-dead gorgeous. But I don't know if she ever talked to anyone. She didn't even talk to me much, and she was working with my kids. She'd ask for their tests and the textbooks we used, and everything else she did on her own."

Izzy refilled the iced tea pitcher, then rejoined the group. "How did she get back and forth? The famous Ferrari?"

"She wouldn't bring that car on the school grounds. She didn't think it set a good example for the kids. Sometimes she'd park it down the street, but Mr. Santos dropped her off usually. Not long ago, a different guy picked her up once—maybe someone who worked for Santos. I saw her get in the car but just from a distance. I remember it because she seemed nervous that day, distracted, like she had something on her mind besides Spanish.

"And that last week, the week she was killed, she looked like she had the weight of the world on her shoulders. I actually felt sorry for her. I went up to her before class and asked if she needed help. She looked at me, kind of vague-like, then said yes I could. But all she wanted from me were directions. When I gave them to her, she turned around and left, leaving three students sitting in a classroom without a tutor. That wasn't like her at all."

"Where were the directions to?" Cass asked.

"The Delaney plant. Weird, huh? Her husband's competitor. She wasn't sure which road it was on. It's kind of hidden back beyond the marshes."

Another wave of people came in then, and Izzy waved to them over the tops of heads. "Sit anywhere," she said and moved off to greet a couple of lost-looking teenagers.

"Find a place, Jim," Birdie said. "Cass and I are on duty, so if you need help, wave."

"I can't believe Cass can knit. She was pretty good at threading worms on hooks, but knitting?"

Cass wrinkled her nose at him and headed across the room to help Esther Gibson find a chair. As she passed the archway to the front of the store, she stopped short. "Good grief," she said, coming face-to-face with Danny Brandley.

"Is this the right place?" He smiled at her down the steps. "I couldn't find anyone in front to ask—they were all busy."

"This is absolutely the right place if you're into socks. Or not," she added. "You could come just because you like our company."

He laughed. "Ties, scarves. I love this stuff. It's a helluva a lot cheaper than a psychiatrist." He walked down the steps. "I take the T in Boston a lot, and knitting is a perfect companion—forces me to let go of whatever I'm writing, to sit back, watch the world, decompress."

"I'm impressed."

"Don't be." Danny pulled a long, narrow piece of knitting from his backpack. "This is my latest. A necktie for a friend. His baby has ten Uncle Danny bibs. And everyone in the entire Brandley clan has at least two scarves. The more unfortunate have nine or ten. My dad is starting to hang them like flags from the loft railing in his bookstore."

Cass laughed. "A generous knitter. The best kind."

"Oh, it's not that they're begging for my handiwork. I have only mastered the knit stitch. I can't quite get a handle on how to purl—but I'm trying."

At the mention of her name, Purl jumped up on the bookcase, then proceeded to land comfortably on Danny's shoulder and rub her cheek against his.

"Her name is Purl," Cass said. "How can you not know how to purl when our Purl seems to be in love with you?"

A rapping on an iced tea glass broke into their conversation, and Izzy stepped up on her box, a pair of socks in each hand.

"Guess this means business," Cass whispered and pointed to a place next to Birdie at the end of the couch. "Maybe Purl can inspire you," she added, and reluctantly left Danny's side to stand by the door and help out when Izzy called.

The class began with a flurry of chatting, laughter, and questions about the techniques they had used for last week's miniature socks. Newcomers were filled in on what they'd missed, and Izzy checked to be sure they'd all come with double-pointed needles and had picked their yarn appropriately. They would all use the same pattern for the first sock project—later, when they were sock experts, they'd pick out their own patterns and knit up spectacular designs. There was much laughter as the Seaside Knitters moved through the group, helping the knitters divide the cast-on stitches between three needles, encouraging them to ignore the initial awkwardness of balancing three needles at once.

"Just concentrate on the two you're actually working on," Izzy suggested. "You'll get the hang of it. It just takes time. Be patient and don't poke yourself in the eye."

Cass saw her chance and snaked through the crowd to Danny's side. "Slip them onto the needles purlwise," she said. "Don't knit them yet, just slip, but it'll help you get the hang of purling." She leaned over and made sure his right needle slipped into the front of the cast-on stitch.

Danny smiled at his signs of success. "You're a decent teacher, Cass Halloran."

"And you're much nicer without your computer," she whispered, then moved on to help Mary Pisano untwist her stitches.

The hour passed quickly, and the knitters reluctantly began packing away their supplies while Izzy handed out instructions for the coming week. "Once your ribbing is finished, we're into the fun part—turning the heels!" She encouraged music lovers to bring their own playlists and they'd have a variety of music.

"Whew," Izzy said, wiping up spilled iced tea as the last idler walked up the steps. Cass and Birdie moved about the room, picking up stray bits of yarn and gathering scattered knitting supplies. Nell carried two folding chairs to the closet.

"As always," Izzy said, "you were a great help. In the middle of everything going on around here you managed to come to a socks class."

"As did you, dear," Birdie said, packing up her own knitting. "We are in this together, the whole kit and caboodle, from my wayward Ella and Harold to fires to knitting socks. Besides," she added, "these gatherings always reveal tidbits for us to chew on."

"Like Jim Rodriguez?" Nell said.

"Exactly."

Birdie returned from the galley kitchen, a chilled bottle of white wine in her hand. Cass headed for the glasses. "Jimmy's a good guy. More perceptive than I'd have guessed when he was a kid. His description of Sophia that last week or two was interesting."

"Izzy—come!" Jillian screamed from the front of the store.

Izzy dropped her cleaning rag and ran up the steps, followed closely by Nell, Birdie, and Cass.

Good Lord, Nell thought. *Please don't let it be another fire or car crash.*

They found Jillian at the front door, her face plastered to the glass.

"What's wrong, Jillian?"

Rose stood behind the counter, counting the day's receipts, her earphones plugged in, oblivious to her sister's drama.

"It's him!"

"Who?"

"The man who picked up Sophia Santos from school. Her lover."

Izzy pried Jillian away from the door, and Nell opened it.

"That's him." Jillian's finger pointed straight ahead. "He must have been in your socks class, but we were so busy I didn't see him come in."

Across the street, standing in front of McClucken's Hardware Store, a backpack slung over one shoulder and chatting with Ben Endicott, stood Danny Brandley.

Chapter 23

"No way," Cass said. She picked up the wineglass Birdie had filled, took a drink, and then set it back down, a little more forcefully than usual. Amber liquid sloshed against the sides of the glass. "Danny Brandley did not have an affair with Sophia Santos. That's teenage garbage."

"None of us said he did," Nell said calmly. "Giving someone a ride—assuming that he is the person those girls saw—certainly doesn't mean there was romance involved. That's just plain silly." She looked across the room at Izzy. "Do you have any of that Roomkaas cheese left? There's some flatbread in your cupboard, I think. We need something to eat with this wine or we won't be able to think clearly about these developments—or rumors or whatever they are."

While Izzy was getting the cheese, Nell put in a quick call to Ben. Dinner might be late, she told him. But if he'd toss a salad and grill some vegetables, she'd stop at Archie's bookstore on her way home and pick up the latest Grisham thriller that he'd reserved.

"Jillian seemed sure of what she saw," Izzy said. She set the platter of cheese and crackers on the coffee table, then walked over and opened the casement windows above the window seat. Purl purred her approval from her prime spot on the seat cushion and lifted her head to catch the sea breeze. "So it seems the next step,"

Izzy continued, "is to find out why Danny was picking up Sophia Santos at Sea Harbor High."

"And why he told me he didn't know Sophia. Now that I think back, he hesitated when he said it, though it didn't mean much at the time."

"I can't imagine Danny having anything to do with any of this, but we need to find out. Maybe he knows something about Sophia that would help us," Birdie suggested.

"We could ask him," Cass said. "But it's a little tricky. How do you ask someone if he had an affair with a woman who was just murdered?"

"I am sure you will come up with a way," Izzy said.

"We also need to talk about Harold," Nell said. Her voice was quiet, the topic a difficult one.

Birdie sat quietly, her knitting in her lap. "Yes, we do. Ella is afraid we'll think ill of him. Even as angry with him as she is, she loves him. And he loves her. Maybe too much."

Birdie told Cass and Izzy about Harold being at the club that night, in spite of his protestations that he'd been home. "He finally admitted it when he realized others had seen him. He had reached the end of his rope. I think the ankle injury had him a little depressed. He's had too much time to sit and think these past weeks. He imagined Sophia was taking Ella away from him."

Nell listened to Birdie talk and her heart grew heavy. Harold hated Sophia for the way his life had changed. Not only that, they all knew that Harold could fix everything from vacuum cleaners to stoves to cars. In her mind, the circumstantial evidence against Harold was every bit as powerful as that against Julianne Santos.

She thought back to the expression on his face last night. He hadn't regretted his words nor had he tried to hide his feelings. Would a murderer be so open? Admit to hating the woman who died? Accuse her of ruining his life?

"Who knows what pushes someone over the edge," Cass said. "Maybe we're all capable of violence, I don't know."

But the thought of Harold Sampson doing anything so vicious was almost as difficult to imagine as thinking Father Northcutt had done it.

"We know Harold was there," Birdie said. "We know he had motive."

"What time did he say he left the club?" Cass asked.

Birdie thought back. "Early, he said. Around eight."

Cass thought about that for a minute. "If he left at eight, Harold is innocent."

"How do you know that, Cass?" Birdie asked.

"Being around trucks and boats and jalopies all my life, I know a little about leaky fluid. Tommy Porter told me that there wasn't much fluid on the parking lot where Sophia had parked."

"So?"

"So there would have been, if Harold had done it early in the evening. Whoever did it, had to have done it between eleven and when Sophia left, which was about midnight. Tommy says that's the time frame the police are working from."

"You're brilliant, Cass," Birdie said.

"*If* that's really when he left. Harold lied to us about being there. He could be lying again," Nell said with regret.

They were silent for a minute. Then Cass said, "So we'll come up with a way to prove he left when he said he did."

And they would. The thought of gentle Harold Sampson killing Sophia was more than the knitters could dwell on for long. Cass' reasoning was hopeful, but unfortunately they needed more than his word.

"All right, moving on," Birdie said. "We know Liz and Alphonso were there, and they both had motive."

"Liz couldn't have done it. I feel sure of that after talking with Ben. He said almost every second of her time that night could be accounted for. She was putting out fires, correcting waitstaff—"

"Preventing Julianne from bludgeoning Alphonso with a beer bottle," Cass added.

"Right. So I think we can cross her off. Someone would have noticed if she had disappeared for that long."

"Alphonso?"

"That's tougher," Nell admitted. "Lots of loose strings. And we also have Danny Brandley who—if in fact he's the person Jillian saw picking Sophia up at the high school—may have misled us about knowing her . . ." Nell put down her wineglass.

"I think we need to look into Gracie's fire." Cass put the thought out there, happy to move away from Danny Brandley as a suspect.

"I don't know how the fire could be connected to Sophia's murder, dear," Birdie said.

"Me either," Cass said. "But it's another bad thing happening to the same family. Gracie's aunt murdered. Gracie's mother in jail. Gracie's restaurant burned. If Birdie hadn't seen the smoke, the whole thing would have burned to the ground. It doesn't add up. It wasn't even that cold out. And wouldn't he have known someone would see the smoke out of the chimney?"

Cass finished her wine and began slathering the creamy Gouda-like cheese on a piece of flatbread while the others digested her words.

Cass was right. Nell wondered suddenly why they'd all bought the explanation so readily. Was it because they didn't want anything else bad to happen? Was that why they'd greedily taken in the simple, benign explanation?

"Well, we know one thing for sure," Izzy said, breaking the silence. "Julianne didn't set that fire. She has an airtight alibi."

"And it still could have been exactly as the police described it," Birdie added. "But we should tuck it away with the other loose ends, at least until we're sure there's no connection. Frankly, I can't imagine why anyone would want to hurt Gracie's business. It's not like we have competing lobster cafés. And who in their right mind would want to hurt sweet Gracie Santos?"

"So let's go back to Sophia," Cass said. "She didn't like Delaney & Sons—and from what Gracie said, they weren't too crazy about her, especially Davey."

"But if someone from D.J.'s company didn't like the Santos Company, why kill Sophia? Why not Alphonso?" Nell asked.

The group fell silent, caught up in their own thoughts. Nell fingered the Ravenscar cardigan in her lap. She'd almost finished a front panel and the all-seasons cotton yarn was comforting to the touch, not stiff, like some cottons. Comfort. That's what they all needed.

Finally Nell said, "I think we need to think about this, keep our eyes open for something that will help us connect the dots. We have plenty of people who could have done it and had motive, but none of it feels solid. We need to peel off layers of lives of all these people. And maybe, just maybe, we'll find a link or a piece of conversation or something we haven't been looking at that will clear up the muddiness. Like Cass did with the brake fluid."

Izzy stood and began clearing away the crackers and cheese. "That's what we'll do, then—I hear plenty in the shop. We'll ask questions. Birdie and Cass did a great job of interrogating Jimmy Rodriguez before the socks class—and he didn't even know what they were doing."

"True, we found out more about Sophia—especially that she was agitated and worried that last week."

"And left the school to visit the Delaney plant," Nell said. "That's odd."

"Maybe once we can paint a more defined picture of her and what she did that last week we'll find a more concrete answer to who killed her."

"And why." Nell stood up and took her empty wineglass into the galley kitchen.

Izzy followed with napkins and the cheese platter and Birdie and Cass straightened up the back room.

"Tomorrow's a new day," Birdie said, collecting her knitting and slipping the bag over her shoulder. "We're all on edge, but things will be opening up. I feel it." She straightened every inch of her five-foot frame and forced a smile to her lips, spreading a touch of strength to each of them.

Nell stood and watched her friend of so many years they'd stopped counting. Birdie was right. A new day was what was needed. It hadn't even been two weeks, after all. But the fear would linger and fester until they knew for certain who had made the red Ferrari fly off the cliff and into a bed of granite rocks—with Sophia in the driver's seat.

Archie was standing in the doorway of the bookstore talking to Jake Risso when Nell left the Seaside Studio and walked next door to pick up the book for Ben.

"Hey, Nell. How's it going?" Jake asked. He shoved his hands in the pockets of his jeans.

Jake was another one, Nell thought. He'd had motive, it seemed. And wasn't one known for peaceful solutions. Nell pushed the thought away and smiled at Jake. "I heard a rumor about you." She slipped on her glasses and looked at the side of his head. "It looks like it's true. Burned the hair right off your head, Jake Risso. Were you trying to play fireman?"

"It was a hair-raising night, for sure," Jake said, then guffawed, along with Archie, at his pun.

Jake touched the side of his head. "It was the damnedest thing. The burgers were too greasy and the fire got out of control. But those poor fellas at the fire station had a worse night than I did. They no sooner got through with me than they got called to that awful wreck."

"What wreck?" Archie asked.

"The Santos crash. It was the same night what I got my new hairdo. The crew spent two hours with me, then headed over there to a *real* mess."

Jake's fire was the same night as Sophia's murder—that probably explained why she hadn't heard about it. It was pushed from the limelight. Nell thought back over that night. "Jake, what time was the fire at your place?"

"Started burning in the third inning of the ball game—Sox were ahead—so eight thirty or so? Took the fools two hours to put out a simple grease fire. I'd've done it myself, but they wouldn't let me."

So Jake Risso was completely occupied, singed hair and all, at the same time as someone was tampering with the Santos Ferrari. Nell smiled in spite of herself. It felt good to cross Jake off the list. As ornery as he could be, she was quite fond of his son, Andy. She patted his hand gently. "It's time to turn the Gull over to Andy and go fishing. Next time it might be your nose that gets singed."

Archie chuckled and followed Nell into the store. "You gals knitting up a storm over there? Harriet says I'm going to be the proud recipient of argyle socks."

"I'll expect you to wear them with your Bermuda shorts so everyone can see her handiwork. Harriet is a wonderful knitter. And from what I understand, Danny may rival her handiwork."

"Danny? Yep. And I have plenty of ties to show for it." Archie chuckled. "That boy is a wonder."

"Not so much a boy, Archie. Though I guess in our hearts they'll always be that. I'm surprised some gal hasn't lured Danny into settling down."

"Oh, they've tried, believe you me. But he just hasn't taken the time, is how I see it. He has a truckload of interests. Marriage probably doesn't fit into it yet. But soon. My boy turns forty next year, you know. Harriet keeps reminding him. She wouldn't mind having some little ones to spoil."

Nell smiled and walked over to the counter.

"But we're proud of him whatever he decides. You know how that is." Archie's great effort to be positive played across his kindly, lined face. He threw up his hands as if chastising himself. "I know, I know. Sometimes I talk too much and you want to get home to dinner. I put Ben's book in the back—they were going fast, though it isn't as good as his last one. Back in a jiffy."

Archie disappeared to the back of the store. Nell dug in her purse for a credit card and set it on the counter. It was then that she noticed a leather album sitting open on the counter.

Daniel Spencer Brandley, it read on the first page. She smiled at the sentiment. Harriet or Archie must have put together a scrapbook of Danny's achievements, carefully placing them between plastic sheets for all posterity. What pride they had in their son. It was how she felt about Izzy, so inordinately proud and happy for even the smallest thing—a 4-H ribbon for best all-around horsewoman when she was ten, a published letter she wrote to the local paper when her beloved grade school burned to the ground, her first dance recital.

She opened the cover and flipped through the pages. There was a medley of achievements, articles for the high school paper, college and graduate school diplomas, an award for a series of articles Danny had written on the fishing industry. She turned several more pages and was about to close the book when a color photograph at the top of the next page caught her eye.

Sitting in an elegant living room, poised and distinguished, were Alphonso and Sophia Santos. The photograph looked like a realistic painting—had the photographer positioned Alphonso standing with his hand on Sophia's shoulder, Nell would have sworn she'd seen it in the Museum of Fine Arts. A soigné Sophia Santos, her makeup perfect and every hair in place, wore a black dress fitting her to perfection. Alphonso was *GQ*-handsome, his Italian suit perfect and his smile as polished as his teeth.

THE NORTH SHORE'S POWER COUPLE, the caption read. The story had been a feature in the *Boston Globe*, an in-depth profile of Sophia and Alphonso Santos—their origins, their lives apart and together, their achievements, and their dreams. It had been written several years before, when Alphonso traveled frequently between his home on Cape Ann and the townhome on Beacon Hill, just as she and Ben had done when they still held full-time positions in the city.

The writer, the short italicized paragraph at the bottom explained, had spent several months interviewing the Santoses for this story. He had accompanied them on trips and spent time at the Santos Company, using the information gained to enlarge and enrich the most complete profile of the Santos couple to date.

And for the detailed, fascinating article, Danny Brandley had won yet another award.

Chapter 24

The next morning, Mary Pisano's About Town column received more than its share of readers.

TROUBLE IN RIVER CITY?

The Summerfest is nearly upon us. And it's time we hitched the wagon to the cart and cleaned up the mess of murder and distrust in our sweet town so we can welcome summer with open, loving arms.

Some questions remain that we need to ponder as we walk our beaches and stroll our lovely Harbor Road:

Who was seen running from the pier in the early-morning hours as a hometown woman seeks to open a lovely new café?

Is it love or war fueling the construction of the new community center at Anja Angelina Park? This columnist has word that arguments are as plentiful as gulls on any given day.

And speaking of love or war . . . how wonderful to see a leading Sea Harbor couple adding an heir to perpetuate the family's generosity and goodwill.

Ben had the paper spread out on the kitchen table when Nell came down the back steps to the kitchen.

"Mary's on the prowl," he said. "You may need to read this." He handed Nell a mug of strong black coffee.

She wrapped her fingers around the mug and sat down next to Ben, her shoulder touching his. Slipping on her reading glasses, she scanned the About Town column.

"Oh, good grief, Ben," she said when she finished reading the column. Her heart sank. "Poor Liz. What was Mary thinking? This isn't like her. I can't believe she'd do this."

When she had finally arrived home the night before, she and Ben had tried to make sense of Danny Brandley's actions. He had spent intimate time with the Santoses—and yet claimed he didn't know Sophia. Nell was willing to dismiss Danny picking her up at the school as teenage fantasy. But a photo and published article made his relationship with the Santoses far more difficult to sweep under a carpet. What was he hiding?

Both she and Ben wanted it explained easily, benignly, perhaps as a misunderstanding. They had been friends with Danny's parents for longer than they could remember. They were good, solid people. It made the assumptions Danny's actions led them to uncomfortable and distasteful.

"Let's go to the worst-case scenario: he had an affair with Sophia after that article was written," Ben calmly asserted.

"Or during."

"It's a big jump from affair to murder."

"But what if Danny loved her, and Sophia tossed him aside? People have killed for less."

They finally tabled the discussion, uncomfortable with where it was leading them. They cleaned up the dishes and headed up to bed. Ben said he had a lunch meeting the next day with Chief Thompson. He wanted Jerry's advice on some safety measures for the sailing program. Maybe there'd be time to talk about other things. He'd try, he promised.

"Mary, what were you thinking?"

. . .

Nell knew exactly where to find Mary Pisano. She'd become such an early-morning fixture on Coffee's patio that locals studiously avoided sitting at the small round table beneath the corner maple tree. And if they forgot, one look from behind her large sunglasses would send them away, apologies drifting along behind them.

"Which part, Nell?" Mary looked up as Nell pulled out a wrought-iron chair and sat down across from her. The morning paper was spread out on the table.

Although she was in her late forties, Mary still bought her clothes in the preteen department, a fact of which she was inordinately proud. "Half the price," she'd say, making her fisherman husband, Ed, smile and scoop her up in a brawny hug. Today, her knitted top and chambray skirt with the floral sash matched the brightness of her smile. Her brown curls bobbed as she greeted Nell.

Nell started to point to the last line of Mary's column, then pulled her hand back. "I'm curious about all of it, I guess."

Mary Pisano was opinionated and fancied herself an amateur sleuth on the side, but Nell enjoyed her enormously and had always found her kind. Revealing personal information that might hurt someone was not her way. Nell was frankly puzzled.

"Where shall I start?"

"Well, the police didn't tell Gracie someone had been seen running from the fire. Do we know they saw someone?"

"No. That's why I was asking. It seems to me that if someone was inside the building and set a fire in the fireplace, and they weren't there when the fire truck arrived, then they ran off. So I was simply asking all our responsible readers out there to let us know what they saw. People shouldn't be camping in empty restaurants unless they have the owner's permission."

Nell couldn't argue with that.

"Are the arguments at the community center something unusual?" she asked, moving on to Mary's next contention. "None of us thought that building would go up peacefully, not with both Alphonso and D.J. involved in supplying crews and materials."

"Well, I don't know exactly, Nell. My source tells me that the Delaneys have been in an uproar. I don't know why. Sometimes I think D.J. should be firmer with those bullheaded boys of his. They don't think twice about giving you a piece of their minds, sometimes using words that belong in a barroom brawl, not a lovely spot like our new park. There's a nice playground out there. Families picnic and children play. They shouldn't be exposed to the anger of workmen. Davey Delaney sometimes doesn't show good sense."

All around them people chattered about the weather, the water, and the whales that were spotted the day before, out beyond the breakwater. And, of course, the trouble in river city. Nell sometimes wondered if Mary came to Coffee's every day to hear firsthand what people thought of her column. Though it really didn't matter as far as her job went—half the newspapers in the area were owned by the Pisano family, and Mary's column was quite secure. Nell set her cup down. "I guess that leaves the last line, Mary."

"Liz Palazola is having a baby. Alphonso is the father."

"Did Liz want that in the paper? Isn't that an awfully intimate item for your column?"

"Now calm down, Nell." Mary cut her muffin in half and pushed a piece over to Nell on a napkin. "Eat this. It will make you feel better." She took a sip of coffee and continued. "You know as well as anyone that I don't hurt people. At least not intentionally. That is not who I am."

"Of course I know that. That's why this bothers me and I—"

Mary lifted a hand in the air. "Shh. I'll explain. When I heard the rumor at Stop & Shop yesterday, I immediately made reservations for lunch at the club."

"Go on."

"I asked Liz if she would take her break with me. Poor thing looked like she was about to fall down. So I got her some tea and crackers and we sat on the deck in a cool breeze. That perked her up."

"Did you bring up the pregnancy?"

"That was why I was there, you see. To ask her about it, since people in the grocery checkout lane were taking it home with them, right along with their carrots and hot dogs. I thought she should know. Sometimes it's easier to manage things early on, don't you think?"

Nell took a sip of the strong coffee and nibbled on Mary's cranberry muffin. What she thought was that for all her snoopiness, sometimes Mary Pisano wisely got right to the heart of things. And used her heart to get there.

"She got a little teary, but she seemed relieved to have someone to talk to who would be happy with her. Having a baby is a joyful time. Liz is such a sweet thing, so pretty and smart. She told me how much she loved Alphonso. How ecstatic they are about the baby, how she hopes it's a boy to carry on the fine name of the Santos family."

"So they don't mind everyone knowing?"

"I asked her that point-blank. She was quiet for a minute, thinking about it. Then she looked down at her phone, as if she might call the baby's father and ask him what he thought. But finally she decided for herself. She put the phone away and told me that she wanted everyone to know how happy she was. *Sublimely* happy, she said. And she thought I was just the person to let people know that in a discreet, lovely way."

A grant-writing conference call and follow-up meeting filled the rest of Nell's Tuesday. It was the next day before she had a chance to rethink her conversation with Mary Pisano and Mary's contention that things were a bit chaotic out at the community center site. Nell had no clear sense that it had anything to do with Sophia's murder—but it seemed Davey Delaney's name came up far too often to dismiss his connection to it out of hand. Perhaps a hike in Anja Angelina Park was in order.

Birdie was going to the orthopedist with Harold. And Cass was out on the water with Pete, checking lobster traps. But Izzy said she had newfound freedom with the Anderson twins wanting to work every chance they got, and she would love a short hike at Anja Angelina Park with Nell. She'd like to see how the community center was coming along.

Nell put on long shorts and slipped on her sneakers. Then she pulled things out of her refrigerator and piled sprouts, sliced turkey, tomatoes, cheese, and a tangy horseradish sauce onto crusty sourdough rolls and packed them tightly in wrap. She added fresh peaches and bottled water to her sack, ensuring that she and Izzy wouldn't get hungry—and it might give them more time to talk. And then, just as a precautionary measure, she tossed together a third sandwich. Sometimes Izzy ate far more than her slim frame would lead one to believe.

"So why the hike, Aunt Nell? Ulterior motive, or did you feel an overwhelming need to spend time with your niece? And was Mary Pisano smoking pot when she wrote yesterday's column? What was she thinking?" Izzy's words tumbled out as Nell drove north toward the edge of town.

Just before the city limits, Nell turned onto Angus Road, newly named after a favorite Sea Harbor man, Angus McPherran, who had deeded the land to the city. The narrow tree-lined road went only one place, and that was through the land now known as Anja Angelina Park, all the way to the point where a new community center was rising.

Nell opened her window a crack and ocean air filled the car. "I always have an overwhelming urge to be with you, Izzy. And I don't think Mary was smoking anything, though I didn't ask."

Then she filled Izzy in on her conversation the day before. "I thought the same thing you did, Izzy. I couldn't imagine what she was thinking. She redeemed herself nicely, but I have vague uncomfortable feelings about Liz's decision to have Mary reveal it. Frankly, I think Mary wondered, too, but it was news, and she had permission, so she put it in the column. You can't blame her for that."

"I can't imagine doing that without Alphonso knowing."

"I had a fleeting feeling that Liz did it intentionally, though I have no way of knowing that."

"My thoughts exactly," Izzy said. She looked through the windshield as they drove through the wooded area, pondering Liz's action.

From the narrow, winding road, hiking trails wound back through thick stands of pine and willow to the old quarries, once alive with the sounds of hammers pounding on stone as men worked the granite. But now they were as quiet as the bottom of the sea, the deep quarries filled with water and surrounded by scrub brush and wildflowers.

Nell drove slowly, the peace of her surroundings a contrast to her thoughts. "I suppose once the world knows Liz is carrying this baby, Alphonso has to deal with it," Nell said.

"So if he was dragging his feet," Izzy said, "those days are over. It smacks a little bit of forcing an issue."

"But only if Alphonso was dragging his feet. And we don't know that." Nell drove around a bend. Up ahead, where the finger of land was surrounded on three sides by water, was the beginning of the new community center.

Angus McPherran had constructed a small lodge on the point that served as a temporary office and held hiking maps, bottled water, and postcards. Angus himself was often inside to tell stories of the land and the quarries and the granite industry to anyone who cared to listen.

A large parking lot was half-filled on the sunny day. The land was wide open here, with mowed lawns, fire pits, picnic tables, benches, and new play equipment. In the distance, meandering through magnificent garden areas, were tended pathways to the sea.

"This place is a bit of heaven," Izzy said, climbing out of the car. "Breathe in the smell, Aunt Nell." She stretched her arms above her head, then pulled her sun-streaked hair back and bound it with a scrunchie. "The magical mix of salt and sea and sunshine. Invigorating. What's first? Food?"

Nell laughed. "How did you know I brought food?"

"Because you'd never invite me anywhere and not have food. At least not usually." Izzy turned toward the community center. "It's going to be beautiful."

The five-sided building was low to the ground with windows everywhere. The frame was natural pine and granite, and Nell immediately felt she was at camp in the northern Minnesota woods. It had a wonderful feeling about it—natural and healthy and good.

"Imagine what this will means to kids," Nell said.

"Hey, you two, wait up!" Willow Adams' voice floated across the parking lot.

"What are you doing here?" Willow asked, stopping to catch her breath.

"We brought lunch," Nell said. "Can you join us?"

"Did you make it?" Willow asked. Her brows lifted.

Nell laughed. "It's just sandwiches."

"Sandwiches-by-Nell? There's no 'just' in that."

"There's a free picnic table over there," Izzy said. "Let's grab it. We can hike later."

The table was near the construction site, but they could see the ocean waves crashing against the shore in the distance.

"It's beautiful down on the beach today," Willow said. "Big whitecaps crashing against the rocks. I've been taking photographs for inspiration. And I got a great idea for a series of fiber-art pieces that feature waves and the sea. These photos guide me. It's going to be for the new center," she said with a touch of pride.

"That's terrific, Willow," Izzy said.

"And Jane tells me your gallery is going gangbusters."

Willow knocked on the table. "So far so good. I think my dad's carved mermaids are what keep me going. So what are you two doing here besides feeding me?"

Nell pulled out the sandwiches and fruit and passed them around. "I've been wanting to see this." Nell's look took in the gardens and building under construction.

"Fantastic, isn't it? I've been hanging around—the guys even gave me my own hard hat. I want my art to be integral to the architecture and materials used in the building. I love what they've done."

"So the construction is going well? No fistfights that you've seen?"

Willow's black eyes lit up with laughter. "You read Mary's column. She seems to think it's a hotbed out here. There've been some heated words, but I'm not sure it has a thing to do with the building."

"What do you mean?"

"Well, a couple weeks ago there was some talk of the Delaney & Sons subcontractors. I don't think it referred to the center really. Just a general rumor. A reporter had gone to the Delaney plant and asked about projects going over budget and maybe cutting corners, that sort of thing. It sent Davey Delaney to hell and back. He was one furious fella." Willow waved at a man walking by.

He lifted his large sunglasses, squinted at the group, then waved and strode over to the table. D.J. Delaney held out a large hand. "Nell, Izzy—good to see you folks. Well, what do you think? Terrific?" His ruddy face was dotted with perspiration.

"It's wonderful." Nell looked over at the half-finished structure. "How is it going, working with the Santos Company?"

D.J. shrugged. "It's okay. We're managing the construction, but Santos sends crews over to help. We both gave materials at cost. The committee that raised the money oversees what's spent and they are the ones involved with the architect."

"That sounds like a decent plan."

"It works."

A group of workers started up the path to the new building, catching D.J.'s attention. He looked over, then called to one of them. "Davey, over here. We've got some visitors." He waved his son over to the group. "I come out to check on things," he said to the group. "Santos doesn't have much time for that sort of thing unless he thinks we're doing something wrong. Hell, I've been in this business as long as he has. Damn rumors can kill a guy." D.J. shook his head. Then he thought about what he said and retracted it slightly. "Alphonso isn't half-bad, I suppose, if you can get by the fancy suits and cars. But that wife of his was trouble, at least in recent days. Don't mean to speak ill of the dead, but the way she went about things, she was asking for something bad to happen."

Nell saw Davey's face harden at his father's words, but he stood politely next to him, his demeanor more that of a young man than a forty-year-old.

"Why don't you take these ladies around, Davey? Show them the great work we do. I'm heading back to the office. Joey and I are trying to make sense of the damn figures. It never ends."

Nell noticed a shadow fall over Davey's face and his chin hardened.

"Take charge, son."

"Sure, Pop." Davey pushed a polite smile in place and motioned for them to follow him over to a trailer. He pulled hard hats out of a box and gave them each one.

They followed Davey through the opening into the framed building and around stacks of lumber and cutting equipment. The shape of the main lobby and a theater and gymnasium just beyond it were defined. Skylights and a labyrinth of rooms and open spaces would allow a free flow of classes and activities.

"You can almost hear the kids racing through here, the creative energies unleashed," Willow said. "I love it."

"I hear you're handling a lot of company responsibilities these days, Davey," Nell said.

He shrugged. "We're the best in the business. Don't let anyone tell you differently." Davey led them through the back area where an outdoor stage would stretch across the back of the building and seats would be built into the rise of the ground.

They walked around the outside of the building, then back to where they had begun their tour and stood for a minute, looking up at the structure.

"But this is a combination of Santos and Delaney, right? A dynamic duo." Nell kept her words light, conversational.

Davey stopped walking for a moment. He stood on the rough floor, his feet apart, and stared at Nell.

Nell went on quickly, easing the moment. "I mean, you've all done a wonderful job. It's such a good thing for the Sea Harbor community."

"We always do a good job. It doesn't matter what the job is, we build strong buildings. We sure don't need the Santos Company for that."

"Of course."

Davey stood quiet for a moment, then looked at Nell straight on. "Did you come out here to check up on us?"

Nell took a step back. "Davey, of course not. We came to see this magnificent community center."

Davey's eyes narrowed. "Did anyone send you?"

"Send us?"

"Hey, Davey," Izzy broke in. "This is a great place. Looks like it's well built. No one sent us, but if they did, that's what we would tell them."

He stepped back then, his hand clenched at his side, and Nell could see the anger crawl up his thick neck and color his cheeks. "For the record, our condos and houses and shopping centers are the best in this whole area, bar none. We don't cheat. We're careful. My dad is the best in the business."

His eyes narrowed and he looked at the three women as if they were coconspirators in a B movie. One stout finger waved at them. His words shot out like bullets.

"And as for inferior subcontractors or whatever . . . that miserable, conniving poor excuse for a woman was dead wrong. She was out to destroy us. Drove around in that Ferrari like she was some hot thing. What did she know about Ferraris? Nothing, that's what. Didn't know a Brembo brake from the gas pedal. And she tried to tell us we didn't know our business. Hah." Davey took a step away, as if he'd said his piece, done his duty. His temples throbbed. And then he started in again, his brows nearly touching each other and his eyes closing to narrow slits.

"She was hateful. And thank the Lord that the god of Ferraris sent her straight to hell. May she rest in the pile of trouble she made for herself."

His words still hanging in the air, Davey Delaney turned and stomped off toward the workers' trailer, shouting back over his shoulder to leave the hard hats on the steps. They were the property of D.J. Delaney & Sons.

Chapter 25

The day began easily enough, sunny and warm as predicted, but the peace that hovered over Nell's first cup of coffee was not to last.

Birdie's call came at eight, just minutes before Nell planned to run by Father Northcutt's church with some canned goods for his soup kitchen.

"Nell, dear, can you please run on over here?" Birdie asked.

Nell frowned at the sound of Birdie's voice.

"It's Ella," she said. "Harold said she never came home last night."

Nell didn't get a ticket, but she knew it was because Tommy Porter would have been embarrassed to stop her. She spotted him out of the corner of her eye, waved as if she were obeying the law, and sped on to Birdie's house.

Birdie was out in the drive when she pulled in.

"She never came home? Where did she go?" Nell slid from behind the wheel.

"She went for a walk," Harold said, hobbling up beside Birdie. His haggard face spoke of a sleepless night.

"Stella came today to help. She's out looking for her."

"Where is she looking?"

"The woods, the cove, up the road. Wherever she could walk from here."

Harold looked down the long driveway. "She left while I was watching *Jeopardy*. She was on her phone for a bit. Then she left, like she was going outside to read, and I thought that was okay because she doesn't like television so much. She likes to sit on that little patio out near the garden where I put the gaslights in. She's there a lot, reading that book of her friend's."

Her friend. The words stood out from the rest. Even beneath his worry, Harold's feelings about Sophia Santos rose to the surface.

"I thought that was a good thing," Harold said. "If she was reading, maybe she'd stop being so obsessed with finding the murderer. She thinks she's the next Sherlock Holmes." He tried to mask his feelings with a play of anger.

"Who was she talking to on the phone?" Birdie asked.

"I don't know. I thought it was you, Miss Birdie."

"No, she didn't call me."

Nell looked around. In the distance she could hear Stella's voice calling out Ella's name. And from farther away, Jake Risso's voice bellowed out. Stella had gathered reinforcements. Good for her. As unpleasant as Ella had been to her, Stella was not going to hold a grudge.

"She did this once or twice before so I wasn't too worried at first. She wouldn't come back up to our apartment because she was mad at me about something. Mostly because of her friend. Ella never got mad at me before."

"That's true," Birdie agreed. "She'd sleep in that small spare bedroom near the kitchen. I already checked there. The bed hasn't been touched."

"What about the other apartment you have above the gardening shed? Or the garage?"

Nell felt she was grasping at straws. But as she talked, she walked across the pebbled drive to the main garage. "Your garages are nice enough to live in," she called back to Birdie. "Maybe she just wanted to be alone, or fell asleep."

Birdie stayed put and shook her head. "Ella never went in the garage. She considered that Harold's domain. She didn't like the smell of grease."

Nell was already to the garage and opening the side door. Her heart was beating fast and she dreaded looking around, no matter what Birdie said. Windows lit the area with morning sunshine. Nell looked around at the neat workbench in the back area, the small practical chairs next to it. Sonny had even installed a refrigerator for cold drinks in case someone got thirsty working back there on one of his cars, shining his wheel caps, or . . .

The small, practical Corolla that rarely got driven sat polished in its place. Nell frowned, then took a step back. Her breath caught in her chest. She stepped out of the doorway and looked back at Birdie and Harold.

"Birdie, where's the Town Car?"

"It's right there in front of you," Birdie said, her voice lifting in an effort to make Nell's question a silly one, and she began walking toward the door, her pace turning into a hustle. Of course the car would be right there. Right where it always was.

She stopped at the door, her heart wedged tightly in her chest, and her small voice filled with fear. "But Ella doesn't drive."

Before Nell could get her phone out of her pocket to call Chief Thompson, Birdie's cell phone rang.

Nell waited, watching Birdie's face. What she wanted the caller to say was that Ella was in jail. Driving without a license. Or was found sleeping in a park. Or, perhaps, had gotten herself a fine room at the Emerson Inn and then had no money to pay for it.

"Birdie, dear," Esther Gibson began . . .

They took Nell's car to the hospital in Gloucester, speeding along the narrow roads, and made it in record time. Harold sat in front with Nell, his face gray and his long narrow hands knotted in fists. Birdie sat in back, and Stella followed in her own car.

"Her vital signs are good," the doctor told them. "She's had a concussion and is still unconscious, but we expect her to come out of it anytime. This isn't unusual, though we don't want it to go on too long. She is lucky, frankly, to be with us. Amazingly lucky. She's certainly a tough lady."

"What happened?" Nell asked.

That was the great unanswered question. The police knew the basics, that Ella had been driving the Lincoln along a narrow road Wednesday night, over near a quarry. Driving fast for someone who didn't know how to drive, Tommy Porter observed. She'd swerved to avoid something—maybe a deer, Tommy thought. There were plenty in that area.

The car went off the road, and crashed into a tree.

But that wasn't the bad part, Tommy said—except, of course, for a major dent in the Favazzas' Lincoln Town Car. The bad part happened when a dazed Ella got out of the car and stumbled into the road.

"That's when she was hit. It was a pickup, we think, judging from the tire tracks. It hit her, then seemed to swerve and scraped some bark off a tree."

"So the driver knew he'd hit someone?"

Tommy couldn't say for sure. It was dark, a narrow road, and Ella was probably weaving along the side—her head was bruised from the first impact. The area was deserted—no house or street-lights to speak of. If the driver felt a bump, he might have thought it was a deer or a raccoon. "But he still shoulda stopped, for sure," Tommy said. "She could have died."

"Like I told you," the doctor repeated, "it's kind of a miracle. That lady must have something good to live for."

Nell looked at Harold as the doctor spoke and saw his eyes grow watery. He rubbed the back of his weathered hand across them.

"She's going to be fine—her arm is broken, but it's not too bad. We'll keep a close eye on her because of the concussion, but she's going to come through this fine."

The relief allowed free rein to the questions. Where was Ella Sampson going? And why?

Ella didn't have her seat belt on, according to the report, and upon impact, she flew hard into the windshield, which must have dazed her badly. It was an out-of-the-way road that circled around the marshes and she may have gotten lost. When the car hit her, she landed near a tree, partly covered by brush and undergrowth.

No one saw her until early morning when a young man, out for a run, spotted the car first, and then Ella, unconscious.

By late afternoon the doctor suggested everyone leave. They were moving Ella into a private room, but it was small, and they didn't want it crowded. They would set her arm in the morning when the swelling went down. The rest of her injuries were superficial bruises on her face and shoulders. A lucky lady, they said again.

Harold, as everyone expected, refused to leave Ella's side. He needed to be there when she awoke, he said. She'd be scared if she was alone.

Birdie didn't want to leave either, but Harold insisted. And when Stella volunteered to stay a while longer, promising to get Harold a meat loaf dinner from the cafeteria and make sure he settled down, Birdie knew it would be all right.

She would call the instant Ella woke up, Stella promised, though the doctor said it might not be for a while.

Birdie hugged Stella tightly, and Nell suspected that Stella's college fund for Salem State was now secure. And she'd more than earned it.

The meal for the Thursday-night knitting group would have to be simple, but Nell knew she could have brought peanut butter and jelly sandwiches and no one would have minded. What mattered to all four of them was being together, and that they would be.

Ben, bless him, had stopped at the market on his way home and picked up some fresh Buffalo mozzarella cheese and plump tomatoes. Along with tortillas, basil from her garden, and Parmigiano-Reggiano cheese, she was able to put together summer-fresh pizzas that everyone would like. An apricot torte from her freezer finished off her offerings, and she was ready to go.

Nell pulled into the alley between the Sea Harbor Bookstore and Izzy's shop. She climbed out of the car and came face-to-face with Father Northcutt.

"Good evening, Nell. May I be of service?" the priest asked. "I was just welcoming little Danny Brandley back to town. He's all folded up in one of Archie's chairs, pounding on a laptop like fury."

"Father Larry, Dan Brandley is anything but little."

"But he used to be. Little towhead. He was always such a nice little kid."

"They grow up."

"You seem a slight bit bristly, Nell."

"Sorry, Father," Nell said quickly. There was no reason to share her feelings about Danny Brandley with the priest.

But he did need to know about Ella Sampson's accident and condition.

Father Larry's smile fell away as Nell explained what had happened. "What a terrible thing. Ella is a fine woman." He tugged on a fob and looked down at his round pocket watch. "I'll be up to see her shortly. She has had a hard time with Sophia Santos' murder. Now this . . ."

"You knew Sophia well, Father?"

"I suppose I did. Sophia wasn't an easy woman to know, but I probably understood her as well as anyone. She was a good person. She knew right from wrong and lived by it. Had she lived during the Reformation, she would probably have been a martyr. Sophia didn't back down."

"Don't you think, Father, that sometimes gray has a place in our lives? I don't mean to criticize Sophia. Nor disrespect the Commandments. But sometimes you have to weigh situations and even act from your heart now and then." She thought about Sophia's tough love approach to Julianne and convincing Alphonso to cut off her allowance. And she wondered about the staunch stand she'd taken, blocking the neighbors' access to the beach.

Father Northcutt looked at Nell solemnly. "Yes, Nell. But your heart and Sophia's heart are different. She did what was right for her."

Nell leaned over and lifted out the box containing the foil-wrapped pizzas. She turned back toward the priest.

"Do you think Julianne Santos murdered Sophia?"

To Nell's great surprise, there was no pause before the padre replied. He looked directly at Nell, his clear eyes unblinking.

"No," he said. "Julianne is a lost soul who couldn't kill anyone, not if her own life depended on it. But I believe we will find out who did this terrible thing very soon."

Chapter 26

*N*ell was surprised. Not by Father Northcutt's answer. She suspected there was little that went on in Sea Harbor the priest didn't stay attuned to. She was surprised that the answer had come out so quickly and definitively. There was no question in his mind that Julianne Santos was innocent. For reasons Nell couldn't quite explain to herself, having the priest confirm what the knitters thought added a bit of divine credence to it.

Mae was closing down the receipts when Nell walked into the yarn shop. Father Northcutt's words were spinning around in her head, crowding her thoughts.

"Nell, are you okay?" Mae asked. "You look like you're miles away."

"Not that far, Mae." She looked through the front display window and watched Father Northcutt walk into Scoopers Ice Cream Shop.

Nell shifted her attention to Mae. "I was talking to Father Larry a minute ago, and every now and then he makes me think about things in a new way—or brings to light old truths. Not that I always agree with him, but at least he makes me think."

"Then I suppose he's doing his job, isn't he? He gave a nice homily Sunday. He talked about walking in other people's shoes before we judge them. He quoted Atticus Finch."

"*To Kill a Mockingbird*?"

"That's the one. He said Atticus had the right idea. You can't really understand a person unless you crawl inside her skin and walk around in it—or something like that. It made me think of my daughter Jackie, the one who joined a commune in Idaho."

"What did you think?"

"That I love her to death. But I don't think I'd crawl inside her skin for a million dollars."

Nell laughed and moved on. Cass and Birdie were already putting out plates and a basket of calamari when Nell walked down the steps to the back room.

"I had a craving for something fried," Cass explained. "I think it's how I handle stress." She dipped a crunchy strip of squid into the spicy red sauce. "Birdie filled us in on Ella. How dare someone leave the scene like that."

"Bring the calamari and pizza over here and let's talk," Birdie said from her perch near the fireplace. "I've poured wine."

"Have you heard anything more?" Nell asked. "Ben will check on Harold tonight, although it appears Stella has claimed him as her responsibility."

"This is the craziest thing I've ever heard, Ella disappearing like that," Cass said. "That nice woman barely spoke a few months ago—and now she's taking off in cars she can't drive and crusading for Lord knows what."

"And nearly getting herself killed," Nell said.

"She wouldn't have done that without a terribly important reason," Birdie said adamantly. "I've known Ella Sampson for forty-five years, and I am absolutely sure of that."

"Do you have any ideas?" Izzy said, eyeing the calamari. She put a few pieces on a small plate and settled back in the chair. "Who could she have been going to see?"

"I don't know, but it's connected to Sophia Santos' murder."

Cass, Nell, and Izzy looked at her.

"Saying it out loud makes me sure of it."

"But how?" Nell took a drink of wine, her mind trying to con-

205 · *Moon Spinners*

nect Ella's escapade—and its awful consequences—to the murder of Sophia Santos.

"Because Ella is shy and sweet, just like Cass said. And in my opinion, though Harold might disagree, she hasn't really changed. She found a soul mate in Sophia Santos, however odd a pairing it was. It was probably the one important female friendship she's had in her whole life. She misses that woman terribly, just as each of you would miss me or I would miss you if one of us were no longer here. It would be like a part of each of us was gone. And tell me, truthfully, what would you do if someone murdered me?"

The outrageousness of Birdie's question stunned them for a minute.

Then Cass said, "We'd track the person down and string him up by his toes."

"We wouldn't stop until we found the person," Izzy agreed. "We'd do anything we had to do, move mountains, sacrifice jobs, nothing would stop us."

"Including not knowing how to drive," Birdie said.

Birdie was absolutely right. Ella was out to find her friend's murderer.

"She talked on the phone before leaving," Birdie said. "Either someone was telling her something and she felt she needed to check on it. Or maybe the person on the phone wanted to see her, to give her some information."

"Or it was one and the same."

"A lot of that will be cleared up as soon as we can talk to her," Cass said.

They nodded. She was bound to be terribly uncomfortable and in pain from the break and bruises when she woke up, but hopefully she'd be able to fill in some of the holes that seemed to be widening each day.

Cass headed to the table to unwrap the mozzarella-basil pizzas. At the last minute Nell had added a layer of thinly sliced chicken-and-spinach sausages. The tortilla rounds were still hot and crisp, and Cass carried them back to the coffee table, passing them around. "This is perfect for tonight, Nell. Comfort food."

Nell took a drink of wine and settled back into the chair. "Birdie's way of figuring out what Ella might do or not do is interesting," she said. She repeated her conversation with Father Northcutt and Atticus Finch's dictum to walk in another's shoes. "Maybe that's the key. We're trying to figure out motives and actions from our point of view. But it might be entirely different from what the other person would think or do."

"Or feel compelled to do if threatened," Izzy said. She finished off her pizza and returned her plate to the counter.

"If Sophia thought someone was doing something wrong— morally, ethically, or for whatever reason—she would move to stop it, even if it wasn't her business," Birdie said. She lifted skeins of azure blue and lavender yarn—sea and sky—from her pack and then pulled out the beginnings of her swingy cardigan. The pattern promised it would be perfect for spring and summer and easy to layer in the winter. Soothing colors . . . a perfect antidote for the cloud that hung over them.

"Exactly. That's what she did with Julianne. She convinced Alphonso that giving her money was enabling her and he needed to stop doing it." Nell pulled a wipe from the pop-up container and rubbed her hands, thinking of Sophia and what it would be like to truly see the world in black and white. It was a skin that was difficult to wear. "I have no reason to doubt her intentions. I am sure that she thought that was absolutely the right thing to do."

"Feeling so *right* must be a burden at times," Birdie said softly.

Nell silently agreed. But it was who Sophia was—and she had to be true to that person.

"Davey Delaney said Sophia was spying on their company," Izzy said. "That's hard to imagine."

"Maybe she thought the Delaneys were doing something wrong and felt compelled to do something about it."

"So we need to find out what that was. Davey was vague,"

Nell said. "But that doesn't make sense to me. If she thought they were doing something corrupt or breaking laws, why not just call the police?"

The rhythmic clicking of knitting needles filled in the silence.

"Unless she wanted that information for another reason," Izzy said.

"Blackmail?" Cass tossed out.

No, they all agreed blackmail definitely didn't fit the profile they'd worked up for Sophia Santos.

Cass pulled out a knit hat and laid it on her lap, unfinished. She looked down at it and smiled. It was a colorful combination of brilliant wool yarns.

Nell looked over. "Cass, what is that?"

"It's the fish hat I told you about. I found it on knitty.com. I love it." The mouth of the fish had a bright red border, a hole where someone's face would eventually go. On the sides, fins flapped out in bright green and yellow yarn.

Izzy laughed. "Great hat, Cass. We need to put one in the shop."

"I was going to give them to the guys Pete and I fish with—the ones who have traps near ours. But I had a genius thought the other night. I'll make three fish hats and give them to the Fractured Fish. And then we'll force the trio to put on a winter concert at which, of course, they will wear them. Won't Pete look great in this?"

They all laughed, welcoming the diversion, not to mention the entertaining image of Pete Halloran, Merry Jackson, and Andy Risso playing "Jingle Bells" onstage, their faces ringed with the mouths of their fish hats.

"Time for tart," Nell said, and quickly slipped the slender slices on plates. She talked while she passed them around, picking up the discussion about Sophia.

"There's one thing Sophia did that we've never paid any attention to, and maybe we should. Remember the night of the yacht club party when she came over to our table to insist that Gracie talk to her the next day? Even at the time it seemed a little odd to me. It was like an order, and Sophia was usually so gracious that it seemed an un-Sophia-like thing to do."

"Gracie thought it was very weird."

"Did she say why?"

"I guess Sophia got her hair done at M.J.'s every single Saturday morning, without fail. She'd once canceled a trip to Argentina when she realized the departure was on her hair day. For her to cancel that appointment just to talk to Gracie simply wouldn't happen."

"But it did—or was supposed to. Which must mean it was very important to Sophia."

"Urgent."

"I wonder if Gracie can shed any light on it. Now, I mean," Nell said. "Looking back."

"She probably forgot it ever happened. But I'll see her later tonight. I'll ask. I wonder if Alphonso knew why Sophia wanted to see his niece that morning."

"Another thing Sophia did that still doesn't sit right with me," Birdie said. "Blocking the beach access. She went to considerable expense and effort to do that, and she infuriated the neighbors. Was that a whim? Why would she anger them like that for something that didn't seem so important? I never thought of Sophia as a cruel person—or someone who would want to alienate people."

"Unless she thought it was the *right* thing to do. Ella mentioned that she did it for her sister. It must have been important to her," Nell said. "Do you think it could have had something to do with her murder? Jake seems to have had other ways around it, ignoring her, for one."

"Ella," Cass and Izzy said together. "Ella might know. She worked hard to carry out Sophia's wishes after she died. She even put herself in danger. I thought Jake Risso was going to plow her down right along with those posts the night she tried to stop him."

"But Jake is off the hook. His way of fighting back wasn't mur-

209 • Moon Spinners

derous, thank heavens." She told them about the timing of the fire in Jake's restaurant.

"One more off our list. That's good," Birdie said.

"How would Sophia have reacted to Alphonso's having an affair?" Nell pulled out her sweater and picked up where she had left off. She smoothed out a row on her knees and absently ran a finger along the ribbing design running the length of the sweater.

"Sophia spent almost as much time as my mom does at Our Lady of the Seas—and adultery is considered pretty bad in the hierarchy of sins," Cass said. "I think she'd have been praying for Alphonso's soul, for starters."

Father Northcutt probably knew all about it, Nell thought. The affair, Sophia's anguish over it. She thought about Sophia lighting candles the way Mary Halloran did. It would be a blaze of light—half the candles lit for Cass to find a man, and half to beg for forgiveness for Alphonso.

"A divorce would have been hard for Sophia," Cass said.

"Even with a baby on the way?"

They fell silent then, wondering what would tip the scale for Sophia—the sanctity of marriage or a baby raised by its mother and father. They each had their own thoughts about it, their own inner voices that helped them make such decisions. But what would Sophia Santos have done? What would her inner voice have said?

"Maybe she didn't know about the baby. Do we know for sure that she did?" Cass asked. "Maybe she only knew about the affair, and she made it clear to Alphonso and Liz that there would be no divorce. But the two of them already knew Liz was pregnant, so it put them in a terrible bind without options. No divorce."

"Ella certainly doesn't like Alphonso, but I'm pretty sure she didn't know about the baby. Or even the affair, maybe," Birdie said. "Sophia was so private, but I guess we'll have to ask Ella when we can."

As if in answer to their questions, a cell phone rang.

"It's mine," Nell said, pulling her cell phone from her pocket.

She looked at the name, then whispered, "Ben," and pressed the talk button.

She listened for a minute. Her face lit up and she covered the phone and whispered, "Ella's awake. She's on heavy pain medication right now, but she's awake and talking." Nell turned her attention back to the phone while Ben continued.

"Oh, Ben." Her smile faded.

"When?"

The room grew silent as they waited for Nell to hang up. Finally, after extracting a promise from Ben to wait up for her, Nell closed the phone.

She looked at her three dear friends, sitting in a room crowded with as many questions as balls of yarn.

"Ella is doing fine. They'll cast her arm tomorrow when the swelling has gone down. She's eating liquids and bearing up under the discomfort as we knew she'd do. She is already wondering when she can leave."

"Go on," Birdie said. She spoke abruptly, knowing Nell was keeping something from them.

"She's her old self in some ways. Except for one important one. She doesn't remember anything that happened last night. Not a thing. The doctor said she has lost her short-term memory, not unusual with a blow to the head. The last thing she remembers is telling Harold to wash out his socks last Sunday night."

Chapter 27

*N*ell and Izzy had made arrangements the night before to meet early at Nell's and head for the beach before the swimmers, bodyboarders, and suntanners made their appearance.

Izzy was right on time.

"I haven't run all week," she said. She was bent over in the Endicott family room, her hands grabbing her ankles and pulling her body into an inverted U. She wore short Lycra running shorts and a black tank top. "We need it, Aunt Nell. It will clear out the cobwebs."

Nell slipped her cell phone into the pocket of her version of running shorts—nearly to the knees and loose to accommodate what seemed like a daily reshuffling of her body fat. An old Art at Night shirt fell low on her hips. "I don't know why you put up with me, Izzy. You'd get twice the workout if you didn't drag an old lady along beside you."

Izzy straightened up. "You will never be old." She frowned in an attempt to chastise her aunt.

Nell laughed and gave Izzy a quick hug. "Thanks, sweetie— music to my ears." Nell knew she'd gotten the luck of the draw when it came to genes that kept her reasonably trim, her skin taut, and enabled her to not worry about arms flapping like bat wings when she wore sleeveless tops. But she didn't fool herself, either. She was sixty-three and her body seemed to have a mind of its own. Running with Izzy—at a slower pace, of course—and lots of walking and occasional visits to the gym had become necessary parts of her routine.

They walked out the back door and down the deck steps to the deep yard behind the house. In the distance was the Endicott woods, as neighbors and guests had come to call it, and beyond that, the beach.

Just at the near edge of the woods was the guest house, which always made Izzy pause and wave. "Such happy, happy days," she said, looking over at the friendly gray cabin. "My first kiss was on that porch, right there, under the light."

"I thought it was out on the pier."

"Oh. There was one there, too." Izzy wrinkled her nose at Nell and tucked her arm in her aunt's.

They walked along the narrow, windy path, worn smooth by years of Endicotts making their way to the beach. The shade of giant hawthorns and pine trees quieted the air, heavy with the fragrance of sea, wild roses, and pine needles.

"Any news about Ella?" Izzy asked.

"Birdie said Harold called early and she's doing better this morning. She is headed over there now. She's driving the practical Corolla that has been sitting idle in one of the garages for a long time. The Lincoln will need some cosmetic surgery."

"I wonder why Ella didn't take the small car that night."

"Probably because Harold always used the big one, and at least she'd seen him drive it and could duplicate the movements."

"It's such a mystery why she would head out like that. And then to be hit by someone on top of it."

Nell was quiet. They walked across a narrow road to the beach and stopped at a bench to stretch.

"Okay, I've let you be quiet long enough. What are you thinking?" Izzy leaned over and pressed the flat of her hands into the sand. Her hair fell over her face and she tossed it aside, turning to the side to look up at Nell.

Nell braced one foot on the edge of the bench and stretched from her waist. "It's the hit-and-run scenario—it just doesn't ring true. Doesn't it seem strange that on an out-of-the-way road, someone would be barreling down and not see Ella struggling along the side of the road? Even though it was dark, she had on a bright white sweater—that little cap-sleeve sweater that Birdie knit her last year. Wouldn't the headlights have picked that up?"

Nell straightened and they began their slow run down the beach toward the breakwater, pondering the coincidences of life. And events that maybe just seemed that way.

The tide was low and they ran along the flat sand comfortably, Izzy matching her stride to Nell's.

The yacht club was alive with early-morning sailors headed toward their boats to check the sails and scrub down decks. Looking up at the expanse of windows that filled the whole backside of the club, Nell thought of Liz, working there each day, being lauded for her competence. And she thought of Liz's mother, Annabelle, and how hard it must be to have a murder shadowing the birth of her first grandchild.

It shouldn't be this way, she thought. It should be a joyous time for all the Palazolas. And for all his indiscretion, she supposed it should be a happy time for Alphonso Santos, too. It was his first child, after all, a fact that was easy to forget both because of circumstance, and because he was nearly sixty.

Up ahead, where the club beach ended and a bank of rocks heralded the beginning of the breakwater, they spotted a familiar figure sitting on a rock, looking out toward the horizon. She wore running shorts and a tee.

"It's Gracie," Izzy said, and started to call out a greeting as they came closer.

At that moment, a man emerged from behind a pile of rocks and walked toward Gracie. His broad back was to Izzy and Nell, and at first they didn't recognize him in shorts and a T-shirt. He lifted one foot onto the rock beside Gracie and leaned in, his words private.

Gracie frowned and moved back against the rock. But the man moved with her, touching her arm as he leaned closer.

"Stop it, Davey," Nell and Izzy heard Gracie say as they came within earshot.

"It's not my fault. You just don't get it, do you, Gracie?" The man's voice was louder now. "When are you going to start making good choices? When, huh?"

"Gracie?" Izzy called out, her hand waving as she sensed the tension ahead.

Nell was happy the gesture was made by Izzy. At this point breathing was her priority—gestures would be difficult while running. How Izzy did it was beyond her.

Davey Delaney stepped back and turned around. He frowned as Izzy and Nell came to a stop a few feet away. His brows pulled together in a stare that clearly accused them of meddling in someone else's business.

"Everything okay?" Izzy asked. Beside her, Nell took in a lungful of air.

Davey looked back at Gracie, glared at Nell and Izzy, and then, without a word, his large running shoes hit the sand and took him off in the opposite direction.

Gracie shook her head as she watched him disappear.

"What was that about?" Nell asked. She slipped onto the flat side of a boulder and wiped her forehead.

"It's okay. It's just Davey."

"He scares me, Gracie," Izzy said. "Are you sure you're okay?"

Gracie nodded. "He's harmless, I think. He just gets a little too friendly sometimes, you know? Touching me and saying things like that."

Nell frowned. "Does Joey know?"

"Not from me. There's enough bad blood between those two lately."

"What did he mean about something not being his fault?"

"He thinks he's being blamed for something, projects being

over budget or something, and doesn't want me to think poorly of him."

"He has an off way of gaining your favor, coming on to you like that," Izzy said.

Gracie shifted on the rock. "Enough about the Delaneys. Tell me about Birdie's housekeeper. I heard about the accident—how awful."

"I suppose everyone knows by now."

"It was in Mary Pisano's column."

"Then it's official—everyone knows." Izzy lifted her palms in the air.

"Mary had very harsh words for the person who drove off after injuring Ella. And she also scolded Ella, suggesting the Lincoln Town Car was simply too big a car for her and perhaps she should consider a small hybrid. It would be funny if it weren't so awful."

"We think Ella was doing her own detective work, trying to find Sophia's killer."

"It's nice, I guess, that people are on Julianne's side, thinking she's innocent. But awful that she put herself in danger like that." Gracie pulled up her knees and wrapped her arms around them. She looked out over the blue water, as if contemplating people's kindness to a mother who might not have done much to deserve it.

"Gracie," Nell said, pulling her back. "Remember when Sophia came over to our table at the yacht club that night?"

She nodded. "Cass brought it up last night. So much has happened that I'd forgotten about it."

"You can only hold so much in your head. It's understandable."

"She sounded urgent, that I remember—it was definitely not a 'let's get together for coffee' kind of invitation. She had left me a couple messages earlier that day, too, though we never connected. For some reason, Joey had decided it was a perfect day for a picnic and we spent a good part of the day over at Peach Cove, even though I had a ton of work to do at the restaurant."

"But you don't know what she was calling about?"

"No. But as I thought back on it, I remembered that Sophia had been acting strange for a couple of weeks. She had been in Boston for a few days, staying at their brownstone on Beacon Hill, and when she came back, she asked me to meet her for lunch because she wanted to tell me about it. I thought it was odd because we weren't exactly lunch friends. But then she canceled the lunch, saying she needed a couple more days."

"For what?" Izzy asked.

"My question exactly. I have no idea. And I don't really know what was so urgent the night she died. Cass, Joey, and I talked about it at the Palate last night. We threw out ideas and then picked them apart.

"Joey thought maybe she knew Julianne was going to show up that weekend, and she wanted to help me handle her, give me some advice. Maybe she had run into her in Boston?"

"I suppose that would have been semiurgent," Izzy said.

"Except it had never been an issue before. I never knew when my mother would show up. So why was it an issue now?"

They nodded, thinking, too, of the coveted hair appointment that had been canceled so she could meet with Gracie. Would an appearance from Julianne have merited that?

"Then one of us—Cass, maybe?—thought it could have been that my birthday's coming up, and she wanted to advise me of how to handle things."

"Advise you on how to handle your birthday?" Izzy wrinkled her forehead.

"No." Gracie laughed. "The trust Uncle Alphonso uses to pay Julianne would transfer to my name on my thirty-sixth birthday. It was in my grandparents' will. I just found out about it myself six months ago when the lawyers called a meeting."

"That's a huge responsibility," Nell said. What were her grandparents thinking to place such a responsibility on their grand-daughter? And how awful for Julianne, too. It was one thing to go to your older brother for money, quite another to be asking your child, however grown-up she might be.

"It's not that it's my money or for my use. This trust is only for Julianne—the lawyers were clear about that. There were other things in the will, but that's . . . that's not the issue here."

Gracie hesitated for a minute, then went on. "Anyway, I can't say I was looking forward to handling that. But now, now I guess I hope I get the chance."

They were quiet as the truth of the situation settled on them. If Julianne were sentenced to life in prison, she would have no need for money.

Nell broke the silence, not wanting to dwell on the dire possibility. "As I understand it, Sophia didn't think Alphonso always handled Julianne's allowance the way he should."

Gracie nodded. "And she didn't like the fact that Alphonso was losing control, that's true."

"I wonder why she felt so strongly about it. Julianne wasn't a blood relative and it wasn't her money—and from what you've said, it isn't yours either."

"That's the way Sophia was. She wasn't mean. But she had clear ideas on how things should be done. I honestly think Sophia thought it was her moral obligation to help my mother. And she thought one way to do it was to force her to grow up and get a job. Who knows? Maybe she was right."

"So her wanting to talk with you might not have had anything to do with her murder."

"I can't imagine it did, Nell. And the explanation seemed logical to all three of us. Everyone bought into it but Danny Brandley."

"Danny Brandley? Now where did he come from?"

"The next table over. He had his computer with him, typing away like there was no tomorrow. He's writing a novel, did you know that? Says he likes it better than his day job."

"So he joined you?"

"Not of his own free will. Cass went and got him." Gracie laughed as she recalled Cass' assertiveness. "I've never seen Cass like this. She really wants to get to know this guy better. All she remembers about him from high school is that he was the editor of the school newspaper when she was a lowly freshman, and he never gave her the time of day. She's determined that not happen again."

Nell was quiet. Danny Brandley was hiding something, and it was connected to Sophia Santos. And Sophia Santos had been murdered. The dots were too close for her to rest easy when his name was mentioned.

"Danny seems nice," Izzy said, glancing at Nell.

"He is," Gracie said. "He enjoyed talking to Joey. He said it was nice to meet a Delaney who didn't hate him."

"Who hates him? D.J.?"

"I guess Davey has something against him."

"What?" Nell asked.

"Who knows? I think they were in the same class in high school. Maybe Danny caught more touchdown passes. Davey is competitive. And a hothead, as you may have noticed."

"What does Joey say?" Izzy asked.

"Oh, he knows what Davey is like, but it's his brother, you know? So he doesn't say much. I think Davey always resented that Joey was smarter. He was like his mother, really good with figures. Davey tried to be but always messed up. He was better being the brawn, and Joey the brains."

Nell listened and wondered how Davey must have felt when Joey was also the one who got the girl. From the looks of things today, it might have been heartbreaking.

"What did Danny Brandley contribute to the conversation about Sophia?" she asked out loud. How would he have handled the conversation? As a stranger? Disinterested? Someone who had never heard of the woman? Or someone who might have known her well?

Gracie thought about the question for a minute, then said, "He was polite. He listened to the rest of us make all our suppositions and present our theories. Then he ordered drinks for all of us. But now that you ask, he didn't really say a word."

$\mathcal{N}$ell showered and slipped into a sleeveless blouse and cotton slacks, then joined Ben for a quick cup of coffee before heading to the hospital to check on Ella. She would pick up some flowers on the way and maybe some magazines from Archie's.

The run with Izzy had been a good jump start to the day, even though the encounter with Davey Delaney sent a shiver of fear up and down her spine. "He was almost menacing," she said to Ben.

"Probably because you showed up at a bad time. But Gracie knows him. If she's not afraid, it's probably okay."

He listened while Nell repeated the rest of the conversation they'd had about Sophia's request to see Gracie that Saturday.

"Do you think Sophia wanted to counsel Gracie on handling her mother's allowance?"

Ben took off his reading glasses and frowned. "Frankly, no. That wouldn't have been urgent. But the grandparents put quite a burden on Gracie, whether she'll need advice or not."

"I agree. I can't imagine her having to say no to her mother. Gracie indicated there were other things the lawyers laid out when they told her about this, but she hesitated to go into them."

Ben frowned. "I wonder what they were. I wonder if there was another provision in the will, one for Gracie? Alphonso said his parents were crazy about her. They were such planners—it seems they would have made sure she was taken care of too."

221 • *Moon Spinners*

Nell lifted her brows at the thought. "Perhaps . . ."

"But that still doesn't answer your question about why Sophia wanted to talk to her that next day."

"Here is my problem with it—and Izzy had the same concern. Would I cancel a hair appointment for something that could just as easily be done the day before or later that day or, frankly, at any time? Sophia knew about the will provision for six months—or at least Gracie did. Why was it so urgent she talk to Gracie about it that day? At that time? Hair appointments are hard to get, and Sophia anchored her calendar by hers."

"My barber gets me in on ten minutes' notice, Nell—so the appointment thing doesn't resonate with me. But I see your point. It doesn't sound like an urgent conversation—and not something she'd have to mention that night during a party." He looked over at Nell. "Okay, Nellie, I know that face. What are you thinking?"

Nell was silent. She tried to put herself in Sophia's shoes, then Gracie's. Then Sophia's again. Sophia cared about her niece. Did she know something about the restaurant that she had to warn Gracie about? The restaurant and her mother seemed to be the two big things going on in her life. And a divorce. A friendly divorce that might not even happen, from all appearances. The fire . . . could Sophia have suspected someone might be out to harm her niece?

Nell looked up, shrugged her shoulders, and sighed. "I think we're getting closer. I hope . . ." A niggling feeling—like a pesky gnat—rested just on the edge of her consciousness. It was irritating and real, and it was so small that none of them could see it.

Nell picked up Birdie and headed for the Gloucester hospital.

"Ella is remarkable," Birdie said. "Harold said she's in pain but quite brave and uncomplaining."

"As we would expect. I don't think I've ever heard Ella complain about anything."

"Until she met Sophia. Then she seemed to take a definite stand on things. I think Harold would argue with you mightily if you claimed she never complained."

Nell laughed. "But I think that might have been good for her. And good for Harold in the long run. They're two people, not one, and should act that way."

They found a parking place close to the main entrance and made their way to Ella's private room. It was so filled with flowers that at first they didn't see the slender woman sitting up against the white sheets, her arm in a cast.

"Ella," Birdie said, moving aside a giant bouquet of daffodils that sat on the tray table. "There you are."

"Can you believe these flowers?"

"Who are they from?"

"The whole town, that's who. People I never met, people I don't know. Archie at the bookstore and even the Garozzos. Can you imagine?"

Nell could. She remembered when Angus McPherran was in the hospital a couple years before—an old man who thought the town had passed him by. The same thing happened. People came out of the woodwork to help. And with Mary Pisano making sure everyone knew where—and who—Ella was, she became the astounded recipient of small-town generosity.

"They're beautiful. And you deserve them," Nell said.

"I'm not so sure of that, Mrs. Endicott."

"Now, don't you think we're beyond the 'Mrs.' Endicott? I think the dozens of years we've known each other merit a 'Nell,' don't you?"

Ella's smile was slow, and Nell suspected there were some pain medications making a smile even possible.

"Nell," she said. The word slipped across her lips. "I like that."

Harold limped into the room with a sack of bagels and his face lit up when he saw Birdie and Nell. "What do you think of my gal? Look at these flowers!"

Harold looked like a new man. The frown was gone. Almost losing someone you love can do that for you, Nell thought.

"Miss Birdie," Ella said, her eyes widening. "About your car—Harold won't talk to me about it. But the doctor said I was driving a car. That's impossible."

"The car will be fine, and you will be fine." Birdie moved to the side of the bed and kissed Ella lightly on the forehead. "And yes, I would have said it was impossible two days ago. But you have done the impossible, Ella. Twice. First, driven the car. And second, lived to tell about it. It must have taken something mighty important to get you into that old Lincoln."

A frown added to the wrinkles creasing Ella's brow. Her head moved across the prop of pillows behind her. "I . . . I simply can't remember clearly. It was Wednesday, Harold said. I keep saying to myself, 'Wednesday, what was Wednesday?'

"And I was driving a car. I don't even like cars, except to get me to church and to the store." Ella looked out the second-story hospital window, out across the treetops, her mind wandering. "Sophia didn't like cars either, especially the fancy red car."

She sounded as if she were talking to herself, unaware of others in the room. Nell looked over at Harold. Instead of his jaw setting, his eyes narrowing, Nell saw a husband in love with his wife. Listening to her carefully.

"He gave it to her because he had hurt her," Ella went on. "As if a car would help a wound so deep." Ella sat up slightly, then winced as she moved her arm unintentionally. She settled back but her eyes were still seeing something beyond the windows that the rest of them were not privy to.

"Sophia loved sitting in a hammock, not a car. Never a car." She listened to the rustling of the treetops, as if imagining her friend swaying in a hammock beneath the branches, peaceful, her eyes closed. "If only she could have died in a hammock," she murmured to herself.

She fell asleep, and Birdie and Nell took Harold down to the cafeteria for a cup of coffee.

Stella met them at the elevator. "How's she doing today?"

"Sleeping," Harold said.

"I'll go sit with her until you come back. Just in case she wakes up," Stella said.

"Such a good girl," Harold said as the elevator doors closed.

"Yes, she is, Harold. And don't you forget it," Birdie said.

Harold confessed he hadn't eaten yet that day, and they insisted he fill a plate, then sit with them. Stella would take care of things nicely.

"So has she remembered anything, Harold?"

"She drifts off some, talks about some things that don't make sense. But the past three or four days seem to be lost to her," Harold said between bites of a hamburger and omelet, both piled together on a plate. French fries were stacked on the side. "Ella doesn't let me eat these," he confessed and dug into the fries happily.

"Did she do anything remarkable those days that you remember?"

"Just the usual—the things she's been doing since her friend died. Walking. And reading that book."

"What book?" Nell asked.

"It was poetry, Ella said. Sophia's book."

Nell and Birdie looked at each other over Harold's head as he dug into a bacon omelet covered with melted cheese.

Sophia's poetry book?

When they returned to Ella's room, Stella was holding a glass of water and a straw, helping steer it to her patient's mouth. "Ella's scolded me so I know she's on the road to recovery."

"I don't scold you," Ella retorted.

"Ella, you have been scolding Stella since the day she walked into my house," Birdie countered.

Ella sat back and looked from Stella to Birdie, then back again. Her eyes filled with tears.

"What? What's that face, Ella?" Stella asked. "Now I'm, like, making you cry?" She handed her a tissue. "Geesh."

Ella took it and dabbed at her eyes. "Birdie is right. I was downright nasty to you. I couldn't take it out on the people I should have. Not your sister, not Alphonso. And I thought maybe somehow, maybe you helped her, maybe you were somehow to blame, at least a little bit, because she was your sister . . ."

"Oh, Ella, I am as mad at Liz as you are. It's, like, awful, what they did. It wasn't fair to Sophia, so sleazy. But it's done. It's over. And Liz is my sister. I love her, you know?"

"We never know the whole story, everything that goes on between people, do we?" Birdie mused.

"Ella," Nell asked, "do you think that Liz and Alphonso had anything to do with Sophia's murder?" Nell realized it might not be delicate asking that question in front of Stella. But it was on all their minds. She thought she knew the answer, and getting it out in the open would be a good thing.

The silence went on for seconds longer than was comfortable, and Harold finally got up and moved over to Ella's side. "Do you need another pill, Ella?"

She shook her head, then turned toward Nell. "I don't know," she said finally. "At first I was sure Alphonso killed her. I wanted it to be him because I hated him so. Sophia never talked about Liz to me, but I knew her feelings about divorce."

"So she didn't tell you about the affair?" Stella asked.

"No. Sophia didn't tell me things like that. Intimate things."

"Then how did you know?"

"I saw them. Sophia went to Argentina to visit her family. I was missing her, and I went walking in the woods where we would sometimes talk. They came driving up to the house in that red car—he had just bought it. At first I didn't know who was with Alphonso. I couldn't see and thought maybe Sophia had come home early. I was excited, and I started out across the clearing. And then I saw them, her blond hair. She was crying, and he was holding her so close I don't know how she could breathe."

"Did they see you?"

"Not at first. But then Alphonso heard me, and he looked up—and that's when I saw who it was. I turned and ran away."

"Did you tell Sophia what you saw?" Birdie asked.

"I didn't know what to do. So I talked to Father Northcutt about it in the confessional. What was the right thing to do? Sophia was so proud, I don't know if we could have been friends after that if I had told her. Father Larry agreed. So I didn't tell her."

But Alphonso wouldn't have known that, Nell thought. So he probably told her himself. And gave her a brilliant red Ferrari, one that Liz Palazola would never sit in again.

She wondered if Ella had told anyone else about the affair. She was such a quiet woman, and wouldn't have done it to spread gossip. There was the anonymous caller that Esther had told them about, someone who had sounded strangely like Ella Sampson.

"Ella, the police said someone called them about Alphonso's . . . well, his relationship . . ."

"I was so angry," Ella blurted out, the sudden pinking of her cheeks a contrast to the rest of her pale body. "I thought they should know."

Nell looked over at Stella. She was a mixture of emotions. Nell hoped that mixed up in them was understanding for her sister. Birdie was right. You never knew it all, only what you could see from the outside looking in.

"You're thinking about Atticus Finch again, aren't you?" Birdie said after they said their good-byes and walked down to the parking lot.

"A mixture of Birdie Favazza and Atticus Finch, you might say."

Birdie took her arm. "There isn't a smidgen of what I know about Liz Palazola that makes me think she brought on the affair or encouraged it. Maybe neither of them did. Who knows how these things go? Who knows what Alphonso and Sophia's marriage was like, or if she was really heartbroken about the breakup?"

"Sometimes things happen," Nell agreed. "Even when they shouldn't."

"You live with them, make the best of it."

"And pray to God they don't lead to murder."

Chapter 29

*N*ell drove up the long Favazza driveway and pulled the car to a stop while Birdie climbed out. She was almost to the door when Nell rolled down her window and rested her arms on the frame.

"Birdie," she called out, "I was wondering where the Lincoln is."

"With its adopted father—Shelby Pickard, the best mechanic in town."

"At his garage?"

"Yes. It has quite a bruise on its front bumper. Lots of scratches. Shelby will nurse it back to health, and no one will be the wiser. He's fixed a couple of my own inflicted scratches and dents from time to time. Why?"

"Harold mentioned that Ella had Sophia's book with her when she left the house."

"The poetry book?"

"It sounds like that's the one. If Sophia wrote poetry in the book, maybe she wrote other things, too. Sometimes I do that in my own journal—I'll write short essays or thoughts or work through problems by writing them down. If I want to remember something, I might jot that down, a name, an address."

"So you think Sophia might have done that?"

"It's possible."

"And if she had the book with her, it could be in my car."

"Again, it's possible."

"The police gave me a handful of things they found at the accident—Ella's smashed cell phone and her sweater—but they wouldn't have emptied the car out." She checked her watch. "I'm teaching a tap class at the retirement home at three. I'll run by Shelby's after that and if we can find it, I'll bring it with me to dinner tonight—along with a fine sauvignon blanc that I brought up from the wine cellar this week." With a wave she disappeared inside.

Thankfully Friday cookouts were as much Ben's doing as hers, and he'd be sure to have the coals, ice, and martini fixings ready. The chunks of tuna for the kabobs were already swimming in marinade, and she'd find everything else she needed with a quick stop at the store.

Nell headed down Harbor Road toward the market, stopping at the red light. But when it changed, Nell made a detour.

Afterward she wouldn't be able to explain to Ben why she'd done it.

Maybe it was the realization that Julianne Santos had been in jail an awfully long time. And calm or not, it wasn't a very pleasant place to be.

She'd have to stop at the Seaside Knitting Studio first, but with a little input from Izzy, she'd be on her way in no time.

A hat, Izzy had insisted. It would be the perfect project. But it had to be a pretty one, a happy hat. They found a pattern for the perfect one, an easy roll-brim hat. And Purl herself decided the yarn by leaping into a basket of cashmere wool blends that came in glorious colors. Purl nuzzled her head down, then looked up as if to say, "So? I'm right, aren't I?"

They picked out a brilliant orange yarn with a rich pink accent. Nell tucked the yarn and pattern, along with the needles, into a canvas bag Izzy donated to the cause, and Nell was set to go.

At the door Izzy stopped her with a hand on her aunt's arm.

"What, sweetie?" Nell asked, her brows lifting. She thought she had everything she needed. She looked down at the bag.

But Izzy just shook her head, and then she wrapped her aunt in a fierce hug and sent her on her way.

She hadn't checked jail times, but they hadn't moved Julianne from the local jail yet, and she was confident that if Tommy Porter hadn't arrested her for speeding along Harbor Road the other night, he wouldn't put up too much of a fuss over visiting hours. Besides, she knew Esther Gibson had the Friday shift. None of the men on the force would dare say no to Esther.

A medium-sized woman with blond streaks in her salt-and-pepper hair was walking down the steps as Nell approached the stone building. She looked Nell directly in the eyes, as one would a friend, and smiled. For a second Nell thought it was someone she knew—the smile was welcoming. But then, with a slight, knowing tilt of her head, the woman continued on down the steps.

Nell watched her walk to the parking lot, then disappear from sight. No, it wasn't anyone she knew. But perhaps someone she would like to know.

The visitors' room, as they called the small room behind the front desk, was in use, so after Nell explained to a gleeful Esther what she was about to do, a uniformed woman with a gun in her belt led Nell directly to Julianne Santos' cell.

"Hello, Nell," Julianne said. She had been sitting at a desk, writing, and stood when the guard ushered Nell inside.

Nell started to say hello, then on impulse, replaced the words with a hug. Julianne hugged her back.

"This is nice. Two visitors in one day." Julianne offered Nell the chair and sat down on the side of her narrow bed.

Julianne looked like she had a lost a few pounds, but it only enhanced her beauty, and without the haze of drink or drugs, her eyes were bright and clear. And she seemed eerily calm. Nell had the feeling that if the president or pope had walked in, they would have received the same warm, unsurprised greeting. No exaggerated fuss, no embarrassment over her surroundings, just pleasure in receiving a guest.

"How's Gracie?"

"She's holding up. Gracie is a strong, lovely woman. I hope you get to know that firsthand when all this is over."

Julianne didn't answer, but seemed to savor the thought.

"Here. I brought you something. This keeps me sane, and I thought it might do the same for you." Nell pulled the yarn and pattern from the bag. "Izzy helped me pick out this hat for you to knit."

Julianne reached out and fingered the soft yarn. The pleasure of it was reflected in her face. "This is wonderful. Thank you. I haven't knit since I was young. I'm not sure I remember."

"Problem solved. Esther Gibson is one of the most accomplished knitters in town. She's promised to help you work through any snags along the way."

"Esther is wonderful. She brings me books and spends her breaks talking with me. And she also lets me call Gracie or Mandy if I want to. I think she bends the rules for me a bit."

"Now you can chat about knitting and purling. Our hope is that you will start the hat now—and finish it sitting on the deck of the Lazy Lobster and Soup Café on a bright summer day."

"How is the café coming along?"

"Everyone's pitching in. It's going to be a wonderful little place." A pleased look washed across Julianne's face, hearing about her daughter's efforts, so Nell continued, embellishing the conversation with paint colors, a description of the fireplace, the wooden tables and booths, and the deck that families would eat on, enjoying Pete and Cass' lobsters, served by Gracie's own staff.

Julianne hung on every word.

"Joey has been helping Gracie a lot," Nell added.

"Joey," Julianne repeated. "He's been here to see me a few times. He says Gracie is happy. It sounds like he still loves her."

"Would that please you?"

Julianne didn't answer for a few minutes. When she did, her voice was soft. "I don't have a right to even have an opinion. That's the sad truth, Nell." She shifted on the bed and looked out the small barred window. A single stream of sunlight fell across her knees. "I wasn't around much those few years they were married—but I kept in touch when I had my wits about me. They had a wonderful landlord who became my friend and filled me in on things. It wasn't easy for them, Mandy—my friend—told me. Joey was gone most of the time. Mandy was Gracie's salvation, I think. She kept her company, kept her spirits up. Let her talk."

"The first years of marriage are an adjustment."

"Especially so for Gracie. I've read every child psychology book that Esther Gibson can dig up for me, and I know it must have been difficult for Gracie to trust anyone. She'd been abandoned—and the books say that makes trusting people very hard. And then, in a way, Joey abandoned her because of his job."

"They were married three years?"

"Almost four. When they separated last year, Joey moved back here into one of his father's condos over near Rockport. Gracie stayed in Gloucester until her lease was up. I don't think they even bothered splitting things up. Joey seemed glad to get away, and Gracie was glad to see him go. Or at least that was Mandy's take on it. I saw Gracie that Christmas—we were together briefly for a family meeting. Gracie seemed okay, and was putting her life together."

Julianne fingered the yarn as she talked, pressing a skein against her smooth skin. "This is beautiful, Nell. Thank you."

"It will look lovely on you." Nell shifted on the chair, wondering how Julianne could sleep in the tiny cell. But there was a peace around her that seemed sincere. Maybe she slept just fine. Something had happened to Gracie's mother during the short time she'd spent in the Sea Harbor jail. Perhaps she had been priming herself for some life change. The confinement brought it into focus.

But good or bad, the jail time needed to be short-lived, of that Nell was sure.

Later, Nell thought it might have been that sense of peace and acceptance that made her ask the next question. She didn't think she would upset Julianne, and she knew her answer, whatever it might be, would be honest.

Nell leaned forward, her elbows on her knees, and looked into Julianne's clear eyes.

"Do you have any idea who might have killed Sophia? Or why? You may have known her better than some of us."

Julianne stared at her hands in her lap. She gave Nell's question careful consideration. Finally she said, "I think that when pressed, most of us could kill. If I thought someone was going to hurt Gracie in a terrible way, I think I could kill them.

"So the question, I think, is what had Sophia done or threatened to do that would hurt or frighten or enrage someone enough for them to kill her? Whose life was about to change in an awful way because of her? That's the person who killed her."

Nell listened carefully. This was not the dazed, angry Julianne she had seen in recent weeks. This woman sitting in front of her on a hard jail chair spoke from her heart, with clarity and wisdom.

"Had Sophia done something that severe to me that I would kill her?" Julianne asked out loud. "She made it difficult for me to get money from my brother—and I hated that she had that power over him. But that was all going to change in a few weeks, so it wouldn't make logical sense that I would kill her because of that."

"What was going to change?"

"On Gracie's thirty-sixth birthday she'll receive her inheritance from my parents—they adored Gracie. She'll have control over the other part of the will, too, so Alphonso doesn't have to worry about that."

"So you know about all that."

"We had a meeting about it months ago. Very hush-hush. My parents were peculiar in many ways, and managing money—though I am certainly not one to speak—was one of them.

"But as you can see, my motive for killing my brother's wife is now reduced to the fact that I didn't like her. And you can see where that disastrous logic leads."

They sat in silence for a moment. Nell was stunned. Julianne spoke with the clarity of a judge. And she was absolutely right.

"One curious piece of this puzzle is why someone wants the police to think I did it."

"What do you mean?"

"Someone put incriminating evidence in my car. Books about car mechanics and some tools that would be useful in tampering with brakes. Even some pages printed off the Internet."

Nell had almost forgotten that the trunk of Julianne's car gave the police the last bit of evidence they thought they needed to arrest her. "When do you think the evidence was planted?"

"It had to have been shortly after Sophia died. That night I went to Gloucester to see Mandy—the landlady in Gloucester that I told you about. She'd become a good friend and she loved Gracie.

"When I got there that night I took my backpack out of the trunk, and if there'd been books in there I would have seen them, even in the state I was in. The next day my car wouldn't start—it was on its last leg, so Mandy said I could just leave it there and she loaned me a motorbike to use. I never used the car again. It stayed there until the police came, opened the trunk, then towed it away. But I know one thing for sure—I had never seen any of those things in my life until the police opened the trunk that day."

"Do you have any idea why someone would do that to you?"

Julianne's soft laugh was sad, but it lacked the bitterness Nell might have expected. "Oh, Nell, you are a sweet woman." She leaned over and touched Nell's hand, then sat back on the bed. "I haven't been a very nice person for a long time. I didn't endear myself to people much. And I didn't care. I'm sure there are dozens of people who wouldn't mind me being blamed for Sophia's murder. I couldn't begin to list the people that I've hurt. Gracie and Alphonso just happen to be the only ones I care about."

Chapter 30

$\mathcal{N}$ell drove away from the Sea Harbor jail with Esther's promise that she'd keep an eye on Julianne.

"She'll be out of here soon," Esther had said. "Mark my words. No one in their right mind could possibly think that gentle lady killed Sophia Santos, and that's exactly what I served up for the chief today, along with his doughnuts. Julianne's on her way to being a fine lady. And once we get her knitting, she'll be better than fine."

Nell certainly hoped so. Julianne had left a trail of hurt behind her, but if there was such a thing as redemption, she was a poster child for it.

A soft wind blew through the open window of her car as Nell headed home, following a slow-moving line of traffic. Her thoughts moved from Julianne to Harold and Ella, and the toll the last days had taken on them. Poor Harold. So distraught over his wife's friendship with Sophia that he did crazy things. But how crazy?

Nell imagined him driving the Lincoln back from the club that night—a car nearly everyone knew—worried Ella would find out what he'd done. Would anyone remember seeing the car that night? But even if someone did, would they remember what time they saw it? Nell neared Harbor Road and a sudden thought struck her. She turned in the opposite direction from home, and drove slowly toward Birdie's house.

And there he was, poised for duty at the corner of Elm and Harbor, his uniform nicely ironed and his motorcycle polished to a high sheen. She waved and pulled up across the street from him.

Tommy Porter took off his dark glasses, recognized who it was, and pulled his motorcycle to the other side of the street. "How's it going, Mrs. Endicott? Saw you driving mighty fast down here the other day . . ."

"Bless you, Tommy. Sometimes it's best to look the other way."

"Seemed you were on a mission."

"Say, Tommy, I see you at this spot often. Were you on duty here the night of Sophia Santos' murder?"

"Okay, okay, I know what you're going to say. But I had to do it."

"Go on," Nell said, not at all sure what was coming next.

"He was going plenty fast. Like a bat out of you-know-where. He said Ella would kill him if he didn't get home fast. But I only gave him a warning. I knew he didn't want Miss Birdie to know about it. Mr. Sampson is a nice guy. He just shouldn't drive so fast."

"Do you remember what time it was?"

"It was just getting dark. I remember because he had dark glasses on, and I told him he should take them off."

"So around eight would you say?"

"Couldn't have been much later, because I went back to the station for a break after I sent him along home."

Nell thanked Tommy profusely. "You're one fine policeman, Tommy Porter. Someday you may be chief." She started her engine, waved, and drove on down Harbor Road.

Harold Sampson could be crossed off their list, thanks to a conscientious policeman issuing a warning to slow down. Bless Tommy Porter.

Nell drove off, then pulled into the parking lot of the market. She found an empty parking space and called Ben. Sometimes repeating odd thoughts to Ben was like unwinding a skein of yarn and neatly winding it into a ball. With the loops taken out, it was smoother, easier to work with. Certainly easier to knit back into a pattern.

Ben listened as Nell divested herself of the conversation with Julianne. He asked a question here or there, and then he promised to mull it over as he lit his coals and iced down the martini glasses. But only if she'd run into the market and pick up some spicy mustard and a jar of toothpicks.

The supermarket was busy. The day had been too perfect not to finish it off with a barbecue on the deck or a beach picnic. The aisles were crowded with people planning to do exactly that. Watermelons and buns and bags of charcoal were flying off the shelves as Nell hurried down the condiment aisle.

Davey Delaney saw Nell before she saw him. Had it been reversed, Nell might have chosen a different aisle. But as it happened, they met face-to-face in front of the pickle section, just before an assortment of ketchups and mustards.

"Nell, I was outta line the other day."

"Davey," she said. "Nice to see you. And yes, you were." Nell noticed he had one of the small carts. Just a few items—potato chips, a carton of ice cream, some hot dog buns.

"We always forget something," he said, shrugging his broad shoulders.

"I understand. I'm battling this crowd for a simple jar of mustard."

"But here's the deal. Sure, I have a temper. But people should mind their own business and let us Delaneys run ours."

"Davey, I'm not sure what . . ."

Davey's voice rose a few decibels, and a woman with a toddler in a cart frowned at him. She hurried by with her crowded cart.

"It's the snooping and poking around, and trying to see our books and Lord knows what all, it's all that. People need to just leave it alone. Leave us alone! And if they don't—"

Nell watched the flush crawling up his neck and heading for his cheeks and forehead. The now-familiar pulse in his temple began to throb.

"If they don't, Davey, then what?"

She spotted the mustard Ben wanted and picked it off the shelf.

"If they don't . . ." Davey tightened his jaw, clamped his mouth closed, then opened it again. "If they don't, then they just might find themselves in a heap of trouble, that's what. Bad trouble."

And for the third time that week, Davey Delaney turned away from Nell, this time with a small grocery cart that spun around beneath his powerful grip, crashed into a cardboard display of spaghetti seasonings, and rattled toward the front of the store.

Nell hoped he was heading home. His ice cream was beginning to melt.

"He starts out calm, almost sweet, and then this anger rises in him, Ben. It's a little scary."

"Maybe we're being too critical of him." Ben opened the freezer and took out some ice. "I think sometimes Maeve is hard on him. She wants him to act more refined. But he's a D.J. clone. He's more comfortable drinking beer on the deck than tea in the parlor, and there's nothing wrong with that. And he could do worse than follow in his dad's footsteps. D.J.'s not such a bad sort—I don't suppose Davey is either."

Nell took napkins and silverware from drawers and piled them on the island. She leaned back against the counter and took a sip of her wine. "It's easy for you to say that. You haven't been the object of his ire this week like I have been. Twice. And in the middle— when we saw him trying to put a move on Gracie—the look he gave Izzy and me wasn't friendly."

The sound of voices distracted her, and she turned to greet Izzy, Sam, and Birdie, walking across the room, their arms filled with bags.

"Wine, a new pattern book from Interweave, and a single skein of the most amazing yarn in the world," Izzy announced.

"And a journal," Birdie said triumphantly. She set a green leather volume down on the kitchen island. "And my thanks for discovering Harold's airtight alibi. I knew all along that sweet man couldn't hurt a fly, but I'll forever love Tommy Porter for giving us proof."

Nell looked down at the teal-green book. It was larger than most journals, a size that would stick out of a purse. Which is exactly where she'd seen it before.

"I saw this the day of Sophia's wake," she said. "Ella was coming downstairs with it. She must have gone up to Sophia's bedroom while Alphonso was greeting people and taken it."

"She probably needed something of Sophia's. She was so sad, and Alphonso wouldn't think to give her anything," Birdie said. "He'd probably have sent it all off to Goodwill, just like he did her car."

Nell touched the cover with the tip of her finger. It was soft, expensive leather, and the heavy pages were edged in gold.

"Ella is probably the only one who will appreciate it—much of it is written in Spanish. I took Spanish a hundred years ago but could only make out a word or two."

Spanish. Nell sighed. She wasn't sure what she thought the journal might tell them. Maybe hints into why Sophia was pursuing the Delaneys with such a vengeance. Her edginess the last weeks of her life. Small notes offering bits of insight? She put the book on the counter to keep it out of harm's way and took a platter of cheese and fruit out of the refrigerator.

"Where are Cass and Gracie?" Nell asked. "Is Pete coming? Willow?"

"Cass had a stop to make. Gracie had to talk to Joey about some things but might be by later. I think maybe she's decided to tell Joey what a jerk his brother is. And Pete and Willow came up the back steps while you were talking about the journal. They're on the deck with the martinis."

"Which is where we should all be, dears," Birdie said. "Come."

Izzy plugged her iPod into the dock. Sounds of Earth Wind and Fire poured from the speakers, and she danced her way out to the deck behind the others, her fingers pointing toward the moon.

The smell of hot coals, even before the ginger-spiced kabobs sizzled on the grill, was intoxicating. As Ben handed out icy martinis, one by one, with the thinnest layer of ice floating on top, Nell relaxed, perhaps for the first time that day. She looked up at the sky. The moon spinners were working their nightly magic, winding the strands of moonlight onto their distaffs, moving the world toward darkness. Providing protection in the darkness, or so the legend went. Nell sipped her drink, looking up. Protection in the darkness. Is that what they sought? When the light was pulled down and spun, would they all be safe and their summer whole again?

For this moment, she would let the moon spinners do their work. She'd let go of her concerns and savor laughter and voices spinning around her of those she loved.

Cass still hadn't arrived when Ben began filling plates with chunks of skewered Vidalia onion, peppers, and the juicy tuna. Crisp asparagus in a citrus sauce and quinoa with cranberries and almonds filled plates to the brim.

Pete had already gone back for seconds when the sound of Cass' battered Chevy pickup finally chugged its way to the front of the house.

"That truck's not long for this world," Pete said, glancing toward the noise.

Voices drifted up to the deck as Cass walked along the side of the house on the flagstone walkway.

Nell looked up. Cass wasn't alone. Behind her, his shadow stretching across the lawn, was Danny Brandley.

A chorus of voices greeted them.

"You're late."

"You're here."

"Wow."

The last was from Willow and directed toward Cass' slinky sundress. Her black hair fell loose around tan, bare shoulders, a far cry from her usual cutoffs, baseball cap, and T-shirt.

Cass silenced her with a look.

"Hi, everyone." Danny walked up the steps behind Cass, smiling at the group. He spotted Ben and Nell and walked their way, looking slightly embarrassed. "Cass said this would be all right?"

"Of course," Nell said. "The Brandleys are always welcome."

"I thought we should call first." He looked back at Cass. "But she's one determined woman."

"That's putting it mildly," Sam said. "Watch yourself, Danny. Ask any lobster in town—she's tenacious."

They laughed, and the tension Nell felt when she saw Danny walk up the steps began to ease. It was her home; Danny was her guest. Perhaps there was an explanation for his actions—and for his not being honest. In any case, she and Ben never made a guest feel less than welcome, and Danny wouldn't be an exception. Even though she would prefer him kept at arm's length—both her arm and Cass'.

The others welcomed Danny warmly. Cass fixed heaping plates of food for each of them, and Nell watched them settle in, Danny like an old shoe. She had to admit he was likable. But liars could be likable—when you didn't know they were lying. And Danny had lied about knowing a woman who was murdered. Why?

"How long are you staying around, Danny?" Ham asked. "A summer stay—even a week—can hook a guy. Take Sam here."

"It's true," Sam said. "One summer here and I was sold on the place."

Izzy walked over and straddled the arm of Sam's chair. She looped an arm around his neck. "Okay, Perry, admit it. It wasn't just the sea and the beach and the sailing that kept you here."

"No." Sam rubbed his head against her arm and looked up with teasing eyes. "These Friday nights on the Endicott deck are worth moving across continents for."

The group laughed as Izzy pretended a stranglehold.

"So, okay," Cass said, "the folks here are asking you questions, Danny. A good guest would answer them. How long are you staying?"

"That's probably why she brought you. She knew we'd interrogate you the way she wants to, and she'll come off smelling like a rose." Izzy passed Danny a martini.

Danny laughed at the gentle teasing, comfortable and relaxed. He held his martini in the air, examining the color, the light shining through the thin glass, the chilled stem. "Made by a master. Wonderful."

"You're getting off track, Danny," Cass said.

Danny tugged on a lock of Cass' hair. "I'm not sure what I'll do. I'm a reporter of sorts—mostly freelance stuff, special-assignment kind of jobs. But I'm working on a novel, too, and wishing I had more time for it. I guess you'd say that's my obsession. I just quit a reporting assignment I'd started so I could spend more time on it."

"What kind of novel?" The question was a chorus from Willow, Birdie, and Cass, all leaning slightly forward in their chairs.

Danny took a taste of Ben's martini and smiled in appreciation. "It's hard to talk about a novel before it's been exposed to real life and hard knocks. When no one, like an agent, has had the chance to tell you that you should never, ever admit to writing such drivel. But I did get a nibble from someone who expressed interest in representing it. It's got one foot out of the cradle, I guess you'd say. So maybe it's okay to talk about it."

"It's okay," Cass assured him.

"A mystery. Suspense. The protagonist is a loner but has a love interest. He lives on the ocean. Does a lot of sailing."

"Sailing?" Sam and Ben looked up.

Danny nodded. "I never won the Sea Harbor regatta when I was a kid, but never gave up that dream. So maybe I can give it another try in a book."

"Does the love interest die?" asked Cass, pulling Danny back on topic. Then she added plaintively, "Please don't have her die."

No, please don't have her die, Nell thought. They'd had enough of dying. For one shining night, they had been able to back-burner it a little. And as much as she hated to admit it, Danny Brandley was partly the reason.

The sky deepened to a midnight black, and the music switched to a mellow sound track from *Something's Gotta Give*. Izzy and Sam poured coffee while Ben got out some brandy. Birdie served up heaping slices of rhubarb pie.

And Danny Brandley made huge inroads into the circle of friends sitting on the Endicott deck.

Nell took the last remaining plate into the kitchen and stood at the window for a minute, listening to the chatter and laughter floating through the open window, thanking her blessings, as she often did at such moments.

They had talked a little about Julianne Santos before dessert was passed around. Nell told about her trip to the jail. But the mood kept moving them away from it, to lighter conversation. Tomorrow, she thought. Tomorrow they would regroup and get Julianne Santos out of that tiny cell. And she was beginning to flesh out a direction they could all take.

"Am I interrupting?"

Startled, Nell spun around. Danny Brandley stood at the island, watching her. He set down two empty bowls he'd carried in. In his other hand, he held a glass of Ben's special brandy. "That was a terrific dinner. Thanks for making room for me."

"Of course. We always have plenty."

"Do you have a minute?"

Nell motioned to the stools. "Please—sit."

"I sense something's going on between us, Nell. Do we need

to clear the air? If I've offended you, I'd like to hear about it and at least have a chance to apologize."

That was a fair request. Nell had a list of things that bothered her about Danny Brandley, beginning with his denial of knowing Sophia even though he'd spent weeks with the family, not to mention a recent rendezvous in Sea Harbor.

"Maybe I'll start," Danny said. "I think it involves the Santoses. I indicated that I didn't know Sophia. But you saw the article at the bookstore. My dad told me—proudly—that you were looking at it."

"That's a good place to begin."

"I spent a lot of time with them when I was writing that piece. But when I'd finished the story, I felt I knew Sophia about as well as I know the guy who sells me shoes at Macy's. So I didn't know her. Not really. That part was true, if a bit deceptive."

Nell could identify with his explanation. "Someone saw you picking Sophia up from the high school shortly before she died."

Danny's brows lifted. "Ah, small-town living," he said sardonically. "I'd almost forgotten."

"It has its ups and downs." Nell smiled.

Danny was quiet for a minute, as if fashioning his reply. He answered slowly. "Sophia heard about a series the *Globe* was doing on the construction industry. She was adamant that Delaney & Sons be on our list. She was a source, in a way. We don't like to put people in danger; it's not what we do. So I hedged, out of habit, I guess.

"Anyway, I came and talked to her—it was a good opportunity to see Mom and Dad. She suggested I pick her up at the school that day. She didn't want Alphonso to know about it—he didn't like meddling in Delaney's business, or anyone else's for that matter. But Sophia had an ax to grind, I can tell you that."

"How would Sophia have inside information about the Delaneys and faulty construction?"

"It wasn't about faulty construction, per se. She was more interested in their billings. She was convinced the Delaney books would show creative accounting, as she put it. She thought they were funneling money to a fake company—or one not really doing work."

"Do you know why?"

"No. She wouldn't say. But she was sure we'd find something. It actually was beyond the scope of our article. But she pushed me. And you may know the rest. I went out there one day, asked some questions, and if Davey Delaney had had a shotgun handy, my backside would be full of pellets right now. Or worse."

Nell listened carefully, processing what Danny was saying. Most of what he said made sense. The pieces playing out in her mind started to line up, like reading a complicated pattern for the third time, and suddenly understanding where the shoulder seams lined up.

"So that's why Davey is angry with you. You were the reporter he talked about."

Danny sat quietly on the stool. He nursed the small glass of brandy, looking at Nell. He offered a small smile. "Angry is putting it mildly. And he knew Sophia sent me. So he wasn't crazy about her either."

"But you're no longer on the story?"

He smiled. "You probably think I'm a wimp—that Davey scared me off."

"It would be understandable."

"I've been in worse situations. What I was uncomfortable with was uncovering family secrets in my hometown, a place I might even be moving back to." Danny paused for a minute, took a drink, and then went he went on, his voice quieter. "There was one other thing that was odd about it. I had the feeling Sophia didn't really care about Delaney & Sons. I think she was using me to get at someone or some information for her own purposes. I'm not sure who or what. But she seemed convinced that billings would show charges for services that were never done. It seemed personal to her. Important. She even mentioned a name to look for. Sheridan Technology something. Consulting, I think."

Nell listened carefully, trying to fit Danny's words into a bigger picture. It was difficult.

"Long story short, there were five of us working on the construction series—four now—and those four are a talented group. In the end, their series may make the industry safer for people. But they'll be writing it without me." Danny rested his elbows on the table. A shock of blond hair fell over his forehead, making him look younger than his years. He grinned. "That's it. End of story."

Nell looked at the man sitting across from her. Of course, he could have made it all up. But somehow she doubted it. She lifted a glass of water and held it up in the air. Danny followed with his brandy.

"Many happy returns," Nell said, and clinked his glass with the edge of her own.

"Nicely put."

"And if you're jotting down reasons to stick around, we'd be pleased if Fridays on the deck, or Ben's martinis, or both, were on the list."

"Right at the top. And Hank and Merry's Palate deck is next. How lucky can a guy get to have two decks in his life?"

Nell turned and looked out the window. Birdie was piling glasses and plates on a tray and giving orders to straighten up, her gentle way of saying it was midnight and the chariot was about to lose its wheels.

"One last thing," she said hurriedly, before the kitchen filled with helpful bodies. "Does Davey know you're off the story?"

Danny shrugged. "That part doesn't matter to me. I'm okay if he thinks I'm a bad guy. It's who I think I am that concerns me."

"I can tell you who I think you are, Danny Brandley. A nice human being."

And a nice human being that she'd prefer to remain safe and happy. Having the oldest Delaney son think you're out to destroy his family might not be the best way to go about that.

Chapter 31

The spinners' darkening moon Friday night gave way to bright Saturday sunshine. Perfect for crack-of-dawn coffee, as Izzy called it.

It was too early for tourists to be lining up for whale watching or excursion boats when Izzy, Birdie, and Nell walked down the pier toward Gracie's café. Fishermen, though, had their own clock, and they waved to the women as their rugged boats chugged out to sea.

Before leaving Nell's the night before, they had decided that early coffee would get their day started right. As Birdie had wisely said, "It would be easier to hash things over without a crowd around." She would bring the breakfast.

Hashing things over seemed a priority today—certainly usurping cleaning or errands or shopping. And Gracie's unfinished café would be the perfect out-of-the-way place to do it.

The door to the café was open and they stepped into the cool interior, then spotted Cass out on the back deck, standing in a pool of sunshine. "Come see the pièce de résistance," she called.

The deck was completely finished. Its wide railing was encased in glass and looked out over calm waters and the beach beyond. On the rocky outposts they could see several seals cavorting on the boulders and diving for breakfast.

In the center of the empty deck was a square picnic table with a bench on each of the four sides. "This is perfect," Izzy said. "All of it. Every single bit."

Gracie walked out with a thermos of coffee and a laptop case hanging over her shoulder. "Isn't it? I love it. The rest of the tables will be here in a few days." She looked around with great pride and set the thermos down on the table.

"Are you taking notes, Gracie?" Cass asked, eyeing the computer.

"Nope. Just thought if there was time I'd run some of my marketing ideas by you. I finally stole my laptop away from Joey," she said. She slipped the case to the floor. "We weren't careful about sorting his and her things when we split—he was in such a hurry—somehow he ended up with my laptop." She climbed over the picnic bench. "And my towels. And all those paintings I bought at Canary Cove. I even have a tiny Aidan Peabody fisherman that I found on Joey's bookshelf. I told him I'd fight him to the finish for that."

"And how does one steal from Joey?" Izzy asked, sitting down at the table. Nell sat down beside her on the bench.

"I just made him a nice dinner at his place, brought a bottle of wine, and then took whatever I wanted when I left. He probably doesn't know it's missing." She laughed. She glanced at the small laptop curiously. "It's funny, isn't it? You live with someone for four years and things merge together. I can hardly remember what was mine and what was his. We shared everything. The computer, though, was definitely mine. He used the ones at work."

"So you finally divided it all up?" Cass asked. "You could use some more furniture, Gracie. I hope you took some of the good stuff. Your place is almost as bare as mine."

"No one's place could be as bare as yours, Cass," Gracie said. "But actually, no, we didn't divide things up. I just took a couple things I needed, like the computer." Gracie paused for a minute, an odd look falling across her face. She traced a wavy grain in the wooden table with her finger, then finally looked up again. "Joey and I have been talking a lot these past days, and last night, it was a long one."

"A good long talk? A bad long talk?" Cass prodded.

"Good. At least I think so. Joey's been dragging his feet about the divorce, as you may have noticed. These past weeks he's been canceling meetings with the lawyer Sophia got for us, changing the subject, whatever. He thinks we've both changed. That circumstances have changed. And that a marriage deserves more than maybe we gave it. Last night we went through it all again—and decided it—our marriage—needed a second chance."

"That's quite a conversation," Cass said.

"What do *you* think, Gracie?" Nell asked.

Gracie swept her hair over her shoulder. "I tend to forget the things that pulled us apart. That's the way I am. They're faded, just cobwebs in my head, or buried somewhere, I don't know. I know Joey wanted the divorce at first. We both did. Neither of us was getting what we wanted from our marriage. But I also know that I couldn't have gotten through these recent days without him. He's been there every inch of the way. Whenever I needed him, there he was. He seems to know before things even happen when I'll need him. He even shows affection toward Julianne."

Nell noticed that Gracie switched back and forth when addressing Julianne. Sometimes it was mother, other times Julianne. Those were all part of the process, she supposed. Knitting anything together took time if you wanted it to last. And sometimes you even had to tear it out and start over. Relationships were no different. She touched Gracie's hand. "If that's what you want, Gracie, then we're one hundred percent behind you."

"He wants to meet with the lawyers to make sure everything is in order. He wants me to change my name to Delaney—which I never did. Dot the i's and cross the t's is how he puts it. This from a man who six months ago almost fled the apartment before the word 'separation' was out of my mouth."

Nell listened to the exchange with mixed emotions. More often than not, she'd found that rushing emotional matters didn't fare well.

"Will Joey be involved with the restaurant?" Birdie asked.

"Maybe. Davey would probably be thrilled if Joey disappeared from Delaney & Sons. Joey keeps tabs on how Davey spends money, things like that. Things aren't too smooth between them right now." She shrugged. "Family businesses can be difficult."

"I've never figured out who does what over there," Birdie said.

"Joey is over in sales—and he also has been helping Maeve with the books, billings, keeping track of subcontractors and analyzing what's spent on each project. Davey does the planning, figuring out what each job needs, then making sure the crews are there when needed."

"That sounds like it keeps them separated enough," Nell said.

"You'd think. Who knows? I guess you can't pick your siblings—and personalities can clash." Gracie passed the thermos around the table, then added, "But anyway, thank you all for hanging in there with me during these awful days."

"Where else would we hang?" Nell said. "Which reminds me, I have a quick question for you. I saw Julianne yesterday."

"I know—she loves the knitting project. She's almost finished with the rolled edge of the hat, she said. Esther Gibson was sitting with her, their needles clicking, like fast friends. Julianne was suggesting acupuncture for Esther's back. Who knew my mother knew about acupuncture?" Gracie tossed her hands in the air and laughed.

"Your mother was telling me about a friend of hers—and yours, too. Mandy?" Nell said.

"Mandy White. She owns the apartment building Joey and I lived in. She adopted us—well, me anyway—right along with five stray cats and three dogs. Animals seemed to read an invisible sign on Mandy's window that says, 'Come in. You're home at last.' She's great."

"Your mother likes her, too."

"Julianne came by shortly after we moved in. She was in a bad way that day, disheveled and loud. She'd just had a huge fight with Sophia. Mandy made us all coffee, and we sat around in her living room looking at each other. But they stayed in touch after that. I was embarrassed, thinking my mother was trying to use Mandy in some way, money or something. But Mandy said it wasn't like that. She said Julianne would call to ask about me." Gracie fell silent, as if the memory had been dormant for so long she wasn't sure it was real. "I'd nearly forgotten about that," she said softly.

"Apparently your mother went to Mandy's the night that Sophia died, after she left the club."

Gracie nodded. "I didn't know where she was those first few days. Joey found her. He remembered that Mandy's was one of the few places Mom would be welcome. Mandy sees all sides of people and then manages to work her way around the things she doesn't like or approve of about someone. I guess that explains why she and Julianne get along so well."

"Do you keep in touch with her?"

Gracie nodded. "She's the kind of friend that's there for life— like you guys."

"Did Alphonso and Sophia know Mandy?"

Gracie laughed. "Mandy wasn't the kind of person Alphonso would likely know. And the neighborhood we lived in? My uncle wouldn't know it existed—not unless there was a massive building project connected to it and the building could be bought cheap. Sophia, though, came by sometimes to check up on me, make sure I was okay, and she met Mandy a couple times."

"What about Joey's family? Did they come around?"

Gracie nodded. "The Delaneys thought Mandy was cool. Davey used to hang out with us a lot back then. Too much sometimes. Maeve liked Mandy too. They'd walk down to Sugar Magnolias for breakfast together, walk the boulevard, that sort of thing. I think she was a confidante for Maeve."

"Do you think she'd mind if we called her? Maybe she remembers something that happened those days right after Sophia died. It's probably a long shot, but it can't hurt."

"I know she wouldn't mind. You'll like each other." Gracie pulled out her cell phone and tapped a couple buttons. "There. I texted you her number."

When Gracie went inside for the cream, Birdie asked Nell, "What do you think this Mandy will know?"

"I'm not sure—except it might be helpful to confirm that Julianne was really with her those few days after Sophia was killed. Her car broke down, she said, so she was stuck. And apparently that's where her car was when the police found the evidence they are using against her."

"It's interesting that Maeve Delaney liked her. I wonder what she needed a confidante for?"

"I guess we all need confidantes now and then. Maybe that's how Sophia used her journal," Nell said, pulling it out of her bag and setting it on the picnic table.

Gracie returned with paper plates and a carton of cream. She passed around the plates and Birdie's coffee cake. "I think Sophia had a journal like that for each year. I remember watching her write in it when I lived with them. She told me once it wasn't a diary— she didn't believe in diaries. It was her 'life book,' she called it."

"That's an apt name for it. It looks like it's a mixture of thoughts, her poems, and then some practical, real-life things, like appointments and phone numbers."

Izzy reached over and leafed through the book. Each page had a date at the top in lovely cursive writing. She looked for Saturday, the day after the yacht club party. There wasn't a poem at the top, but Sophie had jotted several names at the bottom, including Gracie's. And after Gracie's name, the word *"urgente."* Izzy pointed to the page.

Alphonso's name was listed below Gracie's, followed by several others, almost as if Sophia were making appointments with people for the day.

"She was making an appointment with her husband?" Izzy said, looking up.

"Maybe just a reminder that she had to tell him something. Maybe whatever she talked to you about, Gracie."

A prominent Boston attorney was listed, along with an office address.

"That's the firm Sophia had us use for the divorce. They handle all Santos affairs—even my grandparents' wills."

Nell leaned over Izzy's arm, reading down the page. "What does she have for Friday? Maybe if we can walk in her shoes through that last week, she'll lead us somewhere."

Izzy flipped back a page. Father Northcutt's name stood out, with a note to send a donation. Another donation to the community center. And YACHT CLUB DINNER, written larger than the other words—seven o'clock.

Nell wished there had been a comment. Had Sophia looked forward to the dinner? Had she dreaded going? By then she had known about Liz and Alphonso for a while. Did she want to stay away, be alone?

But she hadn't stayed away. And she'd been gracious and composed in front of half the town of Sea Harbor. Even in front of her husband's mistress. And then she had died.

Nell continued looking down the page. The name Maeve Delaney, jumped out. Three o'clock. Maeve Delaney meeting with Sophia? That seemed an unlikely pairing.

The page before—presumably Thursday—was smudged. The top was a succession of exclamation points following the words "no marriage." Nell frowned. That's what she'd said at the deli, too. Alphonso and Liz? Or maybe she meant something else entirely. The thought lingered in the back of her head, settling there without resolution.

Izzy pointed to another phone number, this one circled in red.

Nell looked closer. "That's odd, isn't it? Nothing else is in red."

"Ella," Birdie said. "Ella uses a red pencil for everything. Grocery lists, messages, crossword puzzles. She must have needed that number."

Izzy pulled out her phone and dialed the smudged number. The group hushed while the call was answered.

Then Izzy said quickly, "Sorry, wrong number," and hung up. She set her cell phone down and repeated, in a receptionist's voice: "Delaney & Sons, may I help you?"

"So what does that mean?" Cass finally said. "Ella wasn't anywhere near the Delaney plant that night."

"No. But she called someone there, perhaps."

Cass took the book and turned the pages to Monday. "I think figuring out Sophia's week is a good idea. She was collecting information, it sounds like. Maybe if we collect the same information, we'll be a step closer."

"Or more confused," Gracie said.

Nell took a drink of coffee, her eyes traveling over the journal page. "I think Cass is right. We've been trying to follow every Tom, Dick, and Harry. Following Sophia is what we need to do. That last week may tell us a lot."

"Well, I know where she was on Monday," Gracie said. "She went to Boston after she and Ella got home from Mass. I called to see if she wanted to see the café. But she said she had urgent matters in Boston and it would have to be another day."

"Urgent. That seems to be the theme of her week." Cass took a bite of the buttery coffee cake.

"Why did she go to Boston?" Izzy asked.

"They have a Beacon Hill house. Sophia often went in to shop or visit museums and shows. But none of that would be urgent." Gracie frowned and flipped back to the Monday journal page. There was writing at the bottom of the page. 101A Mt. Vernon: SCC.

Nell read it out loud. "Is that the Santoses' house address? Ben and I used to live not far from there."

Gracie looked at it again, then shook her head. "No. Their place is on Beacon Street. But it's the same neighborhood."

"So maybe she was visiting a friend?"

Nell flipped a few pages, then stopped at a name. *Sheridan*. Where had she heard that before? "Sheridan," she said out loud.

Gracie shrugged. "I don't know any Sheridans, but Sophia might have."

Then Nell straightened up. "I remember. Sophia wanted Danny Brandley to find out if Delaney & Sons used a firm with that name in it. Sheridan. Yes, that was it."

"Used it for what?" Izzy asked.

"He didn't know. Some subcontractor. But Sophia was anxious to know. And here's the same name, in her book."

Nell repeated the name in her head and made a mental note to pass it along to Ben to see what he could find out about it.

"So Monday she was in Boston," Birdie said. "Wednesday we know she went to the deli with Ella."

"And Thursday she called Delaney & Sons. Maybe to make the appointment with Maeve?"

"I wonder if Ella can fill in some of those hours for us," Birdie mused.

The sound of heavy footsteps drew their attention from the book to the back door. Sam Perry appeared, a camera in hand. He lifted it, poised to shoot.

"Women at work, I'll call this," he said, and pressed the button. Then he lowered the camera. "I was on my way to shoot some giant cod and saw the open door. What's up? This looks serious."

Gracie noticed the Dunkin' Donuts coffee cup in his other hand and offered him a piece of coffee cake to go with it. "Sit, Sam."

"Don't mind if I do." He straddled the bench next to Izzy and listened carefully as Izzy filled him in on Sophia's journal. Next to it was a piece of paper that Izzy had scribbled names on, crossing most of them off: Harold, Liz, Alphonso, Jake, Julianne. "I see Alphonso is still on your list."

"I don't think he murdered his wife, but we can't prove he didn't," Nell said.

"I have a strictly practical reason why he didn't do it, though it wouldn't hold up in court," Sam said.

"What's that?" Nell asked.

"Maybe you have to be a car person to appreciate this. But Alphonso had special brakes put in that car. Brembo brakes. Someone who loved that car as much as he did wouldn't have messed with the fine technology that he added to it. He just wouldn't have. Think of your most valued knitting creation. Would you destroy it?"

They were silent for a minute, thinking of cherished cashmere sweaters.

"I get that," Cass said slowly. "I have a new GPS for my boat. It's almost sacred to me."

"That's it, Cass," Sam said. "I know that's taking any humane reason out of the equation. When you add that back in—that Alphonso respected and cared about Sophia—well, then you don't have much left."

"Where have I heard about Brembo brakes before?" Izzy asked. She frowned, thinking back over the crowded, confusing days since Sophia's death.

"Davey," Nell said suddenly. "That day in the park."

"That's right. He was ranting about the foolishness of Sophia driving a car that she knew nothing about. And he mentioned Brembo brakes."

"How would he know that the car had Brembo brakes?" Gracie asked. She looked at Sam. "How did you know?"

"I took a photo of them when Alphonso was showing Joey and me the car. We're both a little goofy about toys like that. I took a couple photos of the car for Alphonso's office, so he let us take it for a spin. But Davey wasn't there."

They fell silent. Nell wondered what the others were thinking. There were several directions you could go with this. And she wanted to be sure they headed in the right one. It just might be Boston.

"You know what I think?" Sam asked. He took a last bite of the coffee cake and stood up. His strong face was filled with concern. "I think you're getting too close to the fire." His eyes met Izzy's and he held them for what seemed like a long time. "There's a murderer out there who doesn't want to be found. And trying to find him—or her—could be very dangerous." He paused and looked around the table at each of them, then settled back on Izzy. His voice had none of the playfulness that characterized Sam Perry. "It's not a good idea, Izzy."

Then he suggested he give Izzy a ride to work since it was almost ten and the Seaside Studio would be opening. And Nell suspected his worries would be laid out in great detail to Izzy on the short ride down Harbor Road.

Shortly afterward, Gracie excused herself to work with the appliance men in the kitchen, and Cass left to meet Pete at the dock and make some repairs to their trawler.

Birdie looked at Nell. "How about a ride to the hospital?" she asked.

"My thoughts exactly."

But they both knew the hospital was just a stop along the way.

Chapter 32

*E*lla was sitting up in bed, a lacy white bed jacket covering her shoulders. "Harold and Stella bought it for me," she said proudly. Her demeanor was peaceful, but Nell and Birdie could see lines of discomfort in her face.

"It's almost as lovely as you're looking today, Ella." Birdie set a stack of magazines on the bedside table. "I hear we will be bringing you home in a day or so. It can't be soon enough. We miss you."

Ella attempted a smile.

"Ella," Nell said, "I hope you don't mind that we've read some of Sophia's journal. I know that it's special to you."

Ella frowned as if trying to remember where she'd left the leather-bound book. "I would like it back."

Nell nodded. "Sophia had some appointments written in it, but not for every day. We thought maybe you'd know what she did that week, the week that she died."

Ella drew her brows together and spoke slowly, remembering. "Monday we went to Mass. And then she went to Boston."

"Do you know why?"

"She needed to check something out, was all she said. Sophia was like that. Always careful. Precise. Tuesday we went to Mass, and Wednesday we went to the deli after Mass. Sophia was upset that day, but she didn't talk about it. She said it would be all right and I shouldn't worry. She was finally getting it all together. And she went back again to Boston—Thursday, I think."

"Do you know why she went back again?"

Ella chuckled to herself. "She used an American expression, and it was humorous the way she said it. She said she had to see a man about a horse. And then she added, 'Only the horse is a man, and the man is a woman.'" Ella frowned again. "Or did I get that mixed up?" She rested her head back against the pillows.

"I think you got it just fine, Ella," Birdie said.

"Harold said he has the doctor's okay to start driving again."

"Yes." Birdie nodded. And then she joked, "But not you, Ella dear."

Ella blushed and closed her eyes. "I can't imagine what possessed me."

"Something quite important," Nell said. "We think you may have called Delaney & Sons that day. Perhaps you wanted to see someone there?"

Ella's eyelids lifted and a curious expression played across her face. "Well, yes, I did," she said. "A machine answered."

Birdie and Nell listened carefully.

"And I asked it to call me back."

"Who did you want to call you back?"

Ella wrinkled her forehead in fierce thought. "Yes," she said, almost to herself. "I remember that. Sophia had called there, and I thought it might help me if I knew why. So I called, too. I left a message saying I had found the number in Sophia's journal. And I asked that they call me back. That's what I did. I said, 'Please call me back. It's very important.'"

"And did they call you back?"

Ella leaned back into the pillows. Her eyes closed again and her words slurred as the pain medication took effect. "Yes," she said. "They did."

.   .   .

The Delaney plant was on the western edge of town, out near the old highway. D.J. always said the Delaneys were more true to their roots than the Santoses because they kept their business within the Sea Harbor city limits and contributed heavily to the tax base. The Santos' facility, on the other hand, was over near Danvers.

Ben and Nell were amused by D.J.'s boast, since nearly everyone in town knew that the Santos family trust contributed to just about every town cause—and in extravagantly generous ways.

Nell pulled onto Delaney Road a short while later, and the next turn was into the construction company proper. The complex was surrounded by chain-link fence, but the entrance gate was open and welcoming. A bright red Delaney & Sons sign announced that they were in the right place.

"It looks like a ranch," Birdie said, as they drove up a gravel road to the main building. Beyond it was a series of lumber warehouses, and beyond that, a field filled with trucks and tractors and more construction vehicles than Nell and Birdie had ever seen assembled in a single place.

Nell parked in a visitor's spot and they walked through the front door of the office.

"Hi, Mrs. Favazza, Mrs. Endicott," a cheery redheaded girl sang out from behind a desk.

"Janie Levin, what a nice surprise. I'd forgotten you took a job out here."

"Yep. Pretty soon I'll run the whole place." Janie laughed. "What are you guys doing here? Want us to build you something?"

Nell laughed. "No buildings today, Janie. We were hoping to see Maeve Delaney. Is she in?"

"Mrs. Delaney? Sure. I just put a call through to her. Just a sec." Janie spun around and disappeared down a hallway of offices. She returned a moment later.

"You can go back. Third office on the left. Want some coffee?"

They passed on the coffee and walked down the hall toward

an office with a magnetic nameplate that read: MAEVE DELANEY, RECORDS.

The door was open and Nell knocked lightly on the frame. "Maeve? Are we interrupting?"

Maeve waved them into the small office. "Of course not. What a surprise. What are you two doing out in this neck of the woods?"

"We've never seen your plant. All these years, and I've never even passed by the entrance," Birdie said.

"We're off the beaten track," Maeve said. Her small face was smiling, but she seemed nervous. "It's always a pleasure to show it to people. But usually it's schoolchildren on a field trip. I'm surprised at your interest." She motioned toward two chairs with a small table between. Behind them was a wall lined with filing cabinets.

"Actually, Maeve, we do have some business," Nell began. "It's about Sophia Santos' death."

Maeve slipped off her glasses and set them on the desk. "My heart goes out to Alphonso. His wife dead, and his sister a murderer."

"Maeve, Julianne may not have done it."

"We talked about this the other day, Nell. I thought the police had settled it," Maeve said. Her smile had disappeared, and a frown deepened the lines in her forehead. "So whoever did this may still be around. Is that what you're thinking?"

"That's right," Nell said. "We're trying to tie off some loose ends, hoping that it might help exonerate Julianne."

"We found a journal of Sophia's," Birdie said. "We thought it would be helpful to clarify some of the notes she made that last week or so."

"What do her notes say?" Maeve's voice had an unpleasant edge to it. "Sophia wanted our accounts examined. She was looking for something, spreading awful rumors. Was that in her journal?"

"No, not exactly. But she had some appointments listed in it. And your name was on the list. We thought that knowing what you two talked about—if it wasn't too personal—might be helpful."

Maeve started shaking her head. "We didn't talk about anything. I never met with her."

Nell frowned. "What happened?"

"She said she'd like to have tea with me. I thought maybe it was about the club party that night—maybe a gesture of goodwill. I thought that was nice of her, in spite of the timing being inconvenient, so of course I said I'd come. Janie put it on our calendar out front, and I was planning on going."

"But you didn't?" Birdie asked.

"She canceled the appointment."

"Sophia canceled?"

"Yes. Janie took the call. Anyway, I had plenty to do that day, getting ready for the dinner, making sure the boys had clean ties, and all those other things that seem to fall on mothers. So in the end, it was for the best."

For the best. Except that it happened to be the night that Sophia was murdered. Would having tea that afternoon with Maeve Delaney have changed the outcome of the evening?

"It must be nice to have your boys working in the business with you," Birdie said, changing the topic.

Maeve nodded. "D.J. takes great pride in the boys being a part of it all. Davey loves it as much as his father."

"So will he take over someday?"

Maeve seemed to consider the statement carefully before answering. "He's good at working with the crews and has a passion for building the company."

"Would Joey mind if Davey took over?" Birdie asked tentatively.

Maeve looked uncomfortable with the question and Nell wondered if they had pushed Maeve's goodwill too far.

But Birdie went on. "Davey seems to be the passionate one regarding the business. But sometimes that can cause problems with the others. My second husband had a family business with several sons involved. I can't begin to tell you the difficulties they had."

Maeve smiled now. Birdie Favazza's understanding pleased her. "Joey could have been a bank president or a lawyer, I always thought. But the 'Sons' in Delaney & Sons has always been very important to D.J. You know how that is."

"You want to treat them all the same," Birdie said. "Sometimes that's hard."

"They are so different, those two boys. Davey's so protective."

"Maeve, was it just Sophia making Davey angry—or was Alphonso suggesting things, too?" The question had been needling Nell for a while now. It seemed out of character for Sophia Santos to be waging this vendetta against her husband's rival. As far as Nell could tell, she didn't care that much about the business, so what made her so interested in the Delaneys?

"It was Sophia. She had an agenda. She even sent a reporter out here one day. Why?" Maeve lifted her hands in the air. "This is a family business. We work through our own problems."

Maeve's eyes turned steely when she talked about her family, and for a moment Nell felt like she was talking with someone she didn't know. It was the mother bear, protecting her cubs.

"Problems?" Birdie asked.

"We have many accounts, so many projects. It's a challenge keeping things on budget, hiring the right subcontractors. Alphonso would know that, too. But it's part of the business, and why Sophia thought she had any right to mess in that is beyond me."

Maeve tapped her fingers on the desktop, agitation showing on her face. "Sophia had the loveliest niece in the world. Why didn't she concentrate on the good things in her life, rather than dragging her niece's relatives through the mud?" She pressed her lips together tightly, as if she could keep evil out of their lives by sheer will.

Nell listened carefully and something clicked into place. Sophia didn't want to bring down the Delaney business. That wasn't her plan at all. Sophia's concerns were with people, not companies. Her pulse quickened. Sometimes the clearest facts are those that are the hardest to see. But once you look at them directly, all sorts of things begin to fall into place.

"Gracie says that she and Joey are giving it another try," Birdie said.

Maeve's mood lightened. "Yes. Gracie needs to be in a family that appreciates her."

"I think Sophia and Alphonso did the best they could," Nell began, but Maeve wasn't listening.

"We love Gracie. Davey, D.J., all of us. She always made us feel welcome in their home."

"And you knew her landlord?"

"Mandy White? Yes. She became a good friend."

Maeve looked at her watch, then at the stack of papers on her desk.

Nell caught the look. "We should be moving on, Maeve. But it was nice to see your plant, and especially to see you again."

They left Maeve to finish her record keeping and walked back out where Janie was filing papers.

"Janie," Nell asked, "Maeve mentioned that Sophia called to make an appointment with her, then canceled it. Did you take those calls?"

Janie wrinkled her forehead in thought. "That was the day Mrs. Santos died," she said, recollecting the irony of it. She looked at a large calendar posted on the wall and moved her finger to the day. Maeve's meeting with Sophia, the time, and the location were printed in the square. And then crossed out with a marker.

She looked back at Birdie and Nell. "We're not this backward, honest," she said, pointing to the calendar. "We keep a company calendar on the intranet so people can see when others are out. But not everyone knows how to use it yet, so they mark things here, then I input them. Maeve, especially, likes to check it to know where everyone is. She's a real mother hen. I remember that appointment because I wondered if Maeve would have time to get home, fix her hair, and get dressed for the event that night if she met with Mrs. Santos. She was so nervous about the yacht club party."

"So anyone can look at this calendar and see who's doing what?"

"Not *anyone* . . ." Janie paused, and then said quickly, "Well, yeah, I guess anyone. I showed it to you, didn't I?" She laughed at herself.

"So Sophia called and canceled. That's curious," Nell said.

"Well, no. Mrs. Santos called to make the appointment. Her voice is so distinctive, and I put her right through to Maeve. The cancellation call came over lunch, so the answering machine picked it up. I told Maeve about it when she came back and crossed it off the calendar. It wasn't Mrs. Santos, though. It must have been someone who worked for her. Someone with a cold. I had to listen to him three times."

"Do you use the answering machine often? Ella Sampson called here, too, and left a message."

"She's that poor lady who was hit by a car, right?"

Nell nodded. "Her memory is fuzzy and we're trying to help her figure out where she was going that night. We know she called here and left a message for someone. It was last Wednesday."

Janie frowned, trying to remember. Then she wrinkled her nose. "Wednesday. Yeah. I wasn't feeling so hot that day and stayed home. So the machine was on. Let's see if it's still there." Janie pressed a button and started clicking back to Wednesday's messages.

The women were so intent on the messages, they didn't hear the door open, nor notice Davey Delaney walking up and standing behind them.

"What are you doing, Janie?"

The sound of his voice caused Janie to jump. Nell and Birdie looked around.

"Geesh, Davey, you scared the pants off me," Janie said.

"Hi, Davey," Nell said. "We're trying to help Ella Sampson piece back her memory. She's been fuzzy since her . . . accident. We know she called here, and we thought whomever she spoke with might be able to fill in some gaps."

Davey listened, then asked simply, "How's she doing?"

"She's still in the hospital," Birdie said.

"Found it," Jane exclaimed. She pressed the button again and they listened. It was Ella's voice, polite and cautious. "This is Ella Sampson. I am trying to reach David Delaney. Please call me at this number. It's very important." She went on to say she had a journal of Sophia's and had found the number written in it.

Davey frowned.

"What did she want?" Nell asked.

Davey was staring at the answering machine. "That's the damnedest thing. Why would she call me? I don't even know her."

"What did she say when you called her back?"

Davey looked at both of them. His face was composed, his body still, as if he knew he had reached his quota of angry outbursts for the week. "I never heard this message. I never called that person back. I don't think I ever met the woman. Good day, ladies."

Davey turned, walked past Janie's desk, and strode down the hallway to his office.

Janie shrugged. "Weird, huh?"

Birdie and Nell didn't answer.

"Hey, it's my break time. Want a quick tour? I do it for the grade school kids and can use the practice."

Nell looked at Birdie. "Maybe a short one, Janie. Then we need to get moving."

"Sure, short." Janie pushed open the front door and they followed her across the parking lot, walking at a fast clip.

She pointed out the warehouses and detailed their uses and contents in a quick, efficient staccato voice, then indicated a large building with pieces of new equipment lined up. "The kids love the tractors and trucks. We let them sit on them sometimes." Janie walked around the huge building to wide fields behind. "And then there's this mess—all the trash the guys can't seem to part with. Maeve wants to get rid of the junk and put in picnic tables and a volleyball court. Cool, huh?"

The area was bordered by woods and they could see Maeve's vision, though at present it looked like a city dump, crowded with rusty equipment and old trucks. They walked along the fringes, then started back when Birdie slowed and pointed toward a truck.

Nell followed her look and took in a quick breath.

Squeezed between a backhoe and a front loader was a red Delaney truck. It stood out for two reasons. It wasn't as old as the others, not rusty and leaning on airless tires. But it stood out also because of the bright silver scratches marring the paint—and a smashed rearview mirror, hanging at an angle more awkward than Harold's broken ankle.

Chapter 33

*N*ell and Birdie drove away from the Delaney plant in silence.

Finally, Nell said, "I think we haven't seen the forest for the trees."

Birdie nodded. "And the trees are starting to line up."

Nell didn't answer. She checked her watch. The day was getting away from her. She had a few errands, and cocktails at the club. But an uncomfortable urgency gnawed at her, just at the edges of her consciousness. It was a *seize the moment* kind of feeling.

She glanced over at Birdie. "Are you up for a ride over to Gloucester?"

"You read my mind."

Twenty minutes later Birdie and Nell sat on a comfortable couch in the Lone Gull Coffee Shop in Gloucester, drinking white mocha lattes. Neither Nell nor Birdie could articulate why Mandy White seemed integral to the unanswered questions littering their lives, but she did. It was as simple as that, Birdie said, and suggested that a stop for lattes at the Lone Gull would help them collect their thoughts.

Nell pulled out her phone and called Ben. He knew his way around the Internet better than anyone. "It's Sheridan Consulting or the Sheridan Company, or something like that," she told him and repeated the note in Sophia's journal. "It's the same name Danny Brandley mentioned. I think it's important, Ben," she said.

Nell checked her text messages, looking for the one Gracie had sent that morning. She'd not only sent her Mandy White's phone number, but her address as well. It wasn't far from the downtown area, off Washington Street, according to the waitress at the coffee shop.

They drove slowly up Washington, then turned onto a side street of tall, practical houses built side by side with slender strips of lawn separating them.

Birdie perched her glasses on the end of her nose and read the address aloud from the slip of paper.

Nell spotted the house immediately. It was on the other side of the street, and somehow, even without the address, Nell knew they would have found it. A freshly painted front porch held a swing and four white rocking chairs. There were two front doors, one leading to the second-floor apartment, the other directly into Mandy White's home. She pulled over to the curb.

They looked across the street to the curb in front of the apartment house, the spot where Julianne Santos' broken-down car sat for days while she was told not to leave the Cape. It had sat here, on this quiet side street, unattended, waiting for someone to come and pry open the trunk. Those early days after Sophia's murder seemed a lifetime ago.

"If someone tried to frame Julianne, how did they know where to find her car?" Nell asked out loud.

"Maybe they followed her."

"The only time she drove here was the very night Sophia was murdered. Her car broke down and she didn't use it again. Someone would have had to follow her from the club when she left."

"Or know where she would be staying."

The stillness in the car was nearly suffocating.

"But why?" Birdie finally said. "Why kill Sophia?"

"Because Sophia knew something and was going to act on it. The last piece of the puzzle," Nell said.

Nell looked back at the house just as a woman pulled into the driveway. She turned off the engine of a white Ford convertible, gathered some packages in her arms, and climbed out of the car and up the front steps. Her hair was carefully arranged, poufed, as Izzy would describe it, with touches of blond highlights woven into a salt-and-pepper hairdo. She was of average height and medium build but carried herself in a way that made her attractive in a unique and special way.

At the door, Mandy White turned the key and started to step inside. Then, as if knowing that two women were sitting across the street, watching her, she stepped back out and shielded her eyes from the sun with her hand as she looked across the street.

And then she smiled. A warm and familiar smile. Her expression was one of welcome—and Nell understood immediately what Gracie had said about this woman—and why even cats and dogs seemed to take refuge with her.

The visit with Mandy White was a gift, both Birdie and Nell agreed. It wasn't just the information she provided. They'd met a truly fine person.

Gracie had called ahead, not knowing exactly when Nell would go by—or even why. But Mandy had assured her that it didn't matter. They would be welcome.

"I'm surprised you didn't come sooner," Mandy said, hugging both Birdie and Nell as one would greet old friends.

"We've met," Nell said. "Somewhere . . ."

"Almost," Mandy said. "On the jailhouse steps. You were going to see my friend Julianne."

Mandy led them into her living room—a small but comfortable room with hardwood floors and natural muslin slip coverings. Spider plants and hoyas hung from the ten-foot ceiling and simple bookshelves were filled with novels and psychology texts and environmental works, lined up next to classics and current bestsellers. Fresh lemonade and homemade chocolate chip cookies appeared as if by magic.

Nell knew instantly why Julianne Santos had come to Mandy to be safe.

Mandy seemed to know why they were there more clearly than they knew themselves. And in the time it took to drink the tall glasses of lemonade, they learned about Mandy White, about why pets and people felt at home in her presence, about Gracie and the Delaneys and Maeve Delaney's need for a friend.

"Julianne thinks highly of you."

"She is a dear. I could tell that, even through the haze of her foolishness. I think she's finally on her way to growing up. It takes some people longer than others."

"Were she and the Delaneys friends?"

"No. The Delaneys didn't have much use for any of the family except Gracie. Awhile after Joey and Gracie separated, though, Joey used to take Julianne out for a drink sometimes when she'd come to town. I was very angry with him one night because he brought her back here drunk. He should have known better, though maybe it wasn't his fault—Julianne didn't need much encouragement to drink. It was after Christmas, I remember, because Julianne had to come into town for a meeting with the family lawyers and she stayed with me, like she usually did. I was her hideaway, I think. She was an awful mess that night and I put on the coffee to try to sober her up. Joey stayed, too, sitting with her. When Julianne drank, she talked too much. Sometimes it made sense, sometimes not. But that night I knew she was talking about things that she shouldn't have been telling me."

"What kind of things?"

"About money, legal things. She told me about the family meeting they'd just had, and how she'd finally be free of Sophia because on Gracie's birthday, her daughter would not only receive her own inheritance from her grandparents, but she'd be in charge of Julianne's trust."

Nell looked at Birdie. Part of that wasn't a very well-kept secret. But they hadn't known about Gracie's inheritance until Julianne mentioned it just recently. Nell wondered now who else knew about it.

"Do you think Julianne told others about Gracie's inheritance?"

"Who knows? She could have, though the next day—after she sobered up—she said she had spoken out of turn and not to tell Gracie. I ran into Gracie's aunt one day at the Franklin restaurant and mentioned it to her because I thought she should know. She thanked me; that was about it."

Mandy disappeared for a minute and returned with a fresh batch of cookies. "I think I bake when I'm trying to sort things out. I've been so worried about Julianne and it's resulted in enough cookies for the whole town." She refreshed their glasses with ice cubes and lemon slices. "I suppose Gracie's divorce will be final soon. I hope she watches her step with Davey and doesn't let him wedge himself in there. He'll try, mark my words."

"Gracie has stopped the proceedings," Birdie said.

Mandy's brows lifted in surprise. Birdie and Nell both watched Mandy's expression, but they couldn't quite read it.

"Well, that's news," she said slowly. "I suppose Gracie has thought this through. She's a forgiving person."

"Forgiving?"

"They had different interests, different lives, really. Joey was gone so much. Sometimes I thought Davey was here more than his brother. Once I teased Davey about Joey working so hard while he—Davey—seemed to have a plethora of free time. 'Is that a fair division of company labor?' I asked him."

"What did he say?"

Mandy took a deep breath. "He said I should take my head out of the sand. But he said it far more colorfully than that. And then he walked out of my house like a wild bull. It was the first time—and fortunately the last—that I experienced Davey Delaney's anger."

When they asked about the mysterious subcontractor, Mandy

couldn't explain to Nell and Birdie how the Sheridan name fit into the puzzle. She wasn't familiar with the name—but she had some suspicions she wouldn't mind sharing.

And by the time the lemonade pitcher was drained and the pile of cookies had dwindled, they had learned enough about the Delaneys and Santoses to understand why they had come to see Mandy White—and that many of their suspicions had more grounding in fact than they realized.

Chapter 34

*I*t was late when Nell finally pulled into her driveway, and she was exhausted. She checked her watch. They were supposed to meet Izzy and Sam a half hour ago.

A note from Ben was stuck to the kitchen counter, written on a yellow Post-it.

Sam, Izzy, and I went on ahead to the club. We'll meet you there.

Nell jumped into the shower. The hot water pelted her weary body, washing away the emotions of the day. She shampooed and rinsed her hair vigorously, wondering if the suspicions she and Birdie had pieced together made sense. A few holes remained, ragged and jarring. But they were smoothing out fast.

Nell had almost called Ben from Gloucester and asked him to cancel the club plans in favor of sandwiches at home with friends. The need to share her suspicions and fears was nearly painful. She dried her hair and slipped into a pair of slacks and a light blue sweater. As she pulled her sweater from the closet, a pair of pants fell from a hanger and landed on the floor with a clunk. Nell picked them up and pulled a key chain from the pocket. She stared at it for a minute, then realized it was from Gracie's fireplace the morning after the fire. Had anyone missed the key? It was odd-looking, not exactly like a car key. It didn't seem likely it belonged to the vagrant who set the fire to Gracie's café. And then a second thought ignited a stab of fear. If the fire had been set intentionally, the key might tell her exactly who set it. She hurried downstairs, pushing the fear that pressed for attention to the back of her heart—and the key to the bottom of her purse.

When Nell showed up at the Sea Harbor Yacht Club, a waitress ushered her over to the low round table near the window. Sam, Izzy, and Ben were already there, intent in conversation—with Alphonso Santos.

Alphonso stood and greeted Nell with unusual warmth. Izzy and Sam hugged Nell as well. It wasn't the usual casual night out. There was an urgency, even to their hugs.

"Alphonso was talking about Julianne," Ben began.

Nell smiled to cover her thoughts. What about Julianne? The poor woman was behind bars, in a small cell, willing to be prosecuted for a crime she didn't commit. And what Nell wanted more than anything right now was a private place to talk to Ben, Sam, and Izzy about exactly that.

"Alphonso knows his sister isn't guilty, just like we do," Izzy said. "He wants to get to the bottom of it."

"But I want you to know something first," Alphonso broke in. "I don't talk easily about my personal life. But for whatever reason, you're all connected to this mess, and I know how some things look to you." He waved a waiter over and ordered drinks for everyone.

"Frankly," he went on, "I don't give a damn how I look to anyone. But I do give a damn about Liz. And her mother and family. They're good people."

"We know that," Nell said.

He went on. "I care more than life what kind of world my baby is brought into. I love Sea Harbor. I don't want it tainted by my actions or by murder or by anything else. It's the best place on earth, and I want my child to be brought up here, healthy and strong and loved by all of you. So I need to talk about all this."

He took a stabilizing breath, then continued as if telling a story. "Sophia and I had not loved . . . not in that way . . . for a long time.

We respected each other, but she had become very involved in her spiritual life. I sometimes thought that the life she really wanted was to live in a monastery. Her sister's death was probably the beginning of it, but I didn't realize the depth of guilt she felt until years later."

"Her sister's death?" Sam asked.

"She had a younger sister who drowned on a beach behind the family estate in Argentina. Sophia always felt responsible—she was watching her sister that day—and spent years going to retreats and to religious leaders to figure out how to reconcile with God."

"That's why she closed off the access," Nell said, more to herself than to the group. "Of course."

Alphonso nodded. "Our bedroom windows overlook the cove, and that access pathway kept her awake at night. She couldn't sleep with worry. And when the opportunity came to buy Pisano's strip of land, she snatched it up. And that's why I backed her while she was alive. It allowed her to sleep. But she didn't want the reason for her decision bandied about like a cheap rumor—it was so personal—so we kept it private."

But Alphonso also knew that the cove was a safer place for children to swim than some of the other beaches, and once Sophia was gone, he opened it to the neighbors who loved the spot. It made perfect sense to Nell. Alphonso quietly did what seemed right—both times.

"I'm not sure why she didn't enter religious life, but she didn't. Perhaps she wouldn't have fit in, I don't know. But we fell in love. Somewhere along the way, though, I was competing with a greater power. And I didn't stand a chance."

Nell watched a mixture of emotions pass across his strong face.

"That doesn't mean that Sophia wasn't hurt when she found out about Liz and me," he continued. "She was—and I deeply regret that. And I regret that Liz—who fought the attraction with a ferocity that amazed me—was put in such a bad position, too. She didn't want to fall in love with me." Alphonso took another drink and set his glass down. "God only knows why she did."

"Sophia's sense of righteousness must have made it difficult for her to accept the relationship," Nell said.

Alphonso nodded. "Of course. I was a married man. She wanted everyone's life to be lived the way she lived her own—according to certain standards, her values and rules. None of us escaped that—Julianne, me, Gracie. I think the only person close to her with whom she was flexible was her friend Ella Sampson."

Nell thought of Ella's journey that night, out in a car she didn't know how to drive, determined to right the wrong that had been done to her friend. It was touching—and nearly tragic.

Izzy leaned forward in her chair, her brown eyes focused on Alphonso. "Did Sophia have problems with Gracie?" she asked.

Alphonso thought for a minute. "Not problems. In fact, Sophia used to go over to Gloucester now and then to check up on her. She was married to a Delaney, after all, and Sophia didn't have the greatest trust for that family."

"Did Gracie mind that?"

"Probably not as much as Joey did, though Sophia said he was rarely there. Traveling, she said. When we heard about the divorce, I worried about Gracie, but Sophia didn't—even though divorce wasn't easy for her."

"I know Sophia and Davey had problems," Izzy said.

Alphonso nodded. "In the month or so before she died, she was almost obsessed with the Delaneys. She wouldn't talk to me about it, but said she would when the time was right. I think she was a little afraid of Davey—he yelled at her one night in a restaurant and I had to suggest to D.J. that he keep him away from her."

Alphonso settled back in his chair as if he were finding surprising relief in the conversation. "Now that she's gone, I find myself wondering about a lot of things, but I was pretty preoccupied myself. She asked me about company things—and she never cared about any of that before. She asked me about a subcontractor and then was almost angry when I had never heard of it."

"Sheridan Consulting?"

Alphonso looked at Ben, surprised. "I think that was it. Never heard of the group, but there are hundreds of subcontractors used in construction—electrical, environmental groups, you name it. But why she wanted to know about it is a mystery."

Ben nodded. Nell read his face carefully, wondering what he knew about Sheridan Consulting, but he didn't say.

"Alphonso, do you have any idea who killed Sophia?" Sam asked, shifting the conversation. He rested his forearms on his knees, his fingers wrapped around a stubby crystal glass of Macallan.

Sam was trying to move around the pieces to the puzzle just like the rest of them. Like the shifting tide, new things came to light as sand was swept clean.

"I know who didn't kill her," Alphonso said. "I know I didn't. Nor did Liz Palazola. I didn't go five minutes that night without catching Liz's eye. I was worried about her. She wasn't feeling good from the pregnancy but insisted on working that party. Her staff knew where she was at all times, too. There are plenty of people who would testify to that.

"As for Julianne—she had no motive. Frankly, I thought this whole thing would blow over quickly—I never expected the police to seriously charge Julianne or I would have raised hell sooner."

"How long has Julianne known about the change in administering her trust?" Ben asked.

"She found out at the same time Gracie did. A family meeting in the attorney's office—Sophia, Gracie, Julianne, and me. It was late last December, six months before Gracie's birthday. My parents' will even dictated the date at which Julianne and Gracie would be told about the trusts. I had controlling parents, I guess you'd say."

Alphonso took another long drink of Scotch.

"You talk about more than one trust," Nell said. She felt a twinge of guilt, questioning Alphonso on something to which she knew the answer. But it was a way to get it on the table for the others to hear.

"My parents provided very well for Gracie. They adored her. My father had decided she should come into her inheritance when she was thirty-six—that was the age he was when he made his first fortune so I guess he and my mother thought Gracie would be able to handle it at that age. The truth is that she could have handled both trusts when she was eighteen. She's a bright, capable woman."

"Who else knew about those trusts?" Sam asked.

"No one. Just family. Julianne was okay with the switch, as you can imagine. She was also grateful that Gracie would be taken care of since she herself had never been able to do that. The café is being funded by loans using the trust as collateral—it's her money, not mine. And soon Gracie will have direct control over it."

Nell thought about the restaurant and all Gracie's hard work. It was too bad her grandparents couldn't see their granddaughter at work, with or without a trust fund.

Ben took a drink of Scotch. "Do you think there's anything to Sophia's claims that Delaney & Sons might have bogus contractors?"

It was a serious accusation that Sophia had made, and from the look on Ben's face, she suspected he had done some homework and had his own ideas about it.

Alphonso set his glass down and stared into the liquid thoughtfully. "She refused to discuss it with me. She said that I shouldn't get mixed up in Delaney affairs. It would be bad for my reputation and my business. She was right about that."

"But she didn't mind getting mixed up in it?"

"She told me she had good reasons. And that I would thank her later."

"Did that strike you as odd?" Nell asked.

"No. That was Sophia, plain and simple. She was a good person, but not an easy person. Most things were done her way. And this was one of them. Sophia would move mountains if she thought it was the right thing to do. But she would do it privately and quietly. There was one thing, though . . ."

Alphonso paused as if searching for the right words. Then he finished his thought carefully. "Sophia didn't really care much about business. That wasn't what her life was about. She cared about the way people lived their lives. So she wouldn't have gone looking at anyone's business affairs because the company was a competitor of ours. She wouldn't have cared at all about that. She would only have done it if it was somehow affecting someone personally—either someone she cared about or an innocent person who might be affected by those actions."

Nell sat back, a vague sense of comfort coming from the fact that Alphonso had verified her thoughts exactly.

He left soon after, anxious to stop by Liz's house to check on her. She was still queasy, he'd said. He wanted to be with her all the time, to move her up to the big house or to stay in her small cottage with her, but Liz had insisted that the most important thing was to get his sister out of jail—and to honor his wife's memory by putting her killer behind bars. Then they could talk about the future.

Annabelle had raised her children right.

Chapter 35

Sam and Izzy disappeared soon after Alphonso left. A party, Izzy had explained apologetically. She'd much rather stay in the quiet of their company, but Sam was insisting. She needed a night away from it all, he said. A night with him. But she promised to meet Nell the next morning at the yarn studio to help her with her sweater that was taking on gargantuan proportions.

Secretly Nell agreed with Sam. Maybe it was the disappearing moon that caused the foreboding feeling growing inside her. Maybe it was the growing certainty that they were one step away from Sophia's murderer. But a night of partying—and a night with Sam—would be a good thing for her niece.

A safe thing.

While waiting for a take-out order from the club's kitchen, Nell told Ben about the truck they'd seen in the Delaney yard.

He'd have the chief look into it, he said. It could be something . . . or nothing.

But Nell was through with coincidences. It's something, she assured him, and from the concerned look on his face, he agreed with her.

Over lobster rolls and wine in the quiet of their own home, Nell poured out the rest of her day to Ben. He listened intently, sorting through the pieces with her, and slowly they tried to link them together.

But it was the Sheridan reference that weighed the heaviest on Nell's mind.

"I found something," Ben said. "But not much. No Web site, no advertising. But I did find vague mentions of a company with that name, that address."

It made sense, Ben had to agree, that Sophia's trip to Boston was somehow connected to that company. Danny Brandley hadn't given her what she wanted, so she was finding it herself.

"So I guess that's what we need to do, too," Nell said.

Ben cleaned up their plates and began turning out the lights. "I need more time to look into it. At least find out a name connected to the company. That information has to be somewhere. But you're right. It's a question that needs an answer: Was the Delaney Company paying money to the Sheridan Consulting Group—or to *someone*—for services not rendered? And if so, why?"

He just needed a little more time, he told Nell as they walked up the stairs to bed.

But Nell wasn't at all sure that they had a little more time. She stood at the window and looked up into the blackness of the night. It wasn't just the moon that was disappearing from the sky. Somehow time, too, seemed to be at a premium.

The Seaside Studio didn't open until noon on Sundays, so they'd have a little quiet time before customers filled the shop. Nell walked into the cool, empty shop and was met with the soothing sounds of Chet Baker's magnificent trumpet coming from Izzy's iPod.

She could hear Izzy and Cass chatting in the back and the sounds of coffee perking in the galley kitchen. She walked through the store to the sunny back room.

"Birdie is on her way," Izzy said in greeting. "She needs to knit, she said. 'Desperately,' was the word she used."

"Which means she didn't sleep much either," Nell said. But she wasn't at all sure how much knitting they were going to get in today.

Nell sat on the window seat in a puddle of sunlight. Purl stretched beside her, her tiny paws reaching into the warm air, her tummy waiting to be rubbed.

"Purl, if only life were as simple as you make it look." She pulled the back section of her Ravenscar cardigan from her bag and handed it to Izzy.

"What's the problem?"

"I think it's too wide. I didn't realize it was so full in the back."

In seconds Izzy took a pencil to the pattern and had lopped off a couple inches, showing Nell where to decrease additional stitches. "You might want to take two inches off the bottom, too."

"If only Sophia's murder were as easy to solve." Nell made a couple notes on her pattern and slipped it back in her bag. "Is that Gracie's computer?" she asked, noticing the laptop sitting on the table.

Izzy nodded. "She's designing a Web site for the café and came by early this morning so we could look at some sites together, maybe get some ideas. But she got a call from a workman as soon as she got here and rushed off without it." Izzy started to open the computer when footsteps announced Birdie's arrival.

"Harold's bringing Ella home today," Birdie announced.

"At least that chapter seems to be coming to a close," Nell said.

"Thank heavens." Birdie sat down and dropped her knitting bag beside the chair. "Her memory is clearing up. She said she called the Delaney number because she found it in Sophia's journal. I mentioned that Davey said he didn't call her back, and she was puzzled. She thought the caller said he was Davey, she said, but it could have been D.J.—or the mailman, for that matter. She wouldn't have known the difference. He wanted to talk to her about Sophia and together maybe they could figure this thing out. He suggested they meet right away at that old fish shack out near the marshes. But halfway there, some bright lights coming from the other direction blinded her, and that's when she went off the road. And we know what happened after that."

What had happened was nearly tragic. Again, Nell felt a tightness in her chest. She remembered Sophia's often-used word those last days: *urgente*. Yes.

Nell reached into her pocket and pulled out the key that she'd found the day before. She held it up.

"Here's the key you found at Gracie's, Cass," she said. "I don't know if it means anything, but Ben says it's a motorcycle key. An expensive motorcycle. Not the kind a vagrant would likely be riding."

They stared at the key, their unspoken thoughts colliding in the air.

Nell put it back in her pocket. "But the bigger issues at hand, I think, are why Sophia went to Boston and why she cares about this consulting group. And I think there's only one way to find out."

Nell hadn't planned that they would all go, but no one was willing to stay behind. Izzy checked her watch. "Mae will be here in minutes to open the shop and Sundays are slow. So count me in." Izzy jumped up, then noticed the laptop and quickly closed it, slipping it into a bottom drawer in the bookcase where it would be safe.

"No way am I staying behind," Cass said.

"Besides, it's Sunday—a lovely day for a ride, my Sonny always said."

The traffic was mostly going the other direction, toward the beaches, so the trip to Boston took little time, and before they had finished the sack of Dunkin' Donuts Munchkins that Birdie had pulled out of her bag, they were winding their way through the tree-lined streets of Boston's Beacon Hill neighborhood. Nell slowly maneuvered the car around jaywalking tourists as they admired the hand-carved doors and beautiful facades of the brownstone homes.

"I think that's the street the Santos townhome is on," Nell said, pointing down one of the narrow roads.

"It's close to this place." Izzy squinted out the window, checking addresses. "There," she said, pointing to a beautiful converted brownstone with an awning that stretched over wide glass doors.

Nell slowed down.

"That's odd," Birdie said. "It doesn't look like an office. And I don't see a company sign."

"I have a feeling we're not going to find a company," Nell began.

Just then a car pulled away from the curb, and Nell quickly claimed the space.

They were out of the car in seconds, walking toward a slightly stooped man in a crisp navy blue uniform standing just outside the door of the building. A halo of snowy white hair circled his round freckled head. He smiled at them, clearly pleased to have company.

Birdie leaned forward and read the engraved nameplate pinned to his jacket. "Elliott O'Day. Good day to you, Elliott O'Day. We need help and you seem to be the kind of gentleman who can give it to us—a font of wisdom."

"Well, now, I hope so," he said, clearly taken by Birdie's smile. He matched it with one of his own.

"We're looking for a business at this address," Izzy said.

Elliott frowned and shook his head. His shoulders hunched forward. "You won't find a business here, missy. These are condominiums. Four of them. Fancy." He stretched out the last word. "Used to be two brownstones and they zipped them together and came up with this grand residence."

"Condominiums," Nell repeated.

"The best that money can buy," Elliott confirmed.

Izzy held out the piece of paper with the address on it and showed it to Elliott. He held it up close to his eyes and squinted at it. Then nodded. "Yes, ma'am. That's the right address. That's our penthouse condo. Very nice."

Nell looked up through the glass doors into a tasteful lobby, filled with fresh flowers and scattered Oriental rugs. Another uniformed man sat inside at a carved mahogany desk, reading a book. When the elevator opened, he quickly jumped up and held the front door open for a striking young woman, tan and toned, wearing a crimson running outfit. "You have a fine run, now, Miss Diana," he said in polite tones, then closed the door behind her and went back to his book.

An appropriate name, Nell thought, watching the well-heeled woman disappear down the street. She turned her attention back to Elliott, who was giving Cass, Izzy, and Birdie a history of the neighborhood, complete with directions to Senator John Kerry's home a few blocks away.

"But you don't have a business called Sheridan Consulting located in the building?" Birdie asked.

"Sheridan. Well, now, that's a kicker, isn't it? You're the second ones to ask about Sheridan Consulting."

"Someone else was here?" Izzy asked.

Elliott pulled his white brows together in thought. Finally a bent finger poked the air. "It was a couple weeks past. I'd seen her before because she used to walk past here sometimes, on her way to the park. A beautiful lady, just like the lot of you. Only she was Latin. Spoke in a wonderful accent as if she were from some exotic place."

"A Spanish accent?"

"That's right. She called me *mi amigo*. A classy lady. She came by a couple of times. First just looking around, asking questions, just like you ladies. Then she came back to talk with Miss Diana. I think she knew Miss Diana's man friend because I heard her say she had seen them together, over in the Commons, one day."

"You mean the woman that just walked down the street? That Diana?"

He nodded. "Funny coincidence. Because her name is Diana Sheridan. When I told Harvey about it—he's the inside man—he says sometimes mail comes in for Sheridan Consulting, but it's all Miss Diana's. Just one of those mistakes in a phone book or something, Harvey says. Or maybe the post office—no wonder they're losing business, Harvey says."

"Does Diana Sheridan live alone?" Cass asked.

"You mean does the dad live here? Nosirree, and it's a darn shame if you ask me."

"Diana Sheridan's father?" Birdie's brows lifted.

Elliott laughed and his chin wobbled with the cackle. "No. No. Little Miss Tasha's dad. He comes by now and again. But still, the little girl should have a dad here all the time, don't you think?"

"Little girl?" Cass said. Her voice cracked.

They all stood in silence, sharing Cass' emotion as the saga of Sophia's murderer poured from the lips of kind, innocent Elliott O'Day.

"Sweetest little thing you ever saw," Elliott said. "She turned three last month. Miss Diana's fellow gave her an electric motorcycle that looked just like his—very fancy—and a helmet with her name on it." His face pulled together until it resembled a prune. "He shoulda been giving her storybooks and pretty dresses and a puppy, not a goshdarn motorcycle."

It was closing time when they finally returned to the Seaside Knitting Studio. Mae stood at the computer, tallying receipts.

"You're finally back," she said as they filed in. "Gracie came by for her computer. She was frantic."

Izzy frowned. "Why?"

"Joey needs it for something or other. He didn't know she'd taken it, she said."

"He needs it right now?"

"That's what she said. We couldn't find it, so we figured you had it with you. She had to go back to the café to take care of yet another plumbing glitch—the second today. Joey was going to meet her there. She said to call the second you get in."

Izzy looked over at Nell. And then they all headed for the back room.

Izzy pulled the computer out of the drawer, lifted the lid, and pressed a button. It hummed to life.

The screen had one file on it—a list of Web sites Gracie was exploring for ideas. The finder indicated other folders and files that they scanned quickly. They looked like they were all Gracie's things. Letters. Computer applications. Nothing that looked like it would be a pressing need of Joey's.

"What could be such an emergency? They must have a dozen computers out at the plant he could use."

Cass leaned over Izzy and clicked on the browser, then the word "history" at the top. The window rolled down and they read through the Internet searches Gracie had made recently: restaurant sites, cafés. Facebook. Cass clicked back through the days until she came to the week that Sophia Santos had died.

And there they found what they were looking for. And what Joey was looking for. Ben and Sam's arrival was timely.

"We were worried," Ben said. "You've been gone a long time."

Nell pointed to the computer, and in silence they looked through the list of sites that detailed anything anyone would want to know about brakes. How to fix them. Ferrari brakes.

And they strongly suspected that the printouts found in Julianne's trunk would find their match right here.

They all sat down, and in starts and stops, they laid out the sad and sobering facts of Sophia Santos' death.

There was no doubt in their minds who had done it. And why.

$\mathscr{B}$en said Chief Thompson would be expecting his call. He and Sam had talked to him that morning about their suspicions. Proof and motive, Jerry Thompson said. If only they had that.

And now they did.

They drove over to the café in two cars, a sober entourage, and parked near the entrance to the pier. They spotted Gracie's car nearby. Next to it was a motorcycle.

In minutes Chief Thompson arrived, along with Tommy Porter and several others. Together, they walked down the pier toward the café.

The others followed, their hearts as heavy as the footsteps of the determined police.

As they passed the window, Nell glanced inside. Joey and Gracie were sitting at a small table near the back doors, talking. Joey looked perturbed.

Nell shivered. Ben wrapped her in the circle of his arms and pulled her close.

Jerry motioned to his men, and they opened the door and walked with purpose into Gracie's near-empty café.

Gracie's face widened in surprise.

Joey stood up, knocking over his chair. He reached for Gracie's upper arm, then dropped it immediately. His handsome smile returned, his composure back. "Hey, Chief, how're things?"

The police chief ignored his greeting. His voice was calm, professional. "Joey Delaney, I'm arresting you for the murder of Sophia Santos."

He looked over at Tommy, who calmly, without a single stutter, read Joey Delaney his rights.

Joey looked around, his manner calm, assessing options. He looked toward the back deck, out toward the water. Then quickly turned back toward the front of the café and spotted more uniforms collecting in the doorway.

He spoke to the police chief, his voice cold as steel. "You'll be sorry for this, Chief Thompson. You're making the mistake of your life. You'll live to regret it, I promise you that."

Then, with a smile in place, Joey Delaney walked calmly over to the chief and suggested they leave without causing a scene. It would be the last night the chief would ever wear his badge, Joey told him, so he might as well make the most of it and do this with dignity.

They sat out on the deck, on benches not yet attached to the floor, beneath a dark, velvety sky. Pete Halloran had come by with Willow after a gig at the Gull. They'd seen activity at the Lazy Lobster and thought they were missing a party, so Pete arrived with beer and wine. Sam and Ben convinced the cook at the Ocean's Edge to send down a few of their homemade pizzas.

Gracie was strangely collected. Her straight blond hair was pulled back and tied with a ribbon, her blue eyes filled with immense sadness. Nell wanted to wrap her in an embrace, but it was clear that they had already done that by being there. All of them.

"How was I so blind?" she said slowly. "I hated that he was gone so much, but I never thought it was to be with a high-priced mistress who benefited nicely from our wedding gifts."

"Of course you wouldn't think of that. Who would?"

"I guess when he went through all our money, his only choice was company funds."

Nell nodded. "He invented Sheridan Consulting and tacked it on to various projects, paying Diana Sheridan."

"For doing nothing," Cass added.

"When Nell and Birdie learned from Mandy that your mother had told her—and Joey—that you'd be wealthy soon," Cass said, "things started to fall into place. He could delay the divorce, use your money to rectify the Delaney accounts, pad his pockets a bit more, and no one would be the wiser."

"And that's when he started being so attentive," Gracie said softly.

"Scum. That's what he is," Willow said.

Sam passed around the pizza and put another beer in Gracie's hand. "Joey Delaney has real problems. The guy doesn't have a conscience. No one is safe from that kind of person. If the accountants had discovered the bogus subcontractor before Joey could reconcile it, he had it set up so Davey—his own brother—would be the suspicious one."

"But Maeve may have suspected something of the sort," Birdie said. "She was nervous when we talked to her. I don't think she knew Joey killed Sophia, but she knew there was something not right going on within the company and she didn't want anyone snooping around, revealing family secrets."

"So many things seem obvious now," Nell said. "But until we had them all together, the picture was fuzzy. We finally realized Joey was the only one who knew where Julianne went when she left the club that night," Nell said. "He knew she would go to Mandy's because she always did. And he knew exactly where she lived."

Nell looked out over the water. Who would tell Gracie the most difficult part? It was all unraveling like a poorly knit sweater. You pull one thread and end up with a pile of yarn that only Purl would take delight in.

"Gracie, there's one more thing," Cass said, as if reading Nell's thoughts. She sat next to Gracie in a pool of moonlight. A breeze off the harbor ruffled her hair.

"This woman and Joey had a baby."

"A baby." The word slipped from Gracie's lips and fell into a deafening silence.

"At least it seems that way," Ben said gently.

Gracie didn't blink. She bit down on her bottom lip, her gaze looking off into the harbor.

"We all believed in Joey," Nell said aloud, feeling Gracie's pain. "He has problems, Sam's right. I think your mother—with all this time to read psychology books—was figuring him out, too. And if she hadn't been protected in the Sea Harbor jailhouse, I'm not so sure she wouldn't have been hurt."

"Like Sam says, he doesn't have a conscience, Gracie," Birdie said softly. "He's a charming sociopath who could hoodwink the best of us."

"How did Sophia know?" Gracie said. "How did she know . . . but I didn't?"

Nell had given that great thought. But when you start out not trusting someone and wanting your niece to be safe, you look for things. And so she did. Seeing Diana Sheridan and Joey together in the Boston Commons may have been an accident. But she was looking for it, and that made it easier to see.

"Sophia probably never believed Joey's business trips were real," Birdie said. "She and Alphonso owned the same kind of business, and even in sales, the guys weren't gone like Joey was."

"She pieced it together and became a little obsessed with it," Nell said. "And when she finally was sure—had actually talked with Diana Sheridan herself—she made arrangements to tell you, Gracie. That Saturday. Privately. That must have been the urgent appointment she had set up. She didn't want to tell you over the phone." Nell's voice grew soft. "You were more important to her than her coveted hair appointment."

Gracie smiled and leaned in to Cass' side.

And she was probably going to tell Maeve, too, Nell suspected. Joey saw the appointment on Janie's calendar and canceled it. But that was only a temporary delay, he knew, unless Sophia was no longer around to cause trouble.

Izzy pulled her feet up to the bench and wrapped her arms around her legs. "So Joey suddenly got nice, and he did his darnedest to endear himself to you."

Gracie nodded. "With great effectiveness."

Cass held up the motorcycle key and ring. "We found this in the fire rubble—it's the extra key to his bike."

"Why would Joey burn down the café?" Willow asked.

"It was smart," Izzy said. "And it worked. Sort of." She turned to Gracie. "He was making you depend on him, the one you would lean on, making you forget why you wanted to divorce him in the first place. He always seemed to be there when things went wrong—at the club that night your mom showed up, the wake, the fire, your mom being taken to jail."

"You're right, Iz." Cass put down her beer bottle. "He was always there. And the strange thing is he was never there when Gracie needed him before." She wrapped an arm around her friend and hugged her tightly.

The candles on the deck burned low as the night wore on, and still they sat, reluctant to leave. It was Gracie who finally stood up and faced her friends. "I think we all need sleep. And I know you're here because you don't want to leave me alone. But I'll be okay. I promise. Alone isn't always a bad thing."

"No, it isn't always a bad thing at all."

Gracie spun around. The new voice came from inside the restaurant, just on the other side of the screened door.

Julianne Santos stood in the opening with Alphonso at her side, one arm supporting her back.

"I hope you don't mind the intrusion—the door was open," Alphonso said. He and Julianne stepped out onto the deck. "They usually wait until morning to process release papers, but Judge Wooten is a friend. Not to mention the fact that Esther Gibson wasn't about to let him get any sleep if he didn't 'trot'—Esther's words—down to the station immediately so her new friend could get a decent night's sleep."

Gracie was silent. She and Julianne looked at each other for a long time.

Julianne spoke first. "Mandy White is on her way to pick me up, Gracie," she said. "I'm going to stay with her for a bit while I get my arms around things." She paused, a small smile playing on her lips. "But I was thinking, if you don't have other plans, would you like to meet for breakfast?"

The normalcy of the invitation cut through the tension of the night as cleanly as the blade of a fisherman's knife. Chuckles broke the silence.

"Breakfast?" Gracie repeated, returning her mother's smile. "Breakfast might be nice." Then she tilted her head slightly to the side, feigning hesitation. "Your treat or mine?" she asked.

Chapter 37

*I*n years past, the summer solstice had sometimes brought rain and hail down on the small town of Sea Harbor, Massachusetts, threatening the scientific truth that the solstice is the longest day of sunshine. One year the sun fulfilled its duty, but the temperature dipped so low that Margaret Garozzo's prized pansies froze into tiny purple ice sculptures.

But this year, the day was filled with sunshine and the temperature reached almost eighty degrees. The sky and sea merged together in a glorious backdrop for the solstice picnic near the pier. At night, when the sun gave way to a sky filled with stars, a bonfire would be built down on the beach and families would gather to roast marshmallows.

Nell paused for a moment just outside the Lazy Lobster and Soup Café, looking up at the late-afternoon sky. Against the daylight, the shadow of the moon was visible, a faint silhouette against a blue expanse. The moon had come its full cycle since that tragic Friday evening that now seemed a lifetime ago. Full cycle—it had waned to darkness beneath the delicate pull of the moon spinners as they wound the streams of light onto their distaffs. And now—these weeks later, the threads of light from their washed garments were once again wound back up into a bright ball in the sky.

Not unlike their lives, Nell thought. And their summer. Once again woven together tightly. Complete. Full and shining.

Nell breathed deeply, then smiled at the invisible spinners somewhere out there, standing on a shore with their spindles. And with her heart as full as their spun ball of light, she turned toward the open door of the café.

Gracie stood inside the polished and decorated café, greeting everyone who came by to take a peek. The restaurant wasn't officially open for another couple weeks, but Gracie had invited the entire town to check it out during the solstice picnic. Sea Harbor's finest lobster rolls from the Lazy Lobster and Soup Café would be available for the picnic, her colorful hand-painted sign announced. A gift from Gracie to the town.

Margaret Garozzo had filled Gracie's flower boxes with fresh summer blooms—daisies, sun sprites, miniature dahlias, and long spires of green and gold grasses. And above the boxes, a bright white sign with wooden lobsters on each edge announced to the town: THE LAZY LOBSTER AND SOUP CAFÉ.

The door to the restaurant was held open by a heavy ceramic lobster Jane Brewster had given her as a restaurant-warming gift. Inside, the woven art of Willow Adams hung above the fireplace— a seascape created from knotted yarn in blues and greens and lavender. It swooped and curved against the brick wall, a splash of ocean right there in the restaurant.

Beneath Willow's seascape, a table holding wine and lobster snacks greeted those who came to wish Gracie well.

Nell hugged her warmly. "You did it, sweetie," she said.

Gracie whispered against Nell's shoulder, "*We* did it. All of us."

Birdie and Ben stood with Archie and Harriet Brandley, admiring Willow's art. "I need me one of these for the bookstore," Archie said, making sure Willow was within earshot.

Julianne Santos was standing off to the side with her friend Mandy White. Julianne was gaining some weight, Nell was happy to see. Her beautiful face was lit with hopeful joy. It would take time, Nell suspected—but the buds of a relationship, whatever form it took, had clearly been planted between her and her daughter.

Alphonso and Liz Palazola were there, too, but discreetly so. It was too soon, too fast, for some people to digest everything that had happened, and Liz was acutely aware of people's feelings.

Nell had run into Liz in Izzy's shop the day before the picnic. Liz had finally attended a beginning knitting class. Her face glowed with newly pregnant joy. She fingered the soft cotton yarn Izzy had helped her choose for a blanket and told Nell they knew they had fences to mend, but she and Alphonso would do it, each in their own way.

Ella, however, deserved special care, so she and Alphonso had invited her and Harold to dinner.

Nell had already heard the story from Birdie, but it lifted her heart to hear it again.

They'd gone to a quiet place where they could talk. Fine food, wine, and an attempt to build a bridge. They'd done two things, Liz said, that at least started the process.

Alphonso had thanked Ella sincerely for her friendship to his wife and explained how much it meant to Sophia. Ella's plain, simple acceptance of Sophia had created a comfortable place in which Sophia could be herself. That was a priceless gift, Alphonso told Ella.

Ella hadn't responded out loud, Liz said, but she knew it had touched her.

They'd also brought Ella a collection of items that had meant something to Sophia. A multicolored silk scarf, light and airy as spun sugar. A painting of a flower garden in Argentina, and several pieces of jewelry that Sophia had brought from her country and cherished.

Ella had tears in her eyes, Liz told Nell, though they might have been her own, she wasn't sure.

Nell walked over to Archie Brandley, who was quickly devouring a plate of lobster canapés. "Is Danny here, Archie?"

Harriet immediately appeared at his side. "Not only is he here, but he's staying here."

"As in living?" Nell asked. This was news.

"Of course," Harriet said, her head bobbing happily.

"At least for a while," Archie said, being the realist in the family. "But you never know, do you?" He nodded to the back of the restaurant, where the doors were open to the deck beyond.

Outside, the Fractured Fish were playing an assortment of covers, and all around them toes tapped, heads moved, bodies jiggled, and helium balloons, escaping from tiny fists, floated up to the clouds.

Off to the side, Cass Halloran stood next to Danny Brandley, her face lifted in laughter.

Izzy came up beside her aunt. "Don't stare. It might jinx it. I've not seen Cass this interested in anything noncrustacean since she fell in love with the instructor of our teenage swim team."

"I hear he's staying around for a while."

"Cass told him he had to."

Nell laughed, then glimpsed a familiar face over in the corner, quietly watching the activities. She excused herself and wove her way through the crowd.

"Ella, I'm so glad you came."

Ella smiled proudly, as if the act of coming was in itself worthy of accolade. She wore a long skirt made of a silky blue and green fabric. On her feet were sandals with ankle straps. It wasn't the Ella Nell was used to seeing in Birdie's kitchen.

She had looped a lacy stole across her shoulders and it draped over a white cast on her arm. Ella saw Nell looking at. "This is nothing more than a minor inconvenience. As soon as those white-coats take it off, Miss Birdie is sending me out for driving lessons."

Ella and Nell laughed together. "Speaking of driving lessons, where is Harold?"

"Out there on the deck, the crazy fool. Next thing he'll be wanting to dance."

Nell followed her look and spotted a more youthful-looking Harold standing next to Sam. His pale gray eyes were lit with music.

She turned back to Ella and spoke quietly. "You seem well, Ella. Inside, I mean."

Ella lifted her long chin and half-closed her eyes, weighing Nell's statement. Finally she spoke. "Sophia lit something in me that won't die with her death. That would be denying what she meant to me. I won't do that."

"Friendship," Nell said softly.

"Friendship?" Ella repeated, as if tasting the word, considering it carefully. Then she nodded. And in spite of herself, her shoulders began moving to the rhythm of an old Paul Simon tune. At the microphone, Pete Halloran began singing about being "Born at the Right Time."

Yes, Nell thought. *Perhaps Ella was born at the right time, thanks to Sophia Santos. And in no time she may be dancing, perhaps for the first time in her life.*

Fish Hats

Designer • *Thelma Egberts*

Following are the directions for the wonderful fish hats that Cass is knitting for her brother's Fractured Fish band.

Size
One (will fit both child and adult)

Finished measurements
Circumference: 20 inches, unstretched
Length: 17 inches

Materials
- Any worsted-weight wool or wool/acrylic yarn that can be knitted to the gauge given, can be used. Approximately 350 to 400 yards will be needed in a combination of colors. Use any colors you like, and vary the stripes as you please!
- Recommended needle size: 1 set US #7 double-point needles 1 set US #7 straight needles (optional) (Always use a needle size that gives you the gauge listed below. Every knitter's gauge is unique.)
- Split ring marker
- Small stitch holder
- Black yarn or embroidery floss

- Small amount white felt
- White sewing thread
- Tapestry needle and sewing needles with both large and small eyes

Gauge
18 st/28 rows=4 inches in stockinette stitch

Pattern notes
(Knitty pattern notes can be found online at knitty.com.)

1x1 Rib
(Worked back and forth over an even number of sts):
All Rows: [K1, p1] to end.

Directions
Using desired color for fish lips, CO 90 sts onto double-point needles. Divide sts between needles and join to begin working in the round, being careful not to twist. Once first few rounds have been worked, place split ring marker in work to indicate beginning of round.

Work in stockinette st until work measures 1.5 inches. Break color used for lips and join desired color for head.

Shape Mouth
Mouth is shaped using short rows. It is not necessary to pick up wraps when working wrapped sts on subsequent rows; edge of mouth will be hidden by rolled edge of lip.
Row 1 [RS]: K27, W&T.
Row 2 [WS]: P9, W&T.
Row 3 [RS]: K10, W&T.
Row 4 [WS]: P11, W&T.
Row 5 [RS]: K12, W&T.
Row 6 [WS]: P13, W&T.
Row 7 [RS]: K14, W&T.
Row 8 [WS]: P16, W&T.

Row 9 [RS]: K18, W&T.
Row 10 [WS]: P20, W&T.

Shape Body
Continue as follows, changing colors as desired.
Work 4.75 inches in stockinette st.
Decrease Round 1: [K8, k2tog] 9 times. 81 sts.
Work 2.5 inches in stockinette st.
Decrease Round 2: [K7, k2tog] 9 times. 72 sts.
Work 1.5 inches in stockinette st.
Decrease Round 3: [K6, k2tog] 9 times. 63 sts.
Work 1.5 inches in stockinette st.
Decrease Round 4: [K5, k2tog] 9 times. 54 sts.
Work 0.75 inch in stockinette st.
Decrease Round 5: [K4, k2tog] 9 times. 45 sts.
Work 1.5 inches in stockinette st.
Decrease Round 6: [K2tog] to last 3 sts, k3tog. 22 sts.

Tail
K 3 rounds.
Next Round: K17; place last 11 sts worked on small st holder. First
    half of tail will be worked back and forth over remaining 11
    sts on needles (last 5 sts of current round and first 6 sts of next
    round). If desired, work tail using straight needles.
Row 1 [RS]: [K1, kfb] 5 times, k1. 16 sts.
Even-numbered Rows 2–6 [WS]: P all sts.
Row 3 [RS]: [K1, kfb] to end. 24 sts.
Row 5 [RS]: K1, kfb, [k3, kfb] 5 times, k2. 30 sts.
Rows 7–12: Work in stockinette st.
Row 13 [RS]: K1, k2tog, k to last 3 sts, ssk, k1. 28 sts.
Row 14 [WS]: P all sts.
Rows 15–20: Work as for *Rows 13–14*. 22 sts.
Row 21 [RS]: Work as for *Row 13*. BO remaining 20 sts.
Replace held sts on needle and rejoin yarn with RS facing. Work
    Rows 1–21 as for first half of tail.

Dorsal Fin

Lay hat flat, so that longest parts of short-rowed fish mouth are at center, and shortest parts are at side folds. Mark a column of sts along center of hat; this will be top of fish. Beginning approx. 6 inches above lower edge of hat and working toward tail, pick up and k 15 sts in marked columns of sts, picking up 1 st for each row.

K 1 row.

Next Row: [Kfb] in each st to end. 30 sts. Work 10 rows in 1x1 Rib. BO all sts knitwise.

Pectoral Fins

Mark a column of sts at each side of hat, centered over shortest parts of short-rowed fish mouth. Beginning approx. 6 inches above lower edge of hat and working toward tail, pick up and k 10 sts in one marked columns of sts, picking up 1 st for each row.

K 1 row.

Next Row: [Kfb] in each st to end. 20 sts. Continue as for Dorsal Fin. Repeat for other marked column.

Finishing

Sew each tail half together along shaped edges. Weave in all ends.

Eyes

Cut two circles of white felt with diameter of approx. 1.75 inches. Use white sewing thread and small-eye sewing needle to sew to hat. Use black yarn or embroidery floss and large-eye sewing needle to embroider a black **X** [for deceased fish] or black dot [for alive-but-non-kicking fish] on each eye.

About the Designer

Thelma Egberts is a Dutch knitter who has a thing for weird and funny hats. She mostly uses leftover yarn and yarn from stash (even her grandmother's stash!). That's why she often has to improvise on patterns or design her own.

Please visit knitty.com at the following url for photographs of the hat: http://www.knitty.com/ISSUEwinter08/PATTfishy.php.

For information on Birdie's sexy socks, Nell's cardigan, other Seaside Knitters' pattern information, and for Nell's recipes, please visit sallygoldenbaum.com.

My thanks to Thelma Egberts and to Amy Singer at Knitty.com for sharing the dead fish pattern with the Seaside Knitters and their friends.